THE LIES ALWAYS TOLD

BAKER OAKS
BOOK 4

AMBAR CORDOVA

CONTENTS

AUTHOR'S NOTE

Dear Reader,

I am so happy you're here. Whether because you picked up this book because you've read some of my other work, because you're a Baker Oaks stan, or just because. Whether you're new here or not, welcome, I hope my words resonate with you.

The Lies Always Told is a story of love even when the whole world conspires against you. It's been a story in my heart for quite a while and I'm so happy I finally got to tell it. It is a romance with a happily ever after, but not without fighting through hardships, mental and physical health, and life crisis. These characters were so loud and so adamant about their story that I had to listen and tell it. A story where the characters could want each other all they wanted but life kept throwing curve balls. A story where their biggest enemy was their own thoughts and all the things we can't control. A story where the biggest villain is their head. Their brains.

When I first started writing romance, I wanted to be able to explore relationships with characters that I could relate to. Originally it started with characters I could see myself in physically, and it has continued to grow into characters I can relate with, emotionally. Nellie and Gus share both. Writing them was extremely cathartic and emotional. On one end I shared so many emotional and mental attributes with Nellie, carrying her story deep in my heart and on the opposite end, I shared so many physical and health traits with Gus. Many times I wasn't sure I would see this story through but they were adamant their story needed to be told, so I did. It took months, rounds of alphas, betas, sensitivity readers, and love to get this story out and I hope you love it as much as I do.

Nellie is a school counselor, like her I've worked as an educator or for the school system for thirteen years. She, like many other educators, go into this career with high hopes and dreams of the difference we will make. The difference we can make but then we're thrown into procedures, testing, data, checklists, training, and so much more. Children walk into our rooms carrying so much that we end up doing more than our job requirements and it's so hard to balance it all. We end up being teachers, counselors, friends, listeners, parents, mentors, cooks, and sometimes we carry the guilt of not being enough. Of not doing enough. This book showcases highs and lows and different situations that I hope I offer a window into the perspective of thousands of educators and that they were handled with care.

Gus, like me, has a myriad of health conditions, but there's one I would like to explain before we get into the story. Gus has Hereditary Angioedema which according to the US Hereditary Angioedema Association, Hereditary Angioedema, or HAE, is a very rare and potentially life-threatening genetic condition that involves recurrent attacks of severe swelling (angioedema) in various parts of the body, including the hands, feet, genitals, stomach, face and/or throat. Swelling in the airway can restrict breathing and be fatal. Episodes may be triggered by physical trauma or emotional stress, however, swelling often occurs without a known trigger. I was twenty-nine when I was diagnosed after almost two years of trying to figure out why I was having anaphylactic reactions without any triggers. For two years, my body was going from typical to an angioedema attack swelling my lips, throat, and hands in minutes. HAE is so rare, it took two years and many ER trips, including one that paralyzed me temporarily for us to find answers. The protocol to follow with HAE varies from patient to patient and they also vary when related to other health conditions, like in my case, a congenital heart disease. It has been a journey learning to live with this condition and I'm so happy I get to share it in Gus' perspective too.

HAE attacks are scary and debilitating. Each patient has their own protocol so just know that Gus' experiences are like my own and I'm not a medical professional. If you'd like to know more about it, please visit https://www.haea.org

The Lies Always told is an interconnected standalone but you will see characters from the other books show up and mentions of their happily ever after are present. If you are wondering where in the timeline this story takes place, The Lies Always Told overlaps with The Road Sometimes Taken timeline and it ends after all of the other Baker Oaks books have ended.

This story has themes that may impact readers, and I want you to be cautious and protect your mental health and space while you read. I will list some of the topics, but they might be spoilers, so if you don't have triggers, feel free to skip the next part, I highly suggest you don't though. I highly suggest reading the content themes.

This book includes on-page spice between two consenting adults, slight kink exploration, public sex scenes, light choking, biting, blindfolding, food play, and pleasure-seeking practices. It has a character with cardiovascular diseases as well as Hereditary Angioedema (HAE) both symptomatic. There's on page anaphylactic shock and an angioedema attack, a rescue by boat, hospital and **ICU stay**, mentions of **self-harm**, alcohol consumption and abuse, especially as a coping mechanism. **Miscarriage and infertility** discussion by a side character. There are food restrictions on a child (off page), discussion of **child abuse (mental) and neglect**, discussion of the United States education system from a school counselor's perspective, **gun violence in a school setting** that ends in **death** (not of the main characters), and talk of grief.

Please take care of yourself.

This story has my whole heart and I hope it finds yours.

143,

Ambar

DEDICATION

For the girl who grew up in the shadows of others, the one who felt like she had to beg to be seen for more than a score. For the girl silently screaming for years without anyone noticing. Being seen by him, wanted by him, chased by him, fought for by him feels like winning the lottery. I hope you know you're worthy of being noticed in both the calm and the storm, in the silence between notes, even when you don't speak it.

... and to A, I see you, and I'm sorry he didn't see you too. You deserve better, and I'm so glad you finally saw it. Here's to you finding your Gus <3

PLAYLIST

Music is my love language, and it's Gus' too. When I sat down to write *The Lies Always Told,* I had a playlist with almost one hundred songs, from vibes, to inspiration, to feel good lyrics that spoke to me. A lot of these songs I listened to on repeat while I was drafting, and others came to me at a later time. Each chapter has a song (or songs) that sets the tone for that chapter. You do not have to listen to them as you read, but if you do, it will bring you into an immersive experience. If you want to listen, there's a playlist available on Spotify here, or on Apple Music here. You can listen to the instrumental version as well, here. Happy listening!

- About Damn Time by Lizzo
- Drop It Low by Ester Dean
- Strangers by Kenya Grace
- Lollipop by Lil Wayne
- Tarot by Bad Bunny & JHAYCO
- You're On Your Own Kid by Taylor Swift
- There's No Way by LAUV Ft. Julia Michaels
- Let It Happen by Gracie Abrams

- 2/Catorce by Rauw Alejandro & Mr. Naisgai
- Yonaguni by Bad Bunny
- Or Nah by Ty Dolla $ign, The Weeknd, Wiz Khalifa and DJ Mustard
- Classy 101 by Feid & Young Miko
- Wait by M83
- Breathe Again by Sara Bareilles
- Fix You by Coldplay
- this is me trying by Taylor Swift
- Homeward Boound/Home by Glee Cast
- Wind Up Missin' You by Tucker Wetmore
- Silence by Mashmello and Khalid
- GRAVITY by Matt Hansen
- Dirty Little Secret by The All-American Rejects
- Still Into You by Ashley Tisdale and Chris French
- Talk by Khalid and Disclosure
- Risk by Gracie Abrams
- Dantasias by Rauw Alejandro and Farruko
- Dancing With Our Hands Tied by Taylor Swift
- Better by James Bay
- Do I Wanna Know? by Hozier
- July by Noah Cyrus and Leon Bridges
- Little Things by Ella Mai
- Anyway by Noah Kahan
- Mientes Tan Bien by Sin Bandera
- Mean It By Gracie Abrams
- So Long, London by Taylor Swift
- Dónde está el amor by Pablo Alborán and Kesse & Joy
- Un Beso by Aventura
- Growing Sideways by Noah Kahan
- Someone to Stay by Vancouver Sleep Clinic
- Deep End by Birdy
- Blowing Smoke by Gracie Abrams

- Shake It Out by Glee Cast
- Different Kind of Pain by Sam Barber
- I Know The End by Phoebe Bridgers
- Mad World by Pentatonis
- Everybody Hurts by Glee Cast
- Already Gone by Sleeping At Last
- My Fault by Shaboozey and Noah Cyrus
- Restless Mind by Sam Barber Ft. Avery Anna
- Someone You Loved by Lewis Capaldi
- How to Save a Life by The Fray
- Hallelujah by Pentatonix
- Keep Holdin On by Glee Cast
- Heal by Tom Odell
- This Town by Niall Horan
- Call Your Mom by Noah Kahan Ft. Lizzy McAlpine
- Fire on Fire by Sam Smith
- us. by Gracie Abrams Ft. Taylor Swift
- Good Luck Charlie by Gracie Abrams
- What a Time by Julia Michaels & Niall Horan
- Bleeding Love by Leona Lewis
- Hold Back the River by James Bay
- Somewhere over the rainbow by Christina Perri
- Always Been You by Jessie Murph

Scan for Spotify here:

Scan for Apple Music here:

PROLOGUE

Nellie

MY DAD always said that tragedy comes in threes. I never understood what he meant by that until now. I didn't understand it until I was the one drowning, with the first taste of salt creeping into my mouth and my lungs filling with the cold, sharp sting of ocean water. Except it wasn't water taking me under—it was the entire world that crashed around me, pulling me under and twisting me until there was barely anything left.

He used to talk about the harmful trifecta, and I always thought he meant the painful things children fear—getting lost, hunger, loss, death—but I was wrong. I never knew the hunger I should have feared had nothing to do with food. I didn't know loss and pain could be so deep, it would leave a wound that would never close, that death doesn't only come when a life is lost. Sometimes, it takes a soul as it slowly slips away. You can be alive but not living, and that was part of it all too.

I didn't know tragedy wasn't only something that struck

you from the outside. Sometimes, it's something buried deep inside you, waiting, holding you down until you can barely breathe. I didn't know that when that wave hit, it would feel like a rush, a storm of adrenaline, confusing my brain and making my heart feel excitement as opposed to the panic I should've felt instead.

The first wave came, and I was swept up in the force of it all. I didn't notice the warning signs until it was too late. The second wave came too fast. It was too cold, too powerful. I was drowning with no way back.

Then came the silence, an eerie calm that followed the chaos, an uncanny quiet that mimicked peace. It mimicked a reprieve, but it wasn't. It was hollow, suffocating. It didn't heal, it wounded. It drew from the pain I didn't know was still there. It took from old wounds until I was caught in the undertow.

From that pain came the third wave, mixed with somebody else's pain, making me feel more than I knew I could. I was sucked under again. I lost everything. Everything I thought I had, everything I thought I was. Everything I thought I deserved. If all I could have carried was pain, if all I could give was pain, then I must have deserved it all.

I didn't know tragedy was this close. I didn't know it was this intimate.

I didn't know it could hit me.

Until, one day…it did.

PART 1

THE SHIFT

The wave pulls back, a whispered thrill,
A tidal breath, the calm, so still.
Upon retrieval, the shore reveals
A glitch in time, it's so surreal.

ONE
EXTRA OLIVES, PLEASE
APRIL

***About Damn Time* by Lizzo**

NELLIE

"IT'S NOT EVEN FAIR," Victoria says, grabbing my hand and twirling me around.

"What's not fair?" I place my hands on my hips and raise my eyebrows expectantly, waiting for her answer. This is night three of my twenty-first birthday celebration in Savannah, Georgia, and I've gone from morning drinking to mid-day drinking to night drinking. I'm the youngest in our group—perks of being in grad school at my age, so they're all just happy I'm finally able to drink without worrying about my fake ID. They worry; I sure don't.

"How hot you look in everything you wear. This little black dress will do a number on people, babe. Are you ready?"

"Fucking finally. I've been trying to get laid all weekend, and all of you cockblockers have fucked it up for me. Tonight, though? Tonight's on," I sass as I turn around and shimmy.

"We're not cockblocking you, bitch. We're being good friends here," Bee says, walking into the room with her heels click-clacking.

"You think I look hot? Look at her," I tell Victoria, pointing at Bee—shimmery silver dress fitted to her curves, sky-high heels, her blonde bob as sleek as ever.

"Also unfair, clearly. Lucky bastards, whoever gets to take the two of you home tonight," Victoria adds, pointing at us. She says we're both hot, but to be honest, she's probably the hottest in this trio. She has dark eyes that stare into your soul, plump rosy cheeks, and the darkest of hair, but unlike Bee and me, she's here to make sure we hydrate, don't lose our purses, and don't go home with drunken boys who will turn into more of a problem than a good time. So far, she's done a spectacular job.

"You could come with," Bee says, winking at her and biting her lip gently.

"I'm not attracted to women, babe, and even if I was, I don't share," she replies, winking back.

"Just hush, you two. We all look hot. Tonight's gonna be a blast. Now can we just go?" I stand and walk toward the front door, determination in my steps as I wait for them to get the memo. "The club is not going to come to us. Let's go girls!" They finally grab their purses, ready to go.

We have tonight and tomorrow left on this trip. Originally, we were only supposed to be here for the weekend, but our school being closed longer meant we could stay one more day. After tomorrow, we have to go back to reality—and a good one, at that. I graduate with my master's degree in counseling next month and then hopefully find a job back home in Baker Oaks.

Most people want to move away from their small town. They see college as the escape they need to start their new life, but that's not the case for me. I've been in college for the past four years because I wanted to experience it but that's long enough for me. I love Baker Oaks, I love my little northern Florida town, how close it is to bigger cities, how safe it is. I love it all—except the men. Well, most of them, anyway. There could be someone new who may be worth my time now.

Still, I actually like it there, and I can't wait to be back in my comfort place, where I know where everything is. Where I know what to expect from people. I struggled with finding my footing for so long until I realized what I was missing—routine. Once I learned everything I needed in order to thrive, I realized that knowing what to expect, having the same routine, and having little-to-no surprises are essential for my mental health. My biggest struggle living away from home was the unexpected, so I can't wait to go back to the predictable.

Right now, though, we're walking down Bay Street from the condo we're renting and getting ready to step into Bay Bliss, an upscale bar at the bottom of the Bay Hotel. Everything is packed; it seems like everyone is spending spring break in the city.

There's a line of people waiting to enter the bar, a bouncer not letting anyone in.

"I don't feel like spending my whole night waiting in that line," I tell the girls with concern. I refuse to stand in a long line unless it's for an amusement park ride. Time is the only thing we don't get back, and wasting mine standing in line, especially at a bar in this backless black minidress, is a big no. I bought this dress thrifting with Cara, my older sister, a while ago, and I've been waiting for a good opportunity to wear it. What better opportunity than the birthday when I finally have access to all types of entertainment?

I stole Cara's ID at sixteen and have been using it ever since. People ask about the hair color, and I just say that it got darker as I got older. Cara's naturally blonde, matching her light and airy personality, while I have dark hair, almost black

—darkness surrounds my thoughts constantly, like strong weeds that keep growing no matter what you do.

"Oh, please. Come on," Bee replies, pulling us both by our hands as she steps toward the bouncer without getting in the line. She looks like a woman on a mission, using every weapon in her arsenal before the war begins. She's swaying her hips, moving her head slightly side to side, enough for you to wonder if you imagined it but not enough to tell if she's moving it or not. When we reach the bouncer, she smiles sweetly at him.

"Can I help you?" His voice is deep, and his eyes flare. I don't blame him; if the walk and the dress weren't enough, she's also smiling and discreetly touching his hand over the rail.

"We have reservations for tonight, handsome. We'll miss it if we have to wait in that line, and I really don't want to do that," she purrs.

"They all say the same thing, but unless you're on this list, I'm afraid you're out of luck tonight." He holds the black clipboard up without an ounce of emotion on his face.

"Why so grumpy? I bet my name is on there." She traces her finger slowly down his arm and over the clipboard. "It's Bee."

He raises an eyebrow at her, asking without words if she thinks he's dumb. I wonder how many people try to tell him a random common nickname to see if he'll bite and use a full name. Little does he know, Bee is her full name. Her mom was obsessed with bees when she was pregnant. Weird as fuck, but what do I know?

"Bee Zimmerman," she adds. "Go ahead, look."

"Oh, come on!" someone shouts from the line, clearly annoyed at the situation.

"Oh, shut the fuck up! It's my birthday!" I shout. The collective grunts, claps, and cheers make the space more chaotic. Mr. Grumpy security guard, though? He does none of that and looks down at his list.

"Ms. Zimmerman, you have an ID to verify it's you? I would need IDs for all your friends here too."

We hand him the IDs, and after verifying all of them and eyeing us up and down, he lets out a breath.

"You're all good to go. Happy birthday, Cornelia," he says as he hands me my ID back. I flinch at my full name. Other than the first day of classes, and my mother when she's mad, nobody calls me Cornelia. Cornelia was my grandmother and I happen to be the one blessed with her name. It's sophisticated and posh; neither word suits me.

"Thanks, darlin'," Bee announces as she blows him a kiss.

Walking into Bay Bliss is like stepping into an alternative reality. The sleek, modern interior is bathed in dim lighting that casts long shadows over dark wood floors and what seems like leather upholstery. It has an air of sophistication, with a touch of industrial designs. The loud hip hop music reverberates in the space as the scent of something musky lingers in the air, awakening all my senses.

I look around and see hidden alcoves behind velvet curtains, which I assume may be VIP booths or areas for privacy. *Exclusive and private with a touch of fun* is their slogan, so I'm sure plenty happens behind those curtains that I don't want to know. I've been trying to steer myself away from trouble these past few months, and thinking about all the mischief I can get into here is not going to help me to stay on track.

"Let's go get a drink," I shout over the noise, grabbing both Victoria and Bee's hands. Bee leads us around the sea of people moving, dancing, kissing, and who knows what else. Not my business. We have to cross through the middle of the busy dance floor to make it to the bar, and even though we bump into a few people, we make it there without letting go.

The bar sits in the dead center of the dance floor—convenient for the people dancing, a pain for everyone else. There's a giant neon sign in the middle showing the name of the venue, surrounded by bottles of the most expensive liquor you can think of. This is nothing like the bars we usually frequent. An elaborate chandelier hangs like a piece of art above, and the flickering lights reflect a kaleidoscope of colors across the room.

"This place is incredible!" Victoria says from behind me, loud enough for me to hear.

Walking up to the bar, we're lucky there's a small space for the three of us to reach the counter. Even though there are no empty chairs, we will be able to ask the bartenders for drinks soon.

There are three bartenders on our side of the bar, all men, and from the looks of it, all three of them damn delicious. They're all wearing dark t-shirts and dancing to the beat of whatever this song is.

Cara, my sister, loves music. I bet she could name this song without hesitation. My parents are both musically inclined too. Me? I know if it's a song I can dance, fuck, or cry to. Other than that, unless I already know the artist and lyrics, they all sort of mingle together.

The music shifts, as if on cue, from hip hop to upbeat rap that has everyone screaming and shouting.

"Damn, this song was a whole bop! Do you remember?" Bee asks Victoria, who is mumbling the lyrics, but I just shake my head.

"Not you. You were probably listening to Beethoven all the way until college. Agh, let me get a drink to forget how uneducated I am."

"Bee, just because I listened to classical music doesn't mean I only listen to that. I don't remember this song, but you know better," I reply, grabbing one of the high-top stools that freed up after some girls went to dance.

"It still makes me feel uncool, especially when my best

friend is finishing her master's degree at the same time we're just graduating with our bachelor's," she says.

I finished high school earlier than most people; I took all my high school classes in middle school. Then, in high school, I did most of my undergrad online. By the time I was eighteen, I was only a year away from college graduation, and I entered the master's program immediately. All my life, I've been either too young to hang out with Cara's friends, too young to hang out with my college friends, or too grown to hang out with people my age—hence stealing Cara's ID and pretending I'm older for everyone's sake.

"I don't hang out with uncool people. You're smart, beautiful, and kind." She beams at my praise, and Victoria rolls her eyes. "Now, can we hurry up and order our drinks?"

She turns around to signal to one of the bartenders. I train my eyes on the exchange that's about to happen, because Bee flirting with everything that walks is my favorite thing to watch.

When I met her a few years ago, I had zero clue how to initiate any type of conversation, especially if I was interested in someone. I would just sit with my cute glasses and my drink and watch. The night we met, she tried to flirt with me, and when I told her the only vagina I liked was mine, she practically spit out her drink and sat next to me. We talked for hours that night, becoming instant friends. A few weeks into our friendship, she told me I was awkward as fuck with other people. I laughed so hard at that, explaining how difficult it was for me to not be blunt or read social cues. We talked about some of the challenges that came with being gifted, and after hours of explanation and scenarios, she told me I needed to approach social interactions the same way I learned school subjects: by paying attention. And she was right.

She's the best wing woman, and for months, she would let me watch and practice. She would pose a scenario, and I would act it out. Sometimes, it was a conversation I wanted to continue, and sometimes, it was one I wanted to avoid. She helped me figure out how to deal with both. Some days, the practice went great, earning me a date, an easy lay, or even just a good time. Other days, I wanted to cringe and die. Needless to say, I'm a lot better at it now, but she's still the queen of banter.

"Hey, sexy. Can we have three martinis, doubles, one with extra olives please?"

"For you? Anything, gorgeous. Be right back," he answers with a wink. I don't take my eyes off him, watching our drinks and making sure nothing *extra* gets put into them. I catch Victoria doing the same. One can never be too cautious about these things anymore.

He brings us our drinks, placing them in front of us in a straight line and taking Bee's card to open a tab. I slide my martini over and pop the extra olives into my mouth one at a time.

The bartender brings Bee her card and lingers for longer than any bartender with a bar full of people should, but eventually, he leaves us to our conversation.

"Okay, hot," Bee says, taking a sip of her drink and roaming over the bar with her eyes.

"Alright, ladies. Let's see if we can find our victims for the night," I say, sitting up taller on my stool and looking around the room.

TWO
DON'T TEMPT ME

Drop *It Low* by Ester Dean & *Strangers* by Kenya Grace

GUS

"WHO'S gonna be your girl for the night?" Abraham says next to me, scanning the room. It's our last night in Savannah, and I'm sure he's ready to pick a girl and go. It's the main reason why he's the best guy to go partying with—he has two things in mind at all times: pussy and alcohol. I don't necessarily indulge in the latter, but the first? I can ride that train. I do regularly, actually.

After spending last weekend with my family at my sister Allie's house, this trip was well needed. I love my family, but sometimes, being in the same room for three days straight is too much. Spring break in Savannah, though? So far, so good, but it can be better. Everyone is always asking us if we're ever growing out of this phase, the traveling to find a good piece of ass phase…and maybe would be the right answer, but not this year, and definitely not this weekend.

This is our third bar of the night, and so far, all the girls I've talked to have seemed too eager. I enjoy an easy lay as much as the next guy, but I would love to find a good girl who can do both—talk and fuck. Not too much for a relationship, claramente, but definitely enough to not lose my interest after one conversation.

"You calling dibs, Abraham?" Jean Luis, our other friend, asks. This one doesn't know what he's doing. Recently divorced after marrying his high school sweetheart, he doesn't know how to talk to girls, let alone take the initiative.

"We should all be calling dibs, loco. Last night. Might as well do something about it," I add, roaming the room to see if someone catches my eyes. The place is packed, and the line outside looks like it stays full constantly.

The fiery redhead writhing in the middle of the dance floor raises her glass at me. No, thank you.

I avert my eyes quickly, looking around and meeting somebody else's. Brown skin, dark eyes, champagne glass up high. No, thank you.

Blonde with the mini skirt, licking her lips? Also pass. The two brunettes grinding on each other, dropping their asses low every time the song 'Drop it Low' says so? Also no.

Maybe I've finally made it to the age where the same thing every weekend is not what I want, considering this whole trip has been a complete waste.

"Hey, twelve o'clock," I hear Abraham say over the loud music. When I turn my head, I see three girls laughing while they scan the room. At least, I assume they're all laughing, because one has her back to me, and I can't see her face. Her shoulders are relaxed, and she's holding a martini in one hand while gesturing as she talks.

My eyes go straight to their bodies. The blonde with the big, pretty smile wears an outfit that resembles a disco ball, the fabric so tight, it leaves very little to the imagination. The one with soft-looking brown skin wears jeans and a shirt that hugs her stunning body with curves for days. The mystery girl—I can't tell if she's pretty or not, but her dress dips all the way down the curve of her spine, almost to the top of her ass, so her whole back is on display. The dress looks to be clasped together by a small chain, and I wonder if that chain hooks to the front, or if I could move it out of the way while I bend her over somewhere. I guess that's who I'm interested in. Without seeing her face, just her body, and I know. Maldito perro, my ex Laura called me many times, and maybe she's right.

"You made up your mind, huh?" Jean Luis asks, and when I nod, he continues, "Which one?"

"Black dress is mine. You two can fight over the others." I get up from the leather couch and walk toward the brunette with the most perfect back. I take a minute to observe them as I approach her. There's an art to flirting at a bar, especially a bar like this. There's a fine line between being a creep and being a charming potential suitor. There's a difference between making a woman uncomfortable and making her feel desired. Until I am one hundred percent sure of the best way to approach her, I won't. So, for now, I watch.

I watch as she talks to her friends, and even though I can't see her face, her body language tells me she's having a good time. She sips on the martini she has in her hand while gently rocking her hips to the beat. The song is loud, and it gets louder in the chorus as the patrons scream the lyrics. She continues dancing and sipping on her drink, still not turning for me to get a quick glimpse of her. I don't care; there's something about the way she moves, effortlessly sensual, even from behind, that makes my skin prickle with awareness. A beautiful face would be a bonus to the whole package.

Her drink is almost gone, so I signal the waiter in our area and order another one of whatever she's having, then do the same for her two friends.

"Three girls," I tell my friends, and I grab my tonic water with lime and take a sip.

"One for each," Abraham says, bumping Jean Luis on the shoulder and drawing a scowl.

"I don't know, man. I think I'm good. Not feeling it. I just..." He stops as his gaze moves from the two girls facing each other to the one on the right who just stood. I was right —curves for day—but what we couldn't see was how long her legs are, how her hair falls in the most perfect curls. Jean Luis kryptonite. Looking back at him, we see he's practically smitten, and I smirk.

"You were saying?" I goad him, smacking his shoulder and shaking him. "Come on, don't be a party pooper. Let's go."

"Nah, let them come to us," Abraham states, raising his glass as soon as the blonde gets her drink and the bartender signals her to where we're sitting.

Our VIP booth is far enough away from the bar and the dance floor to give that secluded and mysterious feeling. She talks to her friends, the curly haired one shaking her head, but when Black Dress stands and walks our way, they all follow. They walk almost in sync, as if they have a common goal and they're ready to score.

The pretty blonde smiles big at the bouncer for the VIP lounge, nodding her head our way when he asks her where she's going. When I nod back at him, he lets them in. I finally drag my eyes back to the girl in the black dress, and there's something oddly familiar about her. I can't really put my finger on it, but I have this weird feeling we've met before. Have I fucked this woman before? Doubtful, because with a body as fine as hers, legs for miles, silky dark hair, I sure as hell would've remembered.

"Hello, boys," the blonde says as she slides into the booth next to Abraham. I keep my eyes trained on mystery girl, struggling to figure out how I know her. She looks eerily familiar, but I can't place her. I for sure would remember if I slept with someone as stunning as her. She oozes confidence with every step, and just her eyes on me make me feel more alive. The feeling that I know her just intensifies the closer she gets to me, and it clicks right as she opens her mouth.

"Which one are you?" she asks with sass in her tone, crossing her arms over her perky breasts. Holy shit. Well I'll be damned. Nellie Thompson has grown a hell lot.

"The hot one, of course." I know she's referring to whether it's me or my twin brother, Manny. Even though we're identical, my skin tone is darker, and we wear our hair differently. I don't expect her to know how different we look now, because the last time I saw Nellie, I was twenty or twenty one, and she was still in high school. Sixteen, maybe? I was too focused on building Zabana Enterprises with Manny, and when you're in the middle of losing yourself in work, there's no time to notice how beautiful your mother's best friend's daughter is growing up to be.

"You must be Gus, right? Full of yourself and cocky as shit." She grabs the olive from her drink and twirls it on her tongue before sitting right across from me. Her other friend is still standing by the edge of the booth, and Jean Luis, being the gentleman he is, won't approach her.

"That'd be me, Nellie. I would ask if you're even old enough to be out here drinking, but Cara told me you just turned twenty-one, so I guess congratulations are in order?" At dinner last weekend, my sister's best friend, Cara, mentioned Nellie—her little sister—was going to be in Savannah to celebrate her birthday, but I didn't think any of it. Didn't think that she would be the girl I called dibs on.

"Yes, indeed. Where's my present?" she asks, tossing her hair back and sitting up straight. I was indeed right—the beautiful black dress has a golden clasp right between her breasts, framing the small tattoo adorning her skin, three little vertical dots right where her borderline indecent cleavage is. Downright perfect for her body, too. Her nipples harden under my gaze, and when she clears her throat, I look at her face and remember this is Nellie Thompson. The last thing I should be doing is eye fucking her in this club.

"Like what you see?" she asks, her tone sultry and inviting. Her green eyes are like vines pulling me in, and her perfect, pouty lips, covered by dark lipstick, makes desire flash behind my eyes as I imagine about how perfectly they would fit around my dick. I hate to remind myself that this can't happen, but I have to.

"I can't like what I see, Nellie." I grab her hand, bringing it to my lips and kissing it tenderly. "Have your drink. That's your present. Happy birthday, and let's just forget this happened."

"Nothing even happened…"

"In here," I say tapping my head, "it did… If you'll excuse me."

I get up and walk toward the edge of the booth, where Jean Luis stands.

"Rejected, Gusti?" he asks, a smirk on his face.

"More like that's jailbait. Erase that damn smirk off your face." The music is louder, or at least, it feels like it is.

"Is she a minor?" Jean Luis asks with a frown on his face.

"Nah, just a family friend's daughter. My mom would kill me if I touched her. So would Allie." I finish my drink and try to call the server for another one, but he's already walking my way with one.

"Can't tap that," I tell Jean Luis, who laughs with his drink in his hand. "But you can do her friend. Go talk to her. I'm going to the bathroom. I'll be back."

I step away as the music changes and the crowd goes wild. I don't recognize the song, but the upbeat tempo makes everyone bounce more than before. I walk quickly past the people rushing to get to the dance floor, slipping into the bathroom like a coward, trying to escape this unfortunate situation.

I WALK BACK to the booth, expecting for it to be empty, but I find Nellie sitting by herself instead, phone in one hand, drink in another, and a scowl on her face. I signal the waiter to bring me another drink before I take a deep breath, mustering the courage I didn't have ten minutes ago, and sit next to her.

"Sorry about that. All that water went right through me," I tell Nellie, flashing her a casual smile.

"Cut the bullshit, Gus. It's fine. Our friends are having fun, and you and I are stuck I guess."

"You can also go and have fun. I can watch the goofs to make sure they don't fuck up." The truth is, I trust them more than I trust myself when it comes to girls. We all might be promiscuous, but we're not assholes, at least not completely. They won't do anything without consent, and neither will I.

"Nah, I'm more interested in why you're here than anything else. Plus, I hate this song." She shrugs, and this is the first time I notice she's not moving to the beat. The whole song and half I watched her earlier, she was moving to the beat effortlessly. Her body language was music in itself, matching the rhythm as if she and the song were one, but not this one. She's perfectly still.

"I can tell." *Fuck, Gus. You couldn't stop yourself huh?*

"You can tell what?" Nellie's eyes snap to mine, and I swear, I can see them darken as she waits for my reply. I swallow hard, trying not to think of all the ways I can make them even darker. *Fuck. Fuck. Fuck.*

"You weren't dancing like you were before, so I assume this song doesn't speak to you."

"Oh yeah? What were the other songs telling me, since you seem to know so much about me?" she replies with a smirk, not dropping my gaze.

"That's a secret I'll never tell." I wink at her and notice the waiter walking up with my drink. I grab it and place it on the table.

"That's three that I've seen in what? Ten minutes? Are you going to be fine, or am I going to have to drag your ass out of here and call you an Uber?"

"This?" I hold my drink up and laugh loudly at the assumption. It's not the first time I've gotten a comment on how much I drink or how well I can hold my liquor, but that's just it: I don't drink anymore. "Just tonic water and lime. It's hot as fuck, so I'm trying to stay hydrated. I don't drink."

"Oh, sorry. I just assumed. Does it matter to you if I drink?" She truly seems concerned, worried, which makes me soften the walls I put up the minute I saw it was her. I *don't* get that question.

"If I cared, I wouldn't be at a club, nor would I've sent those drinks. I don't have a problem with alcohol. I just don't consume it anymore."

"Oh good," she adds, taking a sip of her drink and swinging her gaze back to the dance floor. The song changes again, but none of our friends come back to the booth. They keep dancing and seem to be enjoying themselves. I relax on the couch; there's absolutely no need to stay on edge when they're having a good time.

"So tell me, Nellie. How was your birthday weekend?" I ask her, trying to have a neutral conversation and taking advantage of the moment to catch up. I kinda feel like shit I don't know much about her anymore, so there's no better time than the present.

"It was fine. We had fun. Drank too much, slept too little, but overall fine. I was hoping to end it with a bang tonight, so we'll see."

"Figuratively?" I ask, and she arches a brow at me.

"Literally." Nellie smiles, sipping her drink without taking her eyes off me. Her gaze makes this moment so much more sensual, and my body has a visceral reaction. My fingers tingle to touch her, my mouth goes dry at the thought of kissing her, my body uneasy and ready to be near her. I'm fucked; really there's nothing I can do other than sit here and talk to her. She sits up straighter and, like before, my eyes dart down to her chest, to her perfect cleavage, to the little clasp calling my name.

"Gus, you need to make up your mind, my guy. You either stop looking at me like that, or do something about it. Figuring out where I sit between your annoyed stare and your *ready to fuck* stare is getting hard to handle."

This girl. "Are you always this honest?" I ask her, *not* wiping my smirk off my face.

"What's the alternative? Act like you're not stripping me with your eyes? Play coy? Play hard to get? Which one would you prefer?" Her eyes sparkle with mischief and confidence, and her posture reflects it too.

"I would prefer to ignore the fact that Cara's little sister is making me think those thoughts."

"I'm more than Cara's little sister, but you would never know, since you really don't know me." I don't. She's right. She seems hurt, and I try to rectify that.

"No offense, Nellie, but I never thought getting to know you like this was an option."

"It's an option now. How about we start over?" she clarifies, letting go of the glass with her right hand and offering it to me. "Nellie Thompson, nice to meet you."

I could ignore it. I could wish her a good night and head back to the hotel. At this point, anything I wanted to do tonight has been soured by the past thirty minutes. I could do the right thing and say no. But with her looking at me like that, like I hold all the answers to her prayers, it makes me wonder if that's the case. So fuck it, let's find out.

"Hi, Nellie. Augusto Zabana, but please call me Gus. Nice to meet you too." I take her delicate hand and notice how small and slim it is compared to mine. I may be an office guy, but my rough hands would say otherwise. Living my life to the fullest includes sailing and rock climbing, hardening my hands.

"What's your drink of choice, Gus, if you're not an alcohol consumer?" Out of all the questions she could've asked, she chose one nobody has ever asked before. People always assume I'm either an alcoholic or that I just drink soda all the time. She seems genuine, though, and I would love nothing more than to answer her honestly.

"In the morning, tea. In the afternoon, water. When I'm out and about, tonic water with lime, and before going to bed, tart cherry juice."

Her eyes widen before she asks, "Tart cherry juice?"

"So I can sleep like a baby," I reply, relaxing on the couch and crossing one leg over the other. I smile at her and roll my eyes.

"Is there any research to back up that statement?"

"From big pharma? No. From the crunchy groups online? Sure."

"Crunchy groups?"

"People choosing more natural ways to approach life."

"Are you a big ole hippie, Gus?" Nellie asks, leaning forward, getting closer to me. I get a whiff of her soft almond scent, and it makes me want to lean in even closer to see if my guess on her perfume is right.

"More like I have some issues with taking medication for every little thing. I struggle with peaceful sleep, and the cherry juice helps."

"You know what else helps a good sleep? A good fuck right before bed," she adds with a soft but sensual tone that makes my head spin. I cock an eyebrow at her, and she smirks. "It's true."

She's not wrong. I sleep better after having sex, but the women I sleep with usually don't sleep over, and getting up to walk them to the door or convincing them to leave gets me wired again, destroying my chance to rest.

"Maybe…but it's not always the case. I can count on the juice to always be there."

"And you can't count on women?"

"Next topic. How's school going?" I ask, because I know she's in college. I don't want to focus on those other women. Nellie is some sort of genius. When she was younger, her parents were always talking about how challenging it was raising her, the struggle of matching her learning capacity without forcing her to grow up too quickly. I don't know if it's been different now that she's older. I know some kids who show a lot of potential early at school slowly fizzle out as they grow into their capabilities or the school system makes them compliant instead of creative. They tend to make them fit in the box.

"Almost done. I graduate next month."

"Congratulations, what are you majoring in?" I ask, and her smirk lets me know I'm in for a treat. Whatever her answer is, I know it will be the least expected. I can feel it.

"I already finished my bachelor's in Psychology with a minor in clinical psych. I graduate from my master's next month in counseling." Holy shit.

"Aren't you twenty one?" I ask, because how on Earth is this girl graduating that early from graduate school?

"I am, but I finished high school early, so I finished my bachelor's early too. I didn't want to waste any time, so here I am. I'm excited to be done, though, and put my skills to good use as a school counselor."

"A school counselor, huh? You could make so much more money as a clinician, you know that, right?" I ask. It's surprising to me that someone as smart as she is isn't making a more financially-driven decision. Or maybe it's just my finance brain making me think this way.

"Should I pick the career I will spend the rest of my life

doing by how many zeros will be added to my direct deposit, or by what feeds my soul?" she replies, crossing her arms as a barrier between us.

"Not what I meant. Sorry, that's what I do for a living, so sometimes the questions just come out like I would talk to clients."

"'You stick your nose in other people's career decisions for a living?" Nellie snaps back.

"No, I help people make informed financial decisions, so discussing client's choices in career sometimes comes up, especially for their children. I'm sorry, I didn't mean to pry." I'm usually better at communicating, but damn, if she didn't build that wall ten feet tall the minute I mentioned that.

She sits back, relaxing her shoulders, takes a sip of her drink, and closes her pretty eyes gently. "I'm the one who's sorry. I snapped. I have heard the *educators don't make money* spiel for years now, especially when I graduated at eighteen with both a bachelor's and a minor while being a Summa Cum Laude student… Yes, I should think about money, but right now, I want to think about impact. I want to think about what seed I want to plant in society. I'm twenty-one, I have my whole life to make money if I want. Right now, I want to make children's lives better. Not just any children—middle school children specifically. Nobody likes working with them. Nobody has the patience to deal with them. And when you finally find someone who does, they get burnt out and leave their jobs. It's a flaw in our education system—one I'm very aware of, but also one I want to help solve, at least for right now."

Damn. What an answer. "Noted, Nellie. Damn that was deep."

"Just how I like it." She smiles devilishly as she sets her glass down. The fact that she can go from talking about how she wants to make a difference in the world, with an action plan, to making my dick hard with five words is more than I can grasp. "Stop looking at me like that."

"Like what, Nellie?"

"Like I'm the woman of your dreams." I look at her dumbfounded, because it would be stupid for me to even acknowledge that comment. We both know that couldn't even be a thought, and definitely not after one interaction.

"I'm just kidding. Come dance with me. I love this song," she says, standing and stretching out her hand for me to take. I hesitate because I'm not entirely sure this is a good idea. It also catches me by surprise that she noticed the song changing when I forgot where we were.

"Come on, Gus. I don't bite. Just a dance."

"'Promise?"

"Promise," she replies. Her eyes dance playfully while she awaits my reply.

Who am I kidding? As if there was ever another answer than yes. I shake my head and give her my hand. "You're so much trouble."

"The best kind." She drags me out of the VIP booth, her hand tangled with mine, and walks us to a dark corner far away from our friends and the ounce of clarity I may have had before this moment.

THREE

TROUBLE

***Lollipop* by Lil Wayne** & ***Tarot* by Bad Bunny & JHAYCO**

NELLIE

THIS CLUB HAS BEEN PLAYING REALLY upbeat songs all night but then switched drastically to a slow and soulful song I adore. I had to stand up and dance. I'm thankful Gus decided to join me, because this song is better with a partner. I took dance lessons growing up, but as I got older and my academics took precedence, I found a new relationship with music and dancing. I used to dance for an audience in a studio. Little girl, big tutu, glitter all over my face and hair, perfectly polished and put together—that was my life. As the years went by, I lost interest in being the perfect ballerina. I found that my connection to music is more of an outlet than a skilled performance. It's a way for me to give my brain the dopamine it's seeking while moving my body and creating art, even if it's just for me. Now, when I'm lonely, sad, happy, emotional, excited, or even

37

angry, dancing is what my brain and my body both rely on for me to settle. That, and swimming.

This song was made for slow dancing in the corner of a crowded room, so that's exactly where I lead us. The last person I was expecting to see in this club was Gus Zabana. It even took me a good while to realize who he was. It's been years since I last saw him. He was always around while I was growing up, but my interest in romance didn't start until I was eighteen, and I don't think I saw him around then or after. I really don't remember noticing he was this hot. I was too focused on school and all the shit I was going through in my teens to look at anyone with desire, but when I finally did, when I finally noticed how good it felt, there was no stopping it. I'm kind of glad I never noticed this man before, because I don't think I would have been able to keep my hands off him, damn the consequences.

We move together to the beat, my hands wrapped around his neck and his hands solidly on my hips. The height difference between us means he has to bend to place his head by mine. And he does, burying his nose in my neck, my nipples pebbling against his chest. He stops moving as soon as he feels my body's reaction; I'm sure he can because of the goosebumps on his neck, right under my fingertips.

I bring my mouth to the shell of his ear and say, "No thinking, just feeling."

I turn around, grinding my ass against him and tilting my head back to rest in the crook of his neck. His face is still so close to mine, and when I drag my hand up to cup his cheek the subtle stubble on his chin scrapes my hands. I couldn't tell before with his brown skin, but there's a faint line where his beard would be. He smells like something citrusy and woodsy, like sandalwood and ginger. Mysterious and fresh. Dangerous and exciting. Forbidden and spicy.

I wonder what his strong hands could do if he had the chance, or what his lips would feel like on mine. I wonder how his hard dick would feel buried deep within me. As if he can hear my thoughts, he groans at every roll of my hips. What would it take to get him to show me what those hands can do?

The beat never changes. It's slow, sensual, seductive, and dirty all at once, and I take advantage of the moment to let him feel every inch of me. His hands don't move from my hips, even though with every brush of my ass against his dick, he grows harder, his fingers digging into my hip bones, his breath hitching. His pulse quickens under my touch, and I take everything as indication that he's as turned on as I am. I glide my fingers down his arms and peel his hands from my hips, intertwining my fingers with his. I hold tight and slowly drag his hands up my body.

If I thought he was breathing hard before, I didn't actually know what he could sound like on the edge. His breathing deepens the higher I drag his hands, and I don't stop. I slow down. I want to feel his fingertips climbing every inch of my abdomen. I want to move against him painfully slow. If he won't take me back to his hotel room tonight, at least we'll both leave here hot and bothered. I'll make sure of it.

Our hands brush dangerously close to my breast, but I guide his thumb over my sternum, touching the bare skin revealed by the deep-V of my dress. He hisses as I trace small circles, guiding his index finger down my chest and under my breasts.

"Nellie," he whispers, his warm breath against my ear, but this time, his voice is raspy, with a hint of agony, as if it pains him to touch me.

"Do you want me to stop?" I ask, moving my hips at the same time I guide his finger to brush the edge of my breasts, sliding up slowly, under the fabric of my dress, barely touching my skin, just enough to make myself moan at the welcomed touch.

I wait for his reply, holding both our fingers merely an inch away from my nipple, and when he doesn't, I continue.

"I'll stop if you want me to stop, Gus, but if you close your eyes and forget for a minute that our parents are friends, that you're older than me, that our sisters are practically sisters, you can let yourself feel good. If you just close your eyes and breathe, give yourself permission to feel…what would you want me to do?" I move my hips, following the beat of the song. My hands betray the confidence in my voice as they shake slightly keeping his hands in place. All I want is to let his big hands cover my small breasts.

"What's it going to be, Augusto? Are you going to let yourself feel, or am I stopping right now and walking away?"

He shakes his head against mine as he whispers, "Don't call me that." His voice is gruff and raspy, and I think I lost the battle. I won't do something he doesn't want to do, no matter how much I want it. But then he moves his hands up, dragging mine along, touching my needy nipples.

"How much trouble do you want to get into tonight?" I manage to say between a moan and a gasp. People aren't paying attention to what anyone else is doing, but it still feels a little salacious.

"Fuck, Nellie. I don't know if I'll be able to stop." The brush of his lips against the skin between my ear and my neck makes me shiver. "I want all the trouble you're willing to get into with me."

I press myself harder against him, feeling the heat of his breath against my neck. He walks us back until he hits a wall, never moving his fingers away from my nipples or his mouth from my neck. He nips into my neck at first, then opens his mouth and sucks while he pinches my nipples, forcing the tips of my fingers to rub against my breasts too.

"Oh," I let out, breathy, on the verge of snapping. It's taking every ounce of control and self-preservation I have not to turn around and ask him to fuck me right here. I'm also enjoying every single minute, every single second of his hands and mouth on me.

The song shifts, and instead of throwing cold water on this situation, it only intensifies the feelings. This song is even sexier. I don't know this one, but when Gus starts singing in my ear, I realize why. It's a song in Spanish, and this man is singing every lyric as his dick presses against my ass, his fingers relentlessly pinching my nipples. I'm so turned on, if he were to slide those delicious fingers under my skirt, he would find me soaked, and I contemplate telling him exactly that. But if I'm going to get Gus to forget about the complications back home, I need him all to myself, not in this crowded room.

I squeeze his hands, signaling for him to stop, and he does immediately. He tenses against me, waiting for my consent to keep touching me. I don't give it to him, though. I just turn around slowly, look him in the eyes, and lower my gaze to his full lips. I rest my hands on his chest, feeling his heart beating fast, noticing the small droplets of sweat forming around the collar of his black shirt.

I lift to the tip of my toes, bring my mouth next to his ear, and whisper, "You could keep touching me, Gus, but soon, I'm going to need your hands in places that could land us in jail for public indecency. So I need you to make a decision, right now." I bring my teeth to his ear lobe and bite gently before saying, "If you touch me again, I'm going to kiss you. I'm going to kiss you and take every bit you're willing to give me. If I kiss you, I'm going to need you to tell your friends not to go to your hotel room tonight—or better yet, take me somewhere new. If you do that, I'm going to need you to fuck me until I can't walk straight."

I let my words hang in the air and wait for his reply. He doesn't give any. He also doesn't settle his hands back on my body. He just stands there, not dancing, not moving, not touching. I use the last weapon in my arsenal and smooth my hand down his chest to grab his dick over his jeans. He's hard, I can feel it. He's been hard, and I know he must be aching for relief, just as I am. I bite his earlobe again, earning me a shudder.

"Are you going to touch me, Gus? Or am I going to have to go home alone and touch myself? Tick, tock, tick, tock," I say slowly against his ear, and that's when I feel his control snap. His hands dig into my hips and around my ass, slamming my pelvis against his and squeezing tight.

Fuck, yes. I lift my hands, holding his neck and pulling his face down so his lips meet mine. I speak against his lips, "Good choice. Now kiss me, handsome."

He aligns his lips with mine and kisses me gently, slowly and carefully, taking his time learning what I like and dislike. This kiss is painfully slow, making me suffer, as I did to him earlier. His lips linger a little too long, applying soft pressure and drawing out a small moan of frustration. I want him ravenous. I want him wild. I don't want his carefulness. It makes me feel fragile. I want anything but breakable. I want to feel strong and powerful, capable.

I contemplate saying something, but I don't. He keeps kissing me, increasing his rhythm and intensity. The kiss gradually shifts as he responds to my cues and sounds. He drags one of his hands up from my ass to my neck, reaching over with his fingertips to pull at the hair at the bottom of my neck. I tilt my head back, giving him full access to my mouth. He takes the offering, sliding his tongue inside and tentatively brushing it against my own.

His breath quickens as I pull him even closer by his shirt. The heat building between us hushes everything around us completely. Our eyes may be closed, but I feel so seen by the way he kisses me, by the way he touches me. His lips move relentlessly, deepening with every stroke, making it harder for me to breathe. If this is how I die, I wouldn't wish it any other way.

Both his hands are lightly holding my neck. Fuck, I want to tell him to grip harder. He quickly lets go of my mouth, dropping his forehead to mine and whispering an unraveled, "Fuck". His eyes are still closed, and we're so close. I notice his long lashes touching his cheeks. I notice the faint freckles on his cheekbone, and although the strobe lights are blinding, I notice how shallow his breath is right now.

"Gus…" I let my voice trail off as he takes the time he needs to even out his breathing.

"I need a minute, Nellie. That kiss…that kiss was…" *Perfect*, I want to say, but I don't want to sound like a dork, so I don't. I wait for him to finish and hope it's something similar so I know I didn't imagine this, so he can reassure me I'm not imagining this connection.

"That kiss was something. Are you sure you want to get out of here? This could complicate things."

"Calm down, handsome. I'm not asking for your hand in matrimony. I'm asking for one night. My lips are sealed after that." I bring my hands to my lips as I pretend to zip them up and throw away the key. His eyes sparkle with amusement before he closes them again and nods.

"Come on, then. Where's your purse?" he asks, and when I nod and point toward the booth, he walks us both in that direction. I feel like the shittiest friend when I see his friends sitting there talking while we were doing unspeakable things in the dark, but I don't see mine.

"Where are the girls?" I ask them, looking around for them. I grab my phone I left on top of the table at the same time one of them answers.

"Victoria felt sick, and they rushed to the bathroom. I can't go in there, and I wasn't sure what to do. You two looked a little too comfortable for us to interrupt."

"What the hell? I don't know if that's how bro code works, but in girl code, you interrupt. Always. No good lay will come before my friends' safety. No offense," I say, looking at Gus. "If you'll excuse me." I take my clutch and my phone in hand as I rush to the bathroom.

I step in, immediately hearing Bee soothing Victoria, and what I see is even more heartbreaking. She's outside the bathroom stall, whispering, "Victoria, you have to open the door so at least I can hold your hair, girlie."

"Go away. Let me throw up in peace." I notice it as soon as she finishes that sentence, the sounds and the smell.

"What the hell happened?"

"Nice of you to join," Bee spits back.

"Unfair. I didn't even know something happened." I already feel guilty enough; I don't need her guilt tripping me too.

"Sorry, sorry. I know… Also your birthday, I'm sorry. I actually don't even know what happened, but for the past five minutes she's been in here, throwing up. Do you feel fine? It can't be her drink. That guy gave us all the same thing. Maybe the food?"

The toilet flushes, and a second later, Victoria opens the stall door and walks out with her eyes red and her mascara running all down her face.

"Hey," Bee coos. "Are you okay?"

"It's not the drinks," Victoria replies, and we both look at her dumbfounded. We all ate the same thing, so definitely not food poisoning either. "I think I might be sick." She brings her hands to her face and starts crying. We've been together all weekend, and I haven't really seen her throw up, but I have noticed she was acting weird and calmer than usual. If I think about it, this is the first time she's had a drink all weekend, or at least the first time she ordered one. I can't recall if she drank any. She's been ordering pretty bland foods too and hasn't been wanting to go out for walks.

"Oh sweetie, sick? Sick how?" Bee adds, and Victoria looks at both of us with sadness in her eyes.

"Let's get out of here, and we'll talk more back at the hotel," I say, holding my girls by the hand, dragging them out of the smelly bathroom.

We cross the space across the sea of people and almost make it to the door before someone shouts my name. I turn around to see all three boys heading toward us, Gus leading them. "Nellie!" Gus shouts.

I usually wouldn't worry about this. I wouldn't worry about an almost-lay. I wouldn't worry about a man I just met. But Gus is not that. I've known him my whole life, and the connection I felt back there was more than what I usually feel with anyone. For anyone. That felt perfect. Not too much. Not too little. Damn it if the timing is wrong. Right place, wrong time. Definitely wrong person. I have zero self-preservation, though, and I feel it deep in my bones when I turn around and speed walk to them.

"I'll be right back. Don't leave me," I shout to the girls as I reach him.

"What's wrong?" he asks, concern in his voice, looking past me to my friends, who are so ready to get out of here.

"One of them is sick, so we're leaving." I pause for good measure before looking at him head to toe. He cocks an eyebrow, and I smile at him. "Such a shame. It could've been fun." I pull out a napkin and my lipstick from my clutch. I open the matte lipstick and write my number on the napkin before giving it back to him. "My friends come first, but call me sometime. Let's pick up where we left off."

I run back to my friends, half wobbling in my heels as we call a ride and head back to the hotel. The ride is quiet, heavy with worry, Victoria's words hanging in the air. My mind is still spinning, and although I want to focus on her, I can't. My body tingles from the rush of the night, no matter how much I try to dull it to be here with her. We get Victoria to bed and find ourselves thinking about what's going on with her. My gaze keeps bouncing from Bee to my phone, waiting for a text that never comes.

FOUR
YOUR WORST NIGHTMARE

MAY

YOU'RE *On Your Own Kid* by Taylor Swift & *There's No Way* by LAUV & Julia Michaels

NELLIE

"YOU DID IT, babe! A fucking master's degree at twenty-one years old," my sister Cara says as she hugs me tightly. All her hugs are overbearing and slightly suffocating in the best way.

"Cara, language," Mom replies to Cara's little outburst.

"Sorry, habit," she says.

"How are you in the habit of cussing all the time when you work with children every day? Is that how you talk to your students?" I ask Cara, bumping her with my hip jokingly. We keep walking, leaving the restaurant behind as we approach the parking lot. It's so hot today, unusually hot, and between the humidity and the high temperatures, I really could use a swim to cool off. My phone vibrates in my purse, and when I pull it out, careful not to trip as I look away from the sidewalk, I see I have a text from an unknown number.

UNKNOWN:

Congratulations, Nellie! You should be so
proud.

ME:

Who's this?

I type quickly before sliding my phone back into my purse and linking my arm with Cara's.

"When are you going back to Chicago?" I ask Cara as we step closer to my car. Cara's moving back to Baker Oaks this summer, and I plan to move back around that time too. For the first time in a long time, we'll both live in the same town. Finally, I can hang out with Cara and the girls without feeling like an outsider or the baby sister.

"I leave tomorrow morning. I'm driving them to the airport first, though." Chicago is only a few hours from here, so she drove, but our parents came from Florida for this.

"Wait, I thought you two were staying longer," I tell my parents, who are walking slightly ahead of us, hand in hand. They've been married for almost forty years, and they still hold hands, Mom's head on Dad's shoulder while they carry on a conversation in hushed voices. It's so beautiful to witness. One thing's for sure: they set the bar high, and unless I find a man who looks at me the way Dad looks at Mom, I don't want it. Another reason to continue living my life without attachments. Finding something like that is rare. I won't risk failing at it just because it's what's expected. I've dated, obviously, but I often don't make it to the point where feelings get involved, at least not for me. I've never failed at anything, and I wouldn't want to start now.

Except, for the past month, all I've been able to think about is Gus Zabana. I enjoyed his company so damn much— not only the way he touched me, but also the way he listened. The thoughts circling my brain of what could've been are more than I've been able to handle. Watching him listen attentively to what I was saying and fight with himself because he was attracted to me when he knew he shouldn't be was one of the hottest experiences of my life. No matter how much I try to forget that night, I can't, and it's driving me wild. It's one hundred percent in my head because he has my number and nothing, not even a "it was nice to see you" message.

I shake my head and get back to reality when I hear my mom say, "We were, sweetie, but something happened with the fryer at Ronnie's, so we have to go back a day early. I'm so sorry, Cornelia, but we're very excited for you to be back home next month." My parents own Ronnie's, a southern food diner in Baker Oaks, so I'm sure if they say they have to go, they truly need to. I'm disappointed, but I can handle it. Plus, I'll be moving in with them until I find a place, and I can't wait to spend more quality time with them this summer.

"I understand. I love you guys," I say, hugging Mom, then Dad. We're standing outside Cara's rental, so I guess this is goodbye.

"If you go out tonight, call me, Nells. I want to join." Cara hugs me tight again and smiles at me. Her lemon scent engulfs me, reminding me of long summer days and lemonade stands by the park. We're seven years apart, almost eight, which means we were often doing different things. I always felt like I was playing catch up, never playing together. She was always off with her friends, doing things I couldn't, except for the few summers she would set up a lemonade stand, and we'd spend the whole day together. Cara is an amazing sister and friend, but there's only so much time you want to spend with your little genius sister. Her words, not mine.

"I'm tired, so I doubt it, but yes, I'll let you know. Bye, guys. I love you." I wave at them as I walk toward my car and grab my phone to check if the mysterious number has a name.

UNKNOWN:

Gus

My heart races at the sight of his name. I make it to my car, get in, and lock the doors before replying. Usually, I don't want anything more from a guy than the one night, or even the one dance. Usually, the kissing, the touching, the banter is enough…but not with him. Memories of that night flood my brain, and suddenly, I'm acutely aware of how I felt with his hands on me, his low, silky voice singing for me while his hands explored my body. I usually just want a quick fuck, and I didn't even get that with him. I've been wanting to figure out if there's more. I need to find out if it was a fluke—a combination of the environment, the drinks, and his damn cologne —or if that connection could be something more.

ME:

I was starting to think you forgot how to use a phone.

UNKNOWN:

Why?

ME:

It's been a month

UNKNOWN:

Have you been counting?

ME:

Now Gus, I don't like lies. We both know you were counting too.

The worst thing for me about texting is I can't read tone. I can't look at microexpressions. I can't sense the meaning behind what people are saying, and that puts me on edge. I change his name on my phone to G, since I don't have almost anyone's full names on my phone, until I figure out what I want to call him. Not that I think I would be calling him anything else. It took him a whole month to put my phone number to use, and when he does, it's to congratulate me on my graduation? Not how I was hoping he'd use it.

ME:

Don't be shy now.

G:

I haven't.

ME:

Liar.

G:

46,080.

ME:

What's that?

G:

The number of minutes since the last time I saw you.

What the hell?

ME:

Liar.

G:

768.

ME:

What? Hours?

G:

Yeah.

G:

25.

It can't be days, because 768 hours is thirty-two days. I

have no clue what the twenty-five might mean, but damn it, I'm going to ask, because I want to find out.

ME:

I'm out of guesses

G:

The amount of times I typed a text and deleted it.

Okay, this is both sweet and infuriating. Why? Why wouldn't he just text? I thought the whole fuck boy persona ended after twenty five, but apparently, Gus didn't get the memo.

ME:

Why, Gus? I gave you my number. I expected for you to use it.

G:

You know why...

My fingers dance over the screen, waiting and thinking about what I should do next. I felt like a goddess that night under his stare. My confidence was through the roof knowing how he was coming undone with every touch. And that kiss... He was so ready to throw everything out the window to spend a night with me. That man could have any woman he wants, and he chose me. Fuck, Bee would know what to do.

G:

What are you up to?

I leave my phone in my purse and drive to my condo. It's not far from where I am, so I'm home in no time. I walk through the door, leave my shoes in the organizer, and check to see if I'm alone. I know Bee and Victoria had plans with their families too, so I wasn't expecting them. I find Bee in her room, lying in bed with her phone in her hand, but there is no sign of Victoria.

"Knock, knock," I say, sticking my head in her room.

"Guess who I'm talking to?" she asks, sitting up and wiggling her eyebrows. She's sitting in the middle of her bed, wearing a tiny black dress and a full face of makeup.

"Zero clue, but also…where are you going?" I lean against the wall, phone in hand, as I wait for her reply. I don't message Gus back. I need time to think, to figure out what I want the conversation to be. I learned at a very young age that I'm rather impulsive, so time and waiting are my two best friends when my emotions are at play.

"Frat party. Wanna come? Our last party of the academic year, Nellie. Victoria is with her parents, so she's being a party pooper. Are you in?"

I don't want to go. I would rather stay here and read, but maybe going with her will pull me out of the dry spell I've been in for the last month.

"Which one?" I ask. Some frat houses are better than others, and the bad ones have my least favorite people.

"The one house you'd never catch Jack at." Jack's the guy I slept with consistently my freshman year. We were never a thing. He, on the other hand, had no clue. His frat is one I always avoid. He's an ass and can't take a no for an answer. Jack might have a lot of friends, but they aren't at Zeta Beta. The ZB guys hate him—I don't know why and I don't care, because it means I can party at ZB Jack-free. Time and waiting might be my best friends when impulse control is needed, but the perfect addendum to the trio is space. If I'm not put in a tricky situation, I can make rational decisions without issues. I can stop and think. I may be young and sometimes wild, but I'm never stupid.

"Then maybe…" I look down at my phone and remember what I actually came here for. She's still lying on her back, her phone in her hand, and she's smirking, kicking her feet. "Who are you talking to?"

She turns to look at me and smiles giddily. "Abraham."

What the hell? "Gus' friend Abraham?"

"Yup. He might come over tonight."

"To a frat party? Bee, he's a grown man."

"And we're grown women."

I laugh. "No, we're not. We literally just finished college today. He has been adulting for years now." I watch her, hoping she can explain more.

"You are a twenty-one-year-old genius child who just finished a master's degree, and I'm your friend, so adult by association. He can come… Maybe he'll bring Gus' handsome face over, and you can stop acting like the world ended a month ago."

"I have not."

"You have too, and you didn't even fuck him." She cocks an eyebrow my way. I don't need to have sex with the man to know it would be good. I've never felt sexier. I've never felt more desired, and he didn't even undress me.

"I don't kiss and tell…but if I did, I would tell you I felt more from that kiss than I got from many of the men in my bed."

"Then what the hell, Nells? Call him."

"I didn't even know you were talking to Abraham." I change the topic, because I don't want to tell her I didn't get his number. I don't want to tell her that tonight is the first time he's texted. I don't want to sound as pathetic as I feel.

"We text, but I'm dying to have his hands all over me. Nothing happened for me either. He did say he was in town just for tonight, and he wanted to find out if it would be as good as he imagined. He's leaving the country tomorrow to celebrate his birthday for a few days. How fun is that?"

"Super…" I wait in silence to see if she'll add anything

else. I contemplate telling her about Gus's message but opt to ignore it altogether. "Okay, I'm going to get dressed."

"Don't take too long!" she shouts before returning her attention to her phone. I check mine too and see another message from Gus.

ME:

Probably going to bed.

G:

No getting in trouble tonight?

ME:

Me? Never. I'm a good girl.

G:

You and I both know that's not true, but both can be right. You can be a good girl and get in trouble, or am I wrong?

I shake my head and smile to myself, ignoring how giddy his text messages made me feel. I set my phone down and give myself ten minutes to get dressed so I can live my college days for one more night.

"JUST NELLIE, what are you going to do with all that brain inside that head?" Elijah jokes, wrapping his arm around my shoulder after finding me in the only semi-quiet spot in the frat house almost as soon as I walked in.

"Put it to good work helping—"

"One misunderstood child at a time," he interrupts and says the exact words I was going to say. Elijah is one of the first friends I made here. I'm sure I looked as lost as I felt walking through the sea of students, looking as fresh as they come but going to the graduate studies building. He asked me if I needed help, but when I showed him my schedule, he couldn't believe it.

"You look fourteen," he said, his eyes darting from the schedule to my face. His ringlets bounced over his eyes, so I brushed half of them away from his face.

"And you would look a lot better with the hair out of your face. I can't do anything about having good genes and looking young, but you're doing this to yourself." I snatched the paper from his hands and walked in the opposite direction.

"Wait! We started off on the wrong foot. My name is Elijah, not Eli. Just Elijah. Nice to meet you, Cornelia." He extended his hand, allowing me time to do the same and shake it. When he noticed my look of concern, he figured it was because he called me by name, a name I didn't share with him. "It's on your schedule."

"It's just Nellie, Just Elijah.*"*

"Nice to meet you, Just Nellie. *I have to go to class, but we need to hang out so you can tell me the whole story of how you're going to class in that building."*

Elijah was one of the first people in my life who didn't treat me any differently because of my age or questioned why I would choose to live on campus when I could have a condo. He treats me the way I've always wanted to be treated: normal. He's also one of the only people who touches me and doesn't expect me to date or fuck him. His love language is physical touch, so his hands are always on the people he loves. I just happen to be one of them, and it's much welcomed. I crave touch, and he gives it, even if it's not sexual.

"Where's Sam?"

"Oh, you know, being a social butterfly, as usual." Sam is Elijah's partner, and it has been my biggest pleasure watching them fall in love. They're perfect for each other, the true definition of love at first sight. My phone buzzes in my purse a few times, but I ignore it. Nobody should be bothering me right now.

"Nellie who keeps blowing up your phone?" Elijah asks, eyebrow raised, curious to see what's going on.

"I'm actually not sure."

"Are you hiding away from reality again?" he asks, referring to the hundreds of times I completely ignored my family calling to check on me. Being the youngest of two and a wild card, as my sister calls me, sometimes makes them feel they need to know where I am at all times. The tight leash they've had around my neck for years follows me even when I'm hundreds of miles away. Sometimes, silence is my most powerful tool.

He's right, though; I am trying to hide, but from who? My sister, after I told her I wouldn't go out? The guy I slept with two months ago, who won't take the hint? That's debatable. "Maybe…" I reply as I get my phone out and check to see who needs to talk to me so badly. Although secretly, I've been hoping for it to be Gus, I'm still surprised when I see the thread of messages.

G:

I thought you were going to stay home, but I see you're causing trouble.

G:

Huh, I didn't strike blond surfer dudes as your type, but then again, what would I know?

What the hell? Lifting my eyes, I search for him. It shouldn't take me long to find him, considering how out of place he would look at this party. While this place is full of people of all races, ethnicity, and social statuses, it's also full of boys, and Gus is anything but.

My eyes roam the place, and I don't think I'll find him until… I don't know how I missed him. He's sitting in the back of the room, wearing black denim and a navy-collared shirt. His skin looks smooth and dark in this light. His eyes—

intense—bore into mine. I didn't see him before, but now, all I see is *him*.

"Shit, who's that?" Elijah asks with curiosity in his voice, but I can't take my eyes away from Gus, not even for one second, to see his expression.

"Nobody," I reply, and I really should just laugh at how stupid that sounds.

"*That* is not how nobody looks at somebody. *That* is how a man looks at a snack. A snack he's been craving, Nellie. The question is, when did he get the first taste?" His eyes get obnoxiously big, and he smirks like a know-it-all.

I walk toward Gus, letting his eyes pull me straight to him, ignoring Elijah and everyone around me. The chaos, the crowd, the music, the scents—everything disappears while I stride my way to him. This pull, this feeling urging me to him…there's no way to describe it other than his soul calling to mine. It goes beyond what I should be doing or feeling right now. I fear this is inevitable.

"Gus," I greet him.

"Hey, Trouble." He smiles, and my skin tingles. He keeps his composure while I fight with everything I have not to lose mine and climb him like a tree right here.

"What are you doing here?" I ask, crossing my arms over my chest and seizing the ounce of self-control I have.

"I could ask you the same. Just shy of two hours ago, you said you were going to sleep. Did you sleep walk here?"

"I don't owe you explanations," I reply with more bite than I intended. I hate being micromanaged, and I hate surprises too. This feels like both.

"Woah, woah, I didn't mean it like that. I was just surprised you lied to me, Nellie." He raises his hands, palms up, and his smile softens. His shoulders relax, and his eyes go from intense to warm in just one interaction.

"I'm sorry."

"Are you sorry you lied, or are you sorry you got caught?"

he asks as he stands, towering over me and engulfing me in his spicy, leathery scent.

Both? Neither?

I bite my lip and hold back my reply, waiting out to see if he answers the first question I asked him. How did he know I was here, and why is he here? Then, it hits me: *Abraham.*

"I'm sorry I lied. I'm not usually like that, but in my defense, I wasn't planning on going out. It was all Bee's idea."

"Ah, the little devil to your angel, huh?"

"Nah, Victoria is the angel. I'm more like in between."

"Un arcangel[1]," he says, or I think he does, but I'm not very fluent in Spanish. Maybe I misheard.

"More like your worst nightmare." I step closer to him, his body radiating intense heat.

He notices the tentative step I take and grabs my hand, pulling me to him, and taking us both back down to the couch. I land on his lap, and his hand immediately goes up to my neck. My breath hitches, and I gasp when his lips hover over mine, whispering, "Then I can't wait to fall asleep."

He closes the space between us, raking his hand up my back, grabbing my ponytail and tilting my head back as he kisses me fearlessly, leaving me breathy and unraveled.

---

1. An archangel

FIVE
BREATHE FOR ME

LET it Happen by Gracie Abrams* & *2/Catorce by Rauw Alejandro and Mr. Nasgai

GUS

NELLIE'S LIPS on mine feel better than I remember—soft lips and an eager tongue tasting of toasted almond and secrets. There's no way in hell I can tell anyone I can't stop thinking about the club. I don't know how I kept myself from messaging. All the fight is gone with her this close. The way her body molds to mine is the best reminder that we were meant to finish what we started that night, and I'm done fighting it.

She breaks the kiss with a breathy gasp, and when her green eyes lock with mine, they're glossy and enticing, inviting me in for more without uttering a word.

"A girl can get used to being greeted like that," she mocks.

"Better than me acting like a possessive asshole, I suppose."

"And showing up as a surprise, yes." She smiles at me, her eyes roaming my face as she brings her hands up to hold my jaw. "You shaved."

"I was on vacation last time we saw each other. That was the outlier. This is regular Gus." I barely have body hair as it is, so trying to grow a nice beard is out of the question. I usually just go for clean-shaven, but I let it go that weekend in Savannah.

The music is loud around us, and shouts from people drinking and screaming or playing games drown in the background as I focus on Nellie's rosy cheeks and swollen lips.

"You don't like surprises, Nellie?" I ask her, not letting the small remark she made go. Nellie speaks her mind, and I like it.

"I don't, but this one…this one might be good." She doesn't take her eyes from mine, and I like that. Her whole body is a language, conveying feelings with her eyes, sharing words with her mouth and desire with her hands—hands that are currently creeping up my chest and making me feel like a teenager again.

"I'm digging the whole sexy librarian thing you have going on." I pull gently on her silky ponytail and tilt my chin up toward the oversized glasses framing her face.

"What are you doing here, Gus?" she says as she stops exploring my body.

"Changing the topic?"

"Getting to the point. I wasn't putting any effort into coming to this party, hence not wearing contacts, but I still want to know: why are you here?"

"Shit, if this is not putting any effort… You're out to kill when you do, huh?"

"Gus…"

I sweep my hand over my face as I shake my head and let out a breath. "I wanted to say congratulations in person, and I wanted to see you." There's the truth. Lying would be easier;

it comes naturally to me, but I hate it. Years and years of seeing my dad use lies to manipulate situations definitely left a bitter taste in my mouth. I'd rather suffer through the truth this time than be at ease with a lie. Even if it makes me sound like a simp for someone I just showed interest in, I tell her.

"You flew all the way out here for that?"

"Among other things." I roll my thumb over her lower lip and pull it out from between her teeth.

"A piece of ass?" Not any ass—this ass. Alas, a gentleman wouldn't say that.

"Well, Nellie, how presumptuous of you to assume I want to sleep with you."

"Who said anything about sleeping? You and I both know you can't wait to fuck me." Direct, honest, and no elephant in the room; Nellie is here to play, and she's not holding anything back. She, unlike me, has no trouble telling it how it is.

"We shouldn't," I tell her.

"We're both consenting adults, Gus. Who cares? Also, that's what you should've been thinking before you came here and tongue fucked my mouth on this couch." The reason I've been keeping myself away from her is precisely that: it's too complicated. Our families are too close. We live different lives. I'm in a frat house, for goodness sake. My brother has secretly been in love with her sister forever. It's too complicated.

"Stop overthinking. Just feeling, remember? I know you want to feel good. I know you *feel* the connection right here." She taps on my chest. "So stop trying to deny it here." She grazes her delicate fingers over my temple.

"How about you, Nellie? Do you want to fuck me?" I ask, holding her face in my hands and closing the space between us but not kissing her again. If we're fucking tonight, I want her needy and ready. I want her to feel the pulse driving me to her. I want to know that she feels it beyond the way she's looking at me. I've been thinking about this moment for weeks, so I really hope the only answer she has for me is yes.

"So, so, so bad," she whispers against my lips and kisses me again, slipping a leg over my lap and straddling me. She kisses me intensely, deeply as I dig my fingers into her ass, pulling her closer to me. There's no way in hell I've only kissed her once four weeks ago. The way she kisses me, the way our lips are completely in sync, the way her body molds perfectly with mine—it's like she was made for me.

"Get a room!" someone shouts, and we break apart quickly. Fuck, I forgot we were at a party. The room simply blended into the background and disappeared the minute her attention was on me. The same thing happened at the club. No matter what, when her lips are on mine, everything else is irrelevant.

I drop my forehead to hers and whisper against her lips, "Come with me, Nellie."

"My dorm is a few blocks away," she replies. I don't need convincing, so I pull her off my lap, fixing her shirt as I guide her out of the room. We step outside, but we don't make it far before her friend shouts her name. She walks toward us, pulling Abraham by the hand. He's whipped by this girl, looking like a lost puppy being dragged around.

"I'm heading back home," Bee or Bree or whatever her name is says. "Don't wait up." She blows Nellie a kiss and turns around, still pulling Abraham. He shrugs his shoulders my way and smiles before turning around to follow her.

"So I guess the dorm is out of the question," Nellie tells me, holding her hands in front of her.

"Not a problem, sweet girl. I drove here. Come on." I walk her past a couple of houses to where I parked the rental car. I open the door and guide her in, and I'm on the road as fast as possible. I settle my hand on her thigh as I drive us to the hotel room I booked for the night.

"Where are you taking me?" she asks, her arms crossed over her chest and her gaze locked forward.

"To my hotel room. Why?"

"I need to tell my friends where we're going." Fuckin' dumbass; of course she does. She may trust me, but she needs to protect herself. I don't blame her.

"Here," I say, handing her my phone. "It's all in the notes app under today's date."

"No password?" she asks as soon as she unlocks it.

"I have nothing to hide," I reply, when in reality, I don't have a password because I'm not worried about anyone finding my family's information on my personal phone. If anything, I leave it like that for easy access to my emergency contacts. There isn't a lot of personal information to find either way. Aside from work availability updates with Manny, I don't share my life with anyone, especially not the women I spend time with.

She fidgets with the phone and eventually grabs her own, which I can presume is to text her friends the information.

"That's a good rule to have," I tell her, pulling into the parking garage of the prestigious hotel, the best one I could find on short notice in a college town.

"What is?" she asks, handing me back my phone and crossing her legs as she finishes messaging her friends. There's no music playing so the subtle shift in her body echoes through the car, making me acutely aware of her presence. I said Abraham was whipped, but with the way I can't focus on anything but Nellie, I'm whipped too, I guess.

"Having rules about going places with strangers." I'm not a stranger, but I might as well be. It had been years since I last saw her and the least I thought would happen when I did was that I would be lusting over her for a month.

"Yeah, too many psychos out there. But you're not a stranger, Gus. I just want to be careful. What about *your* friend? Is Bee safe with him?"

"I should be asking *you* the same thing. Is he safe with her?"

Nellie laughs, a soft but carefree sound before she tilts her body my way. "Honestly? Probably not. Bee is a force to be reckoned with. He'll be safe, but he might be sore for days. Also…people who sleep with her end up becoming obsessed with her, so I hope you're ready to have your boy down bad for her."

"I fear he's already down bad." I park the car and step out, helping Nellie do the same. I guide her through the lobby and onto the elevators, walking past the buzzing piano bar and the people waiting to get checked in or sitting in the warm-lit area surrounded by plants.

We step through the elevators at the same time she pulls her phone out of her bag and proceeds to text an update to her friends with her location.

The elevator door opens on my floor, and I slide my hand to stop it from closing. I have an irrational fear that someone will get stuck between them. I prompt Nellie to step out, and she walks confidently, letting me guide her toward my room. In the light of the hall, I notice how perfect she looks. She's wearing jeans that hug her body in the right places and a loose top that should hide her curves but instead showcases them under the sheer fabric. Her dark hair, tied in a high ponytail, bounces down her back with every step she takes, and my dick twitches at the thought of her perfect ass on my face.

We make it to my room, a cool blast of air rushing out of the dark room as I open the door. The room is sixty-five degrees, just how I like it. I have a hard time regulating my temperature sometimes, and I sweat more often than not, but I notice Nellie lifting her hands to her arms immediately.

"I can adjust the temperature so it's warmer here." I offer her a smile.

She returns it easily. "Or we can cuddle, and you can warm me up." She walks in, making herself at home, and stands by the window. This hotel has a floor-to-ceiling window facing the impressive atrium. The indoor garden provides guests with a view no matter the weather. It's perfect, and every time I travel, I try to find something like this. It eases my mind. Plants have always had that effect, but feeling like I'm in a tropical paradise, like my home country, without my skin melting from the heat is the best of both worlds. We're on the fourth floor, it's close enough to see everything but high up enough to give us some privacy, as long as nobody looks this way.

Nellie stands with her hands on the window, looking out into the atrium. I take my keys and wallet out of my pockets and set them on the nightstand as I get out my phone and search through my music to play my favorite song. Her body tenses as soon as the song starts, but she doesn't turn around to face me. I walk slowly behind her until my hands slide over her hips, and I capture them, digging my fingers into her flesh. I pull her flush to my body, and her breath hitches, her eyes never leaving the atrium, not even when I whisper the same phrase I sang for her that night at the club.

"That's the song," she whispers, closing her eyes and matching my movements with her body. I hum, my lips on the shell of her ear. "Are you trying for a do-over?" *Jackpot.*

"Are you a mind reader, Nellie?" My hands wander under her blouse, her soft skin the perfect contrast to my rough hands. She has some sort of tight top on under her blouse in lieu of a bra that I carefully pull up. Now, there's nothing between her perfect breasts and my fingertips. When I brush against her nipples, she hisses and grinds against me harder.

"Yes," she moans.

"Yes, you like this, or yes, you can read my mind?"

"Both," she says between a gasp and a moan when I lick the curve of her neck before sucking and kissing gently.

"What am I thinking now?" I ask as I suck her earlobe between my teeth.

"That you'd like to fuck me against this window." Wrong. I would like nothing more than to fuck her as far away as possible from the window, but her eyes won't leave the space in front of us, telling me she likes this.

"Do you want that, Nellie? Do you want me to make you shiver under my hands right here, where anyone can see?"

"Yes." I turn her around so her back is against the window, her eyes full of fire and desire when they meet mine.

"Let me undress you." I hold her gaze, waiting for her to say yes, and when she nods, I follow through, but not before kissing her. The feel of her lips on mine is something words cannot describe, or at least not any words I have in my vocabulary. I pull her shirt off, leaving her in the tight jeans and nothing else. Her perfect, perky breasts out in the open, her peachy nipples hard and ready for attention. She takes her shoes off and tries to unbutton her jeans, but my hands quickly replace hers. *My job, Nellie. My job.*

I pull her jeans down slowly, taking my time to drag my nose down her body, wanting to find out if she smells the same way everywhere, and she does. "Fuck, Nellie. I can't wait to see if you taste as good as you smell."

She lifts her legs, stepping out of jeans and panties, and I toss them aside. She stands still, her legs spread wide, and her pussy right in front of me.

"Well, are you going to?" she asks, and when I look up at her, she looks like a goddess. This is the moment I know I'm fucked.

"Am I going to what?"

"Taste and find out." Fucked, completely and utterly fucked.

She widens her stance a tad more as I move my hands to the back of her legs, sliding them up from her calf all the way to her ass. Taking my time, I hover my mouth over her pussy, licking her once and holding her in place when her knees buckle.

I do it again, but this time, her hands land on my head, keeping it in place. Greedy. I like it. I lick and suck, loving how sweet she tastes. She bucks her hips against my face, and with her hands, she pulls me closer, even if it's not possible. She sure as hell tries, taking the friction she needs while she silently rolls her hips. I won't stop, relentless as I take, take, and take everything she's willing to give me. Every drop is mine. Every gasp is mine. Every goosebump, every shake of her legs, all of it mine, and I'm taking it. My hands hold her ass hard, and with a suck of her clit into my mouth, she shakes under my hold, dropping her head back, hitting the window. I lick until she's limp in my arms and pepper kisses up her body. I kiss her hip, her delicate belly button, and then the three black dots between her breasts. I lick and kiss under her right breast, cupping it in my hand, taking her nipple in my mouth.

She tenses under my touch, but again, no sounds. I climb up her body, holding her tight, and kiss her gently, letting her taste herself on my lips. "Are you okay?" I ask, letting go of her mouth.

"Yeah. Why wouldn't I be?"

"You went quiet on me," I say, pushing her glasses up her nose and moving a loose piece of hair from the ponytail.

"I'm not a screamer," she sasses back, challenging me with her eyes.

"I bet you'd scream for me," I mutter, turning her back to face the window and widening her stance with my foot.

"It's never happened," she replies, her voice low and sensual.

"I like a challenge." I twist her ponytail in my hand and tug her head back, giving me more access to her neck, which I kiss softly. She hums, and I pull harder, testing the waters.

"And I don't like it slow."

"So demanding," I whisper against her ear as I pull out the condom I keep in my pocket and unbuckle my jeans, letting them drop to my ankles.

"I will demand. I want to feel good too," she says. I really like how assertive she is. I like that she doesn't hold back and tells me exactly how she likes it.

"I'm a good student, Nellie. Let me learn your body." I slide the condom on and hold her hips, tilting them back and taking the access the position grants me to fuck her from behind. I slide my fingers into her pussy, finding her wetter than I thought she'd be. Her perfect ass is on display, her pussy red, swollen, and wet, ready for me. "Fuck, baby. You're so wet for me."

She gasps and rolls her hips against my fingers, but I don't sink them in again. I spread her arousal all over, touching her clit with my soaked fingers, teasing her some more.

"Gus," she whispers, trying to add more fiction and chasing my fingers with every move.

"Talk to me. What do you want?"

"I want to come again."

"How, Nellie? How do you want to come? All over my face? With my fingers buried deep inside you? Or with my cock filling you up?"

"Oh, God," she moans, but then she tenses, her head turning quickly to the side. I follow her gaze to see a couple kissing on the balcony next to us. The lights are on in our room, so if they look our way, they'll see us. They'll see her. Her focus doesn't waver.

"You were saying?" I tease her clit again and drag two fingers down to her entrance, sliding them in seamlessly. She's even wetter than before. If her wetness is any indicator, she might like this a lot. The possibility of being caught. The possibility of being watched.

"I don't care. Just fuck me, please."

"'Do you want to move from the window?" I ask, forcing her to tell me she wants to stay.

She shakes her head but doesn't say anything. "Tell me what you want." I know she wants me to fuck her with the possibility of them looking. I push her closer against the window so her nipples touch the cold glass, and she hisses. *Jackpot.*

"Tell me, baby. Use your words."

"No, I don't want to move," she snaps as she rolls her hips. I slide another finger in. My dick is so hard, and with the condom squeezing me, I won't last long, especially as I feel her grow wetter watching the couple kissing as I tease her with my fingers. Is it wrong? Maybe, but the way this girl's pussy has my fingers in a chokehold, I would do whatever she wanted me to just for another orgasm. Fuck, I can't wait to have my mouth on her again. I slide my fingers out, coating the tip of my cock with her arousal, as I thrust in slowly, giving her time to adjust to the size. She tenses and holds her breath, and fuck, she's so tight.

"You have to breathe for me, Nellie." She lets it out, instantly relaxing.

"They're watching," she whispers. I had forgotten about the possible spectators. Forgetting seems to be what happens when my attention is on her.

"Then let them," I reply. I don't think they can see our faces, but they can definitely see what's going on, and to my surprise, I think they're enjoying the view. They pulled out a chair, sitting on the balcony facing us, the man holding the woman on his lap, his hand lost under her skirt. *Well, shit.*

"Are they…?" Nellie asks, and I take this time to use the same words she used on me.

"Just feeling, no thinking." I pull her hair since she liked it earlier, but not too much to where she can't watch them. She melts against me. She may not be a screamer, but her body screams for me.

I slam into her, slow the first few strokes, and then hard, just like she said she likes it. I bring my hands to tease her clit, and that earns me a loud gasp she tries to cover with her hands.

"Oh no, baby girl. If you're going to make sounds, they

belong to me." I pull her hands down, holding them against her back with one of my hands while the other one teases her clit again. I use the leverage of the window to drive my cock into her over and over again.

"Oh, fuck," she moans, louder this time, and when I look over to the balcony, the woman has her hands on her breasts, her legs wide open over the man's lap. That's enough to get me close to the edge. Come on, Nellie. Give me one more.

I tease her clit, pushing her fully against the window as I slam inside her over and over again. "Are you going to come for me? I want to feel your perfect little pussy tighten around my cock."

"Fuuuck," she shouts, and as the other girl closes her legs, trapping the guy's hand between her thighs, Nellie's pussy tightens around me, pulsating, showing me how hard she can come on my cock.

"Oh, God," she moans louder, her head tilting back as her hands lower to my thighs, grabbing and squeezing, I'm sure leaving marks as she comes around my cock.

"Yes," I groan at the shell of her ear and slow my strokes, allowing us both to come down from the high.

"OUT OF ALL THE things I could've gotten you, Chinese food is really what you wanted as a present?"

"Five orgasms and good food sounds like the perfect present to me," Nellie replies as she takes another crab rangoon and shoves it into her mouth. After the window situation, we took a shower, where I made sure she came two more times—once on my fingers, and once with my mouth. Then, we fucked slowly on the bed. She said she didn't like slow, but what she really means is, she needs pressure. She wanted my entire body on her. I was afraid to hurt her, but making sure she felt enough pressure was the key to making her come again. She asked for Chinese food almost immediately after.

"I mean, sure, but what do you actually want as a graduation present?" I ask her, grabbing the water cup from the side of the table and lifting it to her lips so she can take a sip.

"I can get used to this princess treatment," she sasses.

"You know this can't go any further," I reply, reminding her—reminding us—of the reality outside these walls.

"I don't want to think about that, Gus. I want to enjoy this. I want to enjoy us, for as long as it'll last, even if it's just the rest of the night." I can do that, but I don't think I can fuck her again if she wants to walk straight tomorrow, so I laugh.

"What are you laughing about?"

"I think you will be really sore tomorrow if we fuck again."

"Thanks for your candor, handsome. I happen to agree with you. No more fucking tonight. Such a shame, because that—" she points toward the window, then the bathroom, "—was really hot."

"It really was."

She waits silently for a second, then takes another bite of her food and suddenly sits up, closing the to-go container and slapping her hands on her thighs.

"A book shopping spree," she announces with a smile.

"What?"

"For my present. I want a book shopping spree." She's so damn adorable, and it's so funny, because she can be deep, eloquent, and assertive but very playful and charming too.

"Done, but come on, Nellie. You can dream bigger than that."

"Well, I could say take me on a sailboat out somewhere tropical and fuck me senseless for days, but that's unrealistic."

"Unrealistic for who?" I take the containers and put them on the nightstand, handing her the cup of water.

"Well, to most people, Gus. Do you have a plane on standby so you can take me to the Virgin Islands to sail while you fuck me senseless?" she replies with the sassy tone I'm growing used to.

"Doesn't that sound like the best way to spend the week?" I ask nonchalantly.

"We didn't plan for this."

"We're planning now. Do you have a passport?"

"You don't need a passport for the Virgin Islands, but I do have one," she replies.

"Abraham's birthday is this week, and he has a whole celebration planned in the Dominican. We leave tomorrow. Do you have anywhere to be for the next few days?"

She tightens her ponytail and challenges me with her eyes, as if she's wondering if I'm bluffing. Eventually, she replies, "No, I don't. But I don't want you to spend all that money on a frivolous wish."

"A wish is a wish. All you have to do is rub me, and you can call me your genie."

"Oh my God, stop." She laughs at my comment, and I can't help but smile back.

"If money is not meant to be spent, then why have it at all?" It's true. I have more money than I can spend. I donate so much already, and what I keep, I like to spend it living my life. What's the point in working hard and creating business models that make you a lot of money if you can't enjoy it? So one day you can retire? Once one is old and everything hurts? No, I want to live my life now. I don't know how many years I have to live without being confined to infusions and rescue treatments. So, for right now, I live.

"Gus…"

"Nellie…"

"People can't find out."

"It's a discreet event, I promise. Abraham… Well, his parties are a little something, But nobody will know."

"Are you really asking to take me somewhere tropical for a week?"

"And fuck you senseless, remember?"

She smiles back at me, grabbing the pillow and tossing it my way. "Don't get me all excited if you don't mean it."

"I don't say things I don't mean, Nellie. But I do have to ask for one thing.."

"I thought it was my gift." Her eyes are starting to get heavy, but she still smiles and says, "What is it?"

"You have to promise not to fall in love with me." She stares at me before climbing up on the bed and laying her head on a pillow.

"Don't worry, Gus. I won't. Now, let's go to sleep. If you expect me to be vacation ready tomorrow, I need my beauty sleep."

She pulls the blanket over her, and when I turn off the light, she turns her body and climbs up my torso, laying her head on my shoulder and wrapping her arm and leg around me.

There's no such thing as personal space when it comes to this girl, and I like it more than I should. Maybe I need to keep the not falling in love promise front and center too.

SIX
CHOCOLATE COVERED STRAWBERRIES

YONAGUNI BY BAD BUNNY & *Or Nah by Ty Dolla $ign, The Weeknd, Wiz Khalifa & DJ Mustard*

NELLIE

THIS TRIP HAS BEEN DREAMY. We arrived late Sunday night, so we had no time to do anything other than crash in bed. He has a private villa by the water in this northern town called Cabarete. The area is an intimate community with charming villas, each with tropical gardens and private terraces or balconies overlooking the water.

Yesterday, we spent the day exploring this part of the island, spending too much time under the sun. He booked us a private couple's massage, which ended with us immediately getting our hands all over each other as soon as the masseuse left. I can't get enough of him, and he seems to feel the same way. I've been ignoring Cara's text messages, and the only thing I told my parents was that I was doing some traveling before returning home.

Bee is here with Abraham, but we've not seen them much. The party's tonight, though, and they'll be there. The villa is right by the coast, on the prettiest beach I've ever seen— crystal clear water and smooth white sand. This sand is so different than in Florida, even on the panhandle. It's almost translucent, and it doesn't stick to my body.

Gus has practically dragged me out of the water to feed and hydrate me all day. I've been swimming non-stop, other than food breaks and a quick nap earlier. Gus swam for a while too, and we figured out that's something we both have in common, except he swims to exercise and I swim to feel. I've been sensory-seeking my entire life, always trying to find the right amount of pressure or the right amount of pleasure. For years, dance gave me that, and when I didn't have it anymore, I turned to less healthy choices. Let's just say, my body has the marks to remind me that wasn't the right way. My therapist suggested sports that would give me the sensory input I was always searching for, and swimming ended up being the one for me. The feeling of my skin covered in water provides me with constant sensation. The salty water stings my eyes at first, and then it's natural, like I was always meant to be there. Also…who doesn't love feeling weightless?

"Hey, little fish," Gus shouts from the shore. The sun is setting, casting a glow over his dark skin, making him look even better than he does normally. He's wearing white linen pants, and he's holding a water bottle I'm sure is for me. He's taken good care of me on this trip, keeping me full and sated in more ways than one.

"All slippery and scaly?" I shout from the water, turning my body so I can float facing the sky.

"You're probably a prune by now, Nellie. Come out," he says.

"Or you can get in," I add, not bothering to look at him. I'm sure he can see me carelessly floating away.

"As much as I would love to, we should go get dressed for

the party. It'll be night soon." Oh shit, I forgot about that. I get out, feeling the warm breeze on my skin as I walk toward him. The water's dripping from my body, and I grab my hair, twisting it to get the excess out before putting it in a top bun.

Gus' eyes don't leave my body, roaming from top to bottom, incinerating my skin with every look. He makes me feel more than any man ever has, and he's not even touching me. I smile seductively at him, and when our eyes meet, I know I make him feel the same. I don't know how the hell I have chemistry with this man knowing damn well nothing could ever come out of this situationship.

He hands me the water, and then he turns around to grab a towel from the chair lounge I was sunbathing on. "Thanks," I mutter as he opens the towel and guides me into it. He wraps it around my shoulders, tucking it at the corners, squeezing me once it's done.

We walk in silence back to the villa, where I find a table full of delicious treats: chocolate-covered strawberries, cold cuts, cheese, grapes, cantaloupe, some fruits I don't recognize, crackers, and what seems to be an assortment of spreads.

"What is this?" I ask incredulously, looking up at Gus, who's behind me, squeezing my shoulders just the right amount. Always the right amount.

"Fuel. You need to eat. Come on."

I drop the towel over the high-top stool as I sit with the banquet of finger foods in front of us. I immediately feel over-whelmed at the choices. Do I taste something sweet first? Or salty? Or do I try both? Do I grab something new, or do I stay with something safe? My eyes go back and forth, and I tense with indecision.

"What's wrong?" Gus murmurs, his fingers gently cupping my chin, tilting my face up to meet his gaze. His onyx eyes pierce through the dim room, dark and intense, studying me like I'm the only thing that matters.

I swallow, trying to look away, but his gaze holds mine, and it's futile. "Nothing," I lie, my voice a little softer than I intended.

He doesn't let go. Instead, his thumb traces along my jawline, his touch sending shivers down my spine. "Something," he says, his voice low and steady, a quiet command wrapped in warmth. "I can tell. Talk to me."

"Are you always this perceptive?" I ask, trying to sound casual, even though my heart's racing.

He doesn't smile, doesn't break eye contact.

"I pay attention," he says, his voice barely above a whisper. "It's not that hard when your body doesn't hide what's on your mind." His gaze flickers to my lips before returning to my eyes, which I'm sure show confusion. "Your body language speaks volumes. Now, tell me. What's wrong?"

I hesitate, caught in the pull of him. "Too many choices," I finally admit, the words slipping out before I can stop them.

His brow furrows slightly, as if he's pondering it, but his hands never leave my face, holding me in the moment, grounding me. "I can help you with that. I didn't know what you'd want so I told Sonora to get a bit of everything."

Sonora is his housekeeper. She has been with his family for years and goes where needed, or so she said yesterday, when we were talking about why she's at this villa if nobody lives here. She told me she needed to practice her English, so we talked for hours, a warm conversation during which I slowed myself for her benefit.. I liked her a lot, and she told Gus she liked me, so a good thing, I assume.

"It's not that I don't want it. It looks delicious. I just have a hard time picking. It's exhausting."

"Decision fatigue," he adds at the same time I gasp in surprise. I usually have to explain this to everyone, and half the time, people don't get it. Even being able to breathe and not have to explain lifts some weight off my shoulders.

"How did you know?"

"Wild guess. Wait here," he says, walking toward the living room and then coming back with something in his hands.

"Do you trust me?" Is it normal to think yes?

"I think so," I whisper, and he wraps a piece of fabric around me, sliding it over my eyes and tying it behind my head. "What are you doing?"

"Removing the choices. I'll make the decisions for you. You just let yourself go, okay?"

"I don't want to fuck right now, Gus."

He laughs a warm laugh that reaches my soul. It sounds silky and rough at the same time. "Not everything is about us fucking, Nellie. But if that changes, you let me know, yeah?" I nod. "Now open your mouth." There's some movement in front of me, but not enough for me to pick up on whatever he's doing. I hear him come closer as he places something cold and soft in my mouth. It's bigger than I expected, but I close and chew, tasting sweet and slightly salty at the same time.

"Melón y prosciutto," he whispers.

"Prosciutto what?" I mumble between bites.

"And cantaloupe." Fuck, that was a good bite.

I keep chewing, and when I'm ready for another, I open my mouth again. This time, he puts something hard, salty, and chunky in my mouth.

"Cajuiles."

"Cashews?" I ask, swallowing and opening my mouth again.

"Yes. Atta girl." My body shivers at his praise before I feel the next bite cross my lips. This time, I know exactly what it is, because chocolate-covered strawberries are my favorite. They make me horny as fuck, so I usually don't eat a lot of them, but I love them. I don't say anything, though. I wait for him to say it in Spanish, because I love hearing him speak it.

"Fresa con chocolate." Why is that so hot?

"I think I like how you said that more than I liked the strawberry."

He chuckles again, and when I open my mouth, I expect another bite, but I get his lips instead. He kisses my bottom lip, sucking it in between his teeth and then smiling against me.

"Sorry, you had some chocolate there."

"Don't apologize for kissing me." Especially not that kind of kiss.

"Noted. Open for me." I open my legs on command, and he chuckles again. "Behave, Nellie. You said you just wanted to eat, and it will be really hard for me to keep feeding you and respect your wishes if you do things like that."

"Maybe I'm regretting my choices." He slides something new in my mouth. It's salty and shaped like a fry, but it's firmer, and it tastes different.

"Yuquita," he says in between a chuckle and a cough. "I'm taking that as a no."

"It's good, just a little crispier than I expected," I say. I finish it and realize how at ease I feel. I usually like to be in control, but in this moment, I needed somebody else to take over. He knew that.

I don't want to sound trite and start talking about soulmates and shit. Do I believe in them? Yes. Do I think that just because this guy is giving me all his attention, that's what it means? Maybe, but I can't say that out loud. He continues feeding me multiple other things, some soft and sweet, some crunchy and salty, some a mix, some new things I've never had before. After three different bites, he feeds me a chocolate-covered strawberry and kisses me again. I'm entirely too turned on by all of this, and I'm officially regretting my choices.

I can't eat much more anymore, and he probably can sense it, because he has slowed down feeding me. He brings a straw to my lips while he says, "Suck, baby girl."

I squirm in my seat, and he chuckles again. He likes this torture, and he'll be lucky if I don't jump him in this kitchen when he's done with the teasing.

"Not fair," I say, leaning forward to poke his chest as I feel something hard pressing against my leg. Good to see I'm not the only one affected by this.

"I take it back. I definitely want you now." I hear his footsteps as he walks away from me. I could take the blindfold off, but I like not knowing what's happening. I kind of like being at his mercy, and that's a first. I hear the fridge open and close, and then something makes a low snap close to me.

"Open your mouth, Nellie." Gus says, and on command, I obey. A sticky, cold liquid touches my lip, and I stick my tongue out to taste it. *Chocolate.* In no time, his lips are on mine, sucking and cleaning the chocolate with his tongue. Then, he's gone before I can reach out for more. He drips more syrupy chocolate, touching my lip and dripping over my chin which he licks, flattening his tongue and dragging it up, reaching my mouth and kissing me hard. My lips will be bruised if he continues, but I don't care.

His fingers pull the string of my bathing suit, lowering it under my breast, I feel the syrup cover between my breasts, right over the vertical dotted line tattoo that he quickly licks with his warm tongue. He repeats the process, but this time, the syrup touches my nipple, cold, sticky, and abundant. This feels messy, but it also feels so damn good. I try to remove my blindfold, but he holds my hand and says, "What if…you leave that on."

I stop and think about it for a second. My skin buzzes with electricity at the prospect of whatever will happen if I leave it on, if I just…feel.

I nod, and he hums by my ear. "Yes, that's it. Just feeling."

He lowers his mouth over my chocolate-covered nipple with the same determination he kisses my mouth, and fuck, I'm so damn turned on right now. He repeats the process with my other nipple, and after a loud moan, he chuckles against my body. He brings his hands to my torso and lifts me, sitting me higher on the breakfast table. There's some shuffling around, and then he lays me back on the cold surface, keeping my ass on the edge.

"Blindfold stays on," he commands. Oh, I love demanding Gus. Yes, tell me what to do, please.

"Yes, sir." He groans, and my skin tingles with the sound.

"Fuck, Nellie. You'll be my undoing." He unties the string of my bottoms. I feel a gentle breeze over my pussy, and his warm hands hold my ankles, opening my legs, placing my feet on the edge of the counter.

"You're already so wet for me."

"You've been teasing me for the last thirty minutes."

"If I knew your pussy would be dripping this much after some food play, I would've done it sooner." I squeeze at those words, trying to find some friction, and he groans under his breath. *I guess he saw that.*

Cold, gooey liquid drips over my clit, and I hiss at the sensation. Before I can overthink it, his mouth covers me, sucking and biting gently. My back arches, almost coming off the table, but he uses one of his hands to pin me in place as he sucks harder.

"Fuuuuuuuck," I groan, loud. So sexy. So dirty. My own guttural sounds have me unraveling, and I can feel Gus experiencing the same. He hums over my clit as soon as I try to squirm. He licks, sucks, and teases, increasing intensity over and over again. No more chocolate, but who needs that when he's eating me like I'm his favorite dessert? He licks one more time before biting, making my knees close, my hands moving to hold his head in place. I lift my hips, searching for more friction, and he brings his hand to my nipple, squeezing it— gentle at first, then hard—making me come undone.

"Yes!" I scream and cover my mouth, because who am I, screaming over an orgasm? I'm not used to this level of insanity, and fuck, don't I like it.

"There she is. See, I told you. You just needed someone to give you something to scream about." I gasp at those words and his raspy voice, but then he puts the cherry on top when he says, "No, not someone. Me. You needed me."

I take the blindfold off just in time to see him taking his pants off and sliding the condom on. Now, he's buried deep inside me, and I'm bucking off the counter.

And what a sight he is.

His brown skin, kissed by the sun, is perfect, slightly bronze, with beads of sweat on his face. His dark eyes are focused on mine, heating me up more than I already am as he drives inside me over and over again.

"Yes." My voice was barely a whisper as I close my eyes and let the good feelings wrap me up completely.

"Eyes on me, Nellie." I snap my eyes open, and damn it, I like it entirely too much. I like him entirely too much. "Watch me fuck you so hard, you scream again. This time, I want you to scream my name."

"Yes," I moan, wrapping my legs around his toned ass, bringing my hands to his back, pulling him as close to me as I can. I need his hands on me like I need air, and as if he can hear my thoughts, he does it. We're a tangled mess of arms, his mouth on my neck and my nails dragging along his back as he continues to fuck me hard.

He whispers near the shell of my ear, "Come on, baby. I'm so close, but I need you to come again. Come for me, baby. Give me one more."

I drop my head back, closing my eyes and letting this moment engulf me. He presses one hand to my clit, and when he bites my neck, I scream his name as I explode around his dick.

I feel it all. His dick hardens inside me. His body tenses as he comes, his unraveled moan by my ear. His hands press my chest to his, and my heart skips a beat—how the fuck am I ever going to be able to survive not having this again?

"WHAT DID you two lovebirds do all day?" Bee asks from Abraham's lap. I don't think I've seen the two of them without each other the whole time. She's wearing a tiny white dress displaying her assets, and Abraham, in his all-linen outfit, refuses to take his hands off her. He looks pretty good himself. Plus, the daggers Bee has been sending all night to any woman who dares to look his way is too amusing.

"Not lovebirds," I snap back at her, sipping on my rum drink Gus has filled up for me every time I'm at a third of my cup. This is a white party, so he's also wearing linen pants and a shirt called Chacabana. It's also made out of linen, and it looks breathable, but more formal than what a lot of the men here are wearing. He has his initials embroidered on it, *G.Z.*. The contrast of the white shirt against his brown skin is outstanding, and I find myself more attracted to this man by the hour.

"Oh please, look at how down bad this man is for you already," she sasses, wiggling her eyebrows at Gus.

Gus starts to talk, but I interrupt him and say, "Bee, stop it." I give her my sternest look. I don't want him embarrassed, and I don't want him to think I expect a relationship or anything else. Would I want to date him? Yes, I would. Not something I ever thought I would say, but the more time I spend with him, the more I want to be around him. I don't know how I'm supposed to go home in two days and pretend like I just didn't take this life-changing trip with him.

"Oh relax, Nellie Mellie. I'm just joking. I know you don't date, and from what I've read, neither does he. Ooop! Let's go dance." She stands, pulling Abraham by the arm and dragging him to the dance floor, leaving me and Gus in the dark corner.

I let out a breath, forcing my eyes up to him. "I'm sorry

about that. She can be…well, too intense sometimes." I love Bee with my entire heart, but sometimes, I feel like she doesn't know when to stop pushing. This is one of those occasions.

"It's really okay. I know you know nothing can come out of this." I know it, but hearing him say it is a punch to the gut.

"But maybe…" I let the thought drift. I don't want to sound needy. I don't want to sound young and dumb, but can't he see how good we could be together?

"Nellie," he whispers, dragging his hand over his face. "You know there's no way we could work out."

Ouch. Okay.

"I didn't mean it like that," he adds, roaming my face with his eyes. I'm sure he can see all the emotions I'm trying to conceal, all the hurt behind the silence, all the shock I should have seen coming, but it still catches me off guard.

"I know. No need to say anything."

"Baby, please listen."

"No. You don't get to call me baby after you just told me there's no way we could work out. I'm not asking you to marry me. I'm not even asking you for anything, but shit, Gus. At least pretend I'm not just a piece of ass for the weekend." Isn't that exactly what this is? It must be the damn drinks and the good sex getting to my head. I've never had a problem before sleeping around and then going back to normal, so why now? Why him?

"It's too complicated. It has nothing to do with you and everything to do with…well, everything else."

"I get it. Our families are too close. We don't live in the same town. You don't date. *I get it.* I knew what I was getting myself into. No need to apologize." I don't stop spitting out facts to deviate from this awkward conversation. We have the rest of tonight and all of tomorrow before we return to the States, and I just want to enjoy it.

"Please don't be upset."

"I'm not upset. Stop treating me like this."

"Like what?" he asks, completely shutting me out. I know he doesn't want to let me in, and I can't blame him. I went from an almost one night stand, to a one night stand, to a weekend getaway all within a month. That's on top of being the youngest of the family friends.

"Like I'm a spoiled child who can't handle her shit. I'm a woman, Gus." I get up from the chair and walk outside the crowded room to the beach. I know he's right behind me, because I can hear his footsteps following closely, but he doesn't say anything. He's giving me space, and I like it.

I walk past a group of chairs by the water, the soft sound of waves crashing on the shore embracing me in the hug I didn't know I needed. There's a wooden pier ahead, dotted with yachts, sailboats, and other vessels docked side by side, each one more stunning than the last. But there's something about the pier today, a magnetic pull, that makes me want to step onto it. Without thinking, I slip off my shoes, feeling the rough wood under my feet as I walk slowly, taking in all in: the boats, the way they rock gently in the water, their hulls gleaming under the moon as it casts a soft light over everything, the gentle whoosh of each wave centering me— grounding me.

I start reading the names on the sterns, some in English, some in Spanish, until one boat catches my eye. I stop in my tracks, unable to look away. The sailboat before me is breathtaking, so elegant, it almost seems like it belongs in a painting —white, with smooth, sweeping brown curves along its side. The contrast between the two colors is stunning, but it's the deck that really captures my attention. It's polished, the wood glowing with a golden hue, like it's been cared for meticulously over the years. The mast rises high, standing proud against the sky, the sails, crisp, white, pulled tight against it. There's something about the name that's bizarre, almost too obvious, but I still can't grasp it.

I can feel Gus' presence right behind me, quiet and

steady, but I refuse to look back. I look at the beautiful boat, then up at the sky to see it starless and vast. So infinite. So beautiful.

I hear his voice, low and warm. "Come on, let me show you around."

I turn to him, my heart skipping a beat as I lift my eyebrows, everything clicking. "Is this yours?"

Gus grins, his eyes softening just a little. "My family's," he says, pointing to the name painted on the polished surface. It clicks. *Allie and Twins.* "We get to share it, but Allie never comes, and Manny, well…that man never leaves work. So, for the most part, I use it. Come on."

He steps onto the boat, his shoes in hand, and extends his other hand toward me. Without thinking, I take it, stepping onto the deck. The wood feels warm under my feet, and the boat seems to welcome me, like it's been waiting for someone to appreciate it as much as I do.

Like I belong here.

I walk ahead as his hand rests gently on my lower back, guiding me forward. The sensation is unexpected, comforting. There's something in the way he touches me—like he's making sure I feel safe, but since he's showing me something he cherishes, it feels even more special.

Gus walks beside me now, quiet again, his hands gently touching different parts of the boat. There's a kind of unspoken tension between us. He's showing me something personal, something he's proud of, and I'm not sure what to say next. This space, this boat, it feels like it holds more than just wood and sails. It feels like it holds a history, a story, maybe even a part of him. For some reason, it makes me want to know more.

"It's beautiful," I whisper, letting the breeze share my words.

"Just like you." My eyes snap to his, but I don't say a word. I just hold his.

"You can't say things like that after you just told me nothing can come out of this."

"And you can't expect anything more than what I'm willing to give you right now, Nellie. You knew this. It's too complicated. There's too much going on. What happened to just feeling and not thinking?" he asks, laying his body against the mast. He's not wrong. I said I was okay with a hook-up. I was adamant about it. I was clear. And now, I'm throwing a fit like a petulant child.

"What are *you* willing to give me, Gus?"

"An incredible time for the night and tomorrow. Also… you asked for sailing on a tropical island, and I have not kept my end of the deal. This, I can promise: a good time for the rest of the trip and sailing into the sunrise. I can't promise anything else, at least not right now."

I take the time to settle my feelings and remind myself to think like an adult. Technically, I've only seen him a few days, but the thirty days we were apart built a fire within me, and it's about to burn. Just like a real fire, I pour water over it and pretend it's not there. I can't blame him. "Okay."

"Okay, what?"

"That's okay with me," I reply and smile at him as I step forward, holding his gaze. This is too fast, and honestly, it's probably just adrenaline from a very good lay, so I need to chill and just enjoy the moment.

"Promise me you're okay with that." But then he speaks with that soft tone like he cares, and I just want to hug him. How is this sweet and spicy boy single? "Promise me, Nellie."

"I promise, Gus." Maybe I'm starting to lie to myself, but I still give him the promise I don't know I'll be able to keep. He grabs my hand and walks me through the doors to the small cabin below.

SEVEN
BARELY BREATHING

***Classy 101* by Feid and Young Miko & *Wait* by M83**

GUS

NOTHING CAN COME out of this. Nothing can happen after tomorrow. She's a family friend. She lives in a different town. She just finished college. She's starting a new job, a new life. She's beautiful. She's passionate. She's kind. She's funny. She's smart.

Fuck, Gus. Fuck. I drag my hands over my face and cross my leg over my lap as I watch Nellie sound asleep on the bed below deck. We spent the night in the boat, talking, kissing, and having sex. She's insatiable, and I'm happy to oblige. I can't seem to shake it, either. I need to keep myself in check, because after tomorrow, she'll go back to her life, and I'll go back to mine. I doubt I'll be able to do that unscathed, considering how she's been living inside my thoughts for a month. Now that I've had her in my arms, in my bed, now that I know what she tastes like, I don't know if I'll be able to forget her. I have to. I have too much shit going on. She likes fun and honesty, and I can be both of those things, but not for long periods of time. Not without my body breaking in front of her and dragging her into more problems. Another reason why I don't date. I'm not about to give my shitty heart to someone and then expect them to handle it with the care it needs while putting a strain on theirs.

The waves cradle the sailboat, moving it front and back. Nellie is fast asleep, her dark hair a contrast against the white linen covering the bed, her lips slightly parted as she dreams. Or I hope she does. Someone as smart as she is should have dreams that reach the sky and beyond.

I get up and walk to the bed, sitting beside her and whispering, "Hey, sleepy head."

"Go away," she mumbles, moving side to side and pulling the blanket on top of her.

"I want to show you something." I hold her hand and trace small circles on her wrist over a faint scar. Maybe in another life, I could ask her about it.

"Is it even morning yet? Why are you up so early? Did you even go to sleep?"

I chuckle at the questions she's firing off, but I don't answer any of them. "Come on, I made coffee."

"Iced?"

"Yes, come on." I watched her drink iced coffee these past two days as if they were water. She mentioned something about enjoying the taste of Café SantoDomingo, which makes me happy, considering I grew up on it my whole life. Nothing compares to the aroma and the bitter aftertaste. It's not too overpowering, but it definitely tastes like coffee, not like a watered down version. No flavors, no sweeteners, just good coffee.

I hand her the glass, as she's trying not to fall back on her face in exhaustion, but after a singular sip, her eyes snap to mine, and she smiles.

"Perfect," she whispers.

"Come on, let me show you something." I give her my hand, wrapping her in a blanket and guiding her out of the cabin onto the deck. She gaps at the sight.

"Gus…where are we?"

"Mar adentro"

"Translation, please."

"Out in the ocean. I wanted to show you the sunrise, and it's not the same when you're surrounded by the chaos of the pier. Out here, it's just us, the water, the sky, and the sun." I nod forward, and she follows my gaze.

"This is…this is breathtaking." She sits right where she stands, taking it all in. The cloudless sky changes from dark blue, almost black with purple hues, to a lighter blue with shades of orange and yellow. I tilt her head to the right so she can see where the sun is coming up. *"Breathtaking,"* she whispers, taking a sip of her coffee and taking it all in.

The waves crash against the vessel, but it's not too choppy, just enough to create a melody. The waves, the boat, and us. "Inspiring. Wow," Nellie says again. The water starts lightening too, with every ray of sun giving it more life, making it feel more serene than eerie.

"What does it inspire you to do?" I ask, sitting behind her, my legs wrapping around her, pulling her flush against my chest.

"I don't know…to breathe? To live? Cara's always talking about how spending time outside helps her feel more alive, but I usually only feel like that in the water. This? This is something everyone should experience once in their lifetime. Thank you…" She trails off, and I nod as I lie my head on hers. "Is this why your hands are rough? Because you sail?"

I nod. "Sailing and rock climbing. I love them both for different reasons, but my hands don't necessarily agree." We sit, watching, sharing the silence worth more than a thousand words, and let the sun rise until it's high above our heads.

"What inspires you, Gus?" she asks when I least expect it.

How do I tell her nothing and everything? How do I tell her I live inspired by everything around me and by absolutely nothing at the same time?

"It's hard to find inspiration sometimes. If I overthink it, I won't find any at all, so for the most part, I usually try to find something to look up to in the right here and right now."

She tilts her head back, resting it on my chest and sliding down my body before she closes her eyes. I kiss her forehead, which makes her smile. She opens her eyes again, looking into mine but reaching directly into my soul. She can see right through me, and in this moment, I know. In this moment, I know I may not be able to move on from these past few days.

"What inspires you right now, then? Don't bullshit me, Gus. Be honest." I know she values honesty, and fuck, so do I, but vulnerability is a tougher one to breach. If we only have this time, these days, then maybe I can give her that.

"You."

She turns around, climbing my body and straddling me. She sits right on my lap and holds my face in her hands. "You can't say things like that and expect me to not think about you after tomorrow."

She looks at me with an intensity I can only compare to lust, because if I think beyond it, I could call it yearning, wanting, *needing*, and we can't have that. *She* can't have that. I have so much going on, so much that will always haunt me. A load that is just mine, one nobody else deserves to carry. My health is complicated, and she doesn't deserve the burden. Nobody does.

"You can't think about me after tomorrow, but…I'm just being honest."

"Maybe sugarcoat it for me next time and tell me it's the sky or something." She tries to laugh it off, tries to cover the pain with humor, but her eyes tell me another story. As if she can tell, she lowers her gaze.

"You want me to lie, Nellie?" I bring my hand to her chin, lifting her face up to look at me again. *Come on, Nellie. Don't leave me.* What a fucking hypocrite I am, but damn it, maybe I need to be a selfish asshole for once and go for what I want.

She sighs. "I want you to be easy with my heart. If all you can give me is today, I want it fully, but I don't want to hurt past tomorrow. So please, just be easy on me, okay?"

"I can do that."

"Promise?" she asks, caressing my cheek and smiling sadly at me.

"Promise." Leave it up to me to find comfort and connection in the one girl I shouldn't. Leave it up to me to be so close to saying "fuck it all", to see what else could happen beyond tomorrow. I don't have time to ponder it anymore, because Nellie pops up from my lap and turns to look at the water.

"The water is calling me. Wanna swim?" Nellie asks.

"I didn't really come prepared to swim. I have swim trunks and towels, but I don't have anything for you. I was only planning on staying half a day, if that."

She looks at the water, and I can see it calling for her just like she said. I can see it in her face how she's dying to jump and let it consume her. She walks closer to the rail and then turns around, smiling and motioning me to her with her fingers.

Her smile is wicked. Her eyes are inviting, and whatever she's thinking, I know I will agree with.

"You know...there's nobody else here, so I don't think there's a problem if we just jump in...naked."

Fuck. "Nellie..." She steps out of the oversized tee I let her borrow last night and stands in front of me in her underwear. "You are so much trouble."

"What's trouble if I'm by myself? Or you can join, and then we can both get in trouble together." She moves her hands behind her back, and in a split second, her bra is on the deck, her beautiful breasts on display. I'm dumbfounded by the whole thing, frozen in place. What did she call it? I'm awestruck by this woman. There's nobody out here, so I'm not worried about her being seen, and neither is she, clearly, but damn. What a move. She pulls her underwear down, and with a quick jump, she gets into the water.

"Nellie!" I shout, rushing to the edge as she disappears. I hold the rail and look over at the same time she pops her head out and laughs loudly. Her laugh is vibrant and pure, reaching every bit of my nerve endings and sparking a fire in my soul. Just one laugh, and I feel more alive than I've felt in a long time.

"Nellie, come back up."

"Why?! The water is perfect. It's early enough that we can swim for a while and still be back in time to explore more like you said you wanted. Come on, Gus. Come swim."

"It would be irresponsible of me."

"What would? Jumping in the water with me? Why? Because I'm naked? News flash, my guy—you've seen me naked."

I shake my head and snicker. "Both of us in the water without clothes. What if something happens?"

"What's going to happen, Gus? I won't bite, and I'm a strong swimmer. If you're worried about drowning, I got you." She lays her head back, letting her legs come up, floating away from the boat and taking all my rational thoughts with her. What I do next has no logic at all. I remove my pants, and I jump in the water with her.

The water is perfectly warm. It's too salty for my eyes, but the temperature is perfect. I tread water, waiting for Nellie to swim back to me, and she does with a big smile on her face. Her soaked hair falls over her shoulders, and her smile brighter than the sun itself.

"Hi, handsome," she whispers, treading water in front of me, only her shoulders out of the water, the rest hidden under the waves. *A wave.* She has a little wave tattooed right under her collarbone. I've been so focused on all of *her*, I've missed the little details. I missed how her green eyes have golden and brown specks intertwined with the most perfect green, how she has two small freckles right above her full lips. Her little wave tattoo and the little three dots between her breasts. The latter, I've noticed before, but not like now, with the water brushing over it. The lack of tan lines or, better yet, faint ones that indicate she either sunbathes naked or tans. Her beautiful ears don't have anything adorning them. Her damn smile—the one she's flashing me right now.

"Hola, hermosa," I reply, out of breath, and not because of the physical exertion. She steals my breath away.

"Promise me you won't ever stop looking at me like that," she says, smiling bigger and reaching for my body with her hands.

"Like what?" I curl my hands around her hips and wrap her legs around my body.

"Like I'm the most beautiful girl you've ever seen."

"You are."

"There are a lot of promises being tossed around here today."

"I hope you're a man of your word and you don't break them. Now, promise me. No matter what happens, I want to feel the same way when your eyes are on mine, always. Even if we're old and married to other people. Even if you don't like me anymore."

"Nellie, I could never not like you. I think our problem has nothing to do with that and everything to do with…well, everything else." She traces my neck and my shoulders with her fingers as she tilts her head and flashes me another smile. This one is a little sad, like she knows this is over before it can even start.

"Even if it kills me…I promise."

She brings her lips to mine and kisses me softly until I

can't hold on anymore. I sink underwater with her body wrapped around mine.

"TELL ME ABOUT YOUR JOB." We've been talking for hours, and it's time to go, but neither of us are ready to burst our little bubble.

"I don't work a lot anymore. The company runs itself, and I just make sure my clients are satisfied and their portfolios are up to date." My brother and I own a finance firm we built from scratch. It works really well, and it made us millionaires before we were twenty-two. I have an "as needed" relationship with it. I go when I need to, and I don't go when I don't. I treat it as a job, as a career, not as my life—unlike Manny, who breathes and lives Zabana Enterprises.

"So you have millions of dollars, and you don't even go to work? How is that fair?" She finishes braiding her hair after combing it with her hands. She's been wearing my shirt since we got out of the water, and she let her hair air dry. She's beautiful, breathtaking, and I love that she's so careless about things other girls I'm usually with care about. Not once she has worried about makeup, her hair, or even her clothes. She did mention needing her glasses, since she didn't bring them to the party, but other than that, she's just enjoying the moment.

"Well…kind of. I still go when I have to, and I oversee a lot of accounts from home. Manny, on the other hand, is always there."

"So he makes sure everything runs smoothly?"

"No, more like he makes sure everything is micromanaged. He's approaching burn out, and he needs to take a break sooner rather than later. I'm worried he might die there, miserable and mad at the world."

"But he'll have money…"

"Wasn't it you who told me just a month ago that you weren't going to choose a career based on the zeros of your bank account?"

"Touché, touché, but don't men always want more? More money, more status, more ass, more women? Isn't that how you measure power? How do you measure success?"

"Not all of us."

"Statistically speaking, though."

"I don't want my brother to be a statistic." A comfortable silence falls between us, letting the conversation drift away. "And to answer your question, the only thing I want more of is health and life. Everything else comes and goes, but how are you supposed to live the latter without the first?"

"You seem pretty healthy to me…"

"I wish I could say I was healthy too…but enough about me. How about you? Are you excited about moving back to Baker Oaks?" I add, changing the topic drastically when I see her visibly concerned. She waits but doesn't acknowledge it. Good. Crisis averted.

"I'm about to interview for my dream job at my dream school, and I can't wait."

"You look pretty happy about that. I hope it ends up being exactly what you hope for and that you get the job."

"I hope so too. I'm damn good at it. My internship was dreamy, and my professors sent outstanding letters of recommendation. That brings me joy."

"What else brings you joy, hermosa?"

"Swimming. I started swimming in middle school, when the school counselor introduced me to the swim team. I've done it ever since. That, and escaping to my friend's house in Georgia. Picture this. Small cabin in the middle of Georgia, not too far from home. Her family doesn't use it much, and I've been escaping there since I can remember. Sometimes, during school holidays, I just drive there and stay by myself for days. I like being able to shut it all out sometimes."

"What are you shutting out?"

"The world. The chaos. The noise. The pain." She lays her head on my lap and grabs my hand. "Being in the cabin is like reading—an escape when the world hurts too much."

I both love and loathe how much I like spending time with her. How is it possible that for my entire life, I've only been able to connect with family and friends, and the first girl who makes me interested in more is one who would come with so many challenges?

She brings her hand up to my lip, and when I look where I would find a smile, I find a frown. "Hey, Gus?"

"Yes?" She sits up and brings her other hand to my eye.

"Are you allergic to anything?"

I've been so focused on Nellie and getting to know more about her, I missed all the signs. *No, no, no.* I didn't notice the tingling right below my lips that comes at first, or tight sensation that seems to focus on my lower lip and on my tongue right before it gets worse.

"I'm sorry, Nellie, for what's about to happen. Just don't freak out, okay?" I stand and walk to the cabin, pulling all the drawers out and looking under the cabinets for my emergency bag. I can't find it anywhere.

"Gus, what is going on?" Nellie asks somewhere behind me, but I can't stop to look at her right now, not until I find my medicine.

My lips feel heavier. I feel the same tingling in my hands too. Fuck, it may be too late. I look one more place, and it's not here. I swear to God, if someone took it out when cleaning and didn't put it back… Fuck.

"I need my phone," I say sharply, looking at her while I plead with my eyes. I don't have the words to explain it right now. I can't explain. Every second is precious, but I can't dwell on it. The higher the stress, the worse the flare. I don't have the luxury right now to think about it.

She fumbles next to the bed looking, and once she finally finds it, she hands it to me. I click the emergency feature on my phone and put it on speaker, waiting for the emergency department to pick up.

"Gus, please. What's going on?"

"I need you to stay calm, but…"

"911 ¿Cual es su emergencia? ¿Me puede decir su nombre?"

"Augusto Zabana. Estamos a aproximadamente a un kilómetro del rompeolas de Cabarete cerca de Playa de Oro. Estoy en medio de un ataque de angioedema y necesito mi medicina pero no la tengo conmigo. Necesito un rescate urgente."

"De acuerdo señor Augusto. ¿Tiene a alguien con usted?"

"Si, Nellie Thompson está conmigo. No habla español." I look at Nellie and see two tears rolling down her cheeks. Fuck, fuck.

"I'm sorry. Nellie, here." I hand her the phone and lie down. The pressure in my throat increases, the subtle tightness that threatens to cut my air supply. It's not much at first, but having gone through this before, I know how bad it will get soon. Nellie speaks with the operator in the distance, but I'm focusing on managing my breathing.

"I don't know. I don't know. How can I help?" Nellie asks, her voice trembling as she's trying to answer the questions I'm sure are being fired her way.

The vicelike grip tightening on my throat and around my mouth is scaring me; they need to hurry up.

There's a pause. I don't hear Nellie anymore, so I turn around and find myself alone in the cabin. I don't want to step out. It's better to stay out of the sun.

"I don't know!" Nellie shouts from the door. She's wearing

the dress she had on last night. Her hair is up, and there are no tears left. She's screaming into the phone over and over again. "I can't answer any more questions. Get help here, now!"

The distant hum through the water tells me something is coming. The boats sway side to side, and in what feels like the blink of an eye, four men are onboard, carrying me out into the orange rescue boat. After Nellie gets her life vest on, she sits on the opposite side from me, and we get going.

Her scared gaze is on me, and I want to let her know I'm okay, but I can't. I need to conserve my energy and let them do their job.

"Tengo la medicina de rescate en mi casa. En la marina." I cough in between words, my breath shallow as we speed through the waves and head the few miles back to shore. She will never forget this, and I will never forgive myself for putting her through it.

No matter what I want or how much I do to keep my triggers at bay, my body always betrays me. There's nothing I can do, other than deal with the death sentence I've been given and make my peace with it. I can feel the tightness in my chest, the skin around my lips stretching uncomfortably. My mind's a mess, foggy, but I'm fighting, trying to hang on.

EIGHT
ARE YOU HIS WIFE?

Breathe Again **by** ***Sara Bareilles*** & ***Fix You by Cold Play***

NELLIE

"LISTEN, I understand I'm the one with the foreign language here, but I don't speak Spanish. No hablo español. Please find me someone who speaks English." I ask as nicely as I can, considering my frustration. The emergency room is full of people coming and going, buzzing around with their own emergencies. Nobody pays attention to the girl with no name, no phone, barely any clothes, and, most importantly, who doesn't know the language. I've never felt more useless in my life.

It's been two hours, and I don't know what the fuck to do. We left the boat so quickly, I forgot my phone. I have no shoes, and I don't know where Gus is. They gave him a shot as soon as we got to the marina, but when we got him to the hospital, they took him through the double doors and left me here without a word. It's busy here today, and I know it's an inconvenience to try to find someone who can speak English or who even has the time.

I approach the nurse's station again, but this time, a different nurse is there.

"Hi. Do you speak English?"

"How may I help you?" the nurse with the blue scrubs asks.

"I need an update on a patient. Augusto Zabana. He…he had an allergic reaction, I think." Do not spiral, do not spiral, do not spiral. Calm, cool, collected Nellie needs to be here.

"Are you his sister?"

"No."

"I am sorry, but we cannot give personal information to non-family members." Did we say earlier who I was? I can't even remember. In the midst of the chaos, I don't even remember if I said my name at all.

"I'm…I'm his wife," I blurt out before I can stop myself. I need to see him. I need to know what happened. I don't give a fuck what people say. She doesn't ask any more questions; she just turns around and signals me to follow her.

We walk down a brightly lit corridor. The hum of the ventilation system in the background has been constant since I got here, and it continues even outside the emergency room. With so much unknown and the chaos of the past few hours, the deep humming has been my best friend. The walls are the same dull off-white of hospitals in the States, and even the light blue drapes giving privacy are the same. I'm definitely checking my privilege right now, surprised by the similarities. I'm not sure if I expected the hospital to be as lifeless as the ones back home. It smells sterile and sharp, definitely the underlying scent of bleach clinging to the air as I remind myself this place is supposed to look like this. Nobody wants to feel comfortable in a place where so many people die. It's supposed to be cold, clinical, and distant, even if the medical professionals are not.

"I'm sorry, I didn't catch your name," I tell the nurse as we continue to move down the hall, our footsteps echoing on the tile floor. I need to talk. I need to ask questions so I don't feel like I'm in an alternate reality, so I feel like what's happening right now is real and not like I'm a ghost floating between rooms.

"Nadia. What about you?"

"Cornelia, but you can call me Nellie." Each step gets me closer. No matter how slow, it gets me closer to Gus. I want to run, but I can't, so I focus on breaking down the task at hand and what I *can* do—place each foot deliberately in front of the other, reminding myself that even baby steps will get me there. This will be where I'll be able to ask questions and hopefully see he's okay. The hallway stretches longer than it is, with the distant sound of footsteps and voices murmuring from somewhere far off. I feel like I'm in a new world.

When we reach the door to another sitting area, a soft breath of air greets me as it opens, the temperature shifting slightly. The waiting area is quieter than the one in the emergency room. There's no noise, other than the machines in the background faintly humming, blending rhythmically with the nurses working on their charts.

"Wait here, Nellie. I will be right back." Nadia disappears behind the nurse's station through a glass door. I stand, because if I sit, I'm afraid I'll cry. If I start crying now, there will be no stopping, and I can't make myself do that. I can't break now.

The room is eerily quiet and empty. Nobody waits in the vacant chairs. Nobody walks or paces. This is either the room where they tell people their loved ones died, or this is a... private wing? Holy crap, Nellie, of course, it's a private wing.

"You can follow me this way." Nadia steps out of the room, and, with a sympathetic smile, she guides me through another set of doors into another long corridor.

This place is a maze, a labyrinth of fears and hopeless dreams.

There are several doors on each side of the wall, but none next to each other, confirming my suspicions on the private wing. All doors are shut, all painted a solid white, not see-through like an ICU would be. We stop in front of door number seven, and after a soft knock, there's a reply from the other side in Spanish. Nadia opens the door after waving her badge, and what I find stops me in my tracks.

Gus. I gasp, but before I can lose it completely, he sits up, looking at me with sadness behind his eyes. Or maybe shock. Or both? What did he expect? For me not to figure out how to make it here?

"Hi. I didn't think you'd come." Yup, exactly that. He thought I would leave him here alone to figure it out for himself.

Nadia says something in Spanish, directing it to Gus. I have zero clue what it is, but Gus' reply makes her stiffen before she says, "My apologies. I should have continued in English. I was asking if you were not supposed to be here, but el señor Zabana assures me you're fine. I will leave you two be." She steps back quickly, closing the door behind her.

"Whatever medical emergency you just had doesn't have to make you an ass. What did you say to that poor girl?"

"I told her that if you said you wanted to be here, you should be here. I don't have the patience for pleasantries right now." Gus lifts his body further and pushes a button on his bed to stay sitting up. He looks perfectly fine. His lip is a little swollen still, full and darker in color than usual, but almost back to normal. His eyes look droopy and tired, but nothing out of the ordinary, and his voice is normal. He's okay.

"You're okay," I whisper, not moving from my spot by the door.

"I'm okay. I'm sorry you had to witness that."

"What happened?"

"Come here." He brings his hand up and motions me to get closer. I take heavy steps toward him, keeping my composure in check so I don't break without knowing what actually happened. All my senses are telling me he had an allergic reaction, but to what, and why did it escalate so quickly?

His hand is palm up, waiting for me to take it, but before I do, he pats the bed, prompting me to sit next to him. My movements are not mine anymore. I'm just following steps, trying to make sense of the whole day. How has today just been one day? It feels like more. It feels longer.

"Hi," he whispers, holding my hand and smiling softly at me.

"Gus, please don't "hi" me. What happened?" I need answers. I need to know. I feel like my heart will jump out of my chest at any moment. Some people are paralyzed by fear, but I want to run as fast and as far away as I can. In this instance, though, I'm trapped.

He lets out a deep breath, looks out the window to the ocean just a few blocks away, and then at me. His eyes hold turmoil behind them. The few golden flecks are practically gone, and all I see is onyx black.

"Are you always in need of answers?" He coughs, covering his mouth. Why is he coughing? Did whatever happen affect his throat? His lungs?

"Birth defect. Stop deflecting, please. That was scary. *Too scary*. Please....please explain." I'm not above begging at this point, even though I can see in his eyes he doesn't want to share. He doesn't want to tell me, but I need to know. I bring my hand up to cup his face and softly rub his cheek. "Please."

He lets out a breath before adding, "I had a flare up."

"A flare up? What are you talking about?"

"This is such a long conversation, Nellie, and I don't know if I have it in me to have it right now. There's so much to what happened today that would take me longer than a few hours to explain, and I feel like you need to hear it all. You say you need facts and answers, and I don't have the energy to give them all to you today."

He doesn't have the time to explain? How dare he? I'm the one who has been here thinking he would die and I'd have to explain to everyone what the fuck happened. Here I was, thinking the first man I'm interested in sharing more than a few nights with might die on my watch.

"I'm not asking you to give me your entire medical history. I want to know what that was and why it happened. You scared the shit out of me, Gus." Petrified me is more accurate.

"It scared me too, but it's my own damn fault for forgetting my meds. I have a hereditary condition that produces inflammation. Sometimes, it's mild, and sometimes, it's drastic. Today's attack, or flare up, was bad. I forgot my maintenance *and* my rescue medication back in the villa, and I didn't think anything of it. I must have had a few triggers, and it just unraveled after that."

Triggers? Hereditary? Rescue medication?

"Rescue medication? What sickness?"

"It's not a sickness. A sickness would imply I can get healthy again, and this, well, this is for life. It's a condition, something I have to live with forever, something that has changed the way I live. I take medication every day to maintain it; I just didn't take it the last two days."

"What is it?"

"It's called Hereditary Angioedema." He's spitting facts, answering each question without hesitation, like I'm conducting an interrogation. Zero emotion. Zero lies. Each word a death blow. Each word building a guard around my heart, protecting it from potential pain.

I wish I could control my need for information, but I can't, and it will trump any emotional response until I have all the facts. "How long have you had it?"

"All my life? But my first flare up was five years ago."

Hereditary angioedema. *Hereditary.* "Hereditary? So do your siblings have it? Does Cara know?"

"They don't, fortunately, and I'm not sure. Maybe? We all share similar heart conditions, but this one is all mine. I'm the lucky one, I guess."

What the hell? Heart conditions? They're so young. "Heart conditions? Gus, please, can you just give me more context?"

He sighs as he sits up straighter. "I have issues with my heart and with my autoimmune system. It sucks. I'm twenty-six years old trapped in the body of a seventy-year-old with the will of a twenty-year-old. It's lovely here."

"You don't look like there's anything wrong," I say, trying to dissect all the information he's throwing my way, trying to decipher it, to understand. But my words cause the opposite effect. I'm trying to understand. I'm trying to be here for him, using my curiosity to show him I care, but my fear is that I'm coming off as an examination.

"That's the thing about a lot of chronic illnesses. You can't see them. I look healthy. I feel healthy, but I live with these every day. I live with the fear that something like *that* might happen at any given time, all the time. Today, unfortunately, you were there to witness it. I'm sorry."

Sorry? Is he sorry? And damn it, I should've known. All the facts and useless knowledge I have in my brain for so many situations, but when I need to understand something major, they just seem to disappear? All my neuron connections short-circuit when my emotions and cognition mix. Empathy. He needs empathy, not questioning right now.

"Why are *you* sorry? I should be the one sorry. I just grilled you to share information after the day you've had. I'm sorry you have to deal with this. It was terrifying for me, but I can't imagine how it feels for you." My emotions are all over the damn place.

"It's okay," he adds, bringing his hand to mine and tracing soft circles on my wrists. His fingers are so delicate on top of my faded scars. His eyes soften as he looks at me, instantly grounding me. This is the moment when I know nothing will ever be the same. I can see myself falling in love with this man, but he won't let me, and if I'm being honest with myself, I don't know if I should.

Somebody knocks faintly on the door, breaking the spell. It's Nadia, the nurse from earlier, and she's wearing a soft smile.

"Your ride is ready." She looks at me and smiles before turning back around and leaving us alone.

"I'm stable now, so we can leave. Let's go home." Gus lets go of my hand and swivels his legs off the hospital bed to stand, walking over to the chair with his clothes and dressing quickly. I sit on the bed, watching him move effortlessly, and I almost lose it just thinking about how bad it could've been if the paramedics were late or if the reaction would have happened in the water. I jokingly said I could rescue him, and I meant it, but looking at his sculpted body and remembering how his weight felt on my body, I'm not sure I would've been able to. What if it happened in his sleep, and we didn't notice? How does he live like this, knowing that at any time, his throat can swell?

"Ready?" he asks, standing by the door with his arms crossed over his chest. I snap out of it and walk up to him. He pulls me into his arms, wrapping around me, and I tense under his embrace. I'm on the verge of losing it, and the hugs might take me there.

"Stop overthinking it, Nellie. I'm okay. I promise. It's not the first time it has happened, and it won't be the last. I was irresponsible, and I should've carried my medicine. You—" he brings his hand to my face, caressing it softly, tilting it back so my gaze meets his. Where mine is probably full of worry, his is calm. "You didn't do anything wrong. Hear that. There was nothing you could've done, and being here is more than I could've wished for. Thank you." He brings his lips to my forehead, kissing it gently, and holds my hand as we walk out of the hospital into the vehicle taking us back to the villa.

NINE
USE ME ANY WAY YOU WANT

THIS IS ***me trying** **by** **Taylor Swift*** & ***Homeward bound/home by Glee***

GUS

NO MATTER how much trouble sleeping I may have, after an attack, it's all I seem to be able to do. It drains all my energy, especially considering my body has to fight so hard just to keep me alive. My muscles hurt, my brain is foggy, the heaviness of it all weighs me down—there's not much I *can* do. By the way the sun is shining through the window, it must be midday. I stretch and turn my head, but I don't see Nellie anywhere. The gentle breeze flows through the open window, but all I hear are the seagulls squawking and the waves crashing on the shore.

The last thing I wanted was for Nellie to witness that. I don't want anyone seeing me in that state, but I can't imagine how utterly shocking it is to see someone becoming a human balloon right before your eyes, let alone without having details on what's happening. Walking out of the room, I see the glass double doors are open, the white curtains flowing in the wind. Behind them, far in the distance, standing by the water, is Nellie.

Her dark hair is in a loose braid falling down her back. A dark top with jean shorts frames her body and makes her skin glow under the sun. Her toes are in the water, but her gaze is somewhere in the distance. No matter how close to her I get, she doesn't look anywhere else. She doesn't turn her body around. She doesn't move. She just stands there, toes in the sand, back straight, face held high.

"Good morning," I say, my voice still hoarse and raspy after sleeping most of the morning. Nellie turns my way, and what I see breaks my heart in two: rosy cheeks, swollen, glossy eyes, and the saddest expression I've ever seen on anyone. Nellie is young, but she's never looked as young as she looks right now. She looks fragile and in need of protection, and the internal beast that lives in me notices before I can use my brain.

"What's wrong?" I ask her, closing the space between us and pulling her to me. She buries her face in my chest and wraps her arms tight around my torso. I bring my hands to her head, gently touching her hair in a soothing motion. I know better than to ask her to calm down, and I know better than to try and have a conversation. Sometimes, all we need is a good cry. All we need is to let the tears flow and cleanse whatever ailment is in our hearts, even if it's not a physical one.

We stand wrapped in each other as I let her do whatever she needs—hit me, squeeze me, scream at me, literally anything she wants to do. I stand and wait. It could be seconds, minutes, or hours, and I wouldn't know, because all I can think is how I need to be here for her no matter what.

She finally lets go of me, and after wiping her tears away,

she looks up at me. Her beautiful green eyes reflect flecks of gold from the light and the tears.

"Thank you," she whispers as another tear falls.

I bring my hand up to cup her face and wipe it away with my thumb. "Thank you for what, baby girl?" The nickname leaves my lips before I can hold it back. I don't know if I have the right to call her that after yesterday's events, considering she's going back to her place tonight. After tomorrow, this little bubble will burst, and we'll be back to regularly scheduled programming.

"For letting me use you as my human tissue box. What a mess."

"You're the prettiest mess. You can use me anytime you want." She holds my gaze, keeping me both grounded and scared shitless about what has her so torn.

"Do you want to talk about it?" I ask, and she nods, holding my hand and dragging us back to the towel she has down on the beach. She's fidgety. Her hands go from holding her elbows and squeezing her skin to her fingers picking at her cuticles. She opens and closes her mouth several times but doesn't say anything.

"Say something, Nellie."

"You scared me yesterday. I didn't know what the hell was happening, and I don't speak Spanish. I felt helpless, and that's the last thing I ever want to feel. You kept me in the dark, and you could've died, Gus. I've been reading about HAE since before the sun came up, and let's just say, I'm even more terrified than I was before."

"I know. I'm sorry. I should've said something."

"You think? God, Gus, what would you have done?"

"I understand why you're this upset. I can't imagine what that must have been like for you, but Nellie, this is not my first flare up, and it won't be my last. It's not too dangerous if I keep it under control. It usually is under control," I add, trying to reassure her but also not sugarcoating it. If she's been reading about it, I'm sure she's seen pictures and read the worst case scenarios.

"How quickly can someone die from it?" she asks, and I don't reply. Something tells me she already knows the answer. "As little as four hours. Four hours, Gus, and we were in the middle of the ocean in a sailboat I didn't know how to maneuver. What would you have done?"

"Send you swimming to shore? You're a strong swimmer, remember?"

"Don't you dare play with me right now. This is serious," she spits with fury behind her words. She's so angry, and I get it, but there's nothing I can do now.

"I'm sorry. I deflect with humor. I understand you're upset. I'm sorry I didn't tell you. To be honest, I usually don't tell people. If I'm not attached to someone, they don't need to know my body attacks itself. They don't need to know that, at any given moment, I can have a flare up and swell like a balloon. They don't need to know that even though I'm young, active, and happy, there's a ticking bomb inside me that gets triggered easily. I'm sorry I kept you out of the loop, and I am so sorry I didn't say anything when I knew I had not taken my medicine. I should have warned you. I should've given you more context, and for that, I'm sorry."

She lets a couple of tears fall down her cheeks as she listens attentively. I hold her hand in mine and gently caress her soft skin. Even with the small, raised scars, it feels like heaven.

"I'm definitely sorry I scared you so much you decided to research instead of swimming on our last day here."

"Ignorance is a bliss I don't have the privilege to maintain. At least now, I'm informed, unlike yesterday." I can see it in her eyes as she dances with turmoil. She looks hesitant. She doesn't hold my gaze, challenging like she usually does. It seems like she's ready to tell me something I don't want to hear, and I don't know how to fix it.

"Again, I'm sorry, Nellie. I am so sorry." We sit in silence, looking at each other as the waves softly crash onto the sand. She tilts her head away from me to look at the waver. The tide is coming in, and the spot where we were standing before is underwater before I can say anything else.

"That's how I felt," Nellie adds, not taking her eyes away from the shore.

"How?"

"Like I was under the water with everything moving around me, both too fast and too slow. So helpless. So useless."

"Don't you dare say that. You are neither of those things, I promise you."

"Don't make promises you can't keep," Nellie adds.

"I can promise you that. You're not useless, and you may have felt helpless, but you were not. I mean it."

"I want to go home," Nellie says suddenly as she stands. She dries her tears and looks at the water before turning back toward me with determination in her eyes.

"Okay?" I ask, not understanding what she means.

"I mean it, Gus. I'm going to pack my bags. I would like to go back now."

Noted. The conversation's over, and she's ready to go back to reality, regardless of what I think. She puts her barriers up and walks inside the villa, not turning back once. I guess we're going home.

THE FLIGHT WAS PAINFULLY long and too quiet. Nellie didn't talk to me much and pretended she was asleep for most of it. I was dreading the moment we had to go back, and now that it's here, I was right to dread it. I'm going to miss her, and I didn't even get to say a proper goodbye.

"Can I see you again?" I ask, holding her suitcase and standing outside her condo.

"I'm sure we'll see each other at the next family function in a few months," Nellie replies, grabbing the handle of the suitcase and pulling it to her.

"That's not what I meant." I know I said this couldn't go any further, but I hate leaving her like this here. I hate leaving *us* like this.

"You said nothing could happen after this weekend," Nellie bites back, pushing the frame of her glasses up and not looking me in the eye.

"Yeah, but I don't want to leave things like this. I don't know, maybe you were right. Maybe we can try to figure ourselves out before discarding the possibility completely."

"I don't think so. If there's a chance for us to be a *thing*, I need time."

"Just three days ago, you said you wanted to see where this would go." Please don't prove me right, Nellie.

"Yeah, but the more I thought about it the more I realized these five days—this long weekend is all I could give you. I'm about to move back home and find a job. I need to stay focused on that, so now the weekend is done, we can both carry on." The warm and flirty Nellie I've come to know is gone. Here is the cold and facts-driven Nellie in her place.

I scoff and shake my head. "Unbelievable. I guess I was right. My issues are too much to handle, huh?"

"It's not that, I promise."

"Don't make promises you can't keep, remember? Isn't that what you said? So this is it?" I ask incredulously, watching as Nellie shuts me out completely, locking the door and throwing away the key before I can even ask if I can keep it.

"It's all I can give you right now." Nellie turns to her front door to unlock it and then faces me again. This time, her lips tremble slightly. Almost imperceptible, but it's there. The small shake. The hesitation.

"So that's it then?" I ask again, trying to see if she'll hesitate again. All I need is a small sign that I can fight for this, even if just yesterday, I thought there was no way. Even if I'm delusional. Even if it's delusional. But I don't get that. What I get is a small smile, and then Nellie rises on her tiptoes to kiss me gently on the lips.

"That's it, Gus. Have a good night. I'll see you someday." She steps through her door, closing it behind her and shutting me out completely. *Message received.*

PART 2

THE RISE OF THE WAVE

When water fades and takes its claim,
A towering wave begins its raise.
At first, it thrills in a wild haze,
Then shatters loud, its roar now spent.

TEN

MISSING HER

JUNE

Wind Up Missin' You* by Tucker Wetmore** & ***Silence by Marshmello and Khalid

GUS

I MISS HER. Why do I have to miss her? I'm so fucked if I can't get her out of my head. It was one week, not even. Five days. It felt like both too long and not long enough, and it's not fair. It's been a month, an entire month, and I still can't stop thinking about her, even though I did this to myself.

How many times did I tell her there wasn't a future for us? To stay away? To guard her heart? I fucking made her promise me she wouldn't fall in love with me, and now I'm, what? Missing her? Craving being with her? Feeling like I lost a part of myself the day I brought her back home? After what…a week?

Something soft, but with a little bit of weight, hits my head, and when I look up, I see Abraham smiling at me from the other side of my desk.

"Alo! Are you daydreaming about Nellie again?"

"What did you just throw at me?"

He points to the ground, and when I follow his gaze, I see his wallet. His damn wallet.

"Finders keepers."

"Like you need it. Spit it out."

I look at him and say nothing.

"Cooooooooñoooo[1], you're thinking about her, aren't you?"

"About who?" I try to play coy.

"Cállate, Augusto. ¿Cómo que no sabes de quien hablo?[2]" I throw my hand in the air, giving him the middle finger, and he laughs, pretending to kiss the air.

"Hola soy Nellie, y tengo a Augusto Zabana aficiaó como un perro,[3]" he says mockingly, his arms around his shoulders, pretending to kiss someone. Fucking jackass.

"All the time," I finally snap.

"All the time what?"

"I think about her all the damn time." I wish it was an exaggeration, but it's not. Everything reminds me of her. And because she likes the water, I can't even swim or sail without thinking about her. So much for being a playboy or whatever. I want to play, alright, but I want to play with *her*.

"Just call her."

"And tell her what? Oh yeah, I told you we couldn't be anything, and now I can't stop thinking about you, and I don't want anyone but you?"

"Well, that's just sad," he replies.

"Well, that's the truth."

"You're fucked."

---

1. shiiiit
2. Shut up, Augusto. How do you not know who I'm talking about?
3. Hi, I'm Nellie, and I have Augusto Zabana in love with me (this is a very Dominican way of saying this sentence).

I nod in reply before dropping my body deeper into my chair, crossing one leg over the other and looking out the window at the St. Johns River. Zabana Enterprises has offices in three cities. For the most part, I work from home, but Manny has been on a roadtrip with Cara for a week now, so I'm popping into our Jacksonville office to keep things flowing. Our business runs practically on its own. I'm just babysitting, overseeing some of the accounts he personally handles because his clients act like spoiled little brats if we're not at their beck and call. I could give zero fucks, but *he* cares.

I meant it when I told Nellie I was worried about him and how he has no life beyond work. So when Allie dared him to take time off to drive Cara, I knew we could make it work. We kept from him the fact that it was a three week road trip, because we knew he would say no, but he usually doesn't back down from his promises. After he said yes, it was checkmate. I want him to be happy and find some balance, and I think he can do that with Cara. She's the opposite of Manny. Where Manny is uptight and work-oriented, Cara wants to spend days outside and take it slow. She loves her job, but it's not her entire life. Maybe they can both learn from each other.

"I told her nothing could happen between us, and then I had a flare up, and she freaked out. She's just starting her new life in Baker. She doesn't need to have to handle medical issues on top of that. Maybe under the right circumstances, it would be different." I haven't been able to stop thinking about those words. *Right circumstances*. Maybe in another timeline, in which our families weren't almost related, or she wasn't ready to dedicate her time to the children who need her. Maybe in one where my body is not broken and someone else doesn't have to carry my flaws.

"Okay then, go out and fuck someone else and move on. But this moping shit is dumb." He gets his phone out and texts someone before getting up. I'm also out of here. This place is depressing.

"Get it out of your system before you get boring," Abraham says. His parents own a private security company that has been passed from generation to generation. He was born with a silver spoon in his mouth, and he takes advantage of it. He oversees the business in the United States, and by *oversees*, I mean he calls his assistant and makes sure he's not needed anywhere he doesn't want to spend at least the weekend. It makes our friendship even stronger, since neither of us nor Jean Luis have to be at work unless we want to.

"I don't want to fuck someone else. Remember what happened last week? I couldn't enjoy the bar even when women kept throwing themselves at me. I was just uninterested."

"Well, that's a first. Listen, we don't have time for this shit. If you're seriously interested in her, tell her. Show up at her house or send her some flowers and chocolate or something."

"She doesn't want me," I reply.

"You are so whiny."

"Why? Because I'm telling you I want someone for once in my life, and I'm trying to respect her wishes? That makes me a decent human, not whiny." I may not be honest about a lot of things with my friends, but my intentions toward others is something I can't hide very well. That's why Manny holds our sensitive clients. He can butter them up. I can't.

"Okay, okay, my bad." He brings his hands up in defense. "All I'm saying is, when have you ever felt this way? Never probably. So then do something about it. Show her you're willing to do more than just give up. Grovel a little. The worst that can happen is her saying no, and then, well, leave her alone. But if you think she's scared because of your health, show her you've got her. Show her how she can take care of you next time. Shit, at twenty-one, I would be scared too after you almost died on her. Hell, at twenty-six, your health still scares the shit out of me."

"It scares me too, but I don't have a choice. She does. And

I didn't almost die." The thing is, that's a possibility any day for me, and maybe I brushed it off too quickly without truly checking in on her. It must have been scary. I know she was terrified, her tears the following day were enough indication. She asked questions, and I answered, but maybe I should have asked questions too. I should have made sure she was okay, truly okay.

"In her eyes, you did. I'll send you the therapy bill. Look at me, acting all grown and shit." He laughs, and I want to as well, but I can't. I'm too stunned about the fact it's been a month, and other than calling her, I haven't apologized once for the whole thing, not since the day after it happened.

"Yeah, you just want me to make up with her so you can see her friend." I brush it off, trying to hide my realization.

"I already see her friend all I want. All she wants, too. I don't need you for that. Adios, Gusti. Figure it out."

Abraham leaves, closing the door behind him, and I don't waste time. If I want to see Nellie again and explore where this thing between us can go, I need to take the first step. I need to act like the man I am…and I have the perfect idea in mind.

ME:

I'm sorry.

She replies immediately.

NELLIE:

For what?

ME:

For not telling you about my health before taking you to another country and out on the water.

I see the dots dancing as she types, but then they stop. A minute passes. Nothing. I'm going erratic here.

NELLIE:

It's okay.

ME:

It's not. Let me make it up to you.

NELLIE:

It's truly okay.

ME:

Please.

ME:

I'll do anything.

NELLIE:

Are you begging, Gus?

ME:

I'm not above it.

NELLIE:

I gotta go. Goodbye, Gus.

ME:

Go with me to a gala tomorrow.

NELLIE:

What?

ME:

Please, let me make it up to you. We'll talk and then go to the gala. Or we can talk at the gala.

NELLIE:

I'm not your girlfriend or one of the models you parade around.

ME:

I'm not asking you to be. Just come with me, and we can talk. I'm being auctioned as a date, and you can buy me.

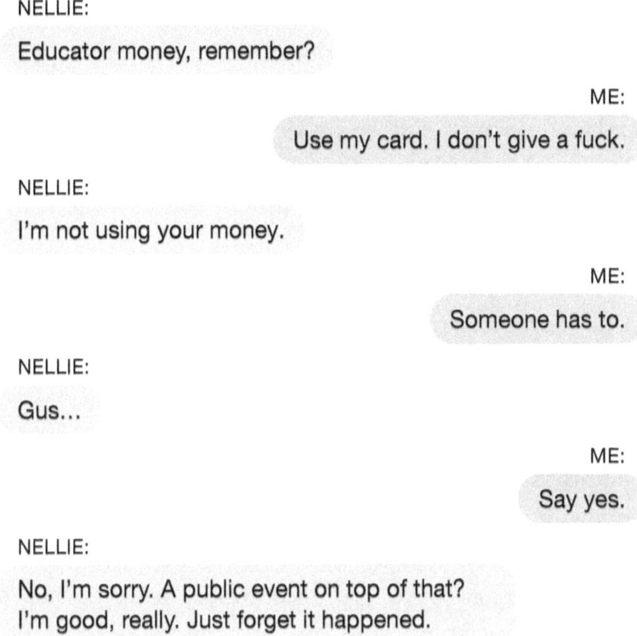

I can't. I wish I could. It would make it so much easier for everyone if I could, but I can't. She wants to just ignore it all and act like nothing happened. The worst part is, *this* Nellie, the Nellie who replied just now, is not the Nellie I know. This is the guarded Nellie who told me she wanted to go home and not give us a try even after telling me she could see herself with me. She went from scorching hot to icy cold in no time, and she seems to have stayed there. Fine. Maybe she needs to see it the same way I did. I'll give her some temptation and see if she'll bite.

I grab my phone and text Manny to give him an update and yell at him for trying to work on the trip. Then, I text Blair to ask her to go with me to the gala tomorrow. Blair is the daughter of Coop's CEO, another local finance company. She's continuing her daddy's legacy while trying to gain status as America's sweetheart. She's good company and who I usually bring to events. We have never slept together, and for the most part, we have a professional relationship. I would call her a friend, but she says she doesn't do friendships, just business transactions. We look like a powerhouse couple, and we both take advantage of it, so we let the rumors talk.

"Lucia!" I shout, propping my feet on top of the desk as Manny's personal assistant shows up.

"Yes, sir?"

"Confirm my attendance at the gala tomorrow with a plus one, and stop giving information to my brother about work. Let me handle it."

"But sir, he specifically said he didn't want me to leave him out of it," she says with a pen to her mouth, her eyes wide.

"I understand, but I'm telling you he needs the break, so please, just let me know. I'll handle it."

"Yes, sir. Anything else?"

"No, you're good to go." She walks back to her desk, leaving the office empty, just me and my thoughts. I hope I know what I'm doing.

ELEVEN
THE AUCTION

Gravity* by *Matt Hansen* & *Dirty Little Secret by The All-American Rejects

NELLIE

RESTLESS. Agitated. Apprehensive. Going out of my mind? None of those words work to describe this feeling, like everything is falling into place just like I wanted, but something is looming over me, making me question if I'm missing something. Someone.

I can't imagine the whiplash he must have felt after I told him I wanted to see what could happen between us and then two days later told him I wanted to go home. How hypocritical of me to demand the truth from him, to demand answers and facts when I lied to him about what I wanted the next day. I dug myself so deep into research and despair, I filled my head with worse-case scenarios, and the only way I could make it stop was by running away. Too much information about what could go wrong, and I couldn't handle it. So, going back home to lock myself in the room for days and cry seemed like the best idea.

Eventually, I called my therapist, because I felt like I was moments away from crawling back into a dark place, where the only way out will scar me again. It was easy for us to figure out the trigger—fear. Fear of the unknown. Too many things out of my control. Fear of that whole situation and the hopelessness I felt sending my mind to overdrive and freak me the fuck out.

Irrational. Baseless. Illogical. Absurd. All the words that fill my mind when Gus' name pops into my head and how much I hate that I like him so much. Protecting my peace has come to be harder than anticipated. I'm telling him with my words to stay away, but my soul wants him. My heart wants to get to know him better. And my body…well, my body wants him constantly.

"Hi!" I smile as Bee and Victoria join the video call. We promised ourselves we would video chat every week. We text all the time, but it's important to me to see their faces, and they love me enough to make it work.

"Did you get the job?" Bee shouts from her bed while looking at the camera upside down.

"Hello to you too, Bee. Why are you upside down?"

"It helps with focus. Don't change the topic. Did you get the job?" she asks again.

"You're looking at the newest Baker Oaks Middle School Counselor!" I add as I sit up straighter, bringing my hands under my chin.

"FUCK YES!" Bee shouts.

"Congratulations, Nells! You deserve it," Victoria adds.

"Thank you! What about you two? What's new?" Bee moved back home to Magnolia Springs about an hour from here, but Victoria is staying in college to finish another year and hopefully graduate with another degree. She's only a few classes away from finishing another bachelor's, so she took advantage of the opportunity.

"The campus is so empty. Even for a summer semester, it feels eerily quiet." Victoria brings her hair up in a ponytail.

"How are you, Vic? How are the flares?"

"They've been under control since I've been on the autoimmune protocol," Victoria says. Victoria got diagnosed with an autoimmune condition. Her doctor put her on an autoimmune protocol to minimize symptoms, and it seems to be working.

"How are you dealing with all of that?" I ask.

"It's been an adjustment, but it could be worse, you know?" She cocks her head to the side and looks at the camera, saying, "Bee, go right side up, for the love of books. You're losing color."

"Alright, Mom!" Bee shouts back.

"Damn, I miss you two." We were inseparable for the past three years. Not having many friends growing up was hard, but I never knew what I was missing. I never knew what friendship really meant. I thought friends were people you gossip with and needed to find things in common to have a good time. Maybe you cry together over boys and definitely drink together over them too. But what I learned with Bee and Victoria is that friends can become family. Friends are the family you choose, and they choose to love you back. Real friendships are some of the best relationships you will ever have in your life. They're your confidants, your voices of reason, your shoulders to cry on, your lifelines. They can be your future maids of honor and your unborn children's aunties. They help you carry your load, and they love you despite all the things you hate about yourself. These girls have shown me how I, or anyone for that matter, deserve to be loved, and I will never settle for less because of them.

"We talk every day, and we'll see each other soon. We promise."

The two of them start asking each other questions as I get lost in my thoughts about the job, the kids, the rest of the summer, and damn it, Gus Zabana too. I don't want to keep thinking about him, and even trying to go out with someone else failed to do what I wanted, what I needed.

"Did you text him?" Victoria asks while I'm lost in my thoughts. Bee doesn't respond, so I assume they're asking me. I look at them through the video chat and see them both waiting. Yup, that was for me.

"Yes."

"Aaaaaand?" Bee asks in a flirty tone.

"I told him we couldn't see each other. To be honest, I was an actual bitch to him. I flinched at the last text I sent him." I lay on the bed and put a pillow over my face. I'm such an idiot. All my confidence went out the window the minute that text came through.

"Why are you fighting yourself so hard not to see him again? You know you want to, so why not? Don't give me bullshit about age. He's five years older than you, not twenty," Bee adds, sitting up straight, all her focus on me.

I don't answer; I just ponder the question. I take pride in being honest and upfront with my friends and people I care about. Even more with strangers, but somehow, I've gone back to my thirteen-year-old self, the scared, self-harm inflicting shell of a human I was then, who needed validation and help. It's been years since I was there, and I'm crawling myself out of that hole I almost put myself in. I don't want to risk it.

"You're scared, aren't you?" Victoria asks, smiling softly at me. Her gentle smile, I've come to love, because I can feel it as if it was a hug.

"I am." There's no point in lying, at least not to them. I may be able to ignore all of Cara's calls and keep Gus at arm's length, but with them, I can be myself.

"Of what?" Bee asks. I never told them what happened, and I don't know if Abraham told Bee. All I know is that Gus' health issues are not mine to share, so I didn't. I can tell them a partial truth, though. A selective truth. I can pick apart everything scaring me and just tell them that. It should be enough.

"I'm not in a great place mentally. There's so much with the new job and everything else, and I don't think adding the pressure of a relationship is a good idea. He owns an empire, and I'm just figuring my shit out." I take a deep breath before continuing, "My sister is moving back home too. I need to try to make friends here. I have to help with the diner. It's too much, and I like him too much to just fuck him every now and then."

"Have you ever stopped to wonder that maybe, he can be one steady thing during this time? You don't have *us* with you. But I mean, you do what's best for you. Just try to find something to make you happy, because you've been sulking for weeks now, and I just want to shake you," Bee says while Victoria nods.

"It's okay. I need to occupy myself and get out of this house." I turn my body sideways, tucking my hands under my head as I contemplate what I just said. I don't even know what I want anymore. How am I supposed to figure it out? I want him, but I'm also so scared that he will have another episode, and I'm supposed to, what? Even if I get trained on his condition and know all the procedures, it's too much. I'm too volatile for his health. He needs stability, and I'm all over the damn place. How am I supposed to be his stillness when I don't know how to stand still?

"Ah!" Bee gasps, snapping me out of it.

"What?"

"Get your phone. I sent you a link."

I follow her directions and click on the link waiting for me in our Burn Book group chat. It's taking me to the American Heart Association's Instagram, where I see they're hosting a gala here in Jacksonville. This must be the gala Gus was talking about, so I click the live to see what's up. The minute it shows me the feed, my heart stops.

They're covering the red carpet for this event, and right smack in the middle of it stands Augusto Zabana in a pristine black tuxedo, flashing his megawatt smile at the camera, a blonde draped over his arm.

I can't tear my eyes away from them. They look good together. Her blue eyes and blonde hair contrast with his black hair and his dark skin. He's so tall and strong. She's slim and tall too, all legs and arms. She's wearing a fitted dress, so I can see her full figure, and suddenly, I've never wanted to be someone else more than now.

Even though they complement each other and they look amazing together, there's little to no chemistry between them, or at least none that I can see. His body is stiff. Yes, his hand is touching her lower back, but it doesn't caress her skin like he did guiding *me*.

She's comfortable around him, and when he smiles to the camera, she keeps her mouth straight and her gaze deadly.

The gala is a masquerade, so they're both wearing masks, but how can you miss him? His strong, freshly shaven jaw, the way he stands confident and powerful, and his midnight stare looking straight into my soul through the screen. My skin prickles at the mere sight of this man, making me question ever saying no to him. I'm left with zero doubts on what I need to do next.

"I gotta go," I tell the girls, and Bee laughs as Victoria says goodbye. I don't care that they know exactly what happened. I need to get there, quick. Volatile? Yes. Do I care? Apparently not.

I hop out of bed and message Martin, the driver Gus told me I could call any time I needed to go somewhere. Then, I start getting ready for this event and hope they allow people to show up last minute.

WELL, five hundred dollars later, I'm sitting at a table at this fancy fundraiser, wearing a dress I stole from Cara's closet. The best part about having an older sister with the same body type as you. It's an emerald green gown with a deep v-cut, showcasing my sternum and my collarbone tattoo perfectly. It has a slit up to my mid-thigh, sheer panels throughout. Cara's taller than me, so I had to wear the highest heels I could find so I wouldn't drag this dress across the floor. I top it off with black high heels and a black mask I found in her room to make me look lethal.

I've been scanning the buzzing room since I got here, and I haven't seen Gus. The blonde from the livestream is sitting at one of the tables, but the chair beside her has been empty. I grab my phone from the black clutch and message him. I changed his contact name to DLS, short for Dirty Little Secret, from a day I kept texting and deleting a text all day. I needed to make fun of the situation, for my sake.

ME:

Remember when you said money was to be spent?

DLS:

Hello to you too, Nellie. Yes, I remember.

ME:

How do you feel about your money being spent for a good cause?

DLS:

It's the best investment. Why?

Because I'm about to bet on a date with you, and I'm hoping you'll pay if it's more than I can afford. He said he wanted me to, so I'm just following his wishes.

ME:

Even if it's your money?

DLS:

Especially if it's my money. Why do I feel like I'm not going to like where this is going?

I'm sure I missed something, because by the time I entered the room, there were plates being removed from tables and glasses taken away. I'm starting to wonder if I missed most of it, but at the soft murmur of the crowd fading to a hush as the heavy velvet curtains at the back of the stage slowly pull open, I know the auction is about to start. It's show time.

Gus steps out from the shadows, tall and confident, his posture straight but casual, the way someone who is used to being watched holds themselves. His hair is just a little too perfect, and the sharp lines of his jaw catch the light in a way that makes the room hold its breath. He's wearing the tailored suit I saw on the live, but in person, I can see how it hugs his frame in all the right places. I'm sure at this moment, it's worth whatever the cost. His eyes scan the crowd as he walks toward the podium, a slight smile pulling at the corners of his lips. There's something about the way he moves, almost as though he's gliding, as if this moment is routine to him, and not like he's stopping everyone in their tracks as we look at him. Cool, cool, cool.

The stage lights shine down, casting a warm glow on his perfectly tawny skin. He stops at the podium, his gaze lingering on the crowd like he's searching. Searching for what, Gus? His presence is magnetic, and for a second, the room feels smaller, like everyone's leaning in just a little closer, drawn to him and everything he represents—class, effortless confidence, money, power.

The auctioneer stands beside him, nodding, a practiced grin on her face. I guess we're starting with the date. *Cool, cool, cool.* Gus turns toward her for a moment, flashing her his panty-melting smile, and she immediately blushes. Good to see I'm not the only one completely smitten by a simple smile from this man. My confidence goes out the window when I realize he doesn't smile like that just for me. I'm not an idiot; I didn't assume he was as starstruck with me as I am with him, but a girl can dream.

"Alright, alright, folks," the auctioneer calls. "We've seen plenty of great items up for bidding tonight, but now, we get to the main event. Let's talk about a special…experience. A once-in-a-lifetime chance. The gentleman you see here beside me is no ordinary man. We're talking about a one-on-one date with none other than Augusto Zabana. Let it be known that Mr. Zabana has been a donor to our cause for years, and every year, this is our highest bidding experience, so get the paddles ready. The lucky winner will get dinner, conversation, and a surprise I'm sure will make a night to remember." So it did start before. Shit, I almost missed his bid.

Gus tilts his head, that knowing smile of his never quite fading. His gaze flickers across the crowd, making brief eye contact with a few people in the front row. He looks like a man used to being admired, desired, and he knows exactly how to wield that power to his advantage.

"Let's start the bidding at five thousand," the auctioneer announces.

Immediately, hands shoot up around the room, the competitive energy palpable. The first bid comes in at five thousand, then another voice rises, offering five hundred more. Gus doesn't react, doesn't even blink, as the numbers start climbing. Holy shit, I'm outbid already.

"Five thousand five hundred!" someone calls.

"Six thousand!" another voice shouts.

Gus shifts his weight slightly, uncrossing his arms, though he remains perfectly composed. The bidding picks up momentum, numbers rising as the audience gets caught in the thrill.

"Seven thousand!" comes a call from the back, a man's voice cutting through the chatter. Holy shit, okay. Wrong from me to assume only women would be bidding.

"Seven thousand five hundred!" a woman at the front counters, and there's a subtle chuckle from Gus, as though he's enjoying the show.

"Eight thousand!" someone else calls out, their voice full of determination, almost as if the idea of losing Gus' attention is unbearable.

"Eight thousand five hundred." The voice is confident, firm, and the crowd quiets as it lands, the number hanging in the air like a challenge.

The auctioneer holds up a hand to signal the highest bid then looks to Gus, who finally breaks his gaze from the audience to glance at the auctioneer. There's a small, almost imperceptible nod, and the auctioneer's grin widens.

Gus pauses for a second before he moves to leave the stage, his eyes briefly flicking toward me. His eyes flare for a split second, almost unrecognizable, but I notice before he covers it up with his calm, collected expression. There's something in the way he looks at me that makes my pulse quicken, even when he's masking whatever it is he's trying to convey. No matter the bids and the voices around us, his gaze never leaves mine.

How much money is too much money? I think it might be crossing the line, so I don't raise the paddle.

"Eight thousand five hundred, going once... Going twice..." The suspense builds as the auctioneer drags out the moment, scanning the room to make sure no one has a higher bid.

"Nine thousand," I shout. Holy shit, I did it. Gus smiles at me, proud. Okay, Gus. Okay.

"Ten thousand," someone shouts.

He raises an eyebrow at me, and when I shake my head no, in silent communication that I won't bid on the date anymore because this is where I draw the line, he smirks and nods softly.

"Ten thousand, going once."

His eyes widen as the blonde hostess looks around to see if anyone would try to outbid the very eager redhead smiling wickedly at Gus. I narrow my eyes at her, closing my thumb between my fingers before looking back at Gus. I find him staring at me with a wicked smile and showing me five fingers. Five? Five what? Five hundred more? My eyes widen, and when I mouth five hundred more to him, he nods.

"Ten thousand, going twice."

He nods again, this time subtly, so I bring my paddle up as I say, "Ten thousand five hundred." I'm going to throw up. This is insanity. He smiles bigger at me, not caring who sees.

Not a girl in the vicinity keeps their eyes on what's happening on stage. They all turn and look at me. I sit up taller, turn my eyes on them, and smile proudly to see if anyone else will raise the bid. Fuck them. If Gus wants me to play, I'm playing, and if he doesn't care who sees he's clearly looking at me, then so be it.

"Twelve thousand," the redhead says, bringing her paddle up and flicking her hair to the back, not looking at me for one second. Okay, girl, it's not my fault you want the same man. The man I had in my bed a month ago. Well, his bed, actually. The man I've been rejecting for a month. The man I can't get out of my head.

Part of the audience turns to look at me, but I'm nervous to bid more. When I look at Gus, I find him smiling wide, two fingers flashing in front of him, his other hand forming a zero. *Twenty thousand dollars?* I know for someone like him, that may not be a lot of money, but that's just insane. He narrows his eyes, as if he can hear my thoughts and hesitations, and moves his fingers even faster. *Fuck.*

"Going on—"

"Twenty thousand dollars," I all but shout, and after some

murmurs from the crowd and nobody else outbidding me, she bangs the gavel with finality.

"Sold! Congratulations!"

I smile devilishly, the crowd erupting in a mixture of applause and murmurs. I feel like a million minutes pass before the music plays, and everyone goes back to what they were doing. I'm suspended in time, Gus' searing eyes on me. Gus steps away from the podium, a graceful pivot, as the lights shift again, and I'm left buzzing with adrenaline. Well, that was insane.

My phone vibrates softly on my lap, and when I look down, I see the text.

DLS:

Meet me by the exit.

I've been summoned. I grab my paddle, the tiny purse, and the courage I mustered out of nowhere today and walk toward the exit, passing the big mahogany doors with my head held high even if I'm shaking inside. I look around until I see Gus standing by the concierge in the lobby. He keeps his eyes on me, searing, dark, and commanding.

I smile at him, a pep in my step that has his eyes roaming my body, stopping briefly where my tattoo rests instead of holding my gaze. My knees feel like they might wobble at any point, but I know I look damn hot in the dress, so I don't give him the satisfaction of showing him how his night dark eyes affect me. Two can play this game, Gus. Let's go.

He opens the door to the baggage storage room, not uttering a word to me or the concierge, who's suspiciously walking away as he ushers me in and slams the door behind me.

He pushes my back against the door, pinning me in place with his stare, and shows me a wicked smile before he leans in and kisses me. His lips are on mine, and it doesn't feel like this is still new. The way he kisses me definitely doesn't feel like we were only together for a long weekend. The way his hands touch my body completely in sync with what I want and what I need feels like he has spent years getting to know me and an eternity away from me. His tongue is pushing into my mouth, eager and starved. I moan against his lips, and when his hand comes to my neck, holding me gently, I arch my back to get closer to him and practically whimper as I bite his lower lip.

He lets go, bringing his mouth to my neck, kissing and biting gently. "You teasing little thing," he whispers against my ear as I roll my hips against him. He removes the mask from my face, and I do the same with his. God, he's stunning, all hard lines and a perfect jaw, dark intense eyes and the most perfect kissable lips.

"And you fucking love it. Did you miss me, Augusto?" I ask in a sultry tone, pausing deliberately as his name eases off my tongue, smooth like butter but lethal like venom. He hates it when I call him that, and I want him to fuck me like he hates me right now. I want him to fuck me like a man possessed. Like I'm *his* possession.

"Don't call me that." He bites with his dark eyes on mine, showing me his lust, want, and need.

"Or what?" I sass back, and his hands tighten around my neck harder. I moan again, and his eyes flare.

"This fucking dress. The fucking sass. The way you've been ignoring me for weeks, and now you decide to show up and make that giant display of what, Nellie? Affection? Jealousy? Lust? What was it, because I'm hella confused."

"All of it, but you forgot possessiveness."

"Oh yeah, please tell me how you go from not wanting to see me again to showing up here?"

"You really want to have this conversation now when I'm pretty sure my panties are soaked from the thought of you fucking me in this closet? With your rough, perfect hand forming the hottest necklace?" He groans, and I smile. "And let's not forget your perfect dick pressing against my hip."

"I'm not taking this further until you answer the questions, Nellie. I'm not."

"Why? Why can't you just fuck me? Why does it have to be complicated?"

"Because you're driving me wild, Nellie. I can't do anything but think about you. I will go fucking insane if I don't fuck you right now, but not before you tell me what changed." He takes his hand away from my neck and brings it to my chin. "Tell me."

"I'm driving you wild? Why didn't you say anything?"

"Because I can be a piece of shit sometimes, and because you scare the hell out of me. Is that enough honesty for you, baby girl?" He pauses, looking at me intensely before adding again, "*You* kept me at bay too. So tell me: why now?" His voice is filled with an emotion almost like hurt. The need. The want. All of it is present in his tone.

"Because I'm done pushing *you* away, at least for right now. I thought I could be okay with only a quick getaway, but clearly, I'm not. If I take this further Nellie, you need to promise me we'll talk after. I'm not giving in to momentary lust to be miserable for weeks." Jesus, he's laying it out straight for me, and now, it's my turn to tell him exactly what I've been too afraid to say, what I've been masking with walls and lies.

"Whatever you want. We can talk. I'm yours all night. I'm done trying to convince myself I don't need you, your hands, or your mouth on me. Now, Gus," I reply, my voice breathy and needy. Our masks are off, both literally and figuratively, and this is all there is for him to see. Just when I think he won't do anything about it, he smiles at me and takes everything I have to offer.

His lips crash to mine, and his hands roam my body. I pull him closer by the lapel of his jacket. I want his hands on every inch of my body. I want his mouth on my lips, on my neck, on my breasts. I want the air he's breathing and I want it now. Like he can hear me, he brings his hand to the plunging neckline, sliding his fingers under the dress and over my right breast. He finds my nipple instantly, rolling it between two fingers as he squeezes gently. His mouth doesn't leave mine as he pulls moan after moan just by playing with my body.

His other hand continues down, past my breasts, over my hips, under the slit of my dress. "This fucking dress. If I knew you were going to look like this, I would have asked you to come to the gala a month ago. Hell, I would have thrown my own formal event to see you like this." His mouth hovers above mine as he utters his praises, and his warm, minty breath caresses my lips, sending shivers across my body and all down my spine.

"Oh yeah, please do tell me exactly how I look in this dress," I whisper, looking at him with the same intensity he's looking at me.

"Royalty worthy. A goddess among mortals." He wastes no time getting on his knees in front of me, slowly lowering my panties down my thighs. His fingers brush the back of my legs, eliciting goosebumps as he lowers himself, whispering, "Your skin is so perfect. So soft." He grabs my ankle and helps me step out of the panties as he leaves my legs spread wide.

He crawls back up my body, sliding his hand up my torso back to my neck, to the sweet spot he was holding me that had me shivering just from his touch. When I tilt my head back, his eyes flare a darker shade of brown as he smirks at me. He starts teasing, running his fingers in between my legs, hovering over my clit and brushing it softly. He tightens his hand on my neck a little more, and I moan, "Gus."

"Shhh, you're going to get us in trouble." He teases my entrance as he kisses my lips raw, and when I moan against him again, he slides two fingers in. Fuck, that feels so good. His eyes heat again before he brings his lips back to mine, pumping his fingers in and out, driving me wild.

"Fuck," I groan, and he stops. He slides his fingers back out and lets go of my neck. *The fuck?*

He tsks. "Oh, I know a way your sweet, sweet noises won't get us in trouble." He pulls something out his pocket—no, not something. My panties. He drags them up my chest, up my neck, to my chin. "I will put these pretty panties in your mouth, and if you drop them…I won't make you come. I want those sweet sounds, but they don't belong to anyone but me. Open up."

He runs his thumb over my lower lip, and when my eyes widen, he cocks an eyebrow. "Relax for me and open up your mouth, Trouble." I do as he says, and with a mischievous grin, he slides the panties in.

He kisses my chin, the sensitive spot right under my earlobe, then whispers, "You were right. Your panties were soaked, and you're so wet, so ready for me. I can't wait to take a taste myself. Do you taste yourself? Can you taste how fucking sweet you are?" My moans are muffled by the lacy fabric, and I can feel his smile against my ear.

Gus looks at me before going back to his knees, his gaze on my pussy, making me clench just with his stare. Damn it; if he can make me feel this hot without even touching me, no wonder I haven't been able to stop thinking about him.

He slides his hands from my calf to the back of my thighs. Even though his touch is feathery, his rough hands on my skin are bringing me to the edge of insanity. He grips my hips, spreads my legs wider, and says, "I'm ready to worship you, my queen."

He's pulling my skirt so tight, I can barely move an inch from the door. As if I would move away from this man. His mouth closes over my mound, immediately making me buzz. His tongue slides out, finding my clit and licking it as he groans. The tingling and vibration intensify, and I know it won't take long. He knows it too, judging by the smile I see on his face.

"Fuck, you taste so good. You taste so sweet. I want to drown right here." I whimper, biting my lip and rocking my hips against his mouth as he continues to lick and bite my most sensitive spot. He doesn't relent. He never stops, not until my legs are jello around his face and he uses his hands to keep me upright. The warm, coiled sensation fills my belly, but I don't want to let go. I want to extend this for as long as I can.

I moan unrecognizable words. He hears it, I'm sure, when he groans again against me. This man is on his knees in front of me, driving me to the peak of my pleasure. The room right outside is full of women willing to pay thousands of dollars just to spend some time with him, and he chose *me*.

"Let go, Nellie."

I shake my head no, not letting go of the fabric between my lips. I bring my hands to his head and hold him where I want him. He takes it as his invitation to press harder. To lick faster. To hum louder. To get impossibly closer.

He grabs my ass with his strong hands. "I know you want to prolong it. I know you want this to last. Me too, but I only paid him to stay away for ten minutes, and I fear our time is running out. We'll have all the time in the world later, baby girl, but right now, I want to see how beautiful you look when you come for me, please."

Please? Did he just—oh, God. He asked with his words, and now he's begging with his tongue. He's moving his mouth against me like his life depends on my orgasm, and there's not much I can do when he flattens his tongue over my clit, pressing hard as his fingers dig into my ass when I feel the pool of desire spill everywhere. I moan his name.

He slows down, dragging out my orgasm until there's nothing more to give. Until *I* have nothing more to give. His hand holds my hips in place as he stands and smiles at me. He runs his hands up my body and pulls the panties from my mouth, putting them in his pocket. "Good fucking girl."

He kisses me again, but this time, it's not frantic. It's not erratic. It's not wild. It's composed and measured, but it brings life back to me.

"Come on, Trouble. Let me take you home." He holds my hand and walks us out of the closet, fixing his jacket but not wiping my arousal from his lips.

"Wait, do I need to pay? I did win a date with you, after all."

"I'll take care of it." He guides us through the quiet lobby into the elevator that will take us to the parking garage. He opens the door to a dark SUV, letting me in before running to the driver's side. He smiles at me, backs out, and holds my hand. He doesn't talk. He doesn't say anything. He just lets the music play, giving me time to think, to realize that this is the moment everything changes. I better start thinking about how the hell we're going to make this work.

TWELVE
ALL OF YOU

Still Into You by Ashley Tisdale and Chris French &
Talk by Khalid

NELLIE

WE ARRIVE AT GUS' place, an upscale penthouse loft in a modern and beautiful building by the beach. I walk straight to the floor-to-ceiling windows facing the water, offering panoramic views of the Atlantic Ocean. Jacksonville Beach is about an hour from Baker Oaks, so not too far, but also far away enough for privacy—the perfect distance to keep the nosy neighbors out of my business. The last thing I need is for someone to tell my parents I was sneaking around town with Gus.

It's late, so the light pouring through the window is misty and subtle from the full moon but breathtaking. I'm sure sunrises here must be stunning, and I can't wait to see, assuming I'm sleeping here. I turn around, walking to the living room, where Gus pours me a glass of wine and himself a glass of water.

I step closer, around the beautiful cream-colored furniture I missed when my eyes were locked on the ocean. Sometimes, I feel like I was made of ocean water and salt, a droplet planted in my mom's belly to grow with feet on the ground, but my soul belongs to the water. I never feel more peaceful than when I swim, especially if it's in the ocean, but sometimes, just looking at it, hearing its waves, is calming.

"Thank you," I say, grabbing the glass of chilled wine he offers me.

"Hold on here. I'll be right back." He disappears behind a giant wooden door, leaving me alone in the quiet of his living room with my wine. I take the time to pace around, looking at what seems like minimalist art on the wall, but when I get closer, I see they're paintings. They're paint-by-number paintings of beautiful landscapes, all in different shades of black and gray. A lion, a zebra, a jungle, and, wait—is that a naked woman?

"La Ciguapa. A Dominican urban legend," Gus says from behind me, his steps getting closer. I can't keep my eyes away from the painting. He stands right behind me and places his chin on my shoulder, sliding his hand over my hip. "Legend says, she'll drive men astray to their demise. This is an ode to her." His accent is beautiful. He has a certain way he says words, a flirty cadence that comes subconsciously. But when he speaks Spanish, his first language, the way he speaks mixes effortlessly with his voice, and goddamn it, if I don't love that. I could listen to him talk for hours.

"You painted these?" I ask, pointing at all the pictures.

"I did. I like to paint on quiet nights, but I'm not great at it. Painting by number comes in handy." Painting by numbers or not, these are stunning. I turn around to face him, taking another sip of the wine. It's almost floral, with a sweet undertone, but it's absolutely perfect. Cold and crisp. He takes the glass from my hand, placing it on the table next to him.

"Turn around," he commands, and I listen. His hands linger on my hips and slowly slide up my ass to my back. His breathing is slow next to my neck, and when I think he's going to kiss me, I hear a quick zipping noise, and the dress immediately loosens around me. He pulls it off my shoulders and lets it fall into the ground. I'm not wearing a bra, and he kept my underwear, so I stand naked in front of him.

"Arms up," he orders, and without asking any questions, I obey. Quickly, I feel fabric draped over me and around my arms. I lower them and look down at the soft t-shirt he put on me. He brings his hands to my shoulders, turning me around and bringing his hands up to my neck. He pulls me closer and kisses me, his hand holding the nape of my neck and sliding into my hair, tugging gently. He stops, lowering to the floor and helping me step through a pair of his boxer briefs. They're too loose on me, but they stay.

"As much as I wanted to keep seeing you in that stunning dress, I figured you wanted to be comfortable. Come on, let's sit." He hands me my wine and holds my opposite hand as he guides us outside through the glass doors to the terrace.

The warm, salty breeze caresses my cheeks as I sit in the chair across from Gus. He looks out into the water for a moment, just a split second, long enough for me to see his stunning features before he looks back at me.

"We need to talk, Nellie." Okay, straight to the point.

"I guess we do. You go first," I add, sinking into the chair and taking another sip of wine.

He lowers down, grabbing my left leg and lifting it onto his lap. His hands brush against my skin as he unbuckles my shoe, sliding it off my foot and placing it on the ground with a soft thud. His full lips are closed tight, and his beautiful thick dark eyebrows furrow as he focuses and does it again with the other. My feet rest on his lap as he relaxes, loosening his tie and sliding it off his neck. I didn't notice how, even though I'm completely stripped from the gala clothes and in utter comfort, Gus is still fully dressed.

"You can take your shoes off too, you know? I could've taken mine off myself," I quip.

"Ladies first," he replies, winking at me and placing his jacket on top of the side table. The gentle warm breeze caresses my skin, and I break out into goosebumps immediately. Gus, of course, notices and hands me the jacket. Without dropping my feet from his lap, I take it and drape it around my shoulders.

"You want to talk, Gus. Talk." I'm done with the slow and careful movements.

"What happened?" he asks directly, as if he's being as clear as day.

"When? Today? We established that. You had a blonde draped around your arm, and I got stupid jealous, used all your money, and then you ended up going down on me in a closet." I take another sip of the wine and cross my arms over my chest.

"Not all my money," he replies, but all I do is smile. "You were jealous?" he asks with a smirk, and I roll my eyes. Jealous? Irrationally so. I was seeing red. It took me ten seconds to realize it, and I did something about it.

"Yes, yes, I was. I know it's dumb, because it's not like you and I are exactly anything, but again, here we are."

"Don't do that," he replies. Is he going to be using more words today, or is he just going to give me the bare minimum?

"Don't do what, Augusto?"

"Don't dismiss what we are, and don't call me Augusto, please."

"Should I call you my dirty little secret instead?" I ask. I know I'm playing it cool. I know I'm acting nonchalant, but he's so tense, this is the only thing that will get him to relax.

When his shoulders sag and he narrows his eyes, I know I'm breaking through those thick walls.

"Is that what I am to you? A dirty little secret?" He looks hurt, but he quickly masks it with indifference, gently raising an eyebrow. He's asking me to be honest while he's hiding behind his questions and his carefully chosen words.

"Is that all you want to be? Answer carefully, Gus." Last time we talked, I did brush him off. I was taken aback by everything that happened in the Dominican. Too much, too soon, too fast. Damn it, Nellie. You should be telling him this, not yourself.

He rubs his face with one hand as he shakes it no. "I thought it was, but it's not. I don't know what I'm doing here, Nellie, but I would like to be more than just a dirty little secret to you. I want to see where this can take us."

"And it took you a month to figure it out?" I ask. Maybe mean and bitchy is his kryptonite, because flirty and sexy just gets him to have sex with me. This Nellie, the spitfire, the won't-hold-anything-back Nellie is getting him to tell me the truth.

"It took me a month to muster the courage to ask. I'm pretty sure I knew the night we danced two months ago. We can take it slow, but I would like to get to know you better." He smiles softly, and it reaches his eyes. He smiles often, at his friends, at his family, at me, but they're all different smiles. This one is sweet, tentative, and maybe even a little shy. It's the first time all night that it dawned on me—he might be scared too.

"What about our families?" I ask, trying to gather as much information as I can. If he needs questions to answer, I'm happy to provide them.

"What about you?" His rebuttal comes quick as he sits up and places his hands on my ankles. "What do *you* want?"

I feel his question bouncing in the walls of my brain,

hitting each side like the choices are playing ping pong in my head.

"I don't know what I want," I answer, barely a whisper, because I'm not even sure I myself believe that statement.

"I think you do know what you want, and you just got scared. I'm sorry you had to witness that, Nellie. I am. However…if you're not willing to look past it, then this—" he points between us with urgency—"is doomed. My medical emergencies are part of who I am. I don't show those parts to everyone, but you're not just anyone. I'm not trying to scare you, but if we're giving this a try, I need to know you're all in. So, I ask you again: what do *you* want?"

I ponder his question. I know I want him, and I know I want more than his perfect body. My heart is aching to get to know him more. Before the incident on the boat, I felt heard, cherished, valued. I felt like he wanted to talk to me and truly listen, regardless of the topic. I don't remember the last time I held a conversation other than with Bee and Victoria about anything not academic. Even my parents tend to revolve our conversations about my achievements. They don't do it on purpose; they just treat me like I'm still the fifteen-year-old girl who measured herself by the awards and prizes she got. Gus made me feel like he just wanted to learn more about me, like he could care less about my academic achievements. I want more of that.

"I want you," I whisper, but I don't think he hears me, because he just sits quietly in the chair for what seems like too long, but it's probably not long at all. He smirks and pulls me by my feet, dragging the chair across the space and closer to him.

"How do you want me? Be specific." His smile is lopsided now, and his posture changes from semi-relaxed to attentive.

"Who's asking for honesty now?" I ask.

"I'm done dancing around this. We either lay all our cards on the table now, or we can say goodbye and move on. What is it going to be, Trouble?" The damn nickname will be my undoing. My thumbs pick at my skin next to my nails while my eyes bounce between his. I try my darndest not to do it, knowing it will hurt my skin, but sometimes, I can't help it. When emotions are out of control, I can control that, the pressure on my fingers and under my nails, the light pain, the outlet I need to act unbothered.

"I want all of you. I want to get to know you better too," I reply, practicing what I preach. If I want honesty, I need to be honest too. He smiles softly back at me, leaning forward and dragging my legs even closer to him. Our chairs are touching at this point.

"Tell me more," he says as he smiles wider this time with his eyes. The tiny flecks of honey in his dark eyes glimmer with excitement. His eyes are so dark, you really have to be close to notice them, or maybe they just glimmer when he's happy. Either way, I'm glad I get to see them.

I drop my legs from his lap and stand. With our chairs so close, I have to stand with my legs wide open and his between them. He cocks an eyebrow at me, and I snort a laugh before I sit on his lap.

"I want your body," I croon as I drag my hands from his hip, up his chest, to rest on his shoulders. "I want your time and your thoughts." I continue the journey with my hands, caressing his neck and holding his face between my hands. He hisses at the contact, and I slide closer to him. From this angle, his face is lower than mine, and he's looking at me through his dark, thick lashes. My breasts are right in front of his face, but he's not looking anywhere but at my eyes, waiting for my next words.

I drag my thumb over his lower lip before adding, "I want your lips on mine and on every inch of my skin. I want to get to know them so well, I could recognize them in the dark. I want my body to know your lips and your hands as if they were my own, as if they're an extension of me." His eyes darken, focused on my mouth, then back to my eyes, bouncing between them. They're full of emotion, and I can tell some of it is lust, but there's a hint of something more.

I lower my hands and let them rest over his chest as I whisper, "But above all, I want to get to know your heart, Gus." He sucks in a breath, and when I smile at him, he does the same before quietly bringing his hands up my back, holding my face.

"I want to try and be all in," I say finally, hoping they're the last words I have to say tonight before he finally believes me.

"Promise?" he asks with comfort and sadness in his voice. I won't break a promise, so when I reply, I know it's not easy.

"Promise."

He pulls my face closer and kisses me breathless.

"ARE YOU DONE PLAYING HOUSE YET?" Gus says in a playful tone. I groan as I look down and notice the soft, dark sheets currently wrapped around my body. That's when it hits me. The auction, the closet, glasses of wine at Gus' condo, and rounds and rounds of sex. Gus. Oh shit, Gus. I don't move so I can continue to listen to the phone conversation.

The voice on the other end of his call replies to his question in annoyance, and it sounds just like Gus, but with a lighter accent. Manny, on Facetime? My head is resting on his chest, and if I don't move, neither of them will notice me here, so I don't. I don't want them to stop talking. I would rather eavesdrop instead. My head is pounding, and I feel like I drank a bar dry while running a marathon. My thighs, my head, my back—hell, even my arms hurt.

"No, Gus. I'm not playing house. That's not what I'm doing here. I'm on a trip with Cara, and I'll be home in less than two weeks. I'll be back to real life." What the hell? With Cara? I jerk, and Gus' hand goes straight to my hair. His abs harden under my touch, but he doesn't stop talking to his brother.

I open my eyes and take in the beautiful room. Dark wooden floors with beautiful cream furniture surround us. Tall windows look out into the beach. The water is calm today, showing barely any ripples in the water.

Gus asks fondly. "Are you liking it, though?"

"Actually, I am," his brother replies. I try to stay still, but I sneeze. I contain the sound, but my head jerks. I hope he can't see I'm awake, but that goes out of the window when Gus mutters *shit*.

"Have some company?" Manny teases at the same time I turn my head to face Gus and mouth a silent "sorry."

Gus looks concerned for a second, but it goes away the minute his eyes land on mine. Without dropping my gaze, he tells his brother, "Yeah, let me call you back, okay? Good luck with the outdoors and…whatever." He hangs up the phone abruptly and tosses it away on the nightstand.

"Buenos dias, Trouble," he whispers, smiling softly at me.

"Sorry, didn't mean to interrupt." Before the words are completely out of my mouth, he brings his hands down and pulls me up so my face is resting below his chin. He tilts his head down for a quick kiss.

"You didn't interrupt anything," he croons. I wrap my legs around him, straddling his warm, naked body. I try to drop my head to his chest at the same time he tries to pull me up or something, because instead of laying on his chest, I end up bumping my forehead into his chin.

"Ugh, Gus!" I groan, twisting my body and laying flat next to him.

"Shit, Nellie, are you okay?" His hands hold my face as I cover my forehead.

"Agh, yes, you hard-headed man." We both laugh, and

when I open my eyes, I find his gaze locked on me, searching and worried with a hint of joy.

"You wanna kill me for real too? I thought death by orgasm would take one of us out, but apparently, just trying to cuddle with you will do that too."

I try to stifle a laugh but lose my battle when he smiles brightly at me. It's then I notice the glass cup next to him with dark caramel liquid I'm assuming is iced coffee.

"Stop being so dramatic, but yeah, sorry about that. Give me the coffee please, because whatever the fuck you gave me to drink last night ruined me. Everything hurts. Everything." He hands me the coffee, and I take a sip. Perfect. Not too sweet, not too salty. No whipped cream, but a tiny taste of cinnamon and maybe coconut sugar? I'm not sure, but I guess I can always go snoop in his kitchen later to find out.

"The wine definitely is to blame for the headache. I stopped you after your second bottle. You were drinking it like water. As for the rest of your body…" He lets his words trail off before smiling knowingly at me.

"Oh, stop. Like you could even," I sass, taking another sip of my coffee.

"Do you need a reminder?"

"Is that a threat?" I ask, leveling him with my gaze. I can't, in this condition, have sex again. My body hums but also hurts, so I need to keep calm or run to take a cold shower.

"It could be a promise, baby girl, but you and I both know your body needs a break. Not forever, but maybe for the day." He smirks and winks at me before getting up from the bed.

"I'm going to the gym, but I'll be back in an hour. Make yourself at home, but please be here when I get back, okay?" he asks, and the sadness behind his words is not lost on me. He thinks I would do that? He thinks I would wait for him to leave and then, what? Leave him again? I thought we talked about this yesterday, about us trying to make this work.

"Gus, I meant it. I want more than just sex with you. I'll

be here when you get back. Any plans today?" I ask, standing and dropping the black sheets onto the bed. My body is on full display before him, and the way he looks at me sparks a fire in my belly. Damn; to be looked at like that forever sounds like the best temptation.

"I want to spend time with you, so whatever you want. We do have to talk about what we're gonna tell our siblings, but for now, I have to go, or I'll miss my group. See you in an hour."

He walks in the opposite direction, but before he leaves the room, I ask, "What group?" What does he mean by group? Maybe he has a team of people he likes to work out with.

"The other climbers. Rock climbing gym. It's better to have friends than go alone, especially when it comes to climbing. Alright, baby girl. See you when I get back."

I toss myself back onto the bed and close my eyes. The stupid smile on my face is a great reminder of how good I feel near him. It makes me feel less crazy about saying fuck it and giving this a try. I wish I could bottle up this feeling.

I get up and walk to his massive bathroom, draw a bath, and sink myself in the nice, warm, soapy water, close my eyes, and let myself daydream about what this could be.

"NOW THIS IS a view I can get used to," Gus says from behind me, making me tense. I was so lost in watching the waves, I didn't even hear him walk in. I turn around and catch myself smiling at the sight. Gus is standing at his kitchen island, wearing dark jeans and an open navy polo. Aviators frame his handsome face, and the smile he's flashing me is worth millions.

"It's your house. You know the view you have," I reply, walking toward him with a pep in my step. After he left, I soaked in the bath for about thirty minutes and then washed my hair using his shampoo that smells just like him—spicy and fresh. He has extremely good hair products for a man with short hair, but I'm not one to complain, especially not after I wrap my arms around his neck, and his hands crawl up the back of my hair, tugging gently.

"Mmm, I meant you, in my house, wearing my clothes….and apparently smelling like me too," he whispers against my ear, his voice groggy, tingling my skin. He tugs at my hair and tilts my head back so my eyes are locked on his face. I bring my hands up and take his glasses off so I can see the dark, intense eyes I love so much. He smells fresh, warm, and spicy, a combination of the shampoo I used on myself, the soap I found in his shower, and something else, lotion, maybe?

"Welcome home," I whisper and close the space between us, kissing him slowly on the lips and earning a groan.

"Trouble…" he groans against my mouth. I kiss his lower lip, pulling it between mine and biting gently. "Your body needs to rest, and we need to talk…for real this time."

"I took a bath, and I'm not sore anymore." A lie. I'm sore as shit, but he smells so good and his skin is so soft, I can't help myself.

"It kills me to do this, but I'm putting your greedy hands in time out. Come on." He kisses my forehead and holds my hand, drawing small circles on my wrist.

"Not fair," I pout, and he cocks an eyebrow at me.

"So greedy."

"And you like it." The smile he gives reassures me he does, but then he takes a deep breath in and lets it out slowly…and the honeymoon is over. "It's time, huh?"

"For us to talk more, yes, but before that, I want to show you something." He guides me to his bedroom and sits on the edge of the bed, right on the side he slept last night, and pulls me to his lap. He pulls open the first drawer of the night stand and pulls out a bag. "Open it," he commands. I look at him, unsure of what this is, but he nudges at me to do it. His soft smile is hiding a little bit of fear, but it's reassuring too. He's letting me in. He's letting me see.

I slide the zipper open and find a few orange bottles, all with different names. I hold the first one in hand, a big bottle with big blue pills in it. "For my high blood pressure. It's controlled, and for the most part, it's nothing for you to worry about," he says before I even ask.

I place the bottle on top of the table and grab another one. This one is smaller, with white pills inside. "That one is a diuretic. I retain liquid, so I need help so I don't blow up like a balloon. It helps my kidneys too."

"Do you have a kidney condition too?" I ask, and he shakes his head.

"No, but I really don't need to develop one. I don't need more comorbidities than what I have. I take care of my healthy organs because I never know if they'll need help one day." Organs…including things like his liver or his stomach, which would make sense on why I always see him eating mostly whole foods.

"Is this why you don't drink?" I ask.

"Protecting my liver." He nods and smiles. I put the bottle next to the first one, and then I find a small box with syringes and a clear liquid. He holds the box and says, "These are my rescue medications. In case of an attack, like on the boat, this is what I need. I have a set everywhere—the house, the cars, the plane, the villa, but I was reckless and didn't think to check if I had some on the boat too."

"Why? Why would you do that?"

"Because I'm human, and I was so lost in you, I forgot about everything else." I lower my head after he says those words, but his fingers hold my chin and lift my face up to see him. "Not your fault, baby girl. Mine. My responsibility. My recklessness, and I'm sorry."

"This," he adds when I nod, blinking away tears threatening to spill as he holds a small container, "is my daily medication for the attacks, or flare ups, whatever you want to call them. Attacks is more accurate, but it's such a rough word, I rather call them flare ups. I take these every day, and it manages my symptoms. If I skip it, well, you saw what happened."

"How often do the attacks happen?"

"It depends, but before the one you witnessed, I haven't had one that severe in over a year. Which leads me to the next thing." He slides his hand in the bag, taking out an EpiPen. "This. This won't stop the attack, but it will keep me alive. I have one of these everywhere, but at the moment, I couldn't remember where I put them in the boat. I would love to show you how to use it," he says.

"I know how. We have training at school for those. I know how to identify the symptoms too." I smile, reassuring him, and open the bag more to see it's empty. "What? No more medicine? I was starting to think this was an endless bag."

He chuckles, and everything is good in the world again. I put all his medicines back in the bag, zip it closed, and hand it to him. I kiss him on the cheek and say, "Thank you for sharing this with me."

"Thank you for listening." He places the bag back in the drawer, closing it with a loud thud.

"It's part of who you are. I'm sorry if someone has ever made you feel like they don't care," I reply, bringing my hand up to cup his face. He closes his eyes slowly, and when his onyx irises meet mine, I can see all the unspoken emotion behind them. "Gus…you know this is not everything you are, right? You're more than all of these conditions, but they *are* part of you, and that's okay too. It's a little scary, yes, but just because of the lack of information. I'm sure it was scary for you too."

"It was. It is," he whispers.

"When I was a little girl, I used to be afraid of a lot of

things. Actually, as I got older and kept learning random shit nobody my age should be worrying about, I got scared of more. A lot more, and you know what someone very important to me told me at twelve years old?" He shakes his head, but he doesn't break my gaze, which I really like. I love that even though his eyes are so intense and all the emotions coursing betweens us are heightened, he still looks at me.

"She told me I didn't have to carry it all on my own. She told me it might be easier if I shared the load, even when I didn't think it was worth sharing. Gus, I'm willing to share yours."

"See, I knew you were trouble. You have no business making me this emotional," he replies, and I smile before bringing my lips to his. I hold his face and kiss him, gently, tentative, and slow as I show him with this kiss that I can be patient for him. I show him with this kiss that I want more than just his body. I don't speed it up, I don't deepen it, I just take my time savoring him. It's emotional and raw, and it feels like layers and layers were just peeled back on this barrier between us. We slow the kiss until our lips are barely touching and we're just breathing each other in.

"Thank you," he whispers.

"For what, kissing you?" I ask.

"For listening." Our foreheads touch before he shakes his head and breaks the contact. His eyes sober quickly, and then he adds, "I'm glad we talked about us and I'm glad we're both on the same page. We want this, we want us." He stops talking, but his dark eyes hold my gaze as his hand caresses my leg from my knee to my upper thigh, the tip of his fingers leaving goosebumps as he moves them.

"But…"

"No buts. I'm just trying to figure out what that means for the rest of the world. Are we dating just for us? Are we letting our families know? How public is this?"

"Gus—" I cock my head sideways and beam at him, "—are you nervous?"

"I just don't want this to be an issue."

"Who the fuck cares what other people think?" I ask, crossing my arms over my breasts.

"It's not that I care about others' opinions, but I'm worried how our moms are going to react, and if I'm being honest, I'm terrified of Allie too." Allie—his sister and my sister's best friend— is a sweetheart, but I can imagine she can be a little mean too…just like Cara. She recently moved back to Baker Oaks as well. I can see how it can be a touchy subject.

"Okay," I say, my voice softening. I take his hand in mine, giving it a reassuring squeeze. "I get it. You don't want to rock the boat with everyone, but listen, we've talked about this, and we want this, right? We're not rushing into anything, and I'm not asking you to make any big declarations until we're ready. But I'm here."

He looks at me for a long moment, like he's weighing what I said. Then, he takes a deep breath, nodding. "So what do you suggest we do? Keep it low-key, see how everything pans out?"

I nod. "Exactly. I think we should keep it quiet for now, just let it breathe a bit, and when we feel like it's time, we'll tell them."

"Allie's boyfriend, Jake, asked me to participate in his proposal next week." I smile as he says that. "I know, I'm excited too. He has this whole thing planned that Manny is helping execute. They will all be in Nashville. I would ask you to come with me, but it would be highly suspicious if you do. How about I go and see if I can talk to Manny and Cara, and we can go from there?"

"But until then, let's keep this between us," I add, and he nods. Gus leans back, rubbing his forehead, looking like he's thinking it through before nodding again.

"You know what that means, though, right?" I ask.

"What?" his head tilts to the side so he's looking at me, and when I smile, he returns it.

"We have some time to sneak around like teenagers afraid of getting caught." For the first time in my life, I'm willing to be selfish and do something for myself. I didn't get to sneak around and have some fun when I should have, so I might as well enjoy it now. He's giving me the space I need to figure this out, and I'm willing to take it.

THIRTEEN

MINDING MY OWN BUSINESS

JUNE— A WEEK LATER

FANTASIAS BY RAUW ALEJANDRO & Farruko & Risk by Gracie Abrams

GUS

MY BIG SIS is about to get engaged. Yeah, yeah, a proposal needs to happen first, but I know she'll say yes. She's been in love with this man for longer than she cares to admit. They had a falling out a few years ago, but once she sat us all down and explained everything that happened, I was pissed, but it made sense. Now, I'm excited to see her live her happily ever after or whatever it is that she likes to read about.

Manny is bringing Allie and her best friends—Cara, Roe, and Natalie—up to this vineyard we were able to reserve for this occasion. None of Allie's friends know; Cara didn't even know Allie and the other girls were coming. Jake wanted to keep it all a secret from them to help make the moment more magical for her. Manny and Cara have also been on a road trip for two weeks, and apparently all the girls have wanted to visit Nashville forever together. It was one of the stops on the trip, so Manny and Jake made it happen. They also made Allie think it was her idea so she wouldn't suspect that all along, Jake was going to propose to her.

For the past week, Nellie and I have seen each other nearly every day. She's spent the night a few times too. We had a routine going. We went swimming and then ate breakfast. Afterward, I ate her for dessert, and then we continued with our day. This went on for almost the entire week until she needed to do some training and state tests for her counselor certification. Now, I've decided that after Allie and Jake have their moment, I'll talk to Manny and see where his mind is at.

Manny and I have a connection that's hard to explain. We're brothers and twins but also best friends. We've been through everything together, and we were also thick as thieves growing up. It was us against the world. When my first diagnosis came, it was like that connection was severed. He thought he would feel there was something wrong with me. He started feeling like it should have been his responsibility to notice the slow progression of HAE. It affected him way more than we both like to admit.

Sometimes, I can't help but worry about him. It's hard not to when all he does is work. He shows up at events or family dinners, but that's it. He needs a break, and seeing how much this trip has helped him realize that has me happy and grateful —grateful to Allie for forcing him to go and to Cara for needing him.

I watch Jake show that cocky grin of his, his eyes practically glowing with excitement as Allie walks up, the girls trailing behind her, hands over her mouth as she reaches him.

We all step closer but still give them the space they need. Something about the way Jake turns serious when they reach the perfect spot—right between the rows of vines—makes me pause. The whole scene feels almost like it's happening in slow motion, but before I can think too much on it, he has dropped to one knee, shared with her why he wants to marry her, and then, it's over. Allie says yes, all the girls squeal, and all the men clap. A good moment, and I'm so happy I got to be a part of it.

I watch from afar as everyone congratulates them before I take the space to do so too.

"Felicidades, hermanita. Te lo mereces[1]." I pull Allie in my arms for a hug and wipe her tears away from her face. This girl is always crying—happy tears, sad tears, angry tears, all the tears.

"Gracias, Gusti. I can't believe you're here," she replies, sniffling and smiling at me.

"I wouldn't miss it for the world. Felicidades, bro, y bienvenido a la familia[2]," I tell Jake as I pull him for a hug too. "I'll give you two another moment alone." I walk back to where I was standing, grab my glass of water, and enjoy the moment. These two finally are getting their happily ever after. I can't wait to see what the future holds for them.

I look around the vineyard, and I spot Manny and Cara talking, so I walk their way. This would be a great opportunity for me to maybe ask about Nellie or something, to see how Cara reacts, see if Manny can tell where my head is at. Maybe his twin sixth sense will pick on the message, and then we can talk.

"You two have always been my favorite girls, Cara," Manny says, completely infatuated with Cara. I'm assuming he's referring to her and Allie. He's had a crush on her all his life, and it's always good to see how lost in her he can get, even if it's just for fun.

"Fancy seeing you here," Cara says as she turns around to see me.

"Only once in a lifetime, your sister gets engaged, Carita,"

---

1. Congratulations, sister. You deserve it.
2. Congratulations bro and welcome to the family

I reply, kissing her cheek and trying to ignore Manny's eyes on me. Whatever that's about. He's been overly broody today, almost guarded, and I have no idea why. I've asked him twice, but he says I'm imagining things, so I try to brush it off as a reflection of myself. Maybe I'm nervous about the whole Nellie situation, and I'm looking too much into things.

"Don't call her that," Manny snaps, his voice sharp. What the fuck? Carita is the nickname we've always used for Cara. Yeah, sure, Manny uses it more, but who does he think he is now?

"She's our Carita. Of course, I can call her that." I wink at Manny and pull Cara closer, hugging her tight, but she tenses under my hold. *Interesting.*

Manny steps forward, his jaw clenched. "She's not, and I said not to call her that." Oh, shit. I know this tone. This is jealousy, raw, deep in your bones jealousy, more than *I have a crush on my sister's best friend* jealousy. I look between both of them, and then it clicks. *They're sleeping together.* Manny shakes his head when he sees it in my eyes and tries to say something, but I stop him, raising my hand.

"I'll leave you two alone so you can figure out whatever the hell it is you have going on." It comes out harsher than I expected, but shit, this just complicates everything.

Cara starts to speak, rushing to say something, I'm sure to deny what's happening, but I cut her off. I need to get out of here and call Nellie. I need to breathe and clear my head, and I can't do that with those two looking at me and each other like that.

"Don't, Cara. Not my business. I have enough of my own to be minding someone else's. Just be careful, both of you." How hypocritical of me when I know damn well what's going on with me and Nellie. What a mess.

I shake my head, walking in the other direction, pulling the phone from my back pocket to text Nellie.

ME:

We have a problem. Call me when you can.

NELLIE:

Is everything okay?

ME:

Unclear. Call me when you can.

NELLIE:

Ok

I drive back to my hotel once we all have dinner and drinks. I try hard to focus on my sister and her night, but all I keep repeating in a loop is how I really want to tell Manny about Nellie, but the whole situation just got a little bit more complicated. We're both adults; it's not like they can act like we aren't. Still, this is turning into a knotted mess, and we need to be on the same page before anything can be said.

"HEY," I say to Nellie, who's walking to my car with a bag in hand. She's wearing a black, one piece bathing suit with some sort of net dress over it, sandals with small bows, and her over-sized sunglasses. Her hair is wrapped in a bun over her head, and she's flashing me the biggest smile I've ever seen.

"Hey, handsome," she replies, opening the door and sliding in. "God, I love this car." She touches the door and the dashboard like she always does, slow and determined, taking it all in, always seeking to feel, wanting to control the how tond when. I find myself wanting to be under her touch.

"So do I, baby girl. So do I." I bought this Barracuda at an auction three years ago, and it has become my most trea-sured possession. I'm very mindful of where I drive this car, and I definitely don't take it out every day, but after Nellie loved seeing the first time, I find myself wanting to find as many excuses as possible to take her in it.

We head down the road, taking the quickest way out of Baker Oaks to the highway, trying to avoid too many people seeing us. Leave it up to me to drive the flashiest car there ever was, but with it being so early, I'm confident most people are sleeping.

"That coffee's yours." I point to the iced coffee in the cup holder, and she grabs it immediately, taking a sip and fluttering her eyelashes.

"Heaven in a cup." I chuckle at her words and continue the silent drive. She's quiet, which is not common for her, and I don't like it. What's going on in that smart brain of hers today?

"Are you ready for today?"

"Did you take your meds?" I flinch at her question, and she immediately softens her features. "I'm sorry, that came out wrong. I'm just a little worried about today."

"What are you worried about?" When I got back from Nashville, I asked Nellie if she'd like to go sailing with me, and she said yes so quickly. Our siblings will be here tomorrow, and things will get a little bit more complicated, so I want to soak in all the time I can with her. But if I'm being honest with myself, I just want to come clean. I want to tell everyone how much I like Nellie, but I need to talk to my brother first. He'd never forgive me if he found out from someone else.

"Well…last time we went out on the boat, you know what happened, and I'm having the hardest time wrapping my head around it." She lifts her glasses and flashes her pretty green eyes at me. I let her words rest between us and continue driving. No music. No sound. Just Nellie's candor between us. She raises her hands in defense when I cock my eyebrows at her. "I'm not blaming you. I promise I'm not. I'm just worried, okay?"

"I know. It's part of the reason why I want to do this

again. Yes, I took my medicine. Yes, I have a bag with all of them here too, and I put a bag with rescue meds to bring on the sailboat. If it makes you feel safer, I'm happy to call Martin to come with us. He can sail." I point to the glove box; she takes the hint and opens it.

"My medicine bag, just like the one in my nightstand. That one stays in the car. If you look back, the black bag on the seat has my rescue meds inside. I was reckless back in the Dominican. I'm not going to do it again."

It's so early, the highway is practically deserted. The midnight blue sky turning into a blend of purple hues in the distance reminds me to show her the calm. She needs answers. She needs control. I can't control my flare ups, but I can give her the tools.

"Thank you," she whispers, sliding the bag back into the glove box, shutting the door, and resting her head back. She closes her eyes, and I take it as an invitation to turn the music on and drive.

Arriving on Amelia Island right at sunrise was perfectly timed. The hour drive from Baker Oaks here was seamless, with very little traffic. After parking and running to open Nellie's door, I feel lightheaded as we walk down the sidewalk to the marina where the boats are docked. I don't own a sailboat here, but I rent one from time to time when I'm homesick and don't want to fly to the Dominican just to sail.

"Are you okay?" Nellie asks when she notices me pinching the bridge of my nose.

"Yes, I'm about to be better once we're on the water." I squeeze her hand and guide her up on the sailboat, where Martin already waits for us. She looks up at me with questions behind her eyes.

"I told you…I want you to feel safe. I don't mind him here, and he can sail. If something happens, he can help. Meds in bag, Martin on deck, a phone call away for a rescue. I'm fine, I promise."

As soon as the last words are out of my lips, she leaps into my arms, almost throwing us backward. "Easy," I whisper into her soft hair, and she wraps me tighter in her arms.

"Thank you."

"For what?"

"For listening to what I said and reading between the lines."

"Draw them for me, and I'll follow them. Wrap your legs around me, baby girl." She's already in my arms, so I might as well keep her there. She does what I ask, and after I drop the bag I was carrying, I bring my hands under her ass and walk us to the deck. I sit us both on the net, and she snuggles against my chest automatically.

"As much as I love you snuggling against me, my little koala, you're going to miss the rest of the sunrise."

"Well, if someone wouldn't have asked me to be awake and ready at 5:00 a.m., I wouldn't be this tired."

"You had your coffee, but also, look—" I point to the horizon, and she follows my gaze. Purple, blue, orange, and pink paint the sky as the wind blows our way, and Martin leads us out into the water.

"Worth it," she says, relaxing her back against my chest and grabbing my thigh. "Damn, Gus. Your skin is so cold."

As if on cue, goosebumps break out on my leg, and I shake the feeling that this is weird. I'm never cold, but lately, my temperature regulation has been off.

"I was missing your touch. I should warm up soon."

She chuckles and says, "You saw me three days ago."

"Three days too many." She shakes her head and turns to face the horizon. I rest my chin on her head and wrap my arms around her. I like how I feel with her. I like how she feels between my legs, resting on my chest, her hands sliding up and down my leg. She feels soft and peaceful. She feels like the piece I didn't know I was missing. She feels like tender moments and wild times. She feels like mine, and I don't know if she should.

We're not going far. It takes about thirty minutes of sailing to get to Cumberland Island, where I plan for us to go. Cumberland Island is a barrier island off the coast of Georgia, only accessible by boat. It's really close to the Amelia Island marina, and because there's no access via land, it's pretty private. Occasionally, people will come on their boats or on tours, but it's rare the island is full of people. It's not Dominican beach and sand, but it's beautiful and peaceful.

We make it as close to the beach as we can, and Martin lowers the anchor, setting us in place. I hop down into the shallow water and open my arms for Nellie.

"Don't let me fall."

"Never," I reply. She jumps down, and I, of course, catch her. She looks at me and smiles.

"My soft place to land." She kisses my lips as her whispered words caress my heart. Yes, baby girl, I want to be that and so much more, and it's terrifying..

"Put me down. I like the salt water on my toes." I do carefully and nod to Martin to hand me the cooler with the food I had made for us, plus the bag with towels and my medicine.

We set up a spot by the water and sit, high enough where the towels won't get wet, but close enough to smell the ocean. Martin stays in the cabin, giving us privacy, and I pull out the mini bento boxes.

"Adult Lunchable, I like it."

"You loved it last time I fed you cold cuts and fruit," I tease, and her cheeks turn rosy immediately.

"I more than liked it… Are you looking for a repeat session, because I can get on board with that." She crosses her arms above her chest and removes the dress as soon as she finishes that sentence. Such a greedy little tease.

"No, ma'am. At least not today, and not here. Not getting

a ticket for licking you out here in the open." She pouts, and I laugh.

"So greedy."

"Only for you." Nellie winks and opens her box, grabbing some crackers and prosciutto and taking a bite. She then grabs another one, adds a piece of cheese on top, and offers it to me.

"Open up," she says, and I open my legs, mimicking her reaction the other day. She laughs and rolls her eyes at me, but eventually, I open my mouth and let her feed me.

My heart is racing, and my chest feels tight, which has been happening more and more lately, so I want to make sure I watch what I eat. I grab a strawberry and feed her, and the same thing happens again. We take turns feeding each other, and with each bite, her body comes closer to mine to the point where she's practically tangled around my lap. My dick is at attention always, and every time she feels it, she giggles. I'm always like this near her. Needy for her. Craving her.

Craving her hands on my body. Her hair on my chest. Her eyes on me and my lips on her. I kiss her gently, tasting salt and sweetness with a faint mint aftertaste on her plump lips. Holding her delicate face between my hands, I try really hard to keep my word not to fuck her on this beach.

"I need you to stop kissing me like that if you're not going to do something about it."

"Kissing you like what?"

"Like you're starving, and I'm your favorite snack."

I chuckle with her lips near mine and give her another quick peck. "I am, and you are. You wanna swim?" I ask her, because I know she must be dying to, and she nods. I take my shirt off and get up, holding her hand and walking with her to the water. It feels like I'm returning the ocean a piece of itself when I bring Nellie back in the water. When I see her smile, close her eyes, and tilt her head back, lifting her feet to float, I know she feels it too.

I sit down, my ass touching the sand. The water hits me at chest level. I rest my hands under her back and hold her up—or pretend to hold her up, since she's floating on her own.

"I love this weightless feeling," she says with her giant sunglasses on her face, little drops of water on them.

"What do you love about it?"

"While I'm floating, I don't think about anything else, other than my body in the water. I don't feel heavy. I don't feel pain. I don't feel chaos. I just feel whole."

"You and the ocean are the same. I called you a little fish the other day, but I think you're a little wave. My little wave." She smiles at my words and brings her arms closer to her body, letting my hands do more of the work, keeping her up, her face above water.

"So what's the plan? Take Cara and Manny out for dinner when they get back and tell them…or are we talking to them separately?" Nellie asks.

"I would rather talk to him in private, personally. He's gonna want to act like an overprotective sibling, especially if he finally told Cara how he feels about her."

"You said he loves her, right?"

"He always has. It's obvious to anyone who pays attention but the two of them." Nellie sits up and lifts her glasses. I've come to realize this is her tell when she's focused. Glasses up, eyes on me. I love it.

"Has he really?" I nod, and she smiles. "Is he a good man, Gus? Like you?"

"He's the better twin. His heart is whole."

"So is yours."

"That's debatable." I mean it in more ways than one. I don't like these little lightheaded episodes I've been getting lately. I don't like this tightness in my chest. I'm worried it has to do with my heart, but I want to be oblivious about it, at least for now. "Cara is safe with him, but I think we should talk to them separately. Then, maybe we can tell our parents together."

"Wouldn't that be something?" Nellie asks, a mischievous smile growing on her face as she adds, "You best friended too closed to the sun, and your children became lovers." She cackles at her own sentence. "We will always be their children, but we're adults now."

"Yeah, yeah. Siblings first, then the parents…okay?"

"Deal. Now, let's go swim," she says, tossing the glasses all the way to the shore and sinking into the water as I follow.

FOURTEEN
WE HAVE TIME

DANCING With Our Hands Tied by Taylor Swift

NELLIE

CARA GOT HOME LAST NIGHT. I heard her door shut late, and I didn't want to bother her. I'm working at the diner today—like I do every summer—so I didn't see her before I left. Her room is directly next to mine in our parents' home, and she's staying there too until she finds a place. She has an offer in on a house, but nothing is set in stone yet.

Growing up, our rooms were always like this, close enough that we could sneak around to talk, but the wall we shared didn't just keep us from snooping on each other. It kept us apart. I love Cara, and I know she loves me, but we're so different sometimes, it feels like we weren't raised by the same people. Maybe we weren't.

Our parents were young when they had her, and then they struggled for years to have me. Once they did, I was a little terror—their words, not mine—and they were tired. With

Cara, it was trial and error and enjoying her bubbly personality. Everything was new, and they got to enjoy parenthood with her. With me, they were overbearing to the max because they wanted me for so long, and when I finally came, I scared the hell out of them with my brain and antics. They already knew what worked and what didn't, and they knew how fast it all went, so they hovered all the time to make sure they didn't miss anything. With my brain developing the way it did, there was no slowing down anything. Their favorite story to tell is when I was two, I stepped out of my play area speaking French. Not fluently, but it was definitely enough for them to question if I was having a stroke. Turns out, they let me watch a few videos with French in them because I would stop babbling and stare, and it stuck. They have hundreds of stories like this until I was diagnosed as gifted. Their "little genius", they said.

Most people think being smart—or academically advanced, I should say—is a blessing, but sometimes, it just feels like it's a burden, a hardship to carry. Sometimes, I just want to be Nellie. Not Cara's little sister Nellie. Not little genius Nellie. Not too smart to become a counselor Nellie. I want to be seen for me. It's one of the reasons I love spending time with Gus. I've never felt more seen, and I'm ready to fall for him out loud. Out in the open. Without restraints. Without barriers. Without secrets.

I know what I need to do. I need to talk to Cara. I need to tell her everything, and then we can talk about telling our parents. If anyone will understand, it's her. I don't actually think our parents will be mad or anything. We're both adults, after all, but out of respect for their friendship with the Zabanas, we need to tell them. My shift is almost over, and I'll go straight home so I can talk to her.

"HEY, CARA," I say knocking on Cara's half-open bedroom door. It's quiet in the house, and it usually wouldn't be a big deal if it wasn't for the fact that I could hear someone sniffle— someone being a very sad Cara on top of her bed. "Hey… what's wrong?"

Her eyes are puffy and red, and her green irises look glossy and sad. Her nose is red; judging by the pile of tissues on her nightstand, she's been crying a long time. It's almost 1:00 pm, so she might have been crying since this morning, and I don't like it.

"Cara…talk to me." I sit next to her on the bed and hold her hand in mine. Cara's always been there for me, and I've never seen her this distraught. The very bare minimum I can do is push for her to share with me what's going on. She's usually pure sunshine, so it must be bad if she's crying this hard.

"I'm okay… It's just—" She sniffles between words as she shakes her head. "I don't know what I'm doing."

"With what?"

"Nothing. It's nothing. Just go."

"Cara, you can tell me. You can trust me. Whatever it is, we will figure it out. Do I need to call your friends? I'm sure they'll be here in no time."

"No!" she shouts, sitting up straighter and opening her eyes wide. "No matter, what don't call them. I'll be fine. I'm just a little sad at the moment."

"Sorry to break it to you, but that many tears and that many tissues are not a little sad. Spill." I take my shoes off and cross my arms over my chest. I mean business.

She takes a deep breath and blurts out the events of her entire trip, the three weeks she was road tripping with Manny before she starts her new life here. She talks for what seems like seconds, but in reality, it's almost an hour, about how she started the road trip upset at him and ended it in love with him.

"I don't understand what the problem is, Cara. You love him, he loves you, you can both live happily ever after."

"He doesn't love me," she replies.

"I'm sorry to break it to you, my girl, but all of that—everything you just shared— shows me he loves you." I have to stop myself from telling her Gus said Manny has been in love with her all his life. My plan to come clean and tell her everything about Gus and I went to shit the minute I saw her crying.

"What's the worst that can happen, Cara?" It's the same thing she used to ask me when I was little and didn't want to take risks, mostly socially. We would play worst case scenario, and then she would make me promise I would at least try, because even the worst case scenario was better than not trying at all.

"I can't compete with his work, Nells, or his lifestyle. I can't offer him anything when he has it all. I can't even offer him stability. I don't want to start something that could mess up our families' relationship you know? My friendship with Allie…that's more important than the what if with Manny."

How do I tell her I understand this so deeply? How do I explain this is exactly where I'm at…except it's not how I might mess up my relationship with Allie, but with her? What if we also don't work out? Or what if we do, and they don't? What then? What a mess. But this isn't about me; this is about her. I can set aside my relationship with Gus and be here for her. We're already hiding it from everyone, so what's hiding for a little bit longer? What is giving Cara and Manny the space they need to figure it out? I don't want to keep sneaking around, but I want her to be happy too, and I don't think if she knows about me and Gus, she'd go through with it. She wouldn't tell Manny how she really feels.

"You don't have to compete with his job or his lifestyle, and you have so much to offer. You just have to be you. Tell him how you feel. You clearly love him, so stop suffering. That asshole ex of yours didn't deserve your heart, but maybe Manny does. If anything, he'll protect it more than you think. You deserve to give it a chance."

"What if I mess everything up?" she asks, tears rolling down her cheeks.

"What if you don't?"

Cara rolls her eyes. "When did you become so wise?"

"I've always been wise. You just never asked." I lean forward and give her a hug, both of us collapsing on the bed. "I love you. You're so, so easy to love, Cara. Let him love you."

She rolls to her back, her eyes trained on the ceiling as she says, "Thanks, Nells… Enough about me. Tell me about you. What's going on with your life?"

Oh, nothing. I'm just falling in love with your maybe-soon-to-be boyfriend's twin brother, who happens to be our mom's best friend's son, who makes me feel more alive than anyone I've ever met, and I'm in so much trouble because I don't even know how to come clean and tell everyone about us. Jesus, Nellie, get a grip.

"Nothing much. I got the job, though." She hugs me tighter before lying back down.

"I'm so proud of you. Those kids are so lucky to have you. I can't wait to see you shine as a counselor."

"Thank you! I'm excited."

"Me too. Just remember to take care of yourself. The first school year is the roughest."

"I promise," I say, smiling at her but thinking about how many promises I've made lately, not sure I can keep them all.

We talk for longer and catch up on everything—everything except the man setting my soul on fire. Everything but my feelings for him. Everything but what I really wanted to tell her. There will be a time, I know it. I'm not going anywhere, and I hope Gus isn't either. We have time.

FIFTEEN
TELL ME ABOUT HER
JULY

July by Noah Cyrus and Leon Bridges

GUS

"SO LET me get this straight. You went on this trip. You found yourself again. You told Cara how you felt after showing her how she deserves to be treated but now you won't fight for her?" I ask my stupid brother, because apparently, someone has to bring him to his senses. He's sitting in his office chair, his foot over his lap, bouncing a stress ball from the desk to his hand without a care in the world.

"I would fight for her. Hell, I would give her the world if I could, but she just spent three weeks telling me how little her ex listened to her, and I don't want to be that same person for her," Manny answers, throwing the stress ball up and down in his hand and looking out at the river through his office window.

"So you're willing to lose her?"

"If you love something, set it free, right?" he asks, and it makes me wonder if I would do the same. Not that I love Nellie, but if I did, would I be willing to let her go if it's what's best for her? I don't think I would. I'm a selfish motherfucker who goes after what I want.

"Enough about me. What's going on with you? I feel like we haven't talked in weeks." Well, I was coming here to tell him I'm falling in love with the love of his life's little sister, but now what am I supposed to do? Sorry you're hurting, but I'm happy with Nellie? Sorry you and Cara didn't work out, but I'm sort of dating her sister, and I want to scream it to the world?

"Not true," I say. Manny hates lies. He and Nellie have that in common. He says our dad lied so much, he learned to abhor it. On the other hand, I spent years covering up the truth about my health to protect him, and it drove a wedge between us. Now, I try not to keep him in the dark, which is why I have to tell him about what's been going with me. The dizziness and weakness is not normal. I fainted yesterday too, and Martin found me after I didn't answer the phone. I need to have someone in the know, at least until I gather more information and figure out if this is something to be concerned about. Manny can help, I know it.

Nellie, though? I have to keep her in the dark for longer. It has to stay like that. It's what's best for everyone, for Manny and Cara and the two of us, especially if we're trying to make this work. I hate that I have to keep this from Nellie, but she needs control, and I can't control anything right now. Calling Dr. Diaz will be step one, but she will want to run tests, and I'm tired of it. I'm tired of the poking, the probing, the medicine changes. I'm grateful for medical advances and the opportunity to give my heart and my body what I need to survive, but sometimes, I just wish I was normal. I just wish I could live my life without having to worry so much about what even too much salt would do to my heart.

"Speaking about weeks ago: what was going on with that

girl at your house?" he asks. I thought I dodged the bullet, but I guess not.

"I thought you would let this one go," I mention, catching the ball he bounces to me. "You didn't ask at the vineyard, so I thought you forgot."

"Nah, no way. You had a girl in your bed in the morning. That's newsworthy, even a month later. Tell me about her."

"You're gossiping like we're in middle school now."

"I'm interested. It's different. Actually, I'm invested. Tell me more." He wiggles his eyebrows before ducking to avoid the ball I throw at his head.

"I may have to keep this one to myself for a while…but I'm seeing someone." Just the thought of saying it was someone else repulses me. The thought of saying it was something casual does too. Ugh, my head. Small dots dance in my vision, and I close my eyes tight. Another dizzy spell.

"What was that?" Manny asks, and I open my eyes to find him looking at me, concerned.

"Are you getting sick or something?

I take a slow breath, but it doesn't help. The dizziness swells, pressing in heavier, making the lights too damn bright. "No, I'm not. Just dizzy."

"Call the doctor." This is why I don't tell him shit unless I have all the answers. He turns into Manny "the fixer" immediately, and sometimes, I just need Manny my brother.

"I'm good. It's just today. I'll have some electrolytes and be fine. I didn't sleep well."

"Long night with her?"

Yes, but I don't tell him. My jaw flexes. "Drop it, man."

A slow grin spreads across his face. "That bad, huh?" He picks up the ball and tosses it back to me, something we always did growing up. Our parents thought we would be good at tennis or ping pong because of it, but really, we just liked whatever would keep our hands busy and us talking.

I fire the ball at him. He barely dodges it, instead catching it. "That good," I correct.

His laughter echoes in the office. "Oh, now I *really* need details."

I rub my temple, trying to push away the lingering dizziness. "Not happening."

"You must care about her a lot if you've seen her more than twice and won't share any details." *I'm falling in love with her. She brings me to life. She's giving me hope that I can share everything with her.*

"Would you share any details about Cara with me?" I fire back.

"Do not compare whatever you have going on to my relationship with Cara."

"Or your lack of one."

He stops tossing the ball and proceeds to slam it on top of the desk. "Mi decisión de decirle a Cara que la amo y ver lo que pasa no tiene nada que ver contigo. Es entre ella y yo. Si no me quieres decir que está pasando con la chica misteriosa, no pasa nada pero no me compares al amor de mi vida con tu chapeadora del mes[1]."

I bring my hands up in surrender. "Let's just drop it, okay? I'm gonna head home. I'm dizzy and tired."

He shakes his head and pinches his nose. "Sorry. Just... don't. Let me handle Cara."

"Let me handle my shit too. Hablamos luego[2], okay?"

"Okay, take care. If the dizziness continues, call the doctor."

---

1. My decision to tell Cara I love her and see what happens has nothing to do with you. That's between me and her. And if you're not willing to tell me what's going on with you and your mysterious girl, it's fine, but don't compare my love life to your piece of ass of the month.
2. Talk later.

"Si, mamaguevo. Adios.[3]"

THAT WAS NOT what I wanted to hear, not what anybody would want to hear. Not at eighteen. Not at twenty six.

"There's something going on with your heart," Dr. Diaz said casually. There's always something going on with my heart. I adore Dr. Diaz, and her practice is good. I feel like her staff listen, and I feel taken cared of there, but damn it, just once, I would like to go see her and leave feeling elevated, like I was finally able to catch a break. But no, my body has to throw another curve ball every time.

Irregular heart rhythms.
Symptomatic.
Ventricular depolarization.
Maybe genetic?
Why didn't it come out before?
We need to run more tests.
Can you come back tomorrow?
Stay away from strenuous activities.
Take it easy.
We need to run more tests.

All words tossed around like I wasn't in the room. Like I wasn't sitting right there, with cables hooked to every part of me. Like I wasn't a human with feelings sitting beside them on a familiar table.

Dr. Diaz is great, but sometimes, it feels as if she can only show her humanity once she has all the answers. Before then, I'm just another case she needs to crack. Still, it beats the countless other doctors who brushed my issues off. It beats the

---

3. Yes, this translates to dick sucker, BUT in Dominican, it's like calling your friend asshole. Goodbye.

countless other medical professionals who told me to just take an antihistamine or to watch what I was eating. She and her team are solution-oriented, but until they find it, I don't exist as Augusto Zabana. I only exist as case whatever number and symptoms sit in my file.

"Where to?" Martin asks from the driver's side. I can't drive either, or I shouldn't. I told Nellie we should spend some time together, so that's where we need to go.

"Nellie's house."

"Yes, sir," he replies as he heads down the highway, starting the forty-five minute drive to Nellie's house.

"And Martin…"

"Yes, sir."

"Not a peep to Nellie about any of this. Got it?"

He nods and drives, drives us away from here and right into the arms of the woman I'm falling for, who doesn't deserve any of this.

SIXTEEN

MY FAVORITE PLACE

AUGUST

Better by James Bay; Do I Wanna Know? by Hozier Cover; The Little Things by Ella Mai; Anyway by Noah Kahan

GUS

"TURN RIGHT," Nellie says softly. Getting to know Nellie these past few weeks has been more than I could have hoped for. We were waiting for our siblings to get their shit together before telling everyone, but now that they've clearly figured things out, it's time to talk to them. Except now, I'm the one who doesn't want to tell anyone—not because I don't think they'd take it well, but because there's so much unknown with my health. I don't want to add more to anyone's plate.

The dizziness and weakness continued, so Dr. Diaz ran more labs. Now, we're waiting on those results before the next steps. It feels like my health has blown up in my face these past couple of months. After that attack in May, my body hasn't recovered fully, and we're back to figuring out the right medications. Dr. Diaz is worried about the combination messing up my heart and giving me other issues, so we're proceeding with caution, slowly. In the meantime, I'm in limbo without answers. Something's wrong with my heart, and I don't want to put pressure on Nellie, not when she just started her new job. Not when she's trying to get everything in place. Not when I don't have any real answers. So, we're still a secret.

This is why we're on our way somewhere Nellie wanted to show me. She didn't say where or why, only that it was around five hours away from her house—near Atlanta. She also promised me nobody would be there, so we can stop pretending for a few days. We've been exploring a lot of places just the two of us a few hours away from home, days where we get to pretend we're a real couple. My hands never leave hers on our getaways because I need to touch her every chance I get. She's becoming an essential part of my life, taking over the majority of my day. When I'm not with her, she's in my thoughts. I find myself wanting to swim more so I can feel like I'm with her. I want to drive more so I can feel like I'm driving to her. I want to see her all the time, and I'm not sure if it's healthy.

"Thirty more minutes on this road, and then we'll be there," Nellie adds, tilting her head back and lifting her arms, letting her hair dance with the breeze. We're in my Barracuda, and she touches every inch, as she always does. It's like she's committing every part to memory, the same way I touch her… I don't use this car often, but when I do, I'm damn careful of where I go. Going up the mountains in Georgia was not what I had in mind when she asked if I wanted to go for a ride and I suggested taking this car.

The engine growls as we fly down winding roads surrounded by beautiful greenery. The red paint gleams under the sun, and every time we stop at a traffic light, people look at the car. They can't help it; it's stunning. Add Nellie to the mix with the beige top she's wearing, open between her breasts and tied together with thin straps, I'm sure they're looking at her too.

"Oh, I almost forgot. Open the glovebox." Nellie follows suit, and after opening it, she pulls out the small bag I placed earlier in there.

"What is this?"

"Open it." I continue driving down the quiet road while she fumbles with the bag, finally pulling out a small velvety box.

"Gus, what is this?" she asks with concern in her voice, making me chuckle. I guess I didn't think this through.

"It's not what you think. Open it."

After opening the small box, Nellie pulls out a ring.

"Is this…"

"A fidget ring," I interrupt. She puts the ring in the palm of her hand and stares at it, not knowing exactly what to do. "I've noticed you pick at the skin next to your nails. I was reading about it, and it said sometimes, these help."

She stays silent, staring at the ring, dumbfounded. Maybe I messed up. I've never seen her this quiet. Her eyes don't leave the ring either. "If I overstepped, I'm sorry. I figured it didn't hurt to try, but I can return it. It's not a big—"

"It is a big deal." She turns to face me, her eyes glossy and her cheeks pink.

"I'm sorry. I didn't mean to upset you."

"No, no. Stop for a second." I pull over on the side of the road. What is going on? She takes a deep breath and turns her body to face me. The wind blows, taking her dark chocolate hair with it, carrying her soft vanilla scent, wrapping me up in her, in Nellie.

"It's a big deal to me, and not in a bad way." She shows me a soft smile and takes my hand, placing it under hers on her lap. "Sometimes, my thoughts are all over the place, and I need to focus on something small to ground myself. Picking at my skin is not the healthiest, but it helps. People are always asking me why I do it or flat out tell me to stop…but nobody has ever thought to find another way to give me the same input. This, this ring, it does that. You, *you* did that…and I'm just—" she lets out another breath, searching my eyes "—thankful. Thank you. This means the world to me."

She climbs over the middle and gives me a hug. Not a kiss, nothing sexual, just a hug. It takes me by surprise. I tense at first, but as her body melts onto mine, I wrap my hands around her and hold her tightly. I bury my nose in her hair, vanilla and cinnamon. Sweet and spicy. Just like her.

"Well now the thing I got you is going to seem silly in comparison." Nellie turns and grabs something from the back seat after she lets go of my neck.

"You got me something?"

"Mm-hmm. Nothing as thoughtful as this, though, so don't get too excited." She settles back in her seat and hands me a brown bag, sealed shut with dot-printed tape. I open it and find more bags inside, all tied with ribbons. I look at her, confused, and she smiles the soft and beautiful smile I love. So simple, but so her. "Go on, look at them."

They look like make up bags but bigger, soft to the touch and in different colors. I pull one up, and when I turn it around, I see it has letters. *Medicine Bag*, it reads with mini cartoon pills. "You said you have bags everywhere with your medicine, like the one in your night stand and the one here. I figured you'd like them a little bit more fun, like you. It's not jewelry, and they're kinda cheap, so just ignore them," she says, but I don't reply. I just keep looking at the rest of them. Another one says medicine bag, but this one with medical doodles. *All My Medical Crap* the black mesh bag reads right. The next one says *These are my legal drugs,* and I chuckle.

"I can use them if you don't want them. Not a problem," Nellie whispers.

"Nellie…"

"No, for real, it's not a big deal. I'm sure you can buy fancier shit and not these homemade stuff."

"This is the nicest thing anyone has ever done for me. I don't care about money, you know that. But this... You took time to find these for me. That...*that* I care about," I add, holding her hand and squeezing it gently.

"I kind of made them," she says shrugging.

"You what?"

"Yeah, Cara has a Cricut, and I was bored and thinking about you...so yeah."

"Think about me much?"

"Oh, stop. We both know that you do too."

I lift my hand to caress her chin. I drag my thumb over her soft skin and smile at her. "Oh, I'm not hiding it, Trouble. I think about you every moment I'm awake, and in my dreams, you're always there too."

I look at her attentively, intensely holding her gaze and not dropping it. I want her to see the sincerity behind my eyes. I want her to see I mean it. "Do you know the one thing we never get back, Nellie?" She shakes her head but doesn't say anything, letting me continue, "Time. You can buy your way through almost anything, but no matter what you do, you can't go back in time, and you can't buy more of it. You spent time getting these bags and then making them for me. That's nothing small. These, I will treasure all my life. Thank you."

I tilt my face forward, dragging my hand down her neck and pulling her to me so I can kiss her forehead. "Thank you."

If she only knew how time spent doing anything is valuable to me—even more if she's choosing to spend it with me, let alone doing something for me. There's nothing I value more than time, and this gift is not only thoughtful, but she used that one thing I can't buy more of. *The one thing I'm afraid of running out of.* And she thought it wasn't a big deal. How do I keep this girl? How do I keep her without overwhelming her with my health issues? With my health questions?

As if she can spot my thoughts getting out of control, she comes closer and kisses me. It's gentle at first, but then hard, intertwining her fingers behind my neck and holding me in place. I groan. "We're on the side of the road. You're going to get us in trouble."

She chuckles against my lips. "Okay, sorry. Let's go." She settles back on her seat and buckles up, signaling me to keep going after she turns the music back up. Her head lays back on the seat as her fingers twirl the ring she just placed on her thumb. With a smile I continue down the road.

"I love this song too," she says when the music changes to another Frank Sinatra song, the unmistakable opening vibrating through the speakers, the rhythm hits hard, and man, this song never gets old. She smiles as she starts to hum along, and before I know it, she's singing. Her hands fly up in the air, a big smile on her face as she follows along. I would take her to the end of the world if it meant I got to see her like this: carefree, wild, and *mine*.

"You know what I've been thinking the entire way here? For someone who has such varied taste in music, I would have expected you to have a different way to play it."

"What do you mean?" I ask, cocking my eyebrow but not being able to take her seriously with her eyes closed and her hair wild.

"A cassette?" she posits, her voice lilting with amusement.

I let out a short laugh. "You mean an eight-track tape?"

"Yeah, yeah, whatever." She waves a hand dismissively. "You know what I mean." She shifts in her seat, eyes still closed, her head leaning back against the headrest as the wind whips through her hair.

"Think about it. It's actually the perfect way to listen to music. No skipping songs, no endless scrolling through playlists, no notifications interrupting the moment. Just a tape, locked in, playing straight through. Imagine a musical journey the way it was meant to be experienced." I smirk, glancing over at her.

"So you want *less* control over the music?"

"Mm-hmm. This way, you can just listen. No obsessing over what comes next, no shuffling. It's like surrendering to fate. Whatever song plays, that's what you get."

She waits a second, waiting quietly before saying, "Alright, but what if you get stuck with a song you don't like?"

I shrug. "Isn't that how life is too though? Life gives you moments you don't like, and you can't rewind to start them over. You can't skip the painful and uncomfortable moments, no matter how much you want to do it. You can, however, choose a different path when the one you're on is not what you wanted, and I could technically do the same. But if I just let the songs play the way they were intended to be heard… when I push through the uncomfortable feelings or the songs I don't love, I find that it teaches me more than just listening to music. It feels like music speaks to me more this way than the other way around."

She lowers the volume and then looks at me. "So you just play all these deep and cool ass songs, learn from them, and what? Just listen? You don't even sing. You don't move your body to their beat."

I snort a laugh. "You don't have to sing to show you enjoy music. You don't even have to know the lyrics. That's not what music is. It's more than just the sound that fills the air. It's the vibration that dances through our veins and reaches our heart, a rhythm that beats beneath our skin regardless of whether we're dancing. Music is the echo in the back of your mind when you recall a moment. It's the soundtrack to the chapters of your life."

I look at her briefly, and her eyes are open wide, looking back at me. "Go on. That was so poetic," she says.

With a grin, I murmur, "You don't need to sing to know

what the song is conveying. The heart sings louder than any lyrics could. Just like music goes beyond songs playing at any given time. It's the whispers of melodies in the spaces between each breath, or the beat that moves us, even when we're still, when we can't or won't move. You know the melody that lingers long after the last note fades? That's the invisible force, pulling you closer to memories, to dreams, to lessons, to moments, to feelings that can't quite be put into words but you can remember in music. We may speak in language, but we feel in songs."

My words rest between us, letting the hum of the engine and the cars passing us by carry our conversation while Nellie stays quiet.

"I do sing sometimes, though." I look her way and wink. She rolls her eyes as she sits up straight.

"Up there to the right." Nellie points after clearing her throat, and I see a gate leading to a narrow and long driveway. I slow down, taking the turn and drive through pines on either side, their trunks slender and dark. The air is cooler, especially now that we've slowed down. It's summer, so it's still hot as shit, but it's nicer than in Florida.

The further we go, the quieter it gets. The hum of the engine and the rustling of leaves are the only sounds. I can almost hear the whisper of the mountain itself, breathing in the silence. The peace that this place brings. In the distance, I catch glimpses of a valley, dotted with patches of grass.

Then, there it is, a small cabin at the end. "Is this where we're going?" I ask Nellie and wait patiently for her reply.

"What's your favorite place in the world, Gus?" she asks, not answering my question but looking straight ahead at the beautiful cabin tucked in between trees.

"I don't have one, I don't think."

"Well, this is mine."

I exit the car and open the passenger door for her, letting her step out and following her with the bag she made me pack before we left. "Come with me." I have her bag in my hand as I follow her.

The air is crisp against my face as I make my way up the winding trail toward the cabin. The ground is littered with fallen pine needles that crunch beneath my shoes. Nellie runs up the steps, opening the big wooden door. The cabin is rustic, made entirely of dark wood, blending seamlessly with the natural surroundings. A wrap-around porch stretches out from the front, old rocking chairs swaying in the breeze.

As I step through the front door, the scent of wood and earth greets me, a smiling Nellie standing right in the middle of a cozy living room warming my heart. Just looking at her makes me feel both at ease and at war—at ease knowing I might have found the girl who will bring me peace for the rest of my life, but at war because I can't say the same about myself.

The walls are lined with wide, aged wooden planks, and the tall windows flood the room with natural light. The space feels expansive yet intimate, the high ceilings stretching above, making the cabin feel like it's almost an extension of the outdoors. I can hear the creaking of the floorboards as I explore, imagining how many years this place has stood, weathering storms and sunshine, rough and calm days, and who knows how many couples or families. It's timeless and beautiful.

"Is this your friend's cabin?" I ask Nellie, placing our bags on top of the counter, and she nods. She walks around, opening windows and turning some lights on before turning to face me with a smile.

"So, what do you think?"

"I think it's a stunning cabin. I can see why you like it here."

"Let me show you the main bedroom. It has a tub." She holds my hand and winks at me, giggling when I shake my head as she drags me down the long, dark hallway. Nellie turns on the lights as we walk past them. There are no over-head lights here, but lamps are carefully placed in different corners, illuminating the hallway in hushed tones.

We pass two rooms and head straight into the last one. She pushes the door open, and the large room covered in natural light brings a smile to my face. There's a large bed in the middle, white linen covering the top, two nightstands made of cedar, and a large dresser to the right. This room has an open concept, letting me see part of the bathroom to the far left. The windows surround the entire room, floor to ceiling, with very little in between. It feels like you're in the middle of the woods instead of inside a room, with no curtains or any privacy.

"This is—"

"Breathtaking," Nellie interrupts on a quiet whisper. She walks in, taking her shoes off as she strides toward the bath-room. She disappears from sight almost immediately, but when I step further into the room, I see her opening the valve on the faucet of a large, clawfoot tub.

"There are no curtains here," I murmur.

"Nope, but you can't see anything from outside. Plus, this is private property, so someone would be trespassing if they were here. Trust me, though, you can't see anything." She lets the water run in small trickles, almost as if she wants it to take a long time to fill up. She pours some bubble soap from the table behind it and then walks toward me with a big, bright smile and that ridiculously cute outfit. Her hands come up to my neck, and she kisses my lips quickly. "Are you going to join me in there? I can tell you all about why I love this place."

"We won't fit in there," I state, pointing to the tub.

"We will have to get really snuggly." She wiggles her eyebrows and lifts her fingers to her shirt, untying the little knots. Her shirt was loose to begin with, so the minute she unties it, it opens completely, held up only by her perky nipples. She smiles at me wickedly, her gaze roaming my chest before moving her hands to my shirt and unbuttoning it, one at a time.

"I want to soak in the bathtub until I become a prune, and I would love for you to do the same. We can talk all you want, but I want to soak. Soak with me," she coos. How can anyone ever say no to this girl?

I cock my head and smile back when she unbuttons the last one, sliding her fingers under my shirt and over my pecs, brushing the shirt off my shoulders. She knows what she's doing to me—I can tell by the smile she doesn't drop when she notices the goosebumps on my skin awakening with her touch or how her eyes widen when she roams my body and notices my hard dick.

Fuuuuuuck, she will be my undoing.

I can't get enough of her, and the fact that she seems to be insatiable only makes me want her more.

Eager to join, my hands slide her shirt off her shoulders and chase it down her arms as it drops to the floor. Now, she stands in front of me in only sexy as fuck jeans, her nipples hard and needy in front of me. My hands are itching to touch them, so I do just that, pinching them, softly first, then hard, just how she likes it.

Nellie moans and tilts her head back, driving me mad with that little movement and sweet sound. I let go of her nipples as she protests the lack of touch. I chuckle. "Good girls who wait get rewarded."

Nellie moans again at my words. She's so responsive to my touch, my voice, and it fuels both my ego and my need for her. I'm a greedy bastard when it comes to her—I want all her breathy sounds, her moans, her orgasms. I want them all, and I want them all the time.

Unbuckling her jeans, I drag them down her legs, leaving her only in a tiny piece of lacy underwear that makes me groan. It's perfect on her, contrasting with her skin.

"Fuck, Nellie. Look at you," I say, peering up at her as I kneel on the floor between her legs.

"I am," she breathes, my hands climbing up her thighs and grabbing her bare ass. A fucking thong. I turn, following her eyes, and then I see it: the giant mirror behind us. She can see this scene completely, her standing, looking hot as sin, with me kneeling between her legs.

Oh, fuck yeah, *a mirror?* Let's go.

I pull her thong down her legs, and once she steps out of them, I grab her ankles and help her widen her stance, her pussy on display for me to see. For me to feast. I stare at her, at this sexy woman standing in front of me. I never get tired of seeing her, especially like this, needy and ready for me. My hands crawl up her legs again, and I hold her ass as I bring my nose to her slit.

"Oh," she breathes.

"I'll never get tired of the way you smell." My tongue slides against her lips as my hands hold her in place.

"I'll never get tired of this taste," I all but groan against her pussy, and when she moans again, I know I won't be able to take it slow.

"You asked about my favorite place in the world, Nellie?" I take a break from marveling at the most intimate part of her I've come to know so well and look up to find her lusty eyes on mine.

"Between your legs. That's my answer." I continue lapping at her pussy, sliding my tongue from her clit to her entrance, working her until all I hear are moans that grow louder and louder. I hear my name spill from her mouth, needy and ready for more, and I bring out the screams she said she never had. I won't stop until she's a mess of whimpers and gasps in my hands, but for some reason she's holding off. I know she's right there, I can feel it, but she's not letting go. I look up and find her looking ahead, not at me.

Okay, Nellie, you do like to watch. No wonder she was so

turned on that night at the hotel. I snag her waist, lifting her and dragging her down with me.

"Damn it, Gus. You're so strong," she says in between a laugh and giggle, and I can't help but smile too.

I slide her body down, and once she's kneeling in front of me, I kiss her. I don't kiss her hard and wild like I know she wants it. No, I kiss her slowly, taking my time exploring her lips, as if it's the first time I ever kiss them. I take my time probing with my tongue, asking for an invitation to enter her mouth even though I know I have it. I take my time kissing and tasting her lips the same way I want to take my time kissing and tasting her pussy, her ass, every single part of her. She's become my favorite in every sense. Her vanilla and jasmine scent haunts me in my sleep. Her sweet and tangy taste is the aftertaste I want after every meal. Her skin is all I want to touch, and her hands on my body feel better than the most expensive clothes. Her moans, I wish I could bottle to hear over and over again, and she's definitely all I want to see. She's actually *all* I see. Fuck, I may be in love with this girl.

I slide behind her, leaving her in front of the mirror. "Sit down for me," I command next to her ear, and she follows, her bare ass on the wooden floor and her eyes wide as she tilts her head to the side.

"I love that you do as I say. Such a good girl. Feet on the ground and open wide. Show me how wet you are for me." Nellie brings her legs up, opening as I asked, and her perfect pink pussy is reflected in the mirror, waiting. Perfectly needy. Ready for me to touch and make it my own again. I kiss her ear, her neck, her shoulder as my hands roam down her arms, over her breasts, down to her hips. She's ready for me to touch her, and if I couldn't tell by how her breath hitches and her chest rises, I sure as hell can tell by the way her pussy glistens in the mirror.

My hands slide over her, parting the lips between her thighs with my index and ring finger, teasing her clit with my middle finger. She drops her head back to my chest and closes her eyes as she gives me the sweetest, most intoxicating sound in the world—my name on her lips. "Gus."

"Open your eyes, baby girl. I want you to watch yourself come all over my fingers. Watch me give you what you want." She gasps at my words, eyes opening, watching us in the mirror. I'm so hard, it hurts, and I won't need much after this to come. I sure as hell hope I can hold off.

"You're perfect, Nellie. So perfect," I praise in her ear as I work her with my fingers. She's so wet, and I use it to slide two fingers in. Her slick, wet pussy squeezes around them immediately, and when I bring my other hand to cup her breast, she gives me another squeeze. I pump my fingers in and out of her, curving them inside, touching the spot I know will drive her mad. I pinch her nipple and bite her neck, sucking hard.

"You'll leave a mark," she says between breaths, gasping when I add more pressure with my fingers.

"You have a problem with that? Do you have a problem with me marking you for everyone to see?" I don't think she does. I think she likes it.

"No," she moans, confirming my suspicion and granting me the permission I needed. I bite her neck, this time closer to her collarbone. I suck and then lick and kiss the spot. I repeat the motions as I hold her pussy in my hand, two of my fingers inside her, completely soaked in her, my other hand not letting go of her nipple.

"Tell me. Tell me you want it. Use your voice, Nellie."

"I want you to leave marks, Gus. I want to hurt and feel good. I want you to brand me as yours." I bite again, and she moans, pulling a groan from me as soon as her pussy clenches around my fingers again.

"It. Feels. So. Good. It. Hurts. Ugh. So. Good," she adds.

"If you're still forming coherent thoughts, baby girl, you aren't feeling nearly enough. Drop your legs for me," I groan against her ear, and she does. "Good girl. Don't close your legs. Stay relaxed for me. Yeah?" I ask, looking in the mirror, and she nods. My fingers are still inside her, but now that she dropped her legs, I'm touching exactly where I wanted. I slide another finger in, and she moans, holding my face, bringing it to her neck.

"You want me to bite you again, my filthy girl?"

"Yes," she coos, and I continue pumping my fingers as I place my mouth on the other side of her neck and bite. Her pussy contracts around my fingers, harder and harder as I press the tip of my fingers against that spot she loves.

"Fuuuuuck, Gus."

"And *that's* my favorite sound," I moan in her ear, echoing the sentiment from before. "My name unraveling from your tongue." I drop my mouth to the back of her neck and repeat the steps. Bite, suck, lick, suck again. Her pussy clenches harder, and her screams fill the room as I prolong her orgasm.

"You like it when I fuck you with my fingers don't you?"

"Yes. Fuck yes."

"You like it when I'm rough with your perfect little nipples, don't you?" I ask, rolling her nipple between my thumb and my index finger.

"Yes," she moans again, this time a higher pitch.

"This neck," I say against her sensitive skin as I lick up her neck to her ear, "is mine. Your nipples," I squeeze her entire breast and hold it in my palm, "are mine."

"Oh my God, it's too much, it's too much," she says frantically, not taking her eyes off the mirror, trying to close her legs. I shake my head no. I can see how she's fighting whatever she's feeling, but I want her so completely undone that she won't be able to sit up straight. I want her so utterly fucked, I'm imprinted on her body and memory forever. I want to ruin her for everyone else. There won't ever be anyone else, just like she has ruined me.

"This perfect needy pussy is mine." I tighten my hold on her, pressing my palm against her clit and applying pressure as

I pump faster and faster. Her pussy is incredibly tight but still pulsing. She's not relenting, so neither will I. My eyes meet hers in the mirror, and I groan. "So pretty, taking what I give you. So pretty. So perfect. So mine."

"Gus!" she screams loudly. I look at her face in the mirror to find tears streaming from the corner of her eyes. Her legs are shaking, and her arousal soaks my fingers and hand, glistening as it sprays. She tenses, but I don't stop. I just slow my movements, letting her come down from her high.

"You are doing so well. Look how perfect you are. Just looking at you drives me wild, Nellie," I praise her until her pussy stops strangling my fingers and her breathing starts evening out. Her entire body is shaking, so when I slide my hand out, I waste no time holding her, cradling her against my chest. "Such a good girl, baby. So pretty, so beautiful. Eres perfecta. Fuiste hecha para mi. Mi Nellie. Mi mujer. Mi amor.[1]"

Her eyes flutter closed as her breaths even out, and her body slowly stops shaking. "That's it, feel it all. I'm not going anywhere. Breathe." I continue until she's settled, and her body melts against mine. I stand, holding her against my chest, and walk us both to the now almost-full bathtub.

"That was—" she says, but a soft sob escapes her lips as I lower her into the warm water, letting her body sink into it, her head resting on the edge. I turn the water off.

"Shh, we can talk about it later. Now, you soak." Her eyes are still closed, but her breathing is even now, her lips wearing a lazy smile. I kiss her forehead gently and step away to our bags to grab Nellie's water bottle. I'm glad she never goes anywhere without it, because she will need plenty of water when I'm done with her.

I place the straw gently between her lips. "Drink some water," I say, and with a lot of effort, she does. She takes four

---

1. You're perfect. You were made for me. My Nelly. My woman. My Love.

big sips and then sighs, removing her mouth from the straw and smiling again.

She opens her eyes slowly, looking at me through the glazed green eyes.

"I love the color of your eyes," I tell her, caressing her cheek.

"They're just green." Her voice is groggy and lazy; she will need to take a nap soon.

"Do you know what my favorite color is?" She shakes her head, sinking deeper into the water. "Since I can remember, my favorite color has been blue. Blue like the sky before sunset, almost periwinkle. I noticed it for the first time after my first long hospital stay. It was a reminder of how beautiful life can be."

"*That's* beautiful, Gus."

"It is. But it's not the prettiest color I've ever seen, so it changed. It's not that blue anymore."

"Then what is it?" Her eyes snap open to meet mine, and when I smile, she returns it.

"It's Nellie green. My favorite color is Nellie green." Her breath hitches, but I smile bigger. "Remember when I said we feel in music? If your eyes were music, they would be my favorite genre, and if your body were a song, I would play it on repeat." I grab her hand and kiss each finger before kissing the palm of her hand and sliding it in the bathtub again.

"Be careful, Gus. You're going to make me fall in love with you if you keep saying things like that," Nellie says, eyes never moving away from mine. "And you told me not to."

I don't say anything, because I want to tell her to go ahead and fall in love with me. I want to tell her I'm already on the ground after falling for her, ready to catch her. But I don't, because as much as I know I love her, I'm not good enough for her, and there are too many unknowns with my health right now to put on her plate. I fear our time is running out.

"Are you getting in?" she asks, splashing some water at me.

"You probably need to take care of that boner you had earlier."

"*You* already took care of that." Her eyes dart to my pants, and when she sees the wet spot on them, her eyes widen.

"Did you…?"

I nod. "I told you, just looking at you had me fucked. Then my hands were on your body, and that whole thing… was straight out of my dreams. So yeah, I did come in my pants. I'm a grown-ass man, Nellie, and you have me so wrapped around your fingers, I don't know what to do. How's that for some honesty?" I take my jeans off and step into the bath to join her.

"Come here." I motion for her to cross the small space between us and sit between my legs. "I'm the one taking care of you. I need you to let me without worrying about doing something for me, okay? Your pleasure brings me pleasure. Knowing you're taken care of is the highlight of my day. Let me."

She turns her head to look at me but doesn't say anything. "You trust me in bed. You trust me with your body. Trust I'm doing what I want. If I ever want more, I'll let you know." She nods, and I bring her hand to my lips, kissing each finger softly. I cover her body in suds and water, taking my time with every inch of skin I bit, licked, kissed, or touched, taking care of her.

After she's clean and I can feel her heartbeat slow, I help her stand and step out of the tub. I grab one of the towels next to it and open it for her. She walks to it, and I wrap her up, kissing her forehead. Grabbing another towel and wrapping it around my waist, I guide her back to the bed by her hand. She lets out the softest, sweetest yawn, and I smirk.

"You tired me out," she says, blinking slowly at me as I let her sit on the bed. "I had plans for us to play board games and stay up all night."

"And I have plans to take care of you, and right now you need to rest."

"Can you do me a favor?" she asks.

"Anything." She snaps her eyes open to look at me. I give her a gentle smile and draw slow circles on her hand.

"You don't even know what it is."

"It doesn't matter. For you, it will always be yes, no matter what it is." She holds my gaze, her green eyes gleaming.

"What do you need, baby girl?"

I caress her cheek as she closes her eyes and whispers, "Could you get me the lotion from the cabinet in the bathroom? I need to put some on; my skin's been so dry lately."

I get the lotion from the corner of the bathroom sink. I squirt some on my hands and rub it between them, warming it up before I make it back to Nellie. I bring my lotion-covered hands to her arm and spread it gently and evenly over her arm.

"I could have done it," she whispers between a sigh and a moan as I make circles down her arm, spreading the lotion.

"I'll take any excuse to get my hands on your body, any day." I make it to her wrist, turning her hand around and continuing the circular motion, this time over the two tiny, faded scars she has there. She's never told me about them, and I won't ask. I wonder, though, if my assumptions are correct, how much pain was she in to hurt herself like this. How long ago was this, considering these are almost gone? They are so small, almost imperceptible, but I notice. I notice everything about her. I bring her hand up to my lips and kiss her fingers, the palm of her hand, and finally, her wrists. I press my lips gently over the raised skin before lowering her arm. I repeat the process with the other arm, wrist, and hands.

"Lay down," I say. She lays flat on the bed and lets me slather lotion all over her body—her breasts, her abdomen, her legs, her ass, her hips. Here, she has a combination of scars and stretchmarks dancing together, telling a story I wish

I knew, a story I will wait until she's comfortable enough to share with me. I bring my lips to them, just like I did on her wrists, and worship every single one.

"They're ugly, aren't they?" she says, and I can hear the fear and sadness in her voice.

"Nothing about you is ugly," I reply, kissing one of the scars on her thigh.

"They are from a long time ago, back when I had no way out."

"No way out of where?" I ask, still caressing her scars, giving her the space she needs.

"Out of my head." She sits up, clutching the towel like armor around her body.

Her fingers hover over the scars on her wrists, tracing them like old wounds that still whisper when the night gets too quiet. I can see the way her jaw tenses, the way her shoulders pull in, like she's trying to make herself smaller.

"They were my escape," she admits. "My thoughts were too much sometimes, and when everything got too loud, too heavy…this was the only thing I could control."

I don't speak right away. I just watch her, letting her take her time, letting her decide how much she wants to give me, how much she wants to tell me.

She exhales, shaking her head, as if she wants to erase the words, take them back before they make her too vulnerable. But then, she looks at me, really looks at me, and I see it—the years of pain buried beneath her skin, the echoes of a girl who didn't know any other way to quiet the storm.

"I didn't know how else to make it stop," she continues. "The thoughts, the feelings, all of it. It was like drowning in my own head, and this…" she gestures to the scars, her fingers ghosting over them like an old habit, "this was the only way I could breathe."

I reach for her hand, slow and steady, giving her the chance to pull away. She doesn't.

"You don't have to explain," I tell her. "Not to me."

"I know, and maybe that's why I want to. You've never asked, but I still want to tell you." She smiles softly at me and takes a deep breath. "I was eleven the first time I hurt myself. It was the first day of virtual high school classes for me, but I was physically in the middle school building with kids my age. I would sit in the back of a classroom, and instead of taking sixth grade math, I was taking algebra two on Florida Virtual School. It took care of my social needs while academically giving me what I needed, but…middle schoolers are tough. Too many hormones, too many emotions, and when they don't understand something, they usually are mean and angry. They needed someone on the receiving end, and for them, it was me. Things started to get out of control, and I didn't know how to handle it."

Nellie lets out a small, broken laugh. "I don't even know where the thought began, just that it did. So, I took a small blade from my dad's toolbox and cut myself. It hurt, but at least I controlled the pain."

She stops, doesn't say anything else, so I ask, "Then what happened?"

"Well, my mom found out. Instead of freaking out, she just talked to me. She listened to me, she asked questions, and when she finally figured out how to help, she took me to therapy. It changed my life. Swimming helps a ton as well. I haven't done it since I was twelve, even though sometimes it crosses my mind. I like control, but just like I can control pain, I can control pleasure," she says, smiling wickedly at me. Everything makes more sense now. Her pleasure-seeking habits, the way she likes it when I teeter on the line of pain and comfort. She needs it, and lately, she's been handing over control to me.

"If at any point, you think about hurting yourself again, can you tell me?"

She nods and asks, "Can you do me another favor?"

"Anything."

"Please don't look at me differently now. I like how you look at me. You make me feel wanted and desired and beautiful. I believe those things about myself, but it's good seeing it reflected somewhere other than a mirror."

I shake my head. "I could never look at you differently, because nothing you share will make you mean any less to me. Nothing you share will make me want you less. Nellie, you are beautiful. I want *you*. I desire *you*. All of you. I see you. Nothing about you is ugly. I will be grateful forever that you let me in and shared this with me."

She swallows hard, blinking up at me as if she's waiting for me to flinch, to look away, to take it back, but I won't. All I see is someone who is strong and vulnerable at the same time, someone who fought battles no one else could see and found a way around it, who found a healthier way to cope.

I squeeze her hand, my thumb brushing over her knuckles.

"You're still here," I say softly. "That's what matters. I just told you my favorite place was between your legs, but really, my favorite place is where *you* are. All of you."

For the first time since she started speaking, she lets out a breath that doesn't sound like she's carrying the weight of the past with it. She closes her eyes, and in no time, her breathing changes. I get up and put some pants on to go back to the car to get our bags. I get my cherry juice that I don't even need any more since falling asleep next to her, but I take it to bed anyway. Habit, I guess.

She looks so peaceful. No monsters haunting her thoughts. No fears, no pain. And I'm about to, what? Drown her in a health rabbit hole with me? Dr. Diaz hasn't been able to give me an answer, and if my previous medical record is any indication, it could take weeks before they do, even months. I don't want Nellie to have to deal with this when I don't know how to deal with it myself. It's out of my control and out of hers. How would she handle the tests and the doctor's visits on top of everything else? How would she handle bad news? Because no matter how positive I'm trying to stay, I'm waiting for a call that will tell me everything's going to shit. I feel it in my gut.

How could we tell our families if I haven't even told her everything that's been going on with me and my heart lately? She deserves someone who's not going to drag her down. She deserves someone who will lift her up. I don't want this to send her back to where she was when she harmed herself. I don't want her to hurt because of us. *Because of me.*

I slide into bed and pull Nellie to my chest, wrapping an arm around her. She shuffles until she's nuzzled perfectly into me, and with her sleepy voice, she whispers, "I love you." My body tenses, both afraid and relieved. Relieved because at least we both feel the same, but scared shitless that I will hurt her.

SEVENTEEN

TELL ME I'M WRONG

***MIENTES Tan Bien by Sin Bandera & Mean It by Gracie
Abrams***

NELLIE

"MMM," I groan when rough hands touch my calves.

"You need to eat." In between times awake and asleep, I
hear Gus. His hands massage my calves and climb up to my
thighs, but they don't move higher, no matter how much I
wiggle, trying to get him to touch me where I want.

"Nellie, you need to eat." He chuckles and then laughs
when I protest.

"What is this?" I open my eyes and see a tray of fruit, cold
cuts, cheese, and different breads, plus iced coffee and a glass
of water.

"Breakfast."

"No shit, Sherlock. Where did it come from?"

"Delivery," he replies.

"There's delivery out here?" I ask incredulously.

"Where there's a will, there's a way. Now, eat."

"So bossy."

"When it comes to your well-being? Yes, I will be. Now, eat."

"You're never this pushy. Also, what time is it? I feel like I've slept for an entire day." I look out the window, and it's not morning sunlight coming through. The light is different, warmer. It's that golden midday glow for sure. The sun's rays filter through the trees, casting little dancing shadows across the wooden floor. I can feel the warmth of it on my skin, like a gentle reminder that the day has moved on without me.

"It's noon." I almost choke on my food. So I slept all night and half the day. That's new, but I guess me squirting all over his hand after the longest, most intense orgasm of my life was new too. My body is sore in the best way, and my heart is both soaring and crashing.

"Well, I guess you've turned me into everything I never thought I'd be: a pleasure seeking girl who sleeps most days."

"Sorry to break it to you, but I'm pretty sure you were pleasure-seeking before me, baby girl. I just learned to provide it." He winks at me with his flashy smile and that glimmer in his eyes. He's so beautiful, it hurts.

"What gave it away?" I take a bite of the prosciutto and the cheese. Provolone? Not sure. I sip on my coffee.

He looks at me intensely, melting the few defenses I had left in place. "For starters, the breathy sounds you make every time you like something. The way you close your eyes when you sip on coffee made just right. The way you press harder against my hands when I touch a spot you like, and no, not just there," he adds, pointing between my legs. "Your thighs, your neck, even your shoulders. The way you sleep better when I wrap you tight in my arms or when you're surrounded with pillows cocooning your body. It's the way you moan softly at every lick or tease of my lips. You enjoy pleasure, *as you should*, and I enjoy giving it to you."

"A perfect match," I reply, and for some reason, that shifts his demeanor. I ignore it, pretending I didn't read that micro expression, pretending I don't know what it means. I've been terrified of asking him when we're telling people about us. With me starting my job last week and kids starting Monday, my time sneaking around hiding a whole-ass relationship will need to come to an end. I need to bring it up. I can't keep doing this, but subtle things like what just moved across his face make me doubt we're even in a relationship at all.

I try to change the unspoken topic and bring some levity to the situation. "Gus? What was your favorite meal as a child?"

"Random question, but rice and eggs, why?"

"I would think it was Lunchables, considering you always make me charcuterie trays for food."

He smirks, but the smile doesn't reach his eyes. "It's quick and easy. I don't know how to cook–" He stops talking when his phone vibrates in his hand, and he mumbles a curse. "Sorry, I need to answer this." He gets up from the side of the bed and steps outside.

Whoever it is, he doesn't want me to listen, and it hurts a little. Here I am, thinking I'm ready to tell everyone about us, and he won't even let me in on a phone call. Telling him last night to be careful because I was going to end up falling in love with him was a lie; I know I'm already in love with him. He listened so attentively as I poured my heart out for him. There are only a handful of people who know about the scars, about those dark years in my life, and he didn't run. He stayed. He listened. He kissed each and every one as if I'm a treasure he needs to safeguard. I hate that I feel so much for him, and I can't even tell him because of fear of losing *him*.

It was our decision to keep us a secret, but it's getting hard to contain. I've been lying to everyone about it. Lying to my family about him. Lying to my friends about how seriously gone I am. Lying to him about what I feel. Lying to myself, thinking I could hold off for much longer. My brain feels like it's in overdrive from getting ready for my new job, feeling like I won't make the difference I want to make because I'm too preoccupied with my love life, all the secrets, and the guilt that comes with it all.

"Sorry about that," he says as soon as he walks in through the door and snaps me out of my thoughts. He looks completely different than when he left this room. His body is stiff, and he doesn't say anything else. He just looks at me with his onyx eyes, darker now than ever, and then lowers them to avoid my gaze.

"What was it?" I ask, getting up from the bed and putting some clothes on.

"Nothing, but I do need to get back to town. I'm sorry, but I have to cut our stay short."

"Why?"

He shifts a bit on his feet. "Nellie…"

I notice in the way he says my name. Something happened. It wasn't just a hunch. It wasn't just a guess. It's a fact. It's written all over his face. "What changed, Gus? You were here, and now you're definitely not."

"Nellie…" He whispers my name again, and I snap.

"Fuck, Gus. Just tell me. Just be honest with me. What was that about?" I swear, I'm about to lose my shit on this man. I laid out my heart and soul last night, and I thought we were finally getting somewhere.

"It's just a work thing." *The motherfucker.* He's actually lying to my face.

"Bullshit. I call bullshit on that." He finally snaps his eyes back to mine, and the same eyes that were soft and welcoming yesterday are intense and cold now. I wish I was like him. I wish I could just flip a switch and turn it all off. I wish I could just decide I don't feel.

"Tell me I'm wrong, Gus." He still doesn't say anything. *Coward.* "You can't, can you? Because I'm right. So tell me this: why is it that I have to lay my soul bare to you and show you into my heart, but you're still not being completely honest with me? Why is it that you consistently keep me at arm's length when all I want to do is dive deep?"

I'm tired of playing this game. I'm done with the secrets and the lies. Here it is, my heart on a platter for him, and I sure as hell hope he can guard it.

"Nellie…" *Or not.*

"No, no. Tell me, because I'm hella confused. All I've asked is for you to be honest with me. I've been patient. We agreed on keeping our relationship a secret until the timing was right, but it's been right. How long after Cara and Manny got together do you deem it appropriate? How many layers of myself should I peel back before you deem me worthy? I started my job, and you, what? You stopped traveling as much as you used to so you could see me more often, but on what pretenses? You won't see me in public—"

His body stiffens, as if he's ready to argue with me, but when my eyes dare him to say something, he doesn't. Maybe it's unfair because I also made the decision to wait, but nothing about his body language or his words tell me he is ready to love me out loud.

"Taking me to a town where we don't know anyone doesn't count as seeing me in public, Gus. Are you *that* ashamed of me?"

"What? No, Nellie. I could never be ashamed of you."

"Then what is it? What's the excuse now? I know you like me. We have fun together. I love talking to you, and I think you like it too. The sex is great, so what is it? We waited for them to get their shit together, and they did, so good for us for being considerate. I don't want to be considerate anymore. I want to be selfish. What. Is. It?" He holds his hands on his lap, intertwining his fingers and looping his thumbs over and over around each other. It's his tell before Gus the business man comes out. I can count on one hand how many times I've seen him do that, and every time is followed by serious and masked Gus, not *my* Gus.

"You're just so young." His shoulders are tense, his eyebrows furrowed. He looks as if he's in pain. Is he hurting because I'm demanding the truth, or because he's a gentleman and doesn't want to hurt me? I'd rather hurt now than in six months, when my heart completely shatters because he refuses to keep me.

"Bullshit. Don't play the age card on me. Not today."

Gus lowers his eyes. "It's not a card. It's the truth. You have your whole life ahead of you, Nellie."

"So. Do. You. You're twenty-six Gus, not forty-six. You said you have a condition, not an illness. A condition you've learned to live with. I can learn more about it too. Did you lie about that? Are you sick, Gus? Because even if you are, I can handle it. Are you?" He shakes his head, closing his eyes tightly. "Then look me in the eyes and tell me why. Tell me."

He looks at me, and the pain I feel is instant. I know that look. Pity. Goosebumps crawl over my skin as his sorrow-filled gaze holds mine. He searches my eyes for something. *For what? What is it, Gus? Give me a sign, and I will give it to you. What is it you need from me?*

"I don't have a reason other than you have your whole life ahead of you, and you don't need anything or anyone slowing it down. You should take the time to be wild and free, not be caught up in a relationship with me. The summer is over, and maybe we can slowly fizzle out. You can call me when you need me, and we can escape again if you want."

"You want me to be your booty call?" I pace around in the room, ready to break something, ready to scream.

"Nellie, that's not what I meant," he says, getting closer to me and grabbing my wrist.

"Then what?" I snap, pulling my hand out of his grasp and slamming my fists onto my hips. His eyes lower to look at my body, and I scoff. "Eyes up here, Gus."

"Sorry." He looks mortified, and I should put him out of his misery, but fuck, if I don't want to. He deserves to feel whatever it is he's feeling right now.

"You know what I don't understand? You could have had my body as much as you wanted, and it would have been fine. I would have fallen in love with you either way, because how can someone know you and not love you? But I wouldn't have dared to hope for more. I would have given my body to you, but you told me you wanted to get to know me. You asked me to tell you what I wanted, and I told you I wanted your thoughts, your heart, your soul. You made me promise, and I meant it. You've watched me fall in love with you for two months now. And you were, what? Lying this entire time? You asked me about my darkest truth last night—is it too much for you? What happened to seeing *all* of me? Did you wake up and think you couldn't do it? Did that phone call remind you there are better women out there for you? Older? Less wild?"

"Nellie."

"Stop saying my name like that! Full stop!" The first tear falls. Damn it; I was holding it back. He doesn't get my tears anymore. He doesn't get my fears. He gets my rage. I snatch my shirt from the chair and slide it over my body. I walk to the closet and pull out a sweatshirt I always wear when I'm out here. I need to remember to thank Victoria for letting me come here whenever I want, but now, this place might be haunted. I won't be able to come back here again and not think about this, about him.

"You could have had it all, Gus, if you wanted it. And if you never did, shame on you for letting me think the opposite."

"Nellie, please let me talk."

"No. I'm done. I've heard enough."

"You haven't heard anything! You haven't stopped for a second to let me talk." His voice is eerily quiet, eerily still.

How is he able to keep his emotions so fucking contained? How is this not breaking him apart too?

"Will the words out of your mouth be *we will figure it out, Nellie?* Or maybe, *you got it wrong, Trouble?* Or *there's nobody else, Nellie?*" He closes his mouth. I walk up to him, tears burning my eyes.

"You are a coward. You want to love me in secret, behind closed doors, and I deserve better than that. You were appalled when I called you my dirty little secret, and it turns out, that's exactly what I am to you. You don't get to have me when and where you want me, not anymore. Not after I've given you pieces of me I've never given anyone else. I'm done being your dirty little secret. Go ahead, prove me wrong."

He doesn't move. He doesn't even flinch. My words must mean nothing to him. *I* mean nothing to him. My heart is about to leap out of my chest. Not for the reason it usually does when I'm near him, but the complete opposite. It's breaking in the present tense, loud heartbreak thumping in my ears as my hopes disappear.

"You can't because you know I'm right. But let me say one more thing. You broke this before we could see if we could make it work. You led me to believe we could be *us*, just to turn around and slap me with your words—or rather, your lack of them. And now, I'm done. I would like for you to leave."

"How are you going to get home?" he asks, and I see red.

"You need to leave. You don't care about me, so let me care about myself. Get out!" How am I going to get home? *That's* what he's worried about?

"Get out!" I scream at him. I sound irrational, but I don't give a fuck.

"I'm not leaving you here in this state."

I scoff. "I don't give a fuck about what you think you should do. I asked you to leave, so leave." I stomp around him to the front door, grabbing his shoes and dropping them on the steps. "Goodbye, Gus."

He walks out with his shoulders down, without uttering another word. It's taking everything I have not to lose my shit, to not beg him to fight back. But it won't happen, so this is the way it should go. This is the way it has to go.

Gus turns around as soon as he's on the porch. There's a storm brewing in his eyes, but I don't have the brain capacity right now to deal with his feelings when I'm trying so hard to keep mine in check. I will lose it, and I will spiral if he doesn't get out of my sight quickly. I deserve to deal with my broken heart in peace. I deserve to cry and wallow in peace. And he deserves to go straight to hell.

"I really didn't want this to go this way," he says. There's something in his tone, the way his eyes look genuinely sad, the way his lips quiver, I would believe him, except actions speak louder than words, and he truly doesn't want me. At least, not the way I want him. Not the way I need him.

"Goodbye." I slam the door and run to the bedroom, where I lock myself in the closet, slamming my back on the door and sliding down to the floor. I put my head between my knees and cry. And cry. And cry.

The seconds turn into minutes, and those minutes turn into agonizing hours of repeating the past few months on a loop. The laughs, the good memories, the intimate moments. Eventually, someone knocks on the door, and when I leave the closet, I find night has fallen. The moon shines brightly over the cabin and barely illuminates a path to the front door. I look through the peephole. What the hell?

I open the door to find Martin, Gus' driver, standing on the porch with the same serious face he always has.

"Martin? What are you doing here?"

"Good evening, Miss Nellie. Mr. Augusto sent me to take you back home. He asked me to tell you to check your phone, even if it is the last thing you do today. His words are not mine, so I apologize." I roll my eyes. I'm sure I look stupid, but I don't have it in me to care.

"Come on in," I say as I walk back to the room and look for my phone. It's charging. He must have done that when I fell asleep. A slew of missed phone calls await me, some from Cara, one from my mom, and a few from Bee, with dozens of text messages from all of them combined.

And one message from Gus.

DLS:

> I'm sorry. I know you don't believe it, but I mean it. Please let Martin take you home, even if it's the last thing you take from me. Please.

No matter how angry and sad I am right now, I know I need to listen to him. I have no way of getting home. Martin must have left Jacksonville as soon as I kicked Gus out for him to have made it here by now. I grab the small bag I brought and a pair of socks from the drawer of clothes I keep here. I'm taking one of the pillows with me too, because I don't want to do anything but sleep, and what better place to do it than in the backseat of a vehicle taking me back to reality? A reality in which my heart is shattered, and I have to pretend on Monday that I'm whole enough to work with broken-hearted pre-teens.

"Let's go, Martin. I'm ready to go home."

We leave, and with every single step I take, I feel like I'm leaving a version of myself behind that I never even knew I could be. The version of me who believes in love and good things. The version of me who believes I'm enough. With me, I take the version of me I was before, a hollow person looking to have a good time when possible, afraid of relenting control and feeling too much.

PART 3

THE CRASH

There was no warning, no time to prepare.
Too cold, too harsh
Too much, too fast.
I got lost in the undertow,
crying and screaming, out of control.
I heard my heart break like thunder,
and that was the moment I knew.
There was no escaping it.
The wave was already here.
And I was going down with it.

EIGHTEEN
FUCK OFF, BUDDY
SEPTEMBER

So Long, London by Taylor Swift

NELLIE

"CARA'S BEEN TELLING me how you've been killing it at work, Nellie. I still can't believe you're old enough to work, let alone as a counselor," Jake says. Allie and Jake—her now fiancé—host family dinners on Sundays at their place, and because the Zabanas don't know how to do "just dinner," we're currently sitting in their living room, chatting, drinking, and enjoying each other's company. Cara dragged me here today because, and I quote, "You're too young and too hot to stay home alone doing God knows what instead of socializing like regular people." So, here I am, socializing with her friends instead.

Allie and Jake's house *feels* like a home. It's welcoming, and even though I don't want to be here, Gus doesn't either, considering the expression on his face every time I look at him. I can't just leave after they've been so hospitable. I'm plopped in the corner of the couch like a potato, just listening when I can and talking when I'm spoken to.

"How are you a counselor? You're not even old enough to drink," Roe, Cara's other best friend, says. I feel eyes on me that are more than just everyone following along in the conversation, but I ignore them. I'm so fucking tired of people reminding me I'm young. I know I am. But I am not a child. I am a grown woman, and damn it, I just want everyone to stop mentioning my age.

"I'm old enough to drink now—" I lift my glass of wine, not even my first one of the day, "—but also? It's not like it stopped the people at your bar from giving me drinks before." Roe owns the local bar, Saddlers, and for years, she chased me out, saying she wasn't going to suffer Cara's wrath for serving her underage sister. Little does she know, Cara's fake ID got me plenty of drinks when Roe wasn't there.

I wink at Roe before continuing, "Are *you* old enough to own a bar and fight drunk people who act like fools? Because you do, and you don't hear me dismissing your accomplishments because of an arbitrary number." I look over to the other side of the couch, where Gus sits, his eyes on mine. He flinches when he hears the backhanded comment I made about my age.

"I'm so tired of people assuming I'm less than because I'm young. Get over it, all of you," I say, pointing at everyone. "I'm twenty-one, yes, but I'm also damn smart, and I've earned it all. You're just acting jealous because you don't have my brain."

"Who the fuck pissed in your cereal?" Roe asks, and her boyfriend, Thiago or Santiago or whatever the fuck his name is, covers her mouth with his hand, dragging her to sit on his lap.

"Ignore this one, Nellie. She left her manners at home, apparently," he says before I can scream at his perfect girl. We both roll our eyes at him.

"Does she even know what manners are?" I ask, and Allie almost spits out her drink.

"These two are the exact same," Manny says, and Cara smacks him playfully on the arm.

"They are not. They're just too sassy for their own good. Roe at least found Thiago to keep her cool, calm, and collected. This one needs the same," Cara adds. Oh, sis, if only you knew.

I look at Gus as I grab the bottle of wine from the coffee table and top my glass off again. *That could be you,* I convey with my eyes. Then, I narrow them, wishing I could just say, *but you act like a coward and can't handle hard truths.* I take another sip of this perfect wine and cross my legs, hoping for a change of topic.

"How about we move on from this topic?" Natalie says. Thank God. Natalie is also Cara's friend; her daughter, Bella, goes to Baker Middle, so I see her often. Bella is the sweetest kid. She comes to my office a couple of times a week to check-in, and I'm pretty sure she's actually checking on me. I don't doubt for one second that Cara told Natalie, who told Bella, to check on me. Why? Because I haven't been able to do anything other than eat, sleep, work, swim, and repeat. I'm exhausted by the time I come home, and I don't want to do anything. Cara thinks I'm depressed, and rightfully so, because last time I was this much of a hermit, I was. But that was ten years ago, and now, I know how to cope, how to find healthy outlets. Reason 5678 why I've been swimming practically every day for the past two weeks since that day in the cabin.

"Nellie, are you joining us for book club?" Natalie asks, taking the changing of topics into her own hands.

"I'm planning on it. I read the book this weekend," I reply.

"Yesss, bitch! I can't wait. My heart broke into pieces, but it was so good," Cara adds, and Roe rolls her eyes.

"No book club talk until Tuesday. Allie, have you picked a date for the wedding?" Roe asks, changing the topic again.

"Not really. We're looking at venues and then picking a date around them."

"How far out are you looking?" Natalie asks Allie. If I had a dollar for every time I looked Gus's way today and he was looking at me, I would be able to pay for a vacation by now. I don't think he's stopped looking at any point tonight, and it's making me warm and fuzzy. Damn the wine and damn him.

"As soon as possible," Jake says, and Allie giggles. I'm brooding. I'm brewing. I'm boiling. I will burst if I don't figure out how to stop noticing his eyes on me. Why in the world does he make me this fucking irrationally upset? Why do my emotions always heighten when I'm around him? Why can't I keep my cool? His scent finds me over the rest. His quiet chuckle reaches my ears, and I know he's containing his full and perfect laughter. I wish I could turn off the attraction, I wish I could turn off the love, but I can't. So, in the meantime, I cover it with something else—anger. "We don't know when. Why? Is there something you'd like to tell us?" Allie asks, looking at Natalie and smiling. I have a feeling that whatever is happening, Allie already knows, and she's just probing.

Natalie looks to the side at her husband Nick, who's sitting on a chair next to her. He holds her hand and says, "We would love for you not to have a wedding in February."

"I mean, no, we wouldn't want to do that. It's too cold, and also, Valentine's day. Nobody wants to get married on Valentine's Day. That seems like making Cupid work overtime."

I sit silently, looking at the entire exchange, reading everyone's expression, trying to figure out what's happening. Natalie seems nervous. Roe seems annoyed. Cara smiles. Whatever it is, she knows. There's zero surprise behind her eyes. Manny is looking at Cara, and Gus is looking at me. I narrow my eyes at him, and he shows me his phone to signal he called me maybe. I look down at my lap and see I have a text message from him, but I don't read it right away. I don't want to miss whatever they're about to tell their friends.

"Turns out, we will be having a baby then, and it would be kinda sad if the godfather missed out on it. That is, if he accepts. We figured the godmother should be there too, since her best friend would be getting married that day, if she accepts," Natalie says, looking at Jake and Cara. Immediately, there are screams and squeals. The men start clapping each other's backs, congratulating Nick and Natalie. Allie and Cara are both screaming at Natalie, happy tears in their eyes.

But me? I grab my glass of wine and drink it all in one gulp. I take the moment of wonderful chaos to look at my phone because I'm clearly a damn dark cloud now, not the sunshine I need to be.

DLS:

How am I supposed to sit here and pretend I don't know what you sound like when you moan my name?

The absolute guts this guy has. I swear, I could fucking kill him if it wouldn't put me in jail and wouldn't put a damper on this celebration right now. I put my glass down and reply to his message while shooting daggers his way.

ME:

You lost the right to say shit like that when you told me I wasn't good enough for you.

DLS:

I never said you weren't enough.

ME:

Not with your words, but your actions for sure.

DLS:

Not true. We agreed to keep a secret.

ME:

No. We agreed to take it easy because our siblings had their heads up their asses, but look around. Clearly, that didn't last. They found their happy while you, well, I guess you found out.

DLS:

I found out what?

ME:

What would happen if you fucked around.

DLS:

BUT I DIDN'T, Trouble.

ME:

Also lost the right to call me that.

DLS:

Come on, that's not fair. We agreed to be together, you know, fuck buddies, and then everything blew up.

Oh, he did not. He did not just call me that. I look at him, and he looks terrified now. Oh, he knows he messed up. He knows it, and if anyone else isn't completely enamored by the happiness oozing out of Nick and Natalie, they would see it too. I am one hundred percent flashing murder in my eyes, but I collect myself. Maybe I'm grieving losing him. There was shock at first, then sadness, and now, there's rage. Just rage.

ME:

Then fuck off, buddy.

I get up suddenly, pushing the wooden chair backward, making a screeching sound with it. A few heads snap my way, and I shake mine.

"Sorry, sorry, congrats, you guys. Carry on celebrating. I'm just using the restroom." I walk down the hallway until I make it to the guest bedroom. Their house isn't huge, so I can still hear them cheering and celebrating, and I need to breathe. I need to wash my face to cool off. I need…something. I need to not look at Gus so I can be myself again. Seeing him here was like pouring salt on a fresh wound. I open the faucet, letting the cool water run and all but stick my head into it. I wash my face after removing my glasses and look up at the mirror.

"Get yourself together, Nellie. He's just a man. Just a man," I tell myself in the mirror over and over, and maybe I'll believe it someday. I grab the tie from my wrist and pull my long hair up into a ponytail. I fasten it with the tie and dry my face.

"Just a man, Nellie. Just a man," I whisper to myself, opening the bathroom door and seeing said man standing right in front of it. His back is against the wall, his legs crossed one over the other one, a smug smile on his face.

"Who's just a man?" I'm actually going to kill him. I would look good in orange. Who the fuck cares about jail? Not me, that's for sure.

"I'm not having this conversation here, Gus."

"You're not having any conversations with me, Nellie. How is a man supposed to survive?"

"You survived just fine before this summer. Go back to your models and enjoy." I try to walk past him, back to the gathering, but he stops me. His hand brushes mine, sending a spark of electricity up my arm.

"What if I want you?" he whispers against my ear. The audacity. Where did he buy it? I would love to buy some for myself.

I turn around to face him and lower my voice so nobody else hears me. "I'm not a toy, and I'm not playing games. You think you want me, but what you want is my body. I'm more than that. You had the chance to have my body and parts of me, but now, that time has passed. Now, you're left with none of me. Excuse me."

I try to walk past him, but he holds my arms and says,

"Tell me something, Trouble. Have you ever felt like your heart is going to leave your body at any time? Because I have, twice… Once at seventeen, when I got diagnosed with my crappy heart, and again when you kicked me out of that cabin. Tell me…have you ever felt like that before? Have you ever felt the way you do when we're together?"

He waits for me to answer, but when I don't, he adds, "Tell me. Have you?" I shake my head. "Well, neither have I. I don't *feel* for others. I don't *fall* for others. I wanted to be able to leave you alone. I wanted to say I could move on and forget you. God knows I've tried. But damn it, Nellie, I can't. One touch of your lips, and I should've known. I lied to myself. I got scared and pushed you away. Again."

He says his heart leaped out of his chest three weeks ago? I'm sure mine is out of my body. Walking alone. Getting crushed and healed by his words, just for him to crush it again when he gets scared. When he shuts down and pushes me away. I can't do this.

He must see the hesitation in my eyes, because he continues, his voice softer, stopping me in my tracks. "I lied because I thought that's all we were pretending to be, but considering how I can't stop thinking about you or seeing you every time I close my eyes, or smelling your scent on my pillow, on my bed, in my home… Considering how much I like it, considering how much I miss you, you were never that. I couldn't keep lying to myself, Nellie. I tried to keep you at bay so I don't hurt you, but the lies I always told myself were beyond what I thought I could keep you from. You ended up getting hurt in the crossfire, and distance wasn't going to fix it." I stare him in the eyes, searching for the bluff, but I can't find it. He's telling me the truth, but I can't think straight right now, so I shake my head.

"I was wrong. You're so much more, and calling you my fuck buddy earlier was definitely stupid of me. I've realized if you push, I push back, and that's a tough habit to break. Not an excuse…just, fuck, please, Nellie. Give me another chance. Let's talk when you're sober, please. I have more to explain, but I can't do it like this. Please. I'm begging at this point. Pleading. If you just give me the chance, I'll be honest about it all, even if it's scary," he says, his eyes an intense midnight stare.

"I have to think about it," I mumble, crossing my arms over my chest.

"What do you want me to do? How can I show you I know I fucked up? How can I show you I'm ready for more?"

"Everyone out there is going to know if you don't go," I snap at him, looking up and seeing his grin. Stupid, handsome jerk.

"No! You don't get to do that. You don't get to come here and look handsome and shit and say things like that after you basically told me we were only going to sleep together, only to then chase me and tell me you actually wanted to get to know me. Then, you said we were fuck buddies, but ten minutes later, you want me again? You need to get your shit in check before you ask for another chance." He looks so sad, so lost, and I feel like a bitch about it.

No, I'm standing my ground.

"You say you're *gone* for me? Prove it. You say you want another chance? Earn it. I want you to grovel, Gus. I want you to do more than tell me you want more. Show me you do. Until then, goodbye."

I walk past him, and this time, I'm successful. I find Allie standing a few feet away.

"There you are. Cara was looking for you. Is everything okay?" She looks between us, waiting for one of us to answer, but I'm not giving Gus the chance to say anything.

"Yup. We had one of those moments when I tried to go right, and so did he, and when I tried to go left, he did too. It's just awkward but all good. Where's Cara?" I ask, trying to play it off as nonchalant.

"Outside. She said to meet her out there when you're ready."

"Thanks for the lovely day, Allie." I hug her, and she smiles at me.

"Always, sweet girl. Please come next Sunday. You're always welcome here."

"We'll see. Thanks again." I walk past her and wave goodbye to the rest of her friends, all still laughing and talking, with no clue about anything else going on.

It's both a blessing and a curse.

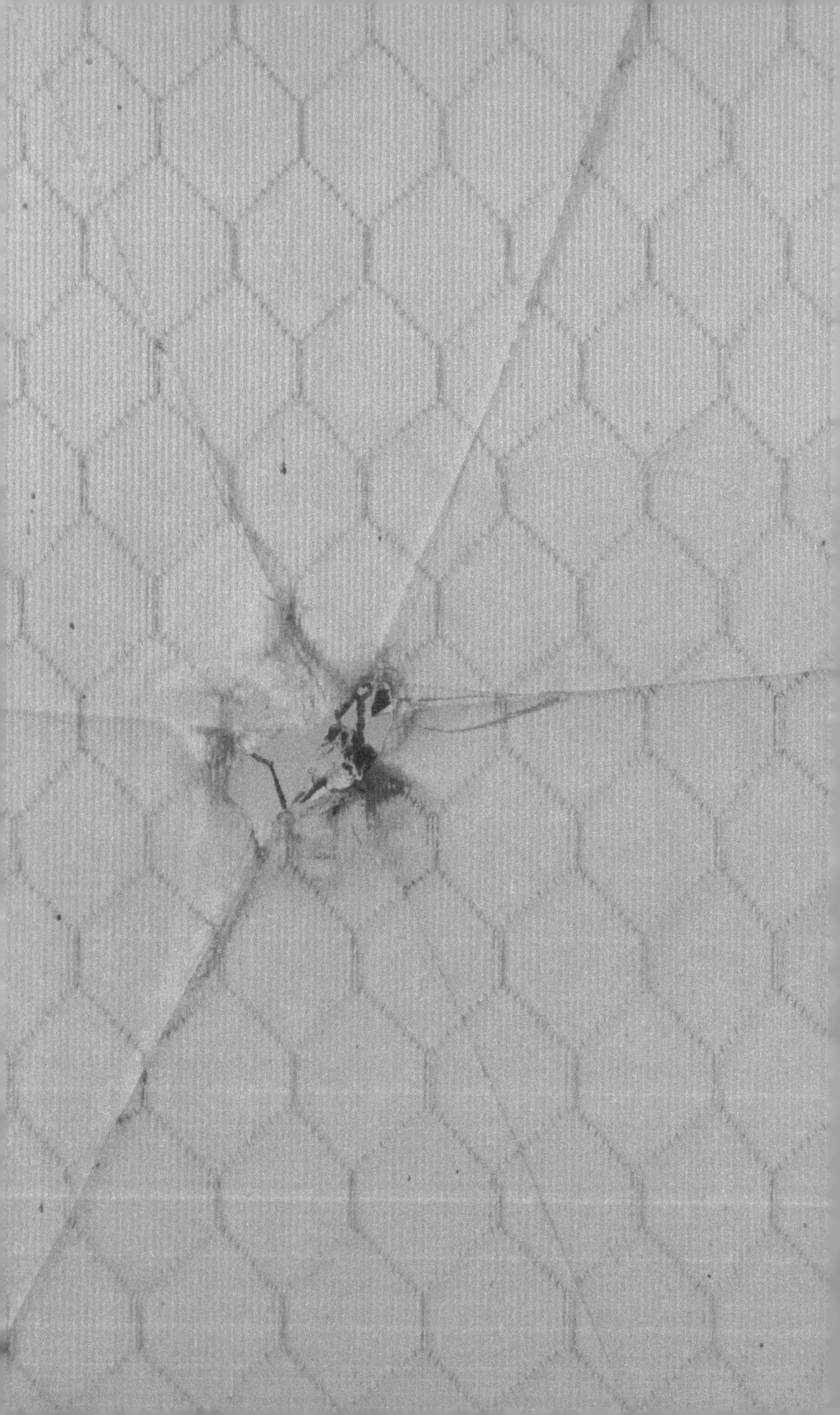

NOT MY FINEST MOMENT

¿Donde Está El Amor? by Pablo Alborán and Jesse & Joy & Un Beso by Aventura

GUS

YOU WANT ANOTHER CHANCE? *Earn it.* Nellie's words echo in my head. They've been looping on repeat since last night. Abraham told me to get my shit together last week. He reminded me of a lot of things, but above all, how my spirit felt better when I was with Nellie, how I'm sulking now that we're not. *Sulking.* The asshole. I feel bad. I should just let her go and stop trying to keep her in this endless back and forth. I know I'm not good for her, but I can't stop thinking about her. I don't think I want to either. I love her, of that I'm sure.

I've fucked so many women in my life. So many have come and gone, but none of them are her. None of them will ever be her. They were easy to forget. Nellie would be impossible. I meant it when I told her I don't feel for anyone the way I feel about her. I don't fall for women, but I fell for her.

Nellie has invaded all my space, all my thoughts, all my dreams. I can't stop thinking about her. The specks of gold in her green eyes. The beautiful smile she shows me every time she catches me staring. The way my brain tickles at the thought of having a conversation with her. The few freckles on her cheeks. I can't let go. The way her dark hair contrasts her fair skin. The way her cheeks turn rosy right before she comes. The way her pouty lips whisper my name before she unravels. The way my heart skips a beat just at the thought of seeing her.

I always fight for what I want. I fought for my business, and I didn't stop until I got it. I just never thought a woman would ever be on the other end of that desire. Of that chase. Not any woman, though: Nellie. Carefree, obsessed with the ocean Nellie. Good listener and beautiful Nellie.

She wants me to show her I mean it, so I will. I made up my mind. I will fight until I get her back, and then I'm not letting go. I've been an asshole, but why? Because of fear? Maybe I just need to tell her that, and we can go from there. My thoughts are all over the place, but when are they not when it comes to her?

I walk through the office doors after being buzzed in at Baker Middle. It's 8:00 a.m., and although some teachers are already here, school doesn't start until 8:30. I hope she's not here yet. The receptionist smiles at me when she sees me. "How can I help you?"

"I'm here to drop this off for Ms. Thompson. Can I leave it here?"

"You sure can. Anything you'd like me to say?"

"No, ma'am. Just don't tilt it, or it might spill." I pass her the bag holding an easy-on-the-stomach breakfast and leave. She seemed tipsy last night. It's not easy to go to work early in general, let alone after drinking, with kids to top it off. I hope she likes it and she doesn't hate me.

I get in my car and head to the cardiologist. It's been

weeks since Dr. Diaz started looking into what's going on with my heart. The first fainting episode happened about a month ago, followed by a HAE attack that left me in the hospital for a couple of days. Hiding it from Nellie was hard, but I didn't want her to worry. Hiding it from Manny was impossible, so I might as well have told him. When I did, he almost turned into a guard dog. Then, it happened again. This time, it was worse. My potassium was low, which is a problem. We fixed that. I went out of town with Nellie, and when I got back, it happened again. Traveling was triggering the attacks, but the fainting has been so bizarre. Blood work, cables, studies, ultrasounds, and a wearable Holter monitor later, the doctors have concluded I was having irregular heartbeats, prolonged QT.

My team of specialists met and found the HAE meds were causing Long QT Syndrome. Today is my follow-up since stopping my oral medicine. Now, I'm working on getting my maintenance meds via shots. The day we were at the cabin, my doctor called to tell me I needed to stop taking the medication. She explained the medicine was most likely causing the Long QTs, but if I stopped taking it, my angioedema attacks would have a higher chance of happening again. I needed to get back into town immediately. I thought about telling Nellie, and looking back, I should have, but I didn't want to have her worrying about me every day as she navigates this new season in her life. I didn't want her to worry, not after she told me how out of control she felt. Unfortunately, I fear my heart may actually be worse without her.

She was so upset, and at first, I didn't understand it completely. Why was it so hard for her to see it all? The big picture? I shut it all down. All my feelings for her. All the what ifs. It was easier to just try to push it away. But I couldn't, no matter what I did. I love her. I'm in love with her. I'd rather go through hardships with her than a lifetime without her. By the time I realized it, I tried to talk to her, but it was too late. She put her walls back up. She closed the door. She threw away the key. She got defensive. She pushed me out. But she loves me. *She's afraid. She's afraid.*

The snapping back without letting me talk. The assumptions. The overall disregard of me showing her how much she means to me without her noticing. It means that she probably doesn't know. The smartest person I know, but also…she can't read social cues easily. She has never learned to read between the lines, and I couldn't flat-out tell her. Or I wouldn't. *We're both running away from the same thing.* We're like two melodies, equally powerful, perfectly matched, endlessly unyielding. Each time one of us introduced a new theme, the other countered with equal intensity. Instead of meshing, we ended up clashing. Instead of building toward a crescendo, our notes became opposites, never blending, leaving only discord and unresolved tension in the air. I need her just as much as she needs me, but neither of us were willing to bring the other one into the mess we think we are. We were vulnerable with each other with a ten foot wall between us. I tried to climb it, but her walls were slippery, and she took away the rope.

I ran.

It's so much easier to let her assume. It's so much easier to be her villain than hurt her. But I still hurt her in the end.

I showed her how much she means to me. Now, I need to tell her. I need to make sure she knows, not just assume she does. I need to win her back. I need to explain it all. I need to trust she can handle it. If it's too much, at least we'll know. Maybe I need to introduce her to Blair too, so she can see nothing is going on between us.

Dr. Diaz's office is always quiet. She has a small private practice in this building where she sees patients twice a week, and then she works at the hospital downtown the rest of the week. I love her as a doctor because she's a practitioner of both Western and Eastern medicine. She balances it all well.

"Dr. Diaz, café para usted." I hand her the coffee I picked up when I grabbed Nellie's, earning me an instant smile.

"We said no caffeine for you until today," she replies. She's playing it safe, making sure everything is on track before letting me have caffeine and other things again.

"I haven't touched coffee, making me sad. I wouldn't be surprised if all your readings today looked like a coffee mug. My heart is missing caffeine." I pout, and she rolls her eyes. She has never been able to resist my charm.

"No, no sadness today. Let's see how the EKG goes. Go take your shirt off and lie down."

I do as she says. The paper crinkles beneath me as I shift onto the exam table, the cushion cold against my bare back. My fingers twitch against my ribs as she fastens the electrodes to my chest, each one a cold, sticky press against my skin.

When I was first diagnosed with HAE, I hadn't thought to mention the Lisinopril I took for my blood pressure. Turns out, it was making everything worse—fueling the swelling, turning minor flare ups into full-blown attacks. It took nearly a year to find a regimen that balanced both conditions. Now, we're back at square one.

The EKG machine whirs to life, translating my heartbeat into peaks across the screen. I try to read the lines, but I never can, so I might as well just let her do her thing.

She doesn't speak, fingers moving across the keyboard. Usually, she fills the silence with small talk unless she's inputting and analyzing data. I like that she focuses so hard when needed. I like that no matter how hard I try, I can never read her face.

I swallow hard. "That bad?" I ask, probing.

"Not at all." She finishes the test and removes everything from my chest, letting me put my shirt back on as she finishes typing the information she needs.

"You can go back to your routine, Gus, but nothing strenuous. Nothing that will spike your heart rate. Got it?"

I cock my eyebrow and smile at her, earning me a shake of her head.

"You know what I mean. For our follow-up. How does three weeks sound?" she asks nonchalantly.

"You don't want to see me again for three weeks. Dr. Diaz, you wound me," I say, shamelessly flirting with her in the most platonic way.

"I would love to only see you twice a year, but we're not there yet. Every three weeks for now. Keep eating the rainbow, keep your stress low, and take your meds. And please, slow down on the dangerous activities, at least for now. I don't need you fainting while climbing a cliff." I nod and leave after that.

If she only knew I haven't been able to rock climb in weeks because of the same reason she's asking me not to. Before, I was careless, but now, thinking about dying without getting to experience love, true love, has me in my head. I have no business doing dangerous shit if I'm afraid. Fear is the biggest paralyzer, and I'm damn terrified of spending another waking moment without Nellie. I can't put more worries on her other than my health, so I'm trying my best to limit the stupid shit I do.

"Hola[1]," I answer the call hands-free on my SUV as I drive down the highway.

"I need you to come in and sign some papers. Lucia has been trying to call you, along with whatever secretary you have this week too. Where is your head at?" Manny asks on the speaker.

"Hello to you too, brother. Yes. I was actually on my way there now."

"How convenient."

"¿Y a ti que te pasa?[2]" He's usually chirpy, or at least, he has been since he came back from the road trip a couple of months ago. He's been a changed man, prioritizing his life

---

1. Yes, sir.
2. What's going on with you?

over work. I haven't heard Manny the CEO Asshole all summer.

"Nada. ¿Date pronto, okay?[3]"

"Si, señor."

The roads are somewhat empty as I navigate the streets of Jacksonville to the corporate office. This is our main office, where we sign new contracts or update old ones, hold staff meetings, or meet with new clients unless they're local to our other two locations.

This place used to be my home, back when I ate, slept, and breathed business. I didn't take care of myself, and it almost killed me. It took me months to break the pattern, and it took me years to look at the building and not feel like it could eat me alive at any second. My relationship with the business is just that now: business. I nourish it, of course, but not as much as I nourish my health.

"Good morning, Zabana Ent!" I call out, my voice echoing as I step through the clear glass doors into the sleek, sunlit lobby. The scent of polished wood and fresh espresso lingers in the air, mingling with the pristine look of this place. The space is open and modern, bathed in natural light pouring in from the floor-to-ceiling windows that offer a great view of the St. Johns River just beyond the building.

"Good morning, Mr. Zabana," Lucas greets me from behind the minimalist black marble reception desk. His posture is always professional, but with a flicker of familiarity in his eyes that makes everyone who meets him feel like family immediately.

"No need to get up—I'll find my brother," I tell him, flashing a quick grin. "Good to see you, man."

He nods, and I head toward the conference room. Manny hired someone to design this space, and it shows. The walls are lined with bamboo panels, a warm contrast to the cool

---

3. Nothing, hurry up, okay?

tones of the polished concrete floors. Clean lines, hidden storage, and furniture that balances comfort with sophistication, just like he always envisioned it. As for me, I don't care. I want this place to feel warm and comfortable for the people who work here, so as long as they feel it, I'm happy.

I take a deep breath, absorbing the quiet energy of the space before pushing the door open. Manny is already inside, standing near the window with his arms crossed, deep in thought. Whatever's on his mind, I have a feeling I'm about to find out.

"Que Lo Que, manin[4]?"

"Gusti," he says, turning around but not smiling at me.

"Siéntate y dime que te pasa porque tengo semanas que no te veo así tan serio.[5]"

"You sit and tell me what the hell are you thinking, fucking Nellie Thompson." Oh, shit. I shake my head and sit down on the oak conference table in the middle of the room. There's no point in denying it.

"You were the one who told me weeks ago that it wasn't any of your business when I was sleeping with Cara, but to remember it was more than our hearts on the line. Then you turn around and fuck her little sister? ¿Que coño te pasa a ti, loco?[6].

"It's not what you think."

"It's not what I think? Are you or are you not sleeping with Nellie?"

"Currently, I'm not." He shakes his head at my use of words. If there's someone I can't bullshit, it's him. He knows me too well. Always has, and I can't blame him. We're not only brothers but twins. We talk every day. We see each other

---

4. What's up bro? (This is a Dominican slang)
5. Sit and tell me what's going on because it's been weeks since I've ever seen you that serious.
6. What the fuck is wrong with you?

often, and until college, we were never apart for more than a day. He knows me too well.

"What the fuck, Gus? *Were* you?"

Just sleeping with her? No. Falling in love with every part of her? Yes. Wishing I could breathe the same air as her? Be in the same place with her? Finding out that my life feels dull without her in it? Also yes. But I don't tell him that. I keep it simple and just say, "Yes."

"I fucking knew it. Since when? June, when you started acting weird and shit? You stopped attending events around that time too."

"Technically May…since her graduation." Well fuck, might as well just tell him everything.

"Cara and Allie are going to kill you," he spits, turning one of the chairs around and sitting opposite from me.

"Why, Manny? I'm a good man. I would be so good for her, so why would they kill me?" A scoff escapes me, because of course I just now realized it, just now figured this out. I've been so afraid of letting others know because of how they might react when I should've been thinking about all the reasons why I'm the perfect man for Nellie. All the reasons why our families would be okay with us being together.

"I don't know, Gus. The mystery girl… It was Nellie all along? What were you thinking?"

I tell him everything, from seeing her at the club and lusting over her before realizing it was her to the events that have happened since. I tell him everything except the things Nellie confided in me; those are none of his business. I tell him about how much I laugh when I'm with her, how unwell I feel when I'm not. I tell him how my heart slows its erratic beatings when I'm near her, how just her scent is enough to bring me peace.

"Coño…you love her don't you?" he asks, raising his eyebrows and relaxing his body. He was so tense throughout the story, wary of what I was going to say, especially considering Nellie is Cara's sister.

"I don't want to answer that question without telling her first." I've told her every single other thing. I feel for her. I want her. I like her. I'm in awe of her. I want to fuck her. *Mine.* But I haven't given her the words I know encompass everything I feel for her—love. I haven't given those words to anyone but my family. I guard them. I don't let them out easily. I don't toss them around. I meticulously keep them inside because I believe in them in a way that maybe not everyone does. So many people say they love, but what they do is lust. What they do is care. What they do is hurt. But love? I've seen it only from some people.

"I've seen it in the way our mother loves us, unconditionally and fearlessly. I've seen it in the way Allie is loved by Jake and the way she loves him back. The way she was haunted by the love they had for each other for a decade until they found each other again. I've seen it in the way Manny loves Cara, first secretly for years, then as loud as someone could show it. I've seen it in the way teachers love students, putting them first, regardless of blood relationships. In the way my grandma loved my grandpa, for decades and decades, through thick and thin, through sickness and health. I respect those three words way too much to just toss them around, but I've always wanted someone I could love like that. I think Nellie is it. I know she is. If it's not love, then it must be insanity. And I'm about to lose her because I've been holding back."

"What are you gonna do?" he asks, challenging me with his eyes.

"I'm trying to win her back. No, not trying, I'm going to win her back. I will nag until I have her again, but it will take time, considering I just called her my fuck buddy at Allie's yesterday."

"You did what?"

"I know, I know. Not my finest moment."

"She can't be one of the women you sleep with and then forget about," he offers.

"Oh, I tried. I tried after the night we just kissed and then didn't talk for a month, but have you ever met her? There's no forgetting Nellie. There's no after Nellie, either. Only *before* Nellie and *with* Nellie. After she's in your life, she's there forever. Trust me, I'd know. I've been trying to fight it, but there's no way I can forget her. She's more than that, Manny. She's incredible. She's everything."

"You need to get yourself together and tell her," he says with a smile on his face.

"I'm trying. She won't listen until I come clean and tell her everything, but I don't want her to choose me because she pities me."

"Because of your heart?"

I nod. "I hurt her. I know I did. So now, I must show her I meant it when I said I was sorry and I won't let her go easily. I need to do what Allie says all the time. Sorry doesn't fix it, so I need a different approach. Where I need space, she needs words, and I need to find a time and a place to say them to her." I'm lost in thought, in my own ramblings, when it hits me. How did he know?

"How did you know?"

"Other than you eye fucking her at the dinner? You weren't interested in joining us until you heard Nellie was going to be there, and you jumped at the opportunity. And then you two were icy cold, sometimes hot too. Looking at each other while simultaneously staying away from each other too. She was shooting daggers at you all day, the way any woman who wants to murder a lover does." *Busted.* "And you…well, you look at her the same way I look at her sister."

"How?" I know what he means, though. I look at Nellie like she hung the moon.

"Like she is your favorite song." Yup, that tracks. My favorite tune, melody, and symphony.

"Does Cara know?" I ask Manny, concerned because I would love to get my shit in check before she finds out.

"No, not that I know of, but I will tell her if she asks. So you need to get your shit figured out before she does. I won't lie to her." And of course, as my twin and best friend, he knows exactly what I mean without me even saying it.

"Understood."

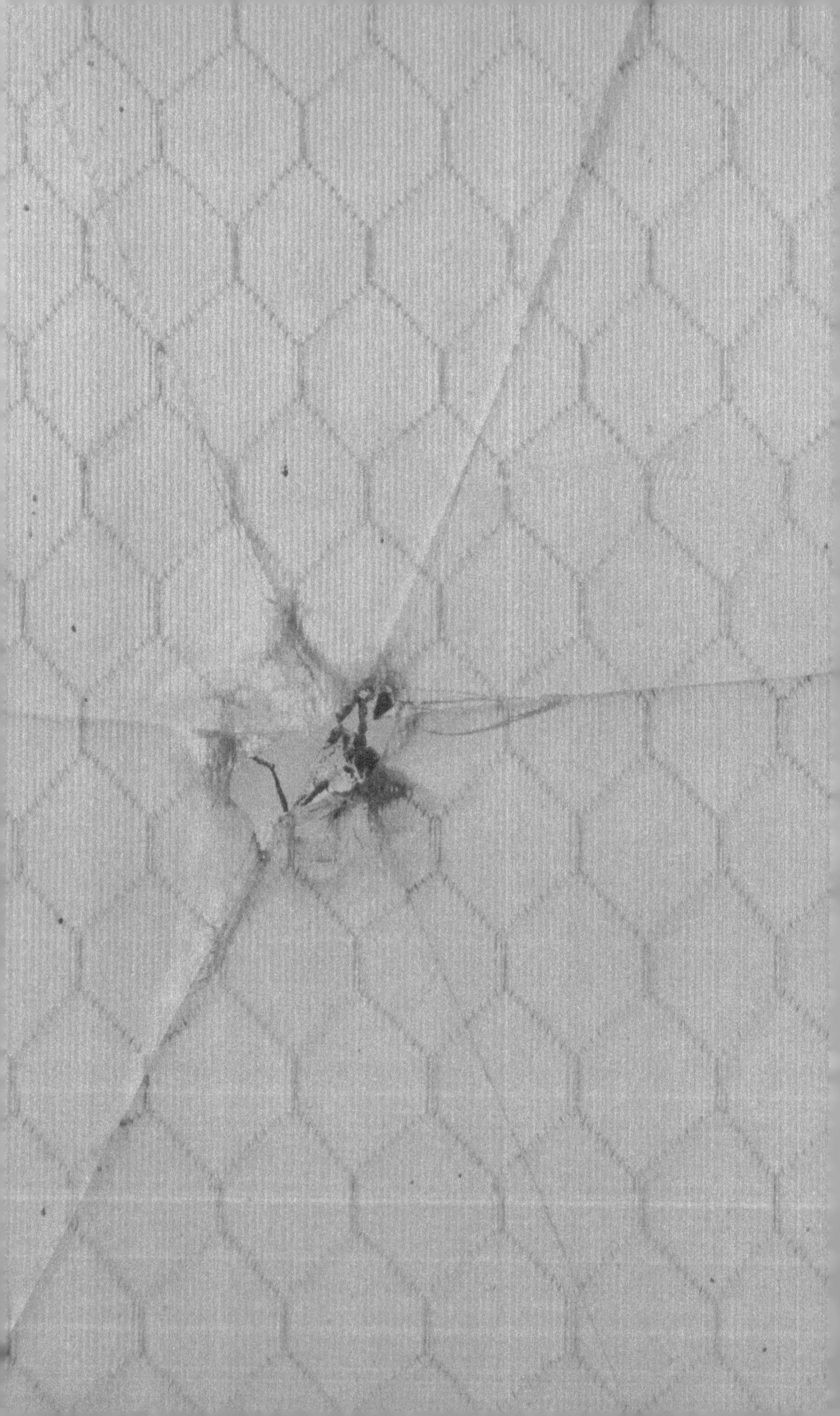

TWENTY

MR. ALBOOTY

Growing Sideways by Noah Kahan & Someone to Stay by Vancouver Sleep Clinic

NELLIE

SO MUCH FOR keeping myself from consuming alcohol during the week. The time of daily drinking and struggling through classes and internships should have remained firmly in the past. Yet, here I am—severely hungover, still grappling with the same overwhelming sense of discomfort I've felt for the past two days, barely able to keep my eyes open. Today might be one of those rare occasions where I remain in my office, buried in paperwork, rather than seeing too many kids.

The chatter from the middle schoolers cuts through the hallway, loud and relentless. They're always loud—too loud, especially today. I love them, I do, but today, I wish they'd dial it down a notch. I move through the entryway, nodding to Ms. Laura, our receptionist. She's been here for decades, and I've known her since my own time at Baker Middle. She's been nothing but welcoming, and for that, I'm grateful.

"Hey Nellie, you have a delivery. Here." She hands me a medium brown paper bag, her voice warm and steady.

I mutter a distracted thanks as I make my way toward the staff room. The noise is almost unbearable now, the buzz of middle schoolers laughing, yelling, the high-pitched squeal of sneakers on linoleum. They always seem so loud, so alive, and I usually love it, but today, my head pounds with each step. I can't help it. I need coffee, something to dull the edges of this hangover. I might even consider hot coffee to see if it would help.

In the teacher's lounge, I make a beeline for the coffee machine, but instead of pouring the scalding liquid into my mug, I set the bag on the table and open it. *What?* In front of me lies a coffee in a to-go cup, something wrapped in tan cellophane, and a note. A letter? Something in a small white envelope. I grab the cup, the warmth of it immediately soothing my hands but not my nerves. I can still feel the remnants of last night creeping up on me, the thrum of alcohol in my veins, the echoes of the conversation with Gus and how many emotions he pulls out of me all the time, even when I don't want him to. I shouldn't have had that last drink. Not the one at Natalie's, but the ones I had at home after I couldn't settle down to go to sleep.

The door to the lounge creaks open, and I hear a familiar voice.

"Ms. Thompson."

I turn to face him. Ben. Ben is a sweet and shy second-year teacher. He's lived in Baker all his life, but he was homeschooled, so our paths never crossed until now. I find it quite interesting he ended up as a public school teacher after being homeschooled all his life. He's smiling as he always does, and I smile back, even if I just want to slowly crawl back to bed and collapse. I was so reckless; I didn't even realize I drank so much. I need to stop. This is so stupid. I acted so stupid, and over what? A man? *A man you're in love with, you idiot. A man who has shown you colors in life you didn't know existed.*

I pull the rest of the contents out of the bag. The carefully wrapped croissant makes me practically moan without even touching it. Buttery and toasty warm deliciousness sounds like exactly what I need. The envelope is sealed, my name written on it. I open it to find two small red and blue packets, each containing two ibuprofen, and a card folded in half. When I open it, I see it's a handwritten note addressed to me.

Hey Trouble,

You asked me yesterday to grovel, and I guess I should start reading some of the romance novels Allie loves, because I don't think I know how. However, for you, I'm willing to learn. Dare I say, I can start by sending you breakfast, coffee, and some medicine for what I assume would be the headache you have today? If I'm out of line, forgive me. If I'm on point, I'm sorry you're hurting, and I hope this helps, if just a little. I would recommend drinking water too.

Con cariño,

Your DLS (hoping to be more than this, though)

PS: I know you prefer iced coffee, but something tells me hot coffee is better suited for headaches. Comfort and all.

I groan, closing the letter and sliding it back into the envelope. It's unbelievable how he knows me this well when I thought he didn't know me at all. *He's been showing you how much he loves you with more than words.* I shake my head, wishing the little voice away.

"Everything okay?" Ben asks from the other side of the dim-lit teacher's lounge. I forgot he was here. I forgot where I was, actually. I hate this feeling, this discombobulated feeling I get when I think about Gus, when I'm near Gus. He makes me feel giddy and irrationally emotional; I don't know if it's a good or a bad thing. Both? Maybe both.

"Yeah. See you later, Ben." I step out of the teacher's lounge, coffee in hand.

"Ms. Thompson, are you free right now?" Bella asks, catching up to me in the hallway as I'm speed-walking to my office.

"It depends. Are you looking for ears, skipping, or advice?" I'm trying to teach these kiddos that I'm not always available just because they want to skip class. I'm happy to be listening ears when needed, but I also have to draw a line so they don't think that because I'm young, they can get away with this.

"Where's your hall pass?" I hear Mr. Alberry ask.

"Here." Bella shows him, and he smiles at me with his gooey gross smile.

"I meant yours."

"Ha, very funny, Mr. Alberry. I work here now."

"I still can't believe it. Little Thompson walking around, counseling children. It was just the other day you were walking these halls yourself." He continues walking and laughing, the stupid laugh that sounds like a whole damn fart.

"So funny, Mr. Albooty," I mumble under my breath, and Bella chuckles. "Don't repeat that." Winning at this counseling thing for sure.

"He was your teacher too?" she asks, waiting by the door. Students are not allowed in the teacher's lounge, but she clearly wants to talk.

"Bella, are you trying to skip class?"

"No, I promise. I want to talk to you about something. Not school related, but I don't know who else to talk to." Sweet girl. Okay.

"Talk to me," I tell Bella as we fall in pace walking toward my office.

"You know my mom is pregnant, right?"

"I do know that, congratulations! Are you excited?"

She stops walking and looks around before shaking her head. "Does that make me a terrible big sister? A terrible daughter?"

"Oh sweetie, no, it doesn't. It just makes you human. Come on in. Let's sit down." I use my key fob to unlock my door and hold it open for her to step inside. This office used to look like an adult's therapy corner: one brown couch in a white room with a desk in the corner. No wonder none of these kids wanted to come in here. Now, it looks cozy, at least in my opinion. A smaller couch, two bean bag chairs, a basket full of floor cushions and blankets, low, warm lights with fairy lights framing the room, and earthy colors that dance together in a perfect blend. I have a small desk with paper, pencils, and some art supplies for the kids who need an artistic outlet. A sensory corner is available, as well as a reading corner. I have some books that vary in genre and topics, and I find myself sometimes just sitting there and reading or journaling, escaping into a fantasy world when the world outside is too much. That is the only corner in this school where I face real feelings about myself; other than that, this is all about them, the kids.

I let students pick what area they want to use before I join them. Bella often prefers the floor, and this time is no differ-ent. She takes her Vans off before walking over to the foam rug to lie down, her face up at the ceiling, her eyes closed. I sit on the bean bag closer to her, take another sip of my coffee, and ask what I usually do before starting, "Am I listening, or am I advising today?" I want them to know I'm here to do both, but sometimes, we need someone to just listen without interrupting. That's my job too.

"Both. Let me talk, and if I ask questions, you can answer, 'kay?'"

"'Kay."

"I'm happy for my parents. They've been wanting a baby forever, but my mom has struggled to get pregnant and has lost some babies too. It destroys her every time, and I don't blame her. That is sad, you know? My dad is her rock. He's always there supporting her, making sure she's okay, but after she goes to sleep, he goes to the living room and prays or cries. Sometimes both. They want this baby so bad, but what if she doesn't make it? I'm scared for them more than I'm happy for them. I don't want to lose them, and I feel like that's what will happen if she doesn't make it." She lets out a breath. This sweet eleven-year-old girl is full of kindness and compassion, full of love for her parents, with so much weight on her shoulders.

"What if *who* doesn't make it?"

"The baby. I have a feeling the baby is a girl, so I call her a she. My mom refuses to call her anything but the baby. My dad doesn't even acknowledge her. I mean, he does rub my mom's belly, but it's so different this time. I think he's scared too."

"It is scary, and you have the right to feel scared too. Your feelings are valid, and you can be both scared and happy. It's totally okay if, right now, you're mostly just scared. Have you talked to them about this?"

She shakes her head no, but she doesn't say anything else.

"Do you want to talk to them about this?"

Bella lets out a breath and stays silent. Her hands scratch the rug before she opens her eyes and looks at me. "I don't know. I don't want to be another burden."

"Oh, honey, you're not a burden. You're their kid, and

they want you just as much as they want that baby. I promise you that."

"They have other things to worry about, and I don't want them to worry about me too."

"Sorry to break it to you, kid, but they worry about you. They do. Most parents do, all the time. But *your* parents particularly love you and worry about you all the time."

"So you think I should talk to them?"

"I think you're their kid, and if you want to chat with them about this, you should. I think you will feel a lot better after you do. And if you don't, my door is always open."

"Promise?" I want to say promise back, but that word now reminds me of Gus, every time. I don't like it. I actually hate that a simple word can bring out so many emotions, mostly anger, and I can't let my emotions overtake me right now. Right now, I'm here for her. I'm her safe space, so I better pull myself together.

"I promise. Even if I'm not personally here, someone will be here. Someone always wants to listen, I promise."

"Okay. Thank you, Ms. Thompson."

"Just doing my job, kiddo. Now, go ahead and go to class. I have a coffee to finish."

"And another kiddo to listen to," she says, finishing the phrase that has become my slogan here. I do more than listen to kids, but it's my favorite part of the job, so I had to let them know.

I hop up to open the door for her, but before she steps out, she gives me a hug. A tight hug reminds me why I wanted to do this job in the first place. "Thank you," she whispers before marching to class.

I flip the sign on my door that says 'Ready to listen' so if anyone needs me, they can just knock and come inside. It's the beginning of the day, so the chances of someone needing me are slim, but you never know. I wish I could just leave the door open, but that's not safe anymore in schools, and it's sad. It breaks my heart, knowing our schools are resembling jails more than the haven they're supposed to be. Outside time has been minimized, and the windows that once were seen as a beautiful opportunity to connect with the real world are now a potential threat in the case of an intruder being at school.

I wish there was a way to fix it all, and I'm sure there is, but there's so much out of my control. All I can do is my part. I can show up here every day and be here for them. I can listen, try to help, and offer advice when needed. I can reach out to others who can help when I can't, and I can also use my voice and my privilege for those who can't.

A light knock on the door startles me and brings me back from my thoughts. There are a few students who stop by to say hello in between classes and some at the end of each day.

I made a corner called Food For Thought. Students can stop by at any time to grab a snack. The caveat? They have to leave me a note. Usually, it's anonymous, but they can write their name too. I check it twice a day, in the morning and before I go home. I open one every day and read it. Some of them have been really funny, and others have been gut-wrenching. Some ask for specific foods, and others ask for prayers. Some ask for a sign. I need to find a system to reply, but I'm afraid they'll stop leaving me notes if I seek them out, and that defeats the purpose.

I open the door to find Cody. Cody is one of the eighth graders who everyone talks about. He's charismatic, the school charmer. Apparently, he'll have a bright future with football one day, but he's also good in class, breaking all the stereotypes that jocks don't study. The outgoing kid who seems to get along with everyone. The social butterfly, as the teachers say. Nobody talks much about his family, just that he has an older brother at the high school who is also a football prodigy. Everyone talks about his football career, but nobody talks about how he's kind. I always see him opening doors for others or helping Jayla, a classmate who has an assistive device, carry her books to class every day. No one ever points out that he always carries extra supplies to share with teammates, or that he stays after practice to help clean up. No one ever said he loves sci-fi novels or that he listens to pop music loudly on his headphones, or that, despite his confidence, he still comes in every day to grab food and leave notes. It took me four days to notice all those things, and now, four weeks later, I know he values our conversations. He trusts me enough to ask for advice when he needs it, even if he doesn't share a lot of deep and personal stuff.

"Hey buddy, what's up?" I ask, smiling at him.

"Hi, can I grab a snack?" he asks, not looking at me. That's weird. He always, always looks at me with a big smile.

"Of course, go ahead." I move from the door, letting him pass. He walks by with his shoulders slightly slumped, as if the weight of something pulls him down. His hands, loosely hanging by his sides, don't swing as he takes every step. His gaze stays on the floor ahead, never quite lifting. This is the saddest thing I've ever seen, and he didn't even say anything. One of my number one rules is not to ask if someone is okay. We're supposed to use assertive language to make sure there's no room for gray areas, so we know exactly our student's state of mind. I try something else.

"Is there anything I can do for you?" He shakes his head until he gets to the Food for Thought corner. I turn around to give him privacy, as I've promised every student I will, and keep myself busy packing my things.

"Thank you," he whispers from the door. I turn around to see him leave without another word. Weird.

"HEY NELLIE. Someone's here to see you," Mom says from the other side of my door. It's open, so there's no need to knock, but I'm not expecting anyone. After school, I went to swim at the local gym, and then I've been laying in bed ever since. It's only 5:00 pm, but it feels a lot later, maybe because I've been in a constant loop of despair all day. Gus brought me coffee and breakfast to school and a note. For most people, that wouldn't be a lot, but for me, it is, because that man could buy me whatever he wants, but he knows I'm not after his money. I care about him and his heart, and the way to mine is the same. Not through the fancy and flashy things, but through the smaller details. I want to be seen; the note, coffee and the sentiment behind it shows me that he sees me. Still, I'm not ready to just forget everything all because he thought of me once today.

"I hear you need an intervention," Bee says walking through my door, and I have to blink twice to make sure it's her. My mom smiles before closing the door and leaving us both here.

"Bee? What the hell are you doing here?" I leap off the bed and into her arms, almost tackling her to the ground.

"A little bird told me you've been a sad baby and needed your bestie fix." Bee only lives an hour away from me, but her new job has had her traveling so much, I haven't seen her since I moved back. She smells like strawberries and long nights talking about our lives. Damn, I miss her. "Stop choking me, you bitch. I'm too hot to die."

I chuckle as I let her go and walk us both back to my bed.

"Nellie, don't you think you're too old to be living in your childhood bedroom?"

"I have zero desire to move anywhere by myself, and here, I don't have to pay rent, so no."

She rolls her eyes and sits across from me. "What's going on with you and that hottie of yours?" We catch up on everything, and by the time I'm done, she has gone through every single emotion known to man. We video call Victoria at some point so she can be in the know with everything too. Victoria, being the emotional one, cries. I think she's more shocked than anything. She's hurting for me because she loves me, but she also understands why I'm in the predicament I am.

"So, as you two can see, I'm fucked either way. If I forgive him, I'm showing him that I'm okay with this freaking whiplash, but if I don't, then what? I'm letting go of the man who has made me feel more than I've ever felt in my life? I feel safe with him, and no matter what my brain tells me, my body and my heart betray me."

"Honey, that's what love is," Victoria says, like I don't already know it.

"Do you know you love him?" Bee asks me, and I give her a dead stare.

"Yes. I thought I made that clear."

"Does he love you?" Victoria asks, and Bee tilts her head to look at me.

"No. Yes. I don't know. Maybe?" I shrug and toss my head back.

"Considering the call I got a few hours ago begging me to come see you? I'd say that man loves you alright," Bee replies and lays flat on the bed.

"What am I supposed to do?"

"What do you want to do?"

I want calm and peace and quiet. I want companionship. I also want a rush and butterflies in my stomach. I want to feel it all. I want everything I had this summer with him, parallel with the life I'm building now. But I don't say any of that. "I want to be happy." Because in the end, it all comes to that— wanting to be happy.

"Does he make you happy?" Victoria asks, always the wise one.

"Not right now, he's not."

"Okay then. Make him suffer until he makes you happy again," Bee shouts, and Victoria snickers. "No, I'm kidding. I think you just need to give him a chance to explain, babe.

Maybe it'll all make sense. And if it does, then be clear about your boundaries. Let him know he gets this one chance and nothing else."

I nod and rub my temples. It's exhausting. All of it. "Enough about me. Tell me about you two."

"I'm fine. Just going through my last internship before applying for jobs," Victoria replies.

"Are you still considering editing?" I ask. She is double majoring in English and Journalism, but she wants to edit mostly.

"That's the goal. There are a couple of places in New York I want to apply. Bee, how's work?"

"Perfect! I truly love it! I can't believe I landed my dream job as soon as I finished college. I guess Nellie and I were lucky like that."

"Nells, is your job everything you wanted?"

I nod and smile. I wish I could smile as brightly as Bee, but the reality is, this job is hard. "Yeah, but I didn't realize how hard it actually is. There's so much I want to do, but it's hard with all the policies and the expectations. For example, I was working with the school psychologist on coming up with a plan for the students without housing, and in the middle of that, we had a code red drill. We knew it was a drill, but we're not allowed to tell the students it is. Their reactions will probably haunt me forever. Not because they were afraid, but because they didn't even bat an eye."

"Code red is a lockdown drill, right? Like if there's an intruder?" Victoria asks.

"Mm-hmm. A code yellow is like a warning. Stay put, don't wander. Sometimes, it might be because of something dangerous nearby, and sometimes, it's just to offer privacy, like if someone had an accident and we had to call an ambulance. A red is an imminent threat. We have to shelter in place. We all have hard corners in every room, which is the safest place to be in case of an active assailant, and we just stay there until we're cleared. It's scary as shit. If you thought it was scary thinking about it as an adult, imagine for the kids...except we've trained them to accept code reds as a natural thing. We've trained them to accept them as their normal so they just follow the motions naturally, as if it's not a big deal."

"That's the whole point, right? Like in case it is real, they have muscle memory to fall into," Victoria continues.

"Yup, but it's so sad that's our reality." They both nod. Bee looks at her watch and gets up quickly.

"No wonder you're all sad and mopey. Oh shit, I gotta go. My sister has an event tonight, and I'm going to be late if I don't leave now."

"Bye!" Victoria waves from the video call and hangs up. I give Bee a hug, and after a kiss on my cheek, she leaves me here. Alone. In the silence.

My phone vibrates on my nightstand stand, and when I look at it, I have two text messages waiting for me.

DLS:

Can we talk?

DLS:

It doesn't have to be tonight, but soon?
Please.

I want to be mean and bitchy and leave him on read, but I also want to know what's going on with him.

ME:

What do you want?

DLS:

For you to give me a chance to talk to you

ME:

you had a chance and you blew it.

DLS:

I know, and I'm sorry.

DLS:

Please, Nellie.

I lock my phone and slam it on the table. This infuriating man. If I continue answering his messages, this will turn into me forgiving him like nothing happened, and I don't think I can. I can't just look past the lies and the secrets. The cold and the hot. The with me one day and not being there the next.

This time, I leave him on read.

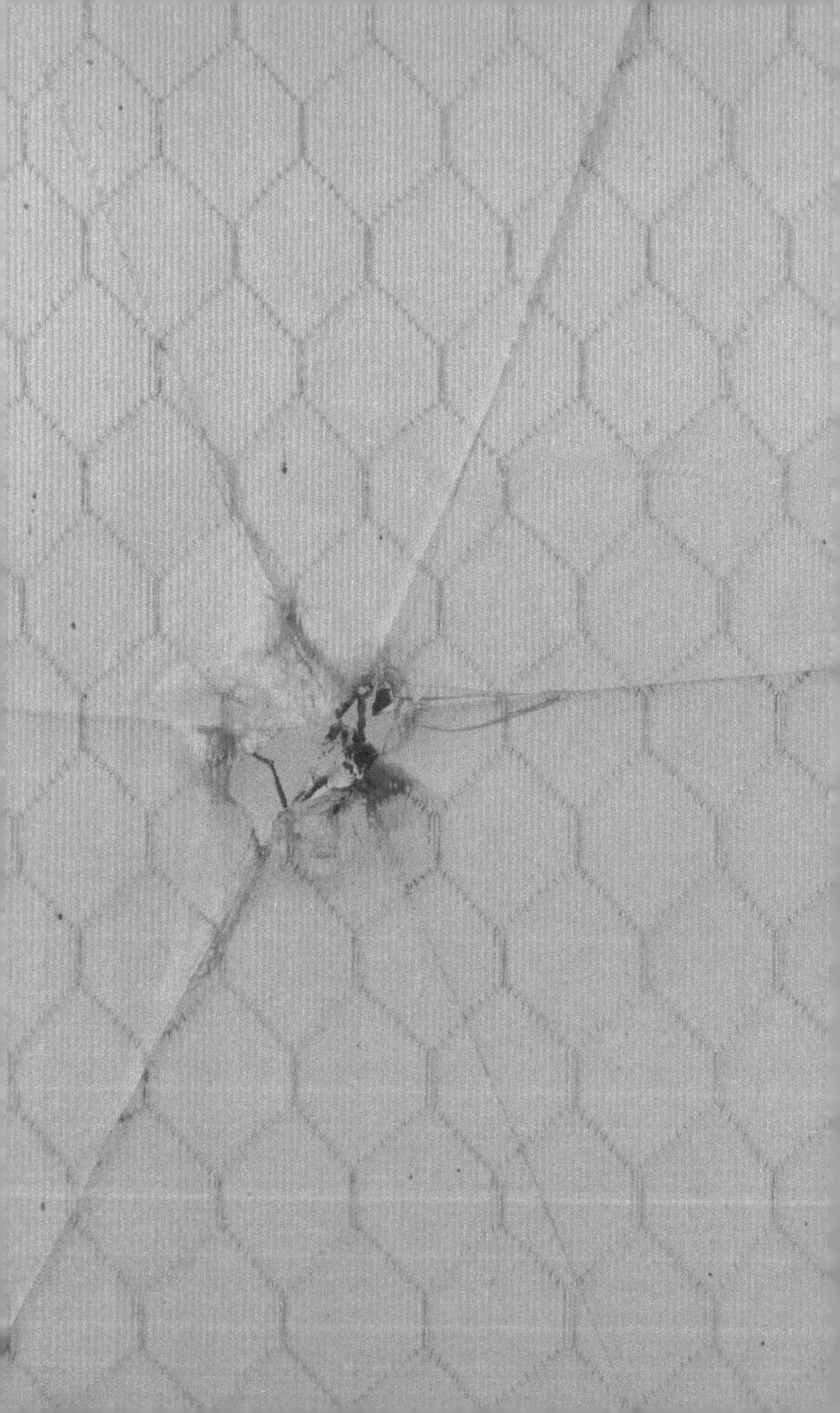

TWENTY-ONE

DEEP END

Deep End by Birdie

NELLIE

SCHOOL WAS NORMAL, just another day, but I didn't feel *normal.* I felt restless, so I drove. I drove to the place where I feel the most like myself without driving for hours to the cabin. It seemed like it took both forever and not long enough at the same time to get to Amelia Island, where I swam today. The pool wasn't going to cut it. I needed the ocean, so I took the hour drive. Neither the swim nor the drive were long enough to calm me down. Not long enough to forget about the fact that I'm hung up on Gus like a teenager, and I need to get over it or forgive him. So, I swam. I swam for about an hour, and now, I'm sitting on top of my beach towel, air drying but not ready to go home yet.

ME:

Facetime, anyone?

BEE:

Can't. Working late tonight. Sorry, boo.

VICTORIA:

Study hall for me. Sorry, Nells.

I miss them, and I feel like all my relationships are dwindling. I just saw Bee; we talk on the phone every day, but it's not the same. At work, I'm fighting hard to step out of Cara's shadow and stand on my own as more than Nellie, the genius child half the faculty taught years ago. Even my parents' diner feels off lately. I feel like the light inside me is slowly dimming, and I hate it.

Going swimming often helps, but today, everything just seems heightened by the weight of the world, my sadness, my anxiousness, and missing Gus. I do know something that will make me feel better: wine slushies and fries. I dry my body and slide the dress back on. I walk up to the beach restaurant with the swing by the bar. They serve wine slushies and the best sweet potato fries around. A beachy view, a swing, the salty breeze, carbs, and frozen wine. Instant mood booster.

I'm trying to relax and only pay attention to my own body rather than much around me. But every man I see, I have to do a double take to make sure it's not Gus. Every laugh I hear, I want to know if it's his. I'm losing my mind, clearly. I've had this ominous feeling all day. A sixth sense, of sorts. Nothing concrete. I can't even put my finger on it, but it's sitting heavy in my gut.

The warm air wraps around me as I walk through the tables in the outside area. The low hum of conversations mixes with the clink of glasses as the sun slowly dips toward the horizon, casting golden and purple hues over everything. My senses are going into overdrive. Laughter rises in bursts, making me move my head from table to table, noticing the different people in conversations. The smell of food and sea salt and the golden rays of the sun are capturing my attention too. It's beautiful and happy, and I feel like a rain cloud walking around. As the sun slides lower, the sky turns pink and lavender, I sit at the bar and wait for the bartender to take my order.

I use the time it takes for him to return with my slushie and food to ponder the kids at school. Cara always says that even if you leave the school behind, it doesn't leave you, and I couldn't agree more. I've only been doing this for a few weeks, but I think about the kids from my internship to this day. Bella's worries, Xavier's anger, Ana's struggles, and Cody's sadness and home life haunt my thoughts as I sip on my slushie and eat my sweet potato fries. At least it's them and not a certain handsome millionaire asshole who won't leave my brain.

An hour goes by, and the sun sets completely, but I had to stay to watch the moonrise and let the wine slushie work its way out of my system. One glass won't do anything, but I'm still hyper-aware of driving, even after just one glass. My rule of thumb is one glass of wine, thirty minutes and four glasses of water before I get behind the wheel. If I ever have more than one, I won't drive. Period. My parents were pretty serious about that growing up, and it stuck with me.

I pay for my bill and get up, ready to walk back to my car, but I need to use the restroom before the hour drive home. I try to walk fast so I can leave faster. At this hour, a lot of people here are dressed in more proper clothes than my tiny, damp dress over a bathing suit. But instead of passing by, I freeze in place when I see the table in front of me.

There's a couple sitting and talking. She's laughing at something he said, and he's shaking his head. She's wearing a teal shirt that makes the blue in her eyes pop, and he's wearing a collared shirt, framing his wide body. Pressure builds behind my eyes as I stare at them—at her fancy glass of wine and the water carefully placed in front of him. When he looks up and sees me, his smile falls.

Right in front of me, at a quiet corner table, looking hotter than sin, sits Gus Zabana, the blonde from the gala sitting directly across from him, smiling sexily at whatever he said. The girl notices his stare, so she turns to the side to see what's caught his attention. She waves and says something to Gus, who tries to get up, but I take a step back instantly. I turn around, trying to speed walk out the same way I came in, but I bump into a server, who drops everything on his tray.

"Oh my gosh, I'm so sorry," I say.

"It's okay," he replies, bending to pick up things from the ground. Nothing broken, but it's still a mess. "I got it, I got it," he adds when I try to help, so I stand and try to leave without making a bigger fool of myself.

"Nellie, wait," Gus whispers, holding my arm as I try to leave. I yank away from him and walk out without saying a word.

I step outside where it's less crowded, so when he shouts behind me, I can hear him loud and clear.

"Give me a minute, please."

"No," I shout back, walking faster. *I'm almost out of here. I'm almost to my car.*

"Let me explain," he shouts again, but this time, it sounds further back. Good. He's not following. Speed it up, Nellie. Speed it up.

I walk as fast as I can until I make it to my car. My phone is buzzing inside my purse, but I don't answer. I just get in my car and drive back home. It took him what? Three weeks? Was he always dating her? Maybe not dating, but fucking her? Clearly.

I drive all the way home in a slight rage. I didn't look at my phone once, so when I finally rinse off the salty water and slide into pjs, I have twelve missed calls from him and one text message.

DLS:

Let me explain.

Three words. Three words I don't want. I grab my phone and immediately reply, just in case whatever the fuck her name is sees it. I'm acting like an irrational, jealous girlfriend. Two of those are news to me, and one of those, I'm clearly not.

ME:

You don't owe me an explanation.

He tries to call, but I decline it. Nope, not talking to him.

DLS:

Stop being so fucking stubborn, Nellie, and answer the phone.

ME:

Don't yell at me.

DLS:

I'm texting, not yelling, and you're infuriating sometimes. Answer the phone.

Fucking hell. Okay. I answer the phone with a loud, "What?"

"Now who's yelling?" His voice carries from the other side of the phone, completely cool, calm, and collected. That pisses me off even more.

"What do you want, Gus?" If this man laughs, I will lose it.

"To explain what you think you saw, but I can guarantee, it's not what it looked like," he says, continuing with his *I don't give a fuck* demeanor.

"And what exactly do you think I thought?"

"That I was on a date with the girl I took to the auction." Pretty on point, I'm not going to lie. "And before you deny it, I know that's where your beautiful brain went. But Nellie, I'm not dating Blair."

"Of course her name is Blair," I mumble, rolling the eyes he can't see.

"I can basically feel you rolling your eyes, Nellie."

"I did not." Now I sound like a petulant child. This man brings out all the stupid emotions in me. All of them. I know this isn't helping. I know I'm showing zero self-control and maturity, the opposite of who I am, but I can't stop. He makes me feel everything more. Happier, angrier.

"Okay, sure." He lets out an exasperated breath. "Nellie… Blair is a business partner of sorts. Her family owns a company that works closely with mine. We have monthly meetings, and we like to meet at restaurants because it looks like we're working together, or like we're together with the public. Good PR. It's a win-win for both our companies. I'm not dating her. Never have and never will."

I stay silent, letting the words hang between us and absolutely hating every single one of them. Is that a rational explanation? Yes. Do I believe him? Yes. Am I still mad? Yes.

"And the reality is, Nellie, I've always had a hard time connecting with people. Not at the superficial, oh I'm friendly level, more at the hard to the core, I might love you forever level. It's always too hard. I'm the one ruining people, the one who can't love right. I thought I didn't know how, but honestly, I think I just didn't have it right. Not until you. So yes, please give me a chance. Give me a chance to show you I am capable of loving right."

"Say something," he says. When I don't, he continues, "Tell me what you want, Nellie. Do you want me on my knees? Do you want me crawling to you, begging? Pleading? Supplicating? I'm ready to do it all. Just please, say something."

"You want me to say something? How about a question… Was she the phone call you took when we were at the cabin?"

"No," he answers, quickly and without hesitation.

"Then who?" This time, the line goes silent, and he doesn't say anything at all.

"Then who, Gus? Who?"

He doesn't say anything. Shocker.

"You said you wanted to explain and to give you another chance just last night. So tell me…who?"

"I don't want to talk about this, not like this."

"You know what…actually, it's none of my business who you talk to anymore. It's none of my business what you do or don't do in your free time, Gus. We're not together, remember?"

"We need to talk about that. We could be, if you would've just called me back. We need to go somewhere so I can explain. Please."

"I'm done talking about it. I know where you stand, and I know where I stand. You want fun and casual, like your friend, Blair."

"Nellie, I already told you. It's not like that."

"And I said I don't care."

"God, woman. You're infuriating. Stop acting your age and listen for a second." Oh, he didn't.

"You know what, Gus? Maybe I do need to act my age for once in my life. What was it you said to me? Oh yeah: I have my whole life ahead of me. You're right. I'm too young and too hot for this back and forth. Goodbye, Gus."

I hang up the phone and park my car. There's zero thinking and all feeling today, especially as I numbly walk inside the house. Maybe that was too harsh and irrational, but damn it, I'm done with it all. I cry and cry until sleep takes over.

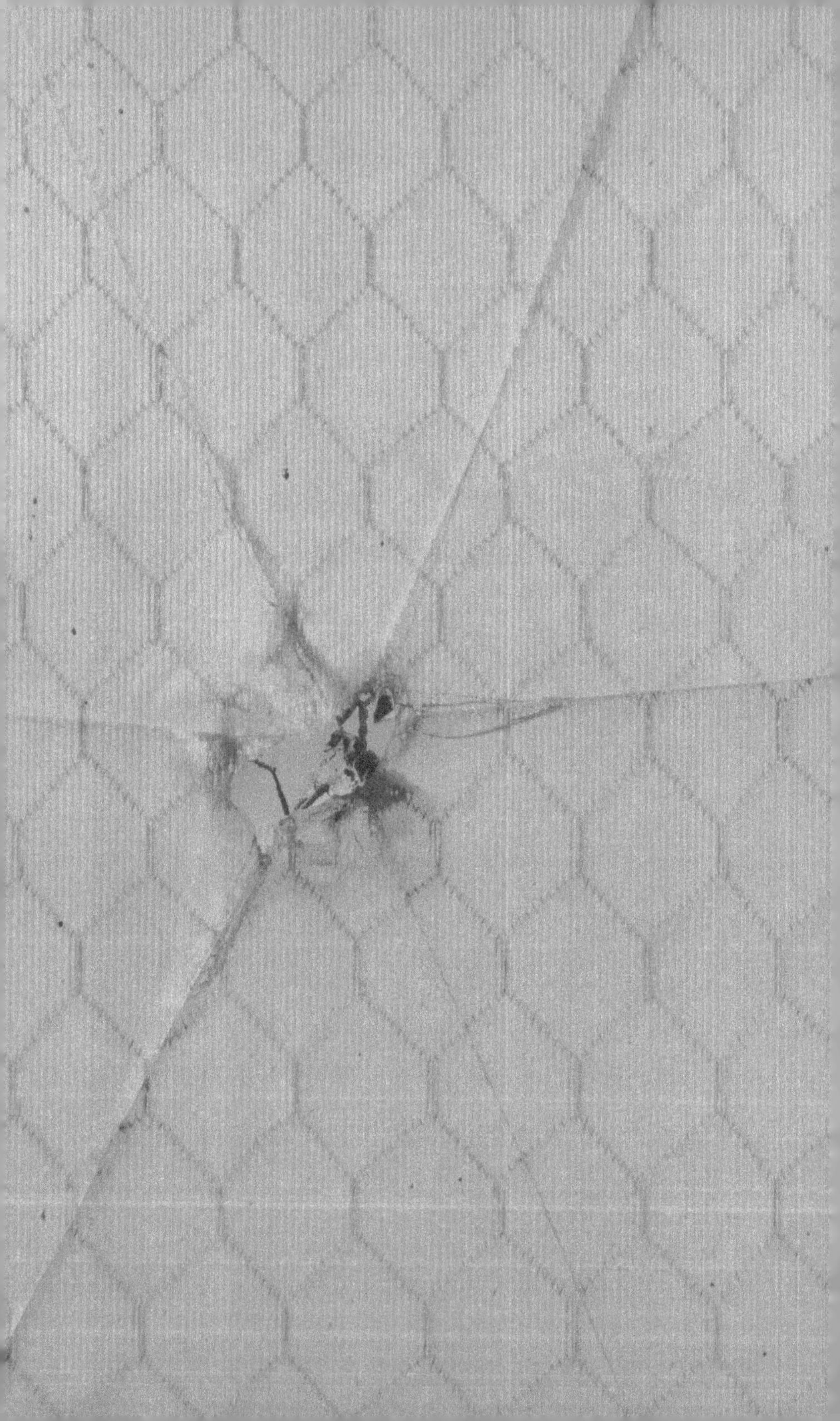

TWENTY-TWO

WHO WILL BE EVEN LEFT TO TELL?

Blowing Smoke by Gracie Abrams & Different Kind of Pain by Sam Barber

NELLIE

"WHAT HAPPENED TO YOU?" Bella asks as we walk together toward my office.

"Good morning to you too, Bella. Do you think that's an appropriate question to ask an adult?" I ask, sliding my sunglasses up to my hair and taking another sip of my coffee. There's not enough caffeine to carry me through the day. I didn't go to sleep at all last night. First, I was crying, and then, I was mad. Then, I was crying again. Eventually, I started deep-cleaning everything I could find, and before I knew it, it was 6:00 am.

The biggest downside of living with my parents is that they're nosy, always worrying about everything. Mom's concerned, and she said she'll call Cara today. I just really wish she wouldn't. What am I going to say? It's not like I can share with her why I'm so dysregulated. I just need to make it through this morning, and then I can sleep all afternoon.

"Sorry. You look like…you didn't rest at all." She's blushing, and now I feel like an asshole for making her feel embarrassed.

"It's okay. Thanks for your candor. I am tired. I didn't sleep well last night, but my job is to be here for you, not the other way around. How are you? Did you think about our conversation the other day?" I ask, stopping by my office, unlocking and propping the door open. I walk in and stay near the door, per school safety regulations, but leaving enough space that any other kid can walk in and grab a snack if needed.

"I needed a day to think it through, but I think I'm talking to them today. I help at my mom's store today, so we'll have time to chat, and then Dad takes us out to dinner on Thursdays, so that works too."

"I'm proud of you. It'll be great. Keep me posted, yeah?"

"I will," she replies, turning around and walking out of my office. She disappears into the hallway, mixing in with the other students seamlessly.

Cody walks in as usual, but today, just like yesterday and the day before, his head's low, and he doesn't say anything before he gets to the food area.

"Hey, Cody."

"Hi, Ms. Thompson," he replies with a hoarse voice. This is a little concerning now. Two days in a row without his usual bright personality.

"How are you, kiddo?" I ask, probing to see if he'd finally open up to me.

"Alive," he replies as he walks out before I can even process anything. The bell rings, and I let the door close behind me, walking to my desk and making notes of the interactions with him. Maybe I need to talk to the district psychologist who visits us weekly and see if there's anything else we can do. Or maybe I need to check his cumulative folder and see if there's any information I don't know about him. I don't like this change, and I don't like those answers.

That same ominous feeling I've had the past few days returns, this time more potent, and again, I can't put my finger on it. It feels like when my head is underwater for too long, right before I come up for air. It's unclear whether I need to breathe or not but knowing that waiting too long can be fatal. This feels like that, but without the sensation of when it's too much or too long or even why. No water in sight, just the drowning feeling.

I walk to the snack area and grab one of the messages. This one is…odd. Usually, these are silly or sweet, maybe even sad, but this one is just bizarre.

Maybe we're all walking in hell.

I bring the note to my desk, placing it inside my planner so I can think on it longer before deciding what to do. There's a knock on my door as soon as I sit down, and at the same time, I get a message. I know it's Gus.

DLS:

I hope you like it.

Like what, Gus? Like what?

I get up quickly and unlock the door.

"Hi!" I say to our school resource officer, who is holding a small bag on the other side.

"This was left for you in the front office."

"Thank you." I take the small white bag and the iced coffee from him and walk back to my desk. I set the coffee on the table, but not before reading the writing on the bag.

Stay out of trouble.

Unbelievable.

I open the bag and, like the other day, there's another note with a small box.

Hey Trouble,

I can't seem to figure this out. It feels like I take a step forward and three steps back. I'm guessing today, you're not tipsy, but pissed. I'm guessing you didn't sleep much last night, and I'm sorry for that. If it's any consolation prize, neither did I. I haven't been able to sleep in weeks. I miss you, and again, I'm sorry. I'm sorry I broke your trust so badly that even when the truth is there, it's hard for you to believe. I'm sorry I did this to us by keeping information from you. I want to tell you everything, but not like this. In the meantime, here's some iced coffee, just how you like it, and a little something that made me think of you.

Con cariño,

Your DLS (hoping to be more than this, though)

PS: They have the same thing with diamonds if you prefer. I'm happy to get you another one, but I figured you didn't want anything flashy.

I OPEN the small box and find a delicate necklace with a small wave pendant in the middle. It's a beautiful, dainty, white gold necklace with a wave that matches my tattoo. I grab it and turn it around to inspect it. There are letters written on the back: "With The Waves."

Does he think he's going to buy me with gifts and coffee? Does he think he can send me treats and apologies, and I'll be able to just, what? Forgive him? *He just wants to talk to you.* Damn you, voice in my head. I'm so irritated, I just want to go home. I look at the clock, and it's only been thirty minutes since school started. Today's gonna be a long day.

SIS:

Are you coming to book club tonight?

CARA'S TEXT COMES THROUGH, and I want to scream as soon as I get it. I forgot about the damn book club, but I promised her and myself I was going to be more social. I still don't have friends here, so I might as well start building stronger relationships with hers. So much for not living in her shadow anymore.

ME:

Yes. What should I bring?

SIS:

Take an Uber and I'll drive you home. Natalie's bringing wine, and since she can't drink, she says it gives her joy seeing others do so.

ME:

I can't drink a lot on a school night. Not again, at least.

SIS:

You won't be able to stop after you taste the first sip. I promise.

ME:

Fine. See you at seven.

We read *Bright Side* by Kim Holden for book club, and I'm in between being in love and completely heartbroken by it. It's such a beautiful story in the most heart-wrenching way. I can't wait to hear everyone's thoughts.

The bell rings, announcing the end of the day, and I immediately let out a breath. I've made it another day. Another day, I've managed to do this job and hopefully not mess anyone's life up. If I hurry and wrap this up quickly, I'll be able to head home and take a nap in the hopes of appearing more human tonight. Nobody comes to get a snack or write messages.

I finish gathering my things and walk to the bowl of messages students have left. Today's reads:

I hope I get to play football this season.

That must be Thomas. He's a goofy seventh grader who walks around like he owns the school but then sits on the bean bag chair and tells me all about how he wants to make his parents proud and that his dad was a football player. I've been meaning to ask Jake and Nick, Bella's dad, to give a pep talk to some of the middle schoolers who are not necessarily playing a lot right now and have barely made it through practices.

The one from earlier was on a light green piece of paper. I wonder if there are more. How didn't I think about it earlier? I could've done this a lot sooner, but the fog in my brain from being tired isn't helping.

I pour the contents of the bowl onto the table and take out all the ones written on the same green paper. There are eight total, two of which have nothing to do with the rest. They're random thoughts, silly. The rest, though? Same handwriting, same feelings, probably same kid.

Who will believe me if I tell?
If there's a heaven, who even goes there?
Those were the cards dealt without any luck or grace.
Who will be left to tell?
Stuck in this hole where nothing feels swell.
Stuck in this mess, lost in this space.

Clearly, whoever is writing these feels lost, but is there a reason for these? Do they seem odd? Sad for sure, but all middle schoolers are sad in one way or another. I leave all the notes on my desk and write myself a sticky note to make a list of my repeat students, the ones that linger and stay here for longer. Maybe one of them is writing these.

I make a mental note about it as I walk through the hallways, trying to get out of this place. Ben is walking ahead of me, but he catches a glimpse that I'm behind him and smiles at me.

"Any plans today?" Ben asks, pushing the double doors open for me and letting me walk in front of him.

"Actually, yes. I usually just swim after school, but today, I have book club."

"Well, I was wondering if maybe I could take you out for dinner once. It doesn't have to be anything super formal, or even tonight, but wanted to throw it out there. Just two people getting to know each other better over food."

I fidget with the ring on my thumb as I look down at his feet. Did I misread this situation? Did I somehow miss that he's trying to ask me out?

"Oh." I wish I could say yes to this sweet man. He seems like the type who would communicate and not keep shit from me, unlike Gus. Unfortunately, I don't want this guy. I want Gus, and it wouldn't be fair to Ben.

"I'm sorry, I…" I, what? I have a boyfriend? That's not true. I have a complicated relationship. Also no. I'm in love with someone else? That's the one, but how am I ever going to get over him if I don't try? I can't, though, for Ben's sake. I can't.

"I can't, Ben. It's sweet of you to ask, though. It's not you—"

"It's *you*, right? I've heard it before."

"Actually, it's not me either. It's my heart that's unavailable. I'm sorry."

"Oh? Oh! I understand. The heart wants what the heart wants. See you around, Ms. Thompson."

"IF YOU DIDN'T CRY, you're dead inside," I tell Roe, who keeps shaking her head no when everyone else is talking about how much this book affected them.

"I am dead inside, actually. I loved the book, don't get me wrong. It was sad too, but like…I still didn't cry," she replies, shrugging her shoulders.

"Well, I couldn't stop crying. Jake thought something had happened. This might be my new favorite book of all time," Allie says, and everyone else nods.

"I'm so glad you all loved it," Natalie states, hugging her arms around her chest and smiling fondly at all of us. "Nellie, since you're new to us, you get to pick the next book."

No pressure. No pressure at all. I just joined this book club for this month's discussion, so I'm not sure what all they've read. I know they prefer romance, but would they read anything else? I love romance, but if they're all avid and ferocious romance readers like both Allie and Cara, the chances they've already read something I suggest are high.

"Has anyone read *Seven Days in June* by Tia Williams or *Heathen and Honeysuckle* by Sarah A. Bailey?" I ask, and everyone shakes their head except for Allie.

"What? I love second-chance romance, so I will always try to hunt those down. Give me an emotional second chance with a dual timeline, and I want them all. I'm happy to talk about it, though. It doesn't have to be an issue just because I read it," Allie says.

"Maybe we can do *Seven Days in June* first and then *Heathen and Honeysuckle*?

"If anyone has an issue with that, raise your hand," Cara

says, and when nobody does, she declares, "Alright, *Seven Days in June* it is."

I smile fondly—maybe because of the friendship I see forming here already, or maybe because of the four glasses of wine I've had tonight.

"Are you and Manny moving in together?" Livie, another one of Cara's friends, asks her, and when my sister's eyes open wide, I giggle.

"What makes you say that?" Cara asks. We all laugh. Cara is the only person who still thinks we don't know how down bad Manny is for her and how much *she* loves him too.

"Is he or is he not at your house right now, waiting for you?" Allie asks through a smile, her lips on her glass. Cara wasn't lying when she said we would not be able to stop drinking the wine. I'm so glad that for once, I listened to my sister and didn't drive here. Because of it, I've been able to enjoy every second.

"Yes, he is, but just because the puppy needs company."

"How often does he sleep over?" Allie asks again. I love that she's not holding anything back. She's just one hundred percent messing with Cara. We all know Manny stays over there all the time, it's just a matter of them pulling the trigger. I stay quiet, because every time I hear Manny's name, I think of Gus, and rage engulfs me whole.

"I mean…often, but it just makes sense," Cara adds again.

"Are all the men hanging out at *your* house with Manny for boy's night or whatever they want to call it?" Allie asks again, and Cara nods, rolling her eyes.

"I think you should just stop acting like you don't want him to move in with you and just do it. It'll be easier on both of you, cheaper too," Roe adds at the same time the doorbell rings.

"Oop, time to go," Cara says, changing the topic and starting to gather her things. The boys were all hanging out together, according to Cara, and by boys I mean, Cara's boyfriend, Livie's husband, Natalie's husband, Allie's fiancé, and Roe's partner. I have no man to add to the combo. I'm just here for the book chats and the wine, single as ever. We all say goodbye to Natalie before walking to the door to be greeted by the boys. I smile as I see their faces, but then, another familiar face shows up next to Manny. Same height, same smile, same eyes, but darker skin and shorter hair, plus a dimple I never noticed until a few months ago, when we started fooling around and I started falling for him. Gus stands next to his twin brother, Manny looking as smug as ever. Fuck my life.

"Gusti!" Allie shouts, walking past everyone to hug her little brother. I'm always happy to see how strong their sibling relationships are. Cara and I are close, but because we're eight years apart, it's hard for us to share the type of bond the twins and Allie share at only two. She genuinely looks happy to see her brother, unlike me. All I want to do is smack him over the head. Yell at him. Kill him slowly. Maybe kiss him. He might be talking to his sister, but every few seconds, his eyes briefly meet mine. I narrow my eyes, but it doesn't stop him from doing the same thing over and over again.

"All the girls are here, and Nellie joined us today too. Isn't she so grown up now?" Allie asks.

"Oh yeah, that she is," Gus replies, walking my way and kissing my cheek. "Hola, Nellie," he whispers. I wish I could hide the goosebumps that crawl up my back or the way my knees weaken at the smell of his cologne. Him being so close makes me want to squirm.

"Hi!" My voice sounds lively, like I'm trying overly hard to say the words, but if anyone notices, they hide it well. Everyone is too focused on their own love lives with light in their eyes to notice the way mine leaves my eyes the minute Gus is around. Once he brought it to life; now, he just let it die. "I'm sorry to rain on your parade, but it's a school night, and I really have to go."

"Oh, no problem. Let's go," Cara says to Manny, who kisses her forehead and guides her out to his car.

"I can take Nellie home. It makes sense, since I just have to drive home, and all of you have work tomorrow," Gus says nonchalantly.

"No!" I spit back quicker than I can stop myself. All eyes are on me instantly, so I probably have three seconds to come up with a reply.

"It's not a big deal, really," Gus says, smoothing over my outburst.

"Are you sure? Cara and Manny can take me." Please dear lord, let this man read between the lines.

"It's no problem. Come on." Why is he even here? Did they all just drive separate cars? Well, Allie and Cara live a couple of blocks away from each other, so maybe that's why only Manny's here. I live on the other side of town, so it does make sense for someone else to drive me, and Roe lives closer to the forest area. Baker Oaks is small, but because each house has acreage, it feels bigger. Cara just bought a house in the same neighborhood as Allie.

"Bye, see you guys soon!" I wave. My hand is a little unsteady as I follow Gus to his car. The Barracuda. His *special occasion car*.

I stumble slightly, still feeling the buzz from way too many glasses of peach wine, and Gus grabs my arm before I can make a bigger fool of myself.

"Easy there, Trouble."

I mutter, "Stop it," and reach for his arm so I don't lose my footing. "What's wrong with you? Why are you even here?" I can barely get the words out, the alcohol muddling my thoughts. He opens the door for me and helps me slide in.

"I will never stop," Gus whispers as he fastens my seat belt with a snap, his fingers brushing my skin and awakening all my senses. Then, he circles the car and slides into the driver's seat, glancing over at me with that damn smile.

I roll my eyes, feeling the weight of his grin. "There are zero reasons for you to be smiling at me."

His smile only widens. "I can think of at least one. The most important one."

"What?"

He smiles again before he says, "I finally have your attention." He winks at me, shifts the car into drive, and pulls out of Natalie's driveway. "Maybe this is the only way you'd actually talk to me."

"Nope, I don't have to talk to you. You can talk, but I don't have to reply. I can just sit here quietly and wait for you to drive me home. It's late, remember?"

"It's ten o'clock. You'll be fine."

"Unlike you, Mr. Rich Man, Forbes thirty under thirty most eligible bachelor ever, I have to go to work tomorrow."

He scoffs as he changes the music and plays an old song I can't put my finger on. "Ten is not that late. We have time to talk."

"Was this your goal all along? Get me alone so you can use secrets and lies to, what? Try to fuck me again?" Maybe the middle schoolers are getting to me, because what the hell was that? I'm twenty-one years old, damn it, not twelve. How do I go from chill to infuriating with this man?

"No, Nellie. Jesus. Get you alone so I can finally explain things. You don't have to reply, but you will listen."

There's no point in fighting him over this. There's nowhere for me to go, nothing for me to do other than sit here and listen to whatever bullshit he's going to tell me. I'm actually a little curious to see what he has to say, since I've been avoiding him or snapping at him at every turn. "Fine, go ahead. Explain."

Part of me expects him to go straight to the girl situation, or at the very least mention it, but the words out of his mouth surprise me more than a lot of things have this year.

"Do you know why I took a step back from my company,

even if it meant delegating a bunch of things?" I don't reply. I don't think he actually wants me to. I think it's more of him explaining whatever it is he's trying to explain.

"Manny and I created this company from the ground up, and it picked up fast, faster than I ever would've anticipated. We worked day and night. All the time. We thought, ate, and slept Zabana Enterprises, and it worked in our favor, considering what the company is now. We both had our ulterior motives for making it work, but mine was so I could make my dad proud. Manny was always patient and kind growing up, so our dad always encouraged me to take the lead on things, and that translated to work. Manny worked hard, harder than me even, but I could produce the same output with half the effort some days. It's not fair, but it's the way it was. We grew up in an environment where our worth was measured by production, so the more we produced, the better. The company was doing great, but I wasn't, and I was terrified to tell anyone, so I hid it. Just like I hid how serious my health conditions are from you at first."

He pulls into my driveway, but instead of driving all the way to the house, he kills the engine and turns off the lights. "I know it sucked that I kept it from you, but Nellie, I don't think you understand how I grew up. My dad...well, he's great with my mom, but he saw illness as a weakness. He sees productivity as power and nothing else. If you cry, complain, or show any sort of what he deems a weakness, it's like you don't exist. All three of us have the definition of daddy issues in one way or another. That's why I don't like being called Augusto—that's his name. I don't want to be anything like him. I don't even realize when I keep things from the people I love. It comes so naturally to me, it's become my automatic response. Everyone thinks I'm an oversharer because I'm funny or whatever, but in reality, I just mask it all. I'm telling you this because I realized how much I fucked up by keeping not only that, but other shit from you. I know you value honesty, and I wish I could say I've been honest with you the entire time, but I haven't. I haven't lied, I just haven't given you everything."

He said *love*. He said people I love. Do I bring it up? Do I ignore it? Did he mean it? I'd rather not. I will just stay in my lane and pretend that was a Freudian slip.

"Your worth goes beyond the amount of money you make." Tears threaten to fall at his confession. Why is this sweet and kind man so afraid of sharing his *faults*, even if they're really not faults at all? It's not like he wanted to get sick or get his condition or whatever. It's sad his dad thinks of him this way.

"I know that, which is why when I had my second big flare up, one that sent me to the ER and kept me hospitalized for weeks, I decided I was simply going to stop. My job was killing me, and I wouldn't rest, so my body made me. My body was talking to me, and it found a way to make me listen. My body made me rest, but it's still hard for me to show others that side of me…and Nellie, you're so young. *Too* young to be dealing with all my medical bullshit."

"You don't get to make the decision for me. I *told* you I wanted to share the load. I *told* you I could handle it. I *showed* you how strong I can be, but you kept me in the dark again. It's not fair that you took the choice away from me. I wanted you. I *want* you, but you took the choice away from me again. You left me in the dark, *again*. I care about you not despite your health issues, but because of everything you are. Everything that makes you, you. Health concerns included. You showed me pieces of you, but only enough to, what? Make me feel like it wasn't all one-sided when, in reality, it has been, right?"

He stays quiet, just looking at me and blinking slowly, his gorgeous long eyelashes framing his dark as night eyes.

"Was it?" I ask. Time passes both too quickly and too slowly, but eventually, he shakes his head.

"No, Nellie. It's not one-sided." His hand comes up to caress my cheek, but I pull back involuntarily.

"What about the blonde? Was that all the truth?" I ask, taking advantage of this moment and how he's opening up to me.

"I told you the truth about Blair. We're just friends. Colleagues, if you will. She's flirty, though, so it makes it look like what it's not."

"Okay," I whisper. Maybe whatever he's keeping from me is something serious, and he just needs time. But why won't he tell me? Why won't he trust me?

"Okay, what? Are you giving me another chance?"

"No, I think we just need to stop. This, whatever this is, is toxic and unhealthy, and I can't." I can't take this again. I can't take the up and down and back and forth, all pushing with a little pulling. I just can't

"Toxic? The way I can't think about anyone else but you? No. Unhealthy? My obsession with you, yes."

"You can't say things like this." I get out of the car, putting physical space between us, since all my body wants to do is melt into his.

"You want me to be honest? This is honesty." He follows me with the car, shouting, "What do you want me to do? How can I show you I know I fucked up? How can I show you I'm ready for more?"

"You're going to wake my parents up," I snap at him, turning around and seeing his grin. Stupid, handsome jerk.

"Good. Then I can tell them how gone I am for their girl."

"No, you don't get to say that either." It's so damn unfair. It's not fair when he's saying all the right things and looks like that.

"You asked me to make up my mind, Nellie, and I did. I don't want a life without you. I don't. I want you. We are end game, and even if it takes me showing you every day for a month, a year, a decade, I will. I don't care. I will show you, one gesture at a time. Life is full of little moments; that's what you said, right? I want to give you a million little more, even if they're all accompanied by coffee dropped at your front office. Please, just talk to me."

"Fine! Talk."

"Not like this. Let's meet tomorrow after school, please. I can even pick you up."

I stand in front of his flashy nice car and look around, as if I'm waiting for the other shoe to drop.

"Fine. Tomorrow."

"Tomorrow," he whispers with a soft smile.

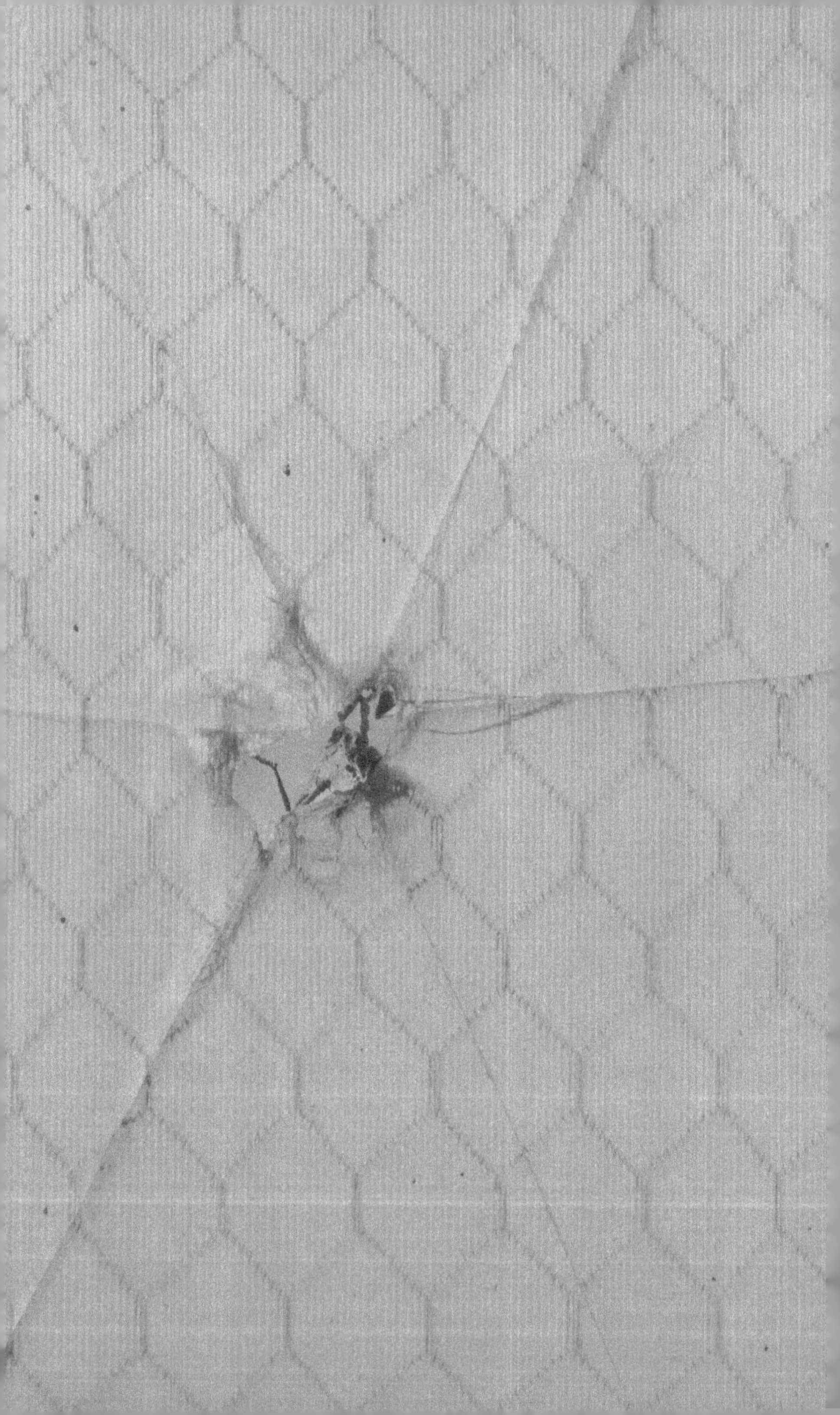

TWENTY-THREE
GUT FEELING

Shake it Out by Glee Cast & I Know The End by Phoebe Bridgers

NELLIE

DAY four of waking up regretting my choices from the day before—coffee in hand, sitting on my office couch, and thoughts swirling in my head. I wish I could just erase that man from my thoughts. I can't keep up with the back and forth and my erratic emotions all over the place. He couldn't make up his mind, but now he has? *I was scared, Nellie.* But what if he truly is scared, and that's why he pushes me away? What if that's what's been going on all along?

All I can think about is Gus and how he makes me feel alive. How he makes all the colors brighter. How he holds space for me. How he makes me feel safe. *I was scared, Nellie…*

Oh my God.

Oh my God.

Nellie, you clueless, clueless girl. If I just stopped being overly emotional and reactive over things for a second, I would have noticed everything he was communicating with me. I thought he wasn't telling me things, when in reality, he has been saying so much with his actions. He thinks in songs and communicates with deeds. The trips, the space, the rings. The physical input I've needed. The way he has made me feel. *Safe.* He has made me feel safe, and he was just scared. What happened, Gus? Why are you scared?

Please, let me talk.

Not like this. I want to tell you.

Please let me explain.

God, I'm so stupid. If I would just have stopped and listened. What else has he shown me with actions and not words? The car? The songs? Has he been communicating through music too? Through time spent with me? He's given me so much, and I have, what? Freaked out and not even let him talk?

What changed, Gus? What happened? I need to call him. I need to talk to him. He said after school today, so maybe I just need to wait and give him this one thing he asked for. A chance to explain.

The feeling comes back, that nagging sense that something's wrong, something's off. I finish my coffee in silence, hoping the taste of comfort will bring me some clarity to what this feeling is. Maybe it has been looming over me because, deep down, I know something is going on with Gus.

Maybe that's not all. I can't put my finger on why I feel like that, but it does. I set my food and bag on my desk and plop myself into the plushie chair I use by my desk. I keep the cup between my hands, as it warms my fingers and keeps me centered on the moment.

There's a faint knock on my door, which is odd, considering first period already started. I set my coffee down and open the door. On the other side stands Cody, his usually bright face drained of color. He's trembling, his hand clutching the door frame as though he might collapse any second. His large frame looks smaller than ever, and his eyes are heavy with something I can't quite describe.

"Cody?" I ask, as if I don't know exactly who he is. He looks so sad. So distraught. So shaken.

He walks in, closes the door behind him, and stands there, frozen for a moment. And then it comes—his voice, small, shaking, unsure. "I…I didn't have breakfast."

Okay? I mean, I have food here, but the school also offers breakfast. "It's okay. You know you can always find food here."

He still stands, unmoving. This is more than just missing breakfast. His eyes stare into space, glossing over and unblinking. He's here, but his mind is definitely someplace else.

"Cody, honey, do you need to talk?"

He keeps looking past me, as if I'm not here. My heart skips a beat. *Something's wrong.* "And my parents…they were screaming at each other again."

Oh, sweet boy. We've talked almost every day for weeks, and this is the first time he mentioned his parents. "I'm sorry. How can I help?" I keep my distance but step aside in case he wants to come in and sit down, but he doesn't.

"They screamed all night, so we didn't sleep. We didn't eat dinner. Plates were shattered all night. We didn't sleep." Okay, but this is more than just parents arguing. He's making no sense. I try to grab my journal from the table so I can take notes, but his eyes snap to it, and he takes a step back. Okay, got it. No writing. He waits. He takes a deep breath and finally raises his eyes to look at me. His pretty eyes look tormented right now.

"My brother dropped me off at school today, but he seemed, I don't know, *off*. He didn't sleep either. He didn't eat. Do you think he has a Ms. Thompson at the high school who can feed him?"

My heart. "School will have breakfast for him." It's the

only thing I can think of saying right now. I can feel tears reaching my eyes, but I can't let them out now. Now, I get to be strong for him and ask questions so I understand what's going on, so he can keep sharing.

"Off? You said your brother was off. What do you mean by that?" I lean forward, my heart catching in my chest.

He nods, eyes wide with something I can't quite place. "Yeah. Distant. Like he wasn't even there, you know? He was hugging his backpack like…like it was all he had left. Even between him and the steering wheel." His voice cracks slightly, but he quickly pushes past it, eyes on the floor. "He was hitting the steering wheel and saying weird things." He shakes his head and continues, "He said weird things. All I could hear was him mumbling and then screaming *I want it all to stop. I just want it all to stop.*"

I take a slow, steady breath, grounding myself before speaking. Cody's voice is small, but the weight of his words is anything but.

I lower my voice, keeping it soft. "Cody, I hear you. I'm really glad you're telling me this."

His fingers twitch, clenching into fists before relaxing again. He nods, but his eyes stay locked on the floor. He walks in and plops on the couch, closing his eyes and shaking his head again.

"Can you tell me more about what your brother was saying?" I ask gently.

Cody swallows hard. "I don't know. It was—he kept saying stuff like 'it doesn't matter,' 'they don't even care', and 'it's too late.'" He finally looks up at me, his eyes glistening. "And he kept gripping his backpack like…like he needed it to breathe."

My stomach twists. This isn't just about a rough morning or an argument at home. This is something else.

"Cody," I say carefully, "I think we should check on your brother. Can we do that together?"

He hesitates. "He-he wouldn't like that."

"I understand," I say, nodding. "But I just want to make sure he's okay. We don't have to do this alone. How old is he?"

"Sixteen."

"Does he go to Baker High?" I ask, and he nods.

Cody's breathing is uneven now, his small shoulders rising and falling too quickly. I lean forward slightly, keeping my tone steady. "Listen to me, Cody. You don't have to carry this by yourself. I can help."

He wipes at his nose, sniffling. "What if he's mad?"

"Then we'll handle that together," I promise. "Right now, the most important thing is making sure he's safe."

A long, shaky pause. Then, finally, a nod.

"Okay," he whispers.

I exhale slowly, already reaching for my phone. "Does he have a cellphone?" The high school doesn't have a phone-free policy. Students are allowed to carry their phones to class as long as they don't text or call during it. Middle school is different, so I'm happy to use my phone with my Telzio extension—a program to make calls to protect our phone numbers. He nods, giving me his brother's phone number, and I immediately call. The phone rings, but nobody picks up. I smile at Cody, reassuring him, but his brother doesn't answer.

"Hey—" I realize I don't even know this kid's name "—it's Ms. Thompson, the school counselor at Baker Middle. I have Cody in my office. He's okay but wanted to check on you. Give me a call back when you can." I hang up after leaving a voice message and get Cody a water and a granola bar. He grabs them both from me without uttering another word. I don't want to press or push, but I really need to find more information. My head is killing me—time for another sip of the coffee I left untouched on top of my desk. I walk to grab it before getting back to the couch area where Cody waits.

"My sister's best friend works at the high school, and I'm pretty sure he's a coach. Your brother plays football like you, right?" He nods but doesn't say anything else. "Can I text her to get his phone number, and maybe just give him a heads up to check on him?" He nods again, so I get my phone out and text Cara.

ME:

Hey Care, do you have Jake or Nick's number? I have a kiddo in my office worried about his brother at the high school.

SIS:

Shared Contact.

Shared Contact.

SIS:

Here you go. All good?

ME:

With me? Yeah. Him? Not sure. I'll text you later.

SIS:

<3

I look up from my phone, and Cody's not shaking anymore. He's just sitting without moving an inch, waiting. Waiting for what? For me to say something, or for his brother to call back?

I sit across from him and study him. His shoulders are slouched, and he's looking between his feet. There's so much sorrow in his posture, so much sadness.

"Is there anything you'd like to report, Cody?" I ask gently, keeping my voice steady despite the unease twisting inside me. I need him to feel safe here, but my gut is telling me this is more than just a bad morning. My gut is telling me there's more going on.

"I don't want to get him in trouble," he whispers, his face strained with the weight of his words. I can hear the guilt in his tone, the fear of speaking up.

"Why would he be in trouble? Who would he be in trouble with?"

"They take it out on him."

"Who, sweetie? Who takes it out on who?"

Before he can respond, the bell rings, sharp, cutting through the tension like a knife. Cody stands, wiping his face quickly, and moves toward the door.

"I'll be okay," he mutters, his voice barely above a whisper. He fumbles getting his backpack and opening the door, but he's so fast, I can't stop him.

"No, Cody, wait." He doesn't listen to me and leaves without another word, the door clicking shut behind him.

I sit back in my chair, the ominous feeling still clinging to me. What was that? I can't shake it. Something's wrong. No amount of training preps you for this moment. What do I do? He's clearly shaken. He's clearly upset, but he didn't say anyone hurt him. He was just worried about his brother. He is upset, so maybe his brother was just upset too. *They take it out on him.* Who? Who? I don't even know the kid's name. I can't even text Jake or Nick because what do I even say?

Should I report this? But report what? Hi, a student said his brother felt off, and his parents were screaming this morning. Is that grounds for a report? That's not technically abuse, right? All the training we go through with scenarios, laws, words for us to identify, and so much more doesn't really prepare you for when you're faced with a real-life scenario, when you're faced with some grey areas. Check this, check that. Active assailant, abuse, neglect, force, code yellow, lockdown, school shooting, locked doors, suicide, risk of harm—all words you hear in training, but nowhere does it prepare you for the ambiguity. Real life is not a checklist of situations; it's a case-by-case scenario.

I rub my temples, trying to push away the unease that settled deep in my chest. Maybe I'm overthinking it, and the headache doesn't help. Maybe it's just a bad morning, a rough patch in their family. God knows plenty of kids walk in here every day with baggage they'll never unpack in front of a teacher. But something about the way Cody said it, the way his voice barely held together—I'll be okay.

I glance at the door, half-expecting him to walk back in. He doesn't.

What if I do report it, and it's nothing? It shouldn't matter, though; by law, I have to, even if just for a wellness check. I don't even know the kid's last name. Oh, duh, Nellie. I can go look at his cumulative folder and see his family history. Maybe I should start there. This. I can focus on what I can do and go from there.

I pace until my thoughts are so jumbled, I can't think straight. The brother doesn't call back. Cody doesn't come back in. I might get sick. I walk to the front office so I can find his folder in the records. I don't want to break his trust, but what if something is seriously wrong? What if they hurt them, and Cody didn't tell me? What if they take food away from them? What if they hurt the brother and not Cody, but he somehow knows?

This is more than I can handle. I need to report this. If I'm worrying about them taking food away from them, then that's neglect. Textbook neglect. *That*, I have to report. Cody might hate me, but I would hate myself if something happened and I didn't say something. Where is the line between guiding the youth and helping them? Where is the line drawn between me listening and just worrying or raising a caution flag?

I knock on Principal Davis' office door. No response. So, I sink into the same chairs I sat in so many times as a student, treading water in the silence. I used to sit here, waiting for someone to pull me to shore—waiting when I was sent to advanced classes, when I picked at my scabs until I bled, when the waves of school life became too much, when I needed someone to notice I was drifting, waiting for someone to see me before I went under.

I promised myself I would never let a child drown in the depths of feeling unseen. I swore I would be the one to throw a lifeline. So why did it take me half a day to act on Cody? To say something? Had I missed the ripples, the small signs of struggle? Had he been struggling just beneath the surface while I, oblivious, let him slip away? And for how long? We've been in school for weeks now, and I never saw it. He's just quiet, I told myself. He looks happy. *But so did I, and nobody saw me either.* What if he has been suffering all along?

The soft hum of the office copier is the only sound as I wait for the principal to get back. I can see Ms. Laura in the front, typing away as usual as I wait in the freezing waiting area. The fluorescent lights buzz faintly overhead as I ponder my life choices, from every single decision I've made this school year to how rough I've been treating my body with the amount of wine I've ingested the past few days.

A loud beep shatters the quiet, and I all but jump in my seat. The Raptor system notification flashes across the computer screens and across the watch I always wear on my right wrist. "CODE RED – LOCKDOWN IN EFFECT. IMMEDIATE THREAT DETECTED."

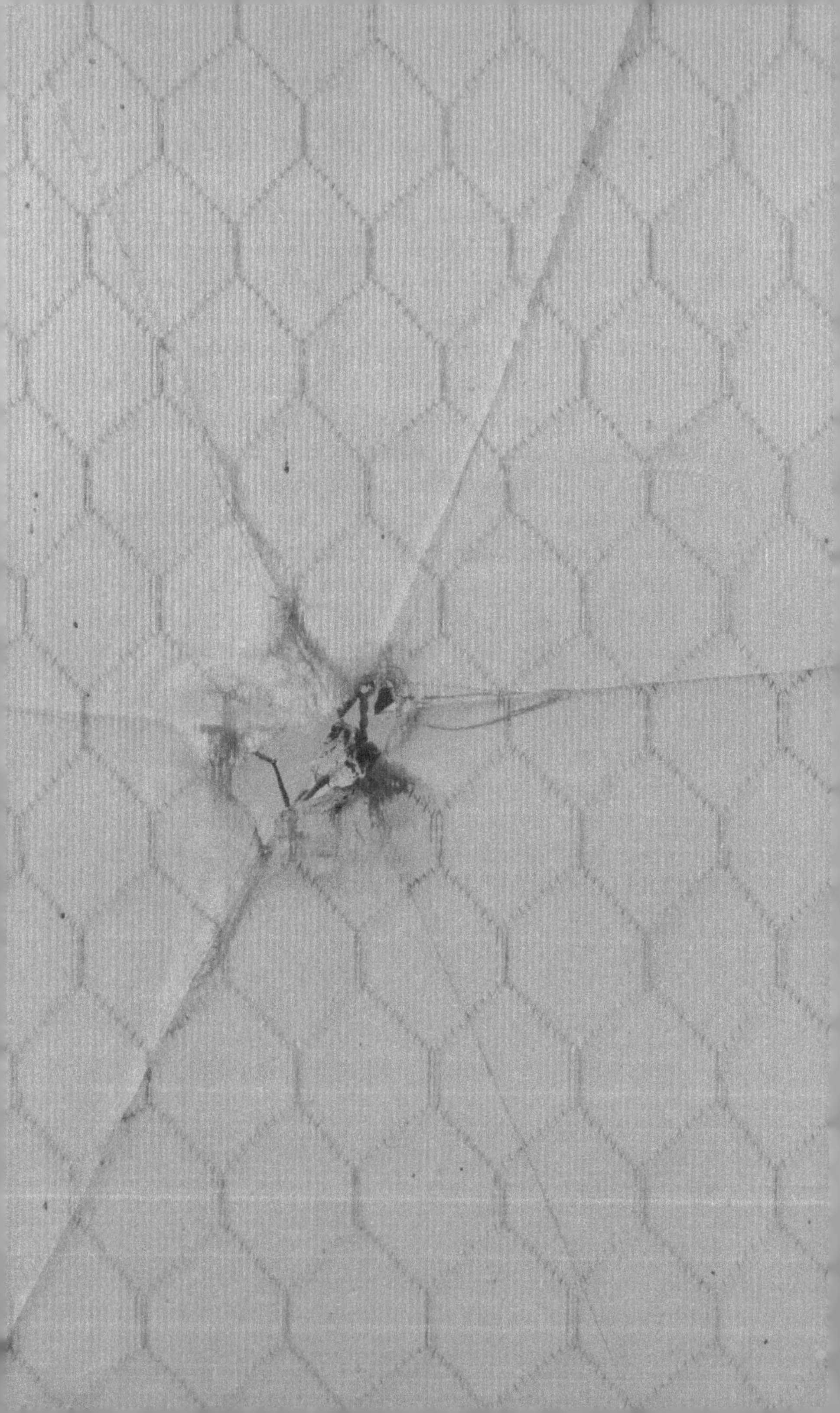

TWENTY-FOUR

RED

Mad World by Pentatonix; Everybody Hurts by Glee Cast; Already Gone by Sleeping At Last

NELLIE

"CODE RED – LOCKDOWN IN EFFECT. IMMEDIATE THREAT DETECTED."

My stomach drops. What the fuck? My breath catches in my throat. This isn't happening. This isn't happening.

From my spot near the front desk, I see Ms. Laura freeze for a second but then quickly retreat from her desk and walk inside, her walkie-talkie in one hand and her phone in the other. She reaches for the landline, her fingers shaking as she dials. She says something, but I can't hear what. I just see her lips moving, her eyes tearing up, and her head bobbing up and down as she listens attentively to instructions.

Outside the glass doors of the main office, the hallways empty in seconds. Teachers pull students into classrooms, doors slamming shut, and the curtains behind them get pulled down. The panic is there just for a moment before everyone goes into action. Then there's me, standing here, not remembering any of my training.

"Nellie, honey, come on," Ms. Laura whispers, holding my hand and walking me to the teacher lounge next to the principal's office, where she shoves me inside and closes the door behind us. "Do you have your phone? There was a message sent on Raptor."

"It's in my office. What's going on?" I ask. If I didn't know I was actually moving my lips and replying to her, I wouldn't recognize the sad, fragile voice that just came out.

"There's a threat at Baker High, not here. However, we don't have a lot of information other than the police are en route there, and considering we're less than two miles from each other, we had to go on lock down too. Are you okay, though?"

Okay? Who could ever be okay during a lockdown? We practice drills every month. We did them when I was in school, and we already practiced our first one of the school year this month. We practice so muscle memory is activated in the case it might actually happen. We practice so we can tell our brain everything will be fine, and we know exactly what to do. Well, my brain is not wired that way. It's totally the opposite. I froze. What if we had an active assailant at school? Would I have freaked out and been unable to move? What if I was responsible for kids? Would they have been safe with me? I froze. I froze.

"Breathe, sweetie. Nobody's here. It's not here, I promise." Not here. Not here. Wait? At the high school?

"What's going on at the high school?" I ask, searching for an answer in her eyes. She looks around the room before holding my gaze, and this is the first time I notice there are more people in this room. They're all sitting where they're supposed to, the safest place in every room, the windowless corner, waiting.

"I don't know," she replies. I twist the fidget ring Gus gave me until it's practically digging into my skin. It's too much. This is too much. I can't breathe. I can't breathe. I can't breathe.

Breathe, Nellie. Breathe. This is just another lockdown. There's not a threat at our school. This is a precaution, not a threat. Just a precaution. Breathe in and out. In and out. The world is closing in around me. Quick. Quick. Quick.

The door jiggles, but it's locked, so nobody comes in. The footsteps outside fade, leaving us back in silence. I walk to the chair in the back corner, careful not to run into anything in the darkness of the room, and sit down. I'm going to break protocol, and I don't care right now. I slide my finger over the screen on my watch and open my text thread with Cara.

ME:

I'm okay but code red. U?

SIS:

Yellow for us. What's going on?

ME:

Something at the high school. G2g. We'll talk later.

SIS:

I love you.

ME:

I love you too.

I bring my knees up and lay my head on them, breathing slowly and evening out my breaths. This day keeps getting worse and worse. First, the headache and the memories from last night, then Cody... *Cody*. Oh no, holy shit.

"I need Principal Davis here, now," I tell Ms. Laura. She hesitates at first, but there must be something behind my eyes that tells her I mean it. She picks up her walkie-talkie and calls him. The seconds feel like minutes, and the minutes feel like hours, but eventually, he's here. He walks in, masking what I'm sure are nerves with a straight face and relaxed shoulders. How many of these events do you have to go through to act so unbothered? How many fires do you have to put out before you're not afraid of the flames?

"Ms. Thompson, you wanted to see me?"

I get up from the cold spot keeping me safe, or as safe as one can feel in this situation. "I need to report something."

His eyes open wide, and he nods. He walks me out of the teacher lounge into his office, and I tell him everything. Even if I think it's insignificant, I tell him. Even if I don't think something's going on with Cody, I tell him. That gut feeling means I have to. That fear that he might not be okay means I should. So, I tell him. The words spill out of me like water from a cracked dam. Once I start, I can't stop. My voice shakes, catches on certain words, but I don't hold anything back. Every interaction, every word Cody said, I repeat, trying to do it justice in case there's something here that means something.

Mr. Davis listens, his face still unreadable, but I can see the way his fingers twitch slightly, the way his jaw tightens. He's good at this—masking whatever thoughts are running through his head. I wonder if he's heard worse. I wonder if this is just another problem on his long list of things to handle today. Does he think I'm stupid? This is clearly stupid.

The air in the office is heavy, suffocating. The dim fluorescent light above hums softly, flickering just enough to be distracting. The walls, lined with bookshelves and framed certificates, seem to shrink, pressing in on me from all sides. My hands are clammy, gripping the edge of my chair like it's the only thing keeping me tethered to reality. I twist the ring so hard, my finger slips, and my nail digs into my skin. I freeze. I can't. I can't start now, or I won't be able to stop it. How can I use any breathing technique not to spiral out of control when the reality is worse than my thoughts right now? A real code red. A real code red. Not a drill. Not training. Something's happening.

Principal Davis exhales slowly when I finally stop talking. I'm still drowning in it—the guilt, the fear, the unbearable weight of it all.

He leans back in his chair, folding his hands together on the desk. "Okay," he says, his voice measured. "I need to call the police."

I nod, unable to speak. I had a feeling it would come to this. He does as he said, and after saying just some of it, he nods and then hangs up.

"They're on their way," he says. His eyes soften, just a little. "I know this isn't easy. But I need every detail so we can handle this the right way." I knew it, but somehow, thinking I knew what would happen and what actually happened are two very different things.

"What's going on at the high school?" I ask, hoping he'll tell me anything. I need to know.

"There's not much I can say, but I can tell you this. The threat has been identified and handled."

"What do you mean by handled?" I ask again. What was the threat? What can they tell me?

"I can't say more. I'm sorry."

I blink once, twice, and then it feels like, suddenly, there is another man in front of me. This one wears a navy blue uniform, asking me questions muffled by the loud thumping in my head. I blink again, and it may sound clearer, but my head is still foggy thinking about it all. It doesn't stop me from actually hearing him this time, though.

"I'm going to need you to go over everything one more time, slowly," the police officer says.

The words sit heavy in the air, but I nod again. My stomach twists, the feeling of drowning pulling me down further. There's no going back now. Whatever happens next is out of my control. All I can do is tell him everything I know. A mandatory reporter, that's what I am, even if I have no clue what's actually happening. I can give the details of what I do know.

Were the notes his? The poem? The pieces of paper shredding my heart to pieces because they were conveying so much meaning? Is this what he was referring to? Oh, God. How long has this kid been showing signs, and I missed them all?

Time passes by naturally, as it always does. Time doesn't shift, because I'm losing my mind. Time doesn't change just because I feel like I might both throw up or pass out at any moment. Time passes until they're about to lift the code red and dismiss the students one at a time. No walking home, no buses, nothing. Parents have to come pick up the children at the office. It will take hours, but this is what they've decided. This is what's best. Nobody has told me or anyone else what happened.

A door opens down the hallway, and two police officers escort Cody out. I keep my head low; maybe if I don't see him, he won't see me. But it's too late—he already has.

"You told them! You told them! You said you were a safe space, but you told them!" he screams at me. I am a safe space, buddy, but if your life is in danger, I have to say something. If others are in danger, I have to say something. Things I want to say but can't, because I'm just frozen in place.

He's trying to walk to me, but the police stop him. He's not handcuffed, so he's not in trouble, so why is he so upset? Why are they taking him? Can't speak. Can't reply. Can't say anything.

"What did you do, Ms. Thompson? You might as well have killed me yourself," he screams again. This time, the taller police officer, one I've never seen before, grabs him by the arm and practically drags him out of the school into a police car.

"Please keep him safe!" I finally shout while someone holds me back. "Please…" I break into sobs. "Keep him safe." Cody and the police officer look back, but where the police officer shows me sympathy, Cody shows me anger.

"Please." Another broken sob. Another silent prayer. I fall onto my knees and cry. A soft hand pats my back, and by the time I look up, they're gone. Time passes, and I stand with my arms wrapped around my body. My nails dig into my skin. I keep counting lines on the tile until I can breathe again, until everyone's gone. The hallway is silent again, and the code red is lifted. Four hours later, all the students have been dismissed, and we, the staff, are sent home.

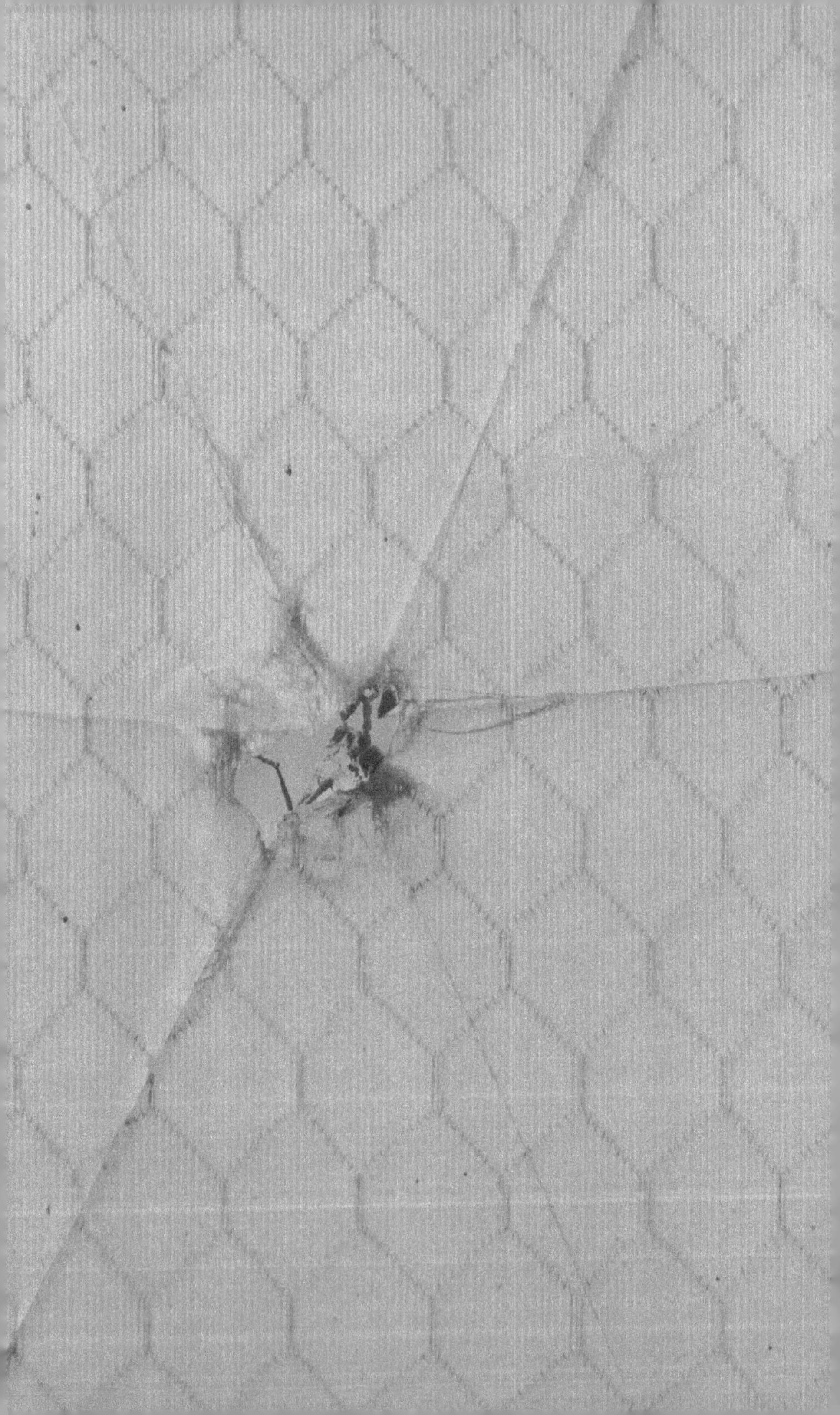

TWENTY-FIVE

ANSWER THE PHONE

My Fault by Noah Cyrus Ft. Shaboozy

GUS

"HERE ARE YOUR KEYS," Santiago says, walking my way to the Baker Auto's waiting room. Jake and his dad own this place, and it's the only place I trust to work on the Barracuda. Even when Jake and Allie were apart, this is where I would take it for maintenance.

"Is it behaving well?"

"You take good care of that beauty, so nothing major. Bring it back in eight to twelve weeks."

"Gracias," I reply, taking my keys and tapping him on the back.

"Can I ask something that is none of my business?" he asks, tilting his body against the wall and crossing his arms in front of him. He's quiet for the most part, and if it wasn't because I know he's kind from being part of the same friend group, I would think he's an asshole based solely on his looks.

Dark eyebrows make him always look mad, tattoos all over the place. Textbook *do not approach*, but he's anything but. Another example of bias and judging a book by its cover.

"Are you dating Nellie?" Oh shit, here we go.

"I better sit down, huh?" There's not an easy answer to that question, because in reality, the answer is no, but how do I explain the physical pain I feel when I'm not with her? How restless I am at the thought of not having her in my arms? How I wish I could turn back time and do it all over again, same but different, just so I don't hurt her, so I could erase this wedge I drove between us. How do I tell him I can't imagine my life without her, but that we're not actually together?

"You don't have to. I know we're not close or anything, and if I'm overstepping, let me know."

"No, no. It's fine. The answer is complicated."

He nods, walking up to the stool in front of me and sitting down. "¿Te puedo dar un consejo?[1]"

"Dale.[2]"

"Whatever it is, if you love her, uncomplicate it. Too much gets in the way of our happiness already without us being in our own way. Life's too damn short to play it safe. So whatever is making it complicated, if it's within your reach, fix it."

"I'm trying…but we're supposed to talk today, so hopefully, it'll be less complicated." I've never used that word as many times as I have in just these few sentences, but yeah, that's exactly what it is. Again…how does he know? "Wait, how do you know?"

He chuckles and shakes his head. "It's obvious to whoever has eyes and is looking for the truth. I wanted to say something because I've seen it happen too many times before; the love and passion are right there, and for whatever reason, one or the other person doesn't make it happen. This is me telling

---

1. Can I give you an advise?
2. Go ahead.

you to make it happen. If she's doubting, unless you hurt her on purpose, prove to her why she shouldn't doubt it anymore. Why she shouldn't doubt *you*."

"I would never hurt her on purpose," I reply, my body stiffening at even thinking those words.

"I know, which is why I said something."

Before I can reply, my phone lights up with a message to my sibling group chat.

ALLIE:

Something's happening at the high school, and I can't get a hold of Jake.

The fuck?

ME:

What do you mean?

MANNY:

Is Cara ok?

ALLIE:

We're fine. We're together, actually. Our school is in a code yellow because of something happening at the high school. There's been no communication other than the high school and the middle school are both in code red.

Holy shit. *Nellie.*

ME:

What can we do?

ALLIE:

I'm sure it's nothing, but I'm getting worried.

ME:

I'm heading to your house. Keep us posted.

MANNY:

Same. Gus, call me.

I look up at Santiago, who's looking at me with questions in his eyes.

"Something's going on at the schools. I'm gonna head to Allie's house."

"Yeah, man. Let me know if I can do anything."

"Will do." I grab my keys and text Nellie before I'm even out to my car.

ME:

Tell me you're okay.

She doesn't reply, but I have no time to wait. I hop in my car and head to Allie's, calling Manny on the way. So much for me telling Dr. Diaz I'd keep my heart rate low.

HOURS HAVE PASSED. Nellie hasn't answered. Allie and Cara stopped answering a while back after they said they were both safe, and Manny and I are just waiting for whatever will happen next. The local news talked about a firearm at school but no casualties. They said someone was severely injured, and they're waiting for more information, then someone was in custody, nothing else. Now, we're just waiting. The hospital will be jam-packed, I'm sure, and the school dismissal seems to be a nightmare too. We just wait.

Allie's door opens, and both Allie and Cara walk through. It's almost dark outside, and I don't even know what time it is. I still haven't heard from Nellie, but the news said nothing about the middle school. Allie looks like she's been crying for hours, and Cara like she's seen a ghost. She walks up to

Manny and collapses in his arms. Allie walks to me, directly into my arms, and hugs me tight.

"Nick's hurt," Allie says between soft sobs while Cara loses it in Manny's arms. He picks her up and brings her to the couch as Allie and I follow. She sits as I go to the kitchen for two bottles of water.

"What do you mean?" I ask, handing her a water and giving the other one to Manny, who currently has Cara curled up on his lap.

"He got shot, and it's really bad. He's in the hospital right now. I don't know many details, but Jake is with him, and Natalie's there. Their daughter is with her grandparents, but we don't know anything else. Jake is clearly distraught, but he couldn't say much. He said he was okay, that was all."

"I'm sorry, Allie. Is anyone else hurt? Doesn't Nellie work at the school?" There, I said it. I asked. Hopefully, it just sounds like genuine concern, not like the truth.

Not like I'm about to lose my goddamn mind if Nellie doesn't reply soon.

"Nellie's okay," Cara answers between sobs. "A student told her something that somehow is related to the situation, so she's been with the police all afternoon. She's on the way home now, though. There's no school tomorrow, so I'm sure she'll sleep in, but I need to check on her tomorrow. She has been working at school for what seems like the blink of an eye and already has to deal with this. Our education system is so fucked up. This is bullshit."

I stay silent, listening to her talk and digesting every word. She heard something. Police interrogation. On the way home. Nellie. My Nellie. And now, she's going home to what—be all alone?

"Do you want me to take you to the hospital?" I ask them, and Allie shakes her head.

"They won't let anyone through unless they're a family member, so we can't. All that is left to do is wait for Jake to update us. Nick was going into surgery, so hopefully after that, we'll get more information," Allie replies.

"I'm staying here until we know more, but you two can go," Cara says as Manny shakes his head.

"I'm staying, but Gus, you should go," he adds, opening his eyes wide and mouthing something that looks a lot like "go to her." Nellie. Nellie's alone. Nellie had to file a report with the police, and now she's all alone.

I kiss Allie on the forehead and squeeze Cara's shoulder as I get up to go. "Let me know the minute you know more," I say, and when Manny nods, I use it as my cue to leave.

I call Nellie, and it rings. It rings and it rings. *Damn it, Nellie. Answer the phone.* Nothing. But she's okay. She's at her parents' house. At home. That's what Cara said, so that's where I go.

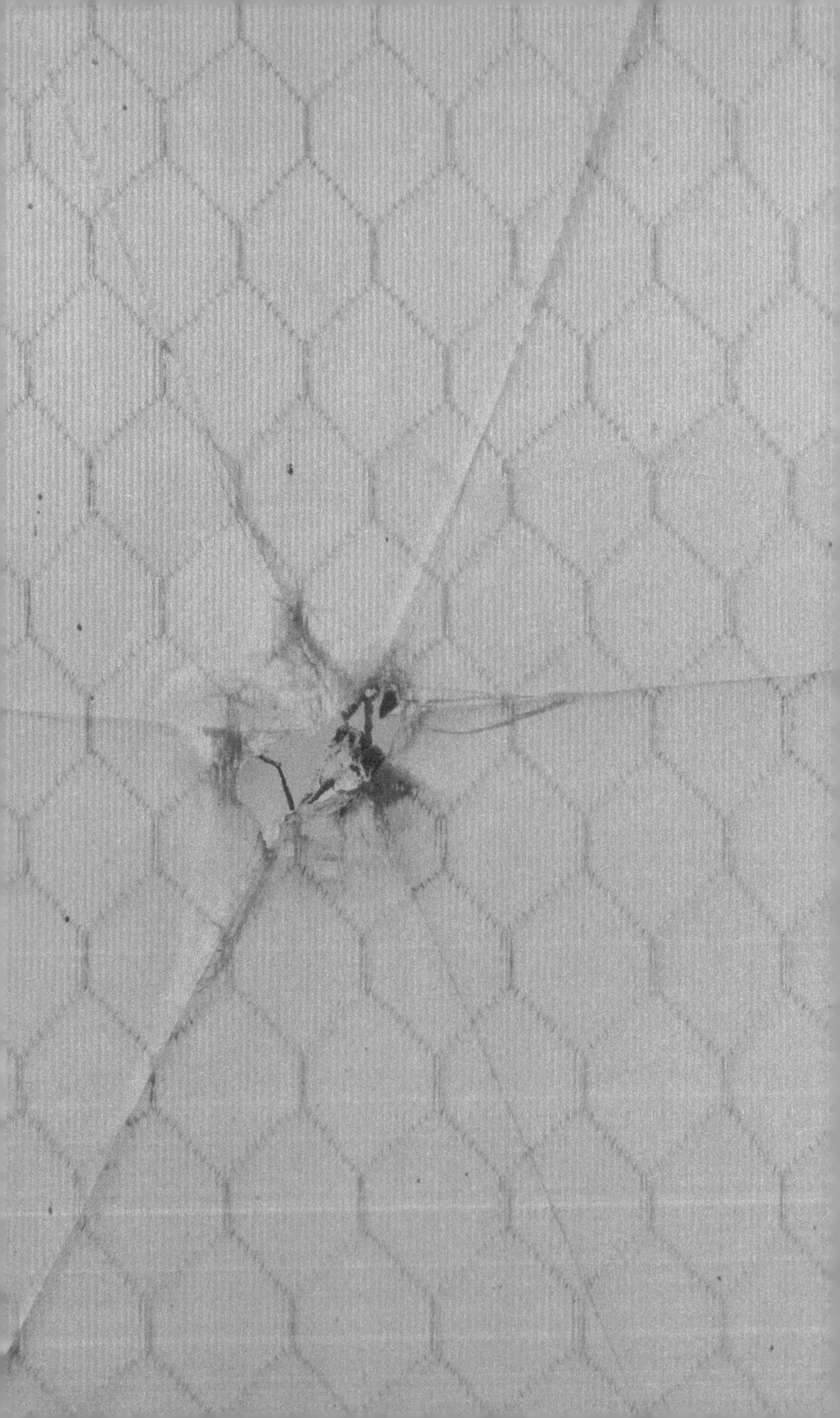

TWENTY-SIX
WASH AWAY THE PAIN

Restless Mind, Sam Barber & Avery Anna; **Someone You Loved, Lewis Capaldi.**

NELLIE

WASH IT ALL AWAY. Wash it all away. That's all I want. To wash it all away. The day. The questions. The news. All of it. Someone's hurt, and it's all my fault. Cody's brother, Josh, is in custody. Someone is hurt. And what about Cody? Is he at home with his parents? Is he at the hospital? Is he with foster parents? Someone's hurt. I wish more information was shared with me. I know they have to protect everyone, I get it, but this not knowing, this not being able to control anything, is driving me wild.

The scalding water burns my skin, but at least it's something. At least I'm feeling something more than numb—numb to today's events, numb to the police interrogation, numb to the feelings, numb to it all.

My skin is raw from scrubbing, and if I don't stop soon I

will hurt myself. It's taking everything in me to actually stop and get out, but I do. Hurting myself won't fix anything. It won't make it go away. Get up. Dry your body, head to toes. Place the towel on the hanger. Put on cotton pajamas. Slide slippers in. All robotic moves I've done before, but I still tell myself each step. I don't need to do a lot, just follow each step. I just need to put one foot forward and take it one step at a time, one action at a time.

I don't remember walking to my room, but suddenly, I'm here. The door clicks shut behind me, and the silence presses in like the deep pull of the ocean before a tidal wave strikes. My bed is unmade, my blankets twisted from last night's restless sleep, when I thought my biggest worry was whether I should or shouldn't give Gus another chance. Now, that might as well be miles away. The soft knock on my door brings me back to reality, and Mom walks in without waiting for me to give the go-ahead. She's worried, I can see it in her face as she brings me a mug and walks with me to my bed.

"I brought you some tea," she adds with tears behind her eyes as she sits on the edge and holds my hand.

My hair is wet from the shower, cascading over my shoulders, still dripping tiny droplets everywhere, making my pajamas damp. They look like tears falling on my shirt, but I don't think I have any more left. *Someone's hurt, and it's all my fault.* I can't believe I didn't connect any dots. I can't believe I didn't talk to the principal about the conversation we had sooner. Maybe I could've prevented it. Maybe nobody would be hurt.

"Nellie?" Mom asks, snapping me out of my thoughts.

"What? What?"

"I asked if you were okay. As okay as you can be, I guess," she says again. She's trying to be strong for me, I can hear it in her voice, but I can also hear the sorrow, the sadness, the worry.

"I'm okay, Mom. I just need to sleep." Will I be able to?

Only time will tell, but I don't want to talk. I don't want to do anything. I don't want to think about anything.

"I have to ask… Are you safe?" I know what she's referring to. I don't think she would ever stop worrying about me hurting myself. It's been years, almost a decade, but I know she blames herself. Does she know there was nothing she could do? It wasn't her fault. I was going to do it anyway. It was the only way I saw out back then.

"I am, Mom. I promise. I won't hurt myself. Any word about who's injured, though?" I ask. The school wouldn't say anything. The only thing on the news is that it's a teacher.

"Oh honey, he didn't make it," Mom replies. What? Someone died today?

"Who didn't make it? Who was it? Do you know?" I sit up straight, put the tea on the night stand, and hold her hand. She looks at me like she knows, but she doesn't say anything. Is it someone I know? Oh my God. "Mom, please."

She hesitates. I can see it flash in her eyes. I can see it in the way her lips tremble and her shoulders stiffen. Her fingernails dig into the palm of her hands, just like mine would. That's her tell. I hate that I know it all too well.

"Mom, please. I'm going to find out anyway. At least let me hear it from someone who loves me, from someone who cares about me." From someone who won't blame me, I want to say.

She lets out a sigh and says, "Nick."

"Nick?" My voice trembles. Cara's best friend Nick? Natalie's husband Nick? Oh lord, no. Bella's dad Nick? The words land like a crashing wave, swallowing me whole before I can even catch my breath. Mom's voice is soft, but the weight of what she says is suffocating. Why? How? There are so many questions and very little answers, but Nick? Why?!

"I'm sure there will be more information tomorrow, but for tonight, you need to try to rest, honey. Cara is with

Manuel, but we're going to their house tomorrow if you want to come."

Nick.

The name alone knocks the air from my lungs. Natalie's pregnant. Bella is going to be a big sister. Oh lord, Cara grew up with him. They've been friends forever. Oh no, Jake. Their whole friend group. This town. Natalie and Nick are town royalty. Oh my God, *Bella.*

This is too much. It's like standing on the beach, watching a tsunami rise from the horizon, knowing there's nowhere to run. I can't run. I can't run. Nick is gone.

I don't even feel my own breath until it comes back as a shudder.

Nick is dead.

I stare at my mom, but she's already looking away, like she can't bear to see me break. I hate that she's bracing herself for my reaction.

Because she knows. She knows how this will destroy me. It was all my fault, and she knows it too. My body moves on its own, twisting toward her, and she holds me. She holds me in her arms, and I grip her like an anchor, but I'm already lost at sea.

Nick. My sorrow runs deep, killing my voice and coming out as a broken sob.

A husband. A dad. A friend. Gone.

I nod, but it's empty, automatic, like my brain has stopped connecting thoughts to actions. Tomorrow. Like it's just another day. Like the world hasn't just collapsed in on itself. I cry, my head on her chest, surrounded by her love as I look at the floor. I can't look at her, I can't look at anything. My fingers tangle together, restless, around her. *It's all my fault* echoes in my mind, over and over again. I should have seen this coming. I should have done something. I missed all the signs. The thought slams into me out of nowhere, knocking me back, but I don't fight it. I let it take me under.

Maybe if I had called in time. Maybe if I had checked in with Cody or asked more questions. Maybe if I looked into the notes more. Maybe, maybe, maybe.

"You're going to be okay, Nellie. It wasn't anyone's fault. Rest. I'm right here." She repeats it over and over again like a mantra.

The guilt pulls me under, and I let it. I deserve it. Tears burn the edges of my vision, but I don't wipe them away. I just curl up on her chest, pull my knees up, and try to make myself small, try to hold myself together when everything inside me is splitting apart. I think about what my dad always said, about how tragedies come in three, about how I never saw this one coming because I was too enraptured in the waves of the other two—in the waves of life throwing blow after blow, even if it wasn't in the shape of sadness, it lead to it regardless.

I close my eyes, succumbing to the darkness. Shadows will stretch everywhere now, just like they're stretching in my brain, like they're stretching behind my eyes. The air feels too thick, pressing down on me like the weight of the ocean. I keep my eyes closed because the darkness behind my eyelids won't be as dark as what will happen to that poor family. To our school. To everyone. I let out a sob, and Mom holds me tighter. It's like I'm asleep and I'm in a nightmare. Except, it's not. It's reality. The nightmare won't stop. Nick is gone, and it's all my fault. Sleep doesn't come easy, but eventually, exhaustion wins, and I drown.

A WARM BREEZE brushes against my skin, making me toss slightly in bed. The very warm and hard bed. It's never like this. Usually, I'm cold when I wake up because I've tossed and turned so much during the night, the blanket falls. I look around and see I'm in my room, in my bed, but when my eyes dart down, there's an arm wrapping me tight. I must have fallen asleep in mom's arms, and maybe she's still here, because it's so warm and *heavy*. Heavy? Is that her?

What the hell?

I turn quickly, a gasp escaping my lips as my eyes widen when Gus opens his eyes. "Gus?"

"Hey, Trouble," he says. His voice is groggy and sleepy, just like his face. His eyes are heavy and lingering with something I can't quite name. Compassion? Sadness? Worry?

"You're here…" I whisper, blinking and looking around, trying to see if this is real, if he's really here. Did my brain make him up because, deep down, I know what I needed was him? How did he know?

"What are you doing here?" I ask, scooting away from him, my back pressing against the wall, my hair falling over my face.

He brings his hand to my hair, tucking it behind my ear. He smiles and says, "You needed me."

"What do you mean?" I say, searching his eyes for answers. Quickly, the memories from yesterday come to mind, fast, crashing like lightning and burning me from the inside out. I gasp, and Gus' face softens. Tears immediately roll down my face. He knew. Somehow, he knew.

"Shh, it's okay. Come here." His arms wrap around me, immediately pulling me to his chest. He smells spicy and fresh and mine. He smells like comfort. He smells like I can let myself fall, and he'll catch me, like I can show him my walls and he won't tear them down, but rather hold them up. He feels like I would be able to open up a dam, and he'll swim across the current to find me. So I let him. I let him be my rock at this moment. I let him hold me and console me. I let myself feel, cry, and scream against his chest. I let myself do it all, for as long as I want, without feeling like I shouldn't. I don't apologize, I just let it all out and he lets me. He holds me and doesn't let go. My buoy. My lighthouse. My safe space.

For all I know, all morning went by. For all I care, today never came, and I've been stuck in a loop of before everything happened. For all I hope, nothing actually happened. But there's no point in knowing, caring, or hoping, not when the reality is as dark as the deepest part of the ocean. Nick is dead. Cody's brother shot him. Cody might be alone. *Cody.*

Gus keeps soothing me with words like *It's going to be okay. Cry, baby girl. Let it out. I'm here. I'm not going anywhere.* He doesn't stop until I do, until I stop crying and just sniffle against Gus' chest.

"Who told you?" I ask, waiting for his reply. God, it feels so long ago when he was here, begging me for another chance. It was just two nights ago, but the world exploded in between.

"Cara. I was with Manny when she texted."

"Does she know you're here?" I ask. The last thing I need right now is to have to explain to my family what's going on with me and Gus.

He shakes his head. "Manny does. He *knows*, but he won't say anything, not until we're ready."

I nod and bury my head in his neck. I want to get lost in him. I want to lose myself in this moment and never face the world again. I don't want to feel this anymore. There's a buzzing sound in the distance interrupting the moment, pulling me away from my thoughts.

"Do you want me to answer?"

"No, it's okay. Just give it to me." He hands me my phone, but the call drops. It's an unknown number I won't call back. Whoever it is can wait. I sit up straight and regret it. My head is heavy, probably from all the crying, and I don't even want to think of what I look like right now. I don't want to think about anything at all. My phone is full of texts, missed calls, and tags online. I'll deal with them when I can. Right now, I just want it all off. I want to turn it off.

I get up, walking to my dresser and pulling on some

leggings and a hoodie. I slide into them, not saying anything at all.

"Nellie, talk to me," Gus pleads, his voice thick with concern. It comes from behind me, soft but insistent. He's still sitting on the bed—I can hear the slight creak of the mattress as he shifts—but I refuse to look at him. I can't. If I do, I'll break.

I press my lips together and focus on my hands, clenched into fists on my hoodie. I don't want to explain. I don't want to talk. I just want it all off—this feeling, this weight, everything that happened yesterday.

Before I can say anything, another buzzing sound cuts through the space. I whip around, snatching it and answering.

"Hello?" My voice is steadier than I expect.

"May I speak with Cornelia Thompson?"

My stomach knots.

"This is she."

"This is Detective James, calling from the Baker Oaks Police Department. How are you?"

A chill races down my spine, but I force myself to sound normal. "I'm good. What can I help you with?" There's a pause, just long enough for my heart to start hammering against my ribs.

"We were wondering if you could come to the station within the hour so we can ask you a few questions about yesterday's events."

I swallow hard, my mouth suddenly dry. "Is this optional?"

His voice turns sharper, edged with something I can't quite place. "It's voluntary right now, but I can get a warrant if I need to. You're not in trouble. This is not about you; this is about whatever information you may have that can aid this case. Ms. Thompson, someone is dead, and from what we understand, you know more about what happened yesterday. We just have some follow-up questions."

Dead. The word lands in my chest like a stone, heavy

and cold. I grip the phone tighter, my knuckles turning white. My mind races, fragments of yesterday flashing like broken glass.

Gus shifts again, not dropping his eyes from mine. He knows something's wrong. How much does he know? I don't know.

I clear my throat, forcing the words out. "I'll be there."

"Thank you." The line goes dead.

I lower the phone slowly, staring at it like it might burst into flames.

"Nellie?" Gus' voice is careful, hesitant. I turn to face him. His brows are drawn together, worry etched into every line of his face.

"They want me at the station," I say, barely above a whisper.

His jaw tightens. "Why do they need *you* at the station? It didn't even happen at your school."

"My student. No, not my student. My...I don't know, client? I don't even know what to call them." I let out a brutal laugh. "I don't even know what to call them, and I already have to follow up with a report? With a police visit?"

"Why?"

"The kid who brought the gun to school is the brother of one of the kids I see often, and he...well, I think he knew something was going to happen. I missed it, so it's all my fault." I cross my arms over my chest.

"It's not your fault. Do you hear me?" He clasps my face, daring me to look at him and not drop his gaze. His eyes are on me, soft and calming, understanding but serious. "I don't even know what happened, and I can tell you it wasn't you. You didn't do anything wrong."

"Maybe I missed the signs. Maybe I could've done something."

"Did you put the gun in his hand? Do you even know this kid?" I shake my head to each of his questions. "Then you didn't do anything wrong. I promise you. Tell me you understand that."

I don't have the energy to say anything back. I don't have the energy for anything more than what I have to do, and right now, that is going to the police. I nod so he'll drop it, and he does.

"How can I help?" he asks.

"Can you build me a time machine?" My voice cracks, just a little. "Take me back to the day before yesterday?"

He exhales sharply, shaking his head, and I already regret saying it. It's not fair to put this on him. It's not his fault. It's mine. All of it. I talked to Cody every day. I should have known.

I swallow hard. "Can you take me to the station?"

A slow nod. No hesitation. He slides on his shoes, and I do the same. The quiet stretches between us as we step out of the room, out of the house, into the driveway.

"How did you even get in?" I ask, glancing at him.

"I climbed through your window."

"How did you know which one was mine?"

He looks out toward the window and says, "I saw you last night. You were pacing in your room. The street lamp illuminates it just enough for me to see your silhouette. So, I sat out there in my car, waiting until you fell asleep—or at least until you stopped walking around. I'm sorry I hurt you so bad, Nellie. I'm sorry, but we don't have to talk about this now. I'm here for you."

"Why are you?" The word is barely above a whisper. Please don't lie to me. Not about this. Not right now.

"I told you. You needed me." His voice drops lower. "But maybe I needed you too. I needed to see you, to know you were okay, too know you weren't hurting—" He swallows and doesn't finish the sentence, since I interrupt him.

"I'm not," I say, but I won't. I won't do that.

His eyes search mine, dark and unreadable. He nods and asks, "Are you okay?"

No, but I don't say that. Instead, I force a tight, brittle smile, the kind that doesn't quite reach my eyes. "I don't think that matters right now."

We keep walking. When we reach his car, he unlocks it without a word, and I slide into the passenger seat.

The drive is quiet, the kind of quiet that isn't comfortable, too heavy with things left unsaid, things to figure out. When he pulls up in front of the police station, he doesn't move to turn off the engine. We just sit there, staring at the building looming in front of us.

"Do you want me to wait?" he asks, voice barely above a whisper.

I shake my head.

"Nellie."

"Gus," I whisper.

"Please," he pleads.

"I'll call you tonight, okay?" My fingers tighten around the door handle. "There's just…a lot I need to figure out."

His jaw clenches, but he nods. Then, suddenly, he reaches for my hand, brings it to his lips, presses a kiss against my palm like he's trying to leave something of himself there, something I can hold on to.

"Okay," he murmurs. "But please, call me. Please. I'm begging."

"I will."

"Promise me. Promise you will come to me."

I nod, but I don't say anything. I can't promise things I don't know I'll keep. I'm stepping out of the car, the air rushing to meet me, before I know it. I take the steps slowly, one at a time, my pulse thrumming in my ears. I don't know what's waiting for me there.

But I know there's no turning back.

PART 4

THE AFTERMATH

Standing on the shore,
watching the waters recede,
leaving behind the debris of everything,
E v e r y t h i n g,
E v e r y t h i n g,
I thought I could hold on.
What is left but pieces?
There is no perfect return,
no way to make the pieces fit again.
Only time will tell.

TWENTY-SEVEN

SHUT IT ALL OFF

A WEEK LATER

HALLELUJAH, Pentatonix; Keep Holding On, Glee Cast; Heal, Tom Odell

NELLIE

I NEVER THOUGHT I'd be here my first year as a counselor, standing at a funeral, surrounded by friends and family—the funeral of a man I've known my whole life. Someone who is loved, cared for, and appreciated by this community. A father, a husband, a friend. I definitely didn't think he would lose his life at the hands of a student, one who never meant to hurt him. A student he loved.

But here I am.

The September air is thick—humid with grief, suffocating with the weight of things that should never have happened. There's a crackle on the microphone, a brief moment of feedback that makes some people flinch, and then the head football coach's voice drones over the silent crowd. He's guiding the funeral, as he was not only Nick's head coach, but also his high school coach when he played. Coach has been part of their family for years, and it just made sense. He speaks about loss, about tragedy, about faith, about God's plan.

I wonder if he actually believes a word of it. Does he believe this was His plan all along? That Josh was going to be bullied so much, he snapped? That he was so distraught because his parents kept punishing him for his grades, grades he couldn't bring up because he wasn't getting any help? Was His plan to give him access to his parents' gun and for him to bring it to school to scare his bullies into leaving him alone, but it turned into a disaster? A disaster that came at a high cost. A sentence for a sixteen-year-old boy who was hurting so much. A boy whose parents took out their frustrations on him, and he never said anything. A sentence for the sixteen year old boy who needed help and didn't know how to ask. A sentence for that boy's teacher, who now is gone. That boy's teacher and coach who stood between the gun and his students while he was trying to figure out what was going on. A teacher who called for a code red so nobody else would get hurt. A teacher who managed to pull half of his homeroom out of the class-room. A teacher who had been trained on what to do in case of an active shooter, but when put in front of a kid he cared about, he forgot. A teacher who tried to take the gun away. A boy who accidentally fired in fear. A teacher who took a bullet for the kids under his watch. Was it His plan all along?

I'm having the hardest time believing everything truly happens for a reason. What's the reasoning behind this? None —this is just a tragedy. Praying won't turn it around. Praying won't do anything. Actions will. More safeguards in place. More awareness and more consequences. More access to mental health care, more talking to kids about kindness. Maybe we did everything we could here, but Josh was still hurting before any of us knew it. We needed to do more. Not everything happens for a reason. Not everything is fair. This shouldn't have happened. This is unfair.

I stare at the closed casket, but I can't bring myself to look at Natalie standing in the front row, shoulders shaking, her hand over her baby bump. She hasn't stopped crying since she got here. Someone—I think it's her mom—keeps rubbing circles on her back. It doesn't seem to help. Next to her is Bella, equally distraught.

I'm going to be sick.

People say things in hushed voices as they place flowers over the casket. They whisper condolences to his family, to his parents, to Natalie and Bella and into the air. Whispers of him being a hero. That it could've been worse. That he protected the kids. Nobody who goes into education should be choosing this. Nobody should be put in this situation.

But there hasn't been *justice*. A courtroom, a gavel, a sentencing that hasn't come—none of that makes this better. Josh is only sixteen. They want to sentence him, but it's trickier than that. Does he need mental health treatment? Does he need prison? What is the right thing to do here? Nobody knows, and in the meantime, they'll keep looking. Nothing will undo what happened. It doesn't change the fact that a kid brought a gun to school. Nothing changes the fact that he thought that was his only way out. Nothing ever will. He chose to take the gun, even if he didn't mean to fire it, even if he didn't mean to hurt anyone. It's all so complicated and sad. Everything's under investigation, and nobody knows what to do.

There were other victims here. Josh, who needed help. Josh, who had been suffering in silence for years. Josh, who felt he needed to respond with violence. Nick, who lost his life trying to protect others. His family, who is mourning a father in the wake of receiving another daughter. His friends, who will have a Nick-sized hole in their hearts forever. Baker Oaks and our schools that will never be the same after this. Cody, who's being sent to live with his grandparents because his parents are under investigation. A loaded gun at home without a safe. A loaded gun unaccounted for. The perfect family in the eyes of the public but monsters behind closed doors. They were the aggressors, not just this kid. Maybe the true aggressor was the system, the broken system that keeps perpetuating the cycle.

I close my eyes.

Monday, the school will open again. Classes will resume. Teachers will take attendance, lessons will be taught, kids will fill the halls and talk about this in hushed tones, afraid of what others might think or say. I hope I can provide a space for them to share, but will I? Will I be able to get back to things? They'll talk about the funeral, about how Josh, not the shooter as some are calling him, cried because he never meant for any of it to happen. About how Josh's name should be said because we failed him. The adults in his life failed him. Kids will talk about how the bullet was never meant for anyone. Kids will talk about how Josh didn't think the gun was loaded. Some will call him a school shooter. Some will call him an assailant. There will be vigils and rallies and press coverage. His family will talk. They'll try to defend themselves. Nick's family will talk, and they'll want justice. A town divided, torn. Because who's completely in the wrong here? Josh? His parents? The system? What we know for a fact is that every-one's hurting, and Nick didn't deserve this fate.

I feel like I'm falling, like I'm unraveling from the inside out, and no one sees it. This is not about me, so I need to keep my shit together.

I should've done more. I should've seen it coming. I should've *stopped* it. My breath is short, shallow. I can feel the walls closing in, the heat pressing down, the scent of lilies and candle wax making me nauseous. I walk away abruptly, leaving the funeral and walking fast toward my car. People glance at me. I don't care.

And I drive. I drive without focus. I drive until my thoughts are clear. I drive until my tears are dried. I drive. I drive. I drive. I don't even realize where I'm going until I make it there and park.

Gus's house. I asked him not to come. I didn't want to answer more questions, and my family can be so nosy.

By the time I reach his front door, my hands are shaking. I knock once, twice.

It takes a moment, but then I hear footsteps. The door swings open, and Gus stands there, eyes heavy with sleep, hair a mess. His mouth parts slightly in surprise.

"I didn't know where else to go," I say, my voice breaking.

He doesn't ask any questions. He just steps aside, letting me in.

I follow him to his room, the floor creaking under my feet. Neither of us turn on the light. The darkness feels safer. He feels safer. He's been there for me this entire week. He stayed silent and gave me the space I needed. He let me cry, scream, and vent every day and every night for the past week, but tonight, I want him to be loud. Not with his words, but with his hands. With his mouth.

I loop my arms around his torso and hug him, sliding my hands under his shirt and touching his back. I lift his shirt up and over his head.

"Nellie," he pleads. He would let me do whatever I wanted. He would let me take whatever I needed. And right now, I need him.

I kiss his chest, bringing my hands around his neck, and I breathe him in. I pepper kisses along his jaw, and when I thrust my pelvis forward, rolling on him, he hisses. "Nellie, we can't. Not like this."

"Shut it all off, Gus. It was my fault. Shut it all off." He's still tense, and I give him space.

"It wasn't your fault, Nellie. What do I have to do to make you see it?"

"I don't want to talk. I just want to shut it all off. Can you? Can you make me feel something? Anything…other than this?" His eyes are on mine, but the intensity I would usually find is replaced by a feeling I hate: pity.

"Stop looking at me like I'm broken," I whisper.

"I just don't want to hurt you," he replies as indecision washes all over his face.

"I'm already hurting. I want to feel something other than pain. Please," I plead with my voice, with my hands, with my lips.

"I want to feel something, but not this, please," I whisper on his lips. He finally loosens up, melting around me, cupping my ass and lifting me up. We kiss in the dark, quiet and slow. Not rushed, just two people exploring each other. Two people who know each other well. One of them hurting, the other one helping. One trying to be there, the other one using him. One just trying to do the right thing, the other one escaping reality.

This Town, Niall Horan & **Call Your Mom, Noah Kahan & Lizzy McAlpine**

GUS

I WISH I hadn't slept last night. I wish I would've been able to stay up and watch her. Commit her to memory. Trace all her features over and over again until there's no mistaking that every part of me knows her by heart. I want her curves imprinted, the way they feel under my hands. I want to see her every time I close my eyes, feel her lying next to me every time I open them. I want her vanilla-jasmine softness invading my senses. I want her hair on my face. I want to bury my face in it. I want to know exactly how many breaths she takes in a minute, how her pretty closed eyes, with her long lashes kissing the top of her rosy cheeks, take my breath away. I want to see, touch, breath, smell, taste, and feel Nellie. But that's not what happened.

After we made love, I fell asleep with her in my arms. *Love.*

Does she know that's what was happening? Could she understand what I was telling her with my hands? With every touch? With every moan? My heart belongs to her. A shitty heart I've kept to myself all my life, but it has found a home within her. A heart that feels safe with her. I just hope she feels it too.

She's my comfort, there's no denying it. Now, I need to find a way to tell her. I wanted to stay awake. I wanted to see her. But I didn't. My heart, my body, my soul, my mind—it all rests when I'm near her. And now, she's not here. She must have left for school, but fuck, I should've stayed awake. I should've savored it all and waited for her so I could tell her as soon as she woke up. I was so afraid she might lose me, I didn't stop to think what would happen if I lost her.

The phone buzzes on my nightstand. I toss to the side of the bed. ¿Las doce? Coño, ni yo me lo creo[1]. I don't remember the last time I slept past nine, let alone until noon. Manny's calling, and for the looks of it, he's been calling all morning.

"¿Qué[2]?" I answer, my voice snappy and groggy with sleep.

"Where have you been?"

"Sleeping."

"Jablador[3], you don't sleep," he says knowingly. There's no denying the connection we share. He knows me better than most people, sometimes better than myself.

"There's a first time for everything. Is the world burning more than usual. Why are you blowing up my phone?" Nellie's world was turned upside down, but so was Manny's. Nick was one of Cara's best friends. Their entire group of friends has been mourning deeply, and Manny doesn't know what to do. I guess this is what happens when you belong to

---

1. Noon? Shit, I don't even believe the time.
2. What?
3. Bullshit/Liar (Dominican style)

the group by proxy and not because you grew up as friends. We've been talking almost every night, reminding each other that *just being* is enough. Listening to them is enough, even if we don't have any answers. Even if we can hold them. That's enough.

"Have you heard from Nellie?" he asks, anguish in his voice.

"Today? No, why?"

"When was the last time you saw her? She was at Nick's funeral, and then nobody has heard anything from her since."

"I saw her last night," I reply, sitting up in bed, wide awake now.

"Where?"

"Here. She came here last night."

"Why didn't you say anything?"

"Manny, what's going on? I've seen Nellie practically every day all week. Why should I have said anything at all? You know she's been here. She was sadder than usual, but that's expected, considering the day."

"She didn't go to work today. When did she leave your house?" What? I sit up and toss the blanket away.

"I don't know," I add, standing up and grabbing some clothes.

"What do you mean?"

"I don't know because she left, and I slept all morning. I figured she left to go to work. I haven't slept this heavily in a while."

"Well, she didn't show, and her phone's going to voice-mail," he answers.

"Where are you?" I get up from the bed, phone in my ear as I slide shorts on and search for a shirt. I walk around, seeing if she left a message, if she said anything. I look on every hard surface. I look everywhere, and eventually, I see it: a small paper with four words. Four words that should make me feel at ease, but they make my skin prickle and the hair on my neck stand at attention.

Thank you for everything.

"I'm on my way to get an inconsolable Cara from school. We're going to look for her."

"I'll do the same. Call me if you find her, please."

I hang up the phone and immediately call Nellie. *Voice message.* Fuck, okay.

"Hey, Trouble. Could you call me back?" I leave the message with my soft voice. I don't want her to think I'm upset. I don't want her to be more upset. I hang up right after, sliding my shoes on and leaving my place. If they're looking for her at home, I can look for her somewhere else. If she's not at home…where does she feel at peace? Okay, beach first.

IT'S NOW EIGHT O' clock, and I'm almost to the place where I hope she is. We searched for a while; Cara and Manny looked everywhere in Baker Oaks. She's not answering anyone's calls. It's as if her phone has been off all day. I called Abraham, and he asked Bee, but nothing. She wasn't anywhere we thought to look until I heard her voice loud and clear in my head.

What's your favorite place in the world, Gus? This is mine.

I'm ashamed it took me as long as it did to figure it out, but I should've known.

I go there when I want the rest of the world to be quiet, or when I want to escape for a few days.

Please don't shut it all off. Please don't turn it all off. Please don't give into the pain. Please, Nellie.

Pulling up to the driveway of the beautiful wooden cabin

hidden between the trees, I see Nellie's car parked right up front. *Thank God.* I grab my phone to text Manny before I go in.

ME:

I found her. I'll keep you posted, but please don't ask where.

MANNY

Is she okay?

Is she? I don't know. At least not yet. I'm not sure what I'm walking into, but I'm not telling that to Manny.

ME:

I'll keep you posted.

There. Not a lie, but also not the entire truth. I walk up the wooden steps to the porch and lift the frog figurine where Nellie grabbed the key the last time she was here. I'm going to knock first, and hopefully, she'll answer, but if not, I'm ready to walk through those doors and get to her.

I knock. Once. Twice. And wait. Okay, three seconds, that's enough. I open the door and immediately hear the TV playing. There's fighting and screaming on whatever is playing, but I can't figure out what it is. I close the door behind me and walk in to find the last thing I was expecting. Nellie's lying on the couch, her eyes closed and her mouth open. What the fuck? I stop myself from running to her. I need to assess the situation first. The soft snores, the rise and fall of her chest, her fingers moving slightly tell a part of the story—she's sleeping. *She's not dead, just sleeping. She's breathing. She stayed.* I feel like I can breathe for the first time in hours. Is this what it feels like? Is this what it feels like when people say when you truly love someone, you can't imagine your life without them? Because the way my chest has tightened, the way my throat has felt like I can't swallow, the way I feel like I haven't been able to take a full breath since Manny called, it has nothing to do with my heart or HAE and everything to do with the love I have for the woman in front of me.

I stop for a moment and take the whole scene in. She's clearly sleeping, but she's, what? Too tired? Too overwhelmed? Too sad? Her eyes are swollen, her cheeks red. She's been crying, that's for sure, but when has she not cried in these past few days? A big shirt is swallowing her body, keeping every inch of her but her legs covered. Is that my T-shirt? It sure as hell looks like it. I should love the way it looks on her, but damn it, Nellie, why didn't you call *me?* Why wrap yourself with an object that belongs to me and not *me?*

What is she holding? Is that a vodka bottle? It sure is. *She's drunk.* The chocolate wrappers around her body answer the unspoken question of whether she ate something or not. She looks anything but peaceful, and my heart breaks.

I get closer, moving the bottle from her hand, and she complains with a grunt. I move the hair off her face, sliding a strand behind her ears. "Hey, Trouble," I whisper, trying not to spook her.

"The door was big enough for both of them," she mumbles, or at least that's what I think she says.

"What?"

"I couldn't save him, but she could've saved him," she adds. What is she talking about? The movie is so loud, I turn around and finally pay attention to what she's watching: 'Titanic'. *The door, of course.* I turn the TV off and grab her under her arms, helping her sit up. She's in between asleep and awake, mumbling words I can barely discern. I manage to sit her up, but she collapses over my chest. *How much did she drink?*

As I remove the blanket from her legs, there's a crumpled-up paper under it. I grab it, open it, and gasp at what I read.

I lost my brother. I lost my parents. I lost my school. I lost you. Is this what you wanted, Ms. Thompson? Well, congratulations. I'll never see you again.

What the fuck? Is this why she's like this? She's completely out of it. I pick her up, cradling her body against me, and drag her to the shower, opening the faucet with water as cold as it'll go and bring us both inside the stall.

"Stop!" she screams the second the icy cold water falls on her. I'm fully dressed while she's wearing practically no clothes, so I know it must be hard on her skin. This shit is cold, but I don't care. She needs this.

"What are you doing? Let me go! Get me out!" she screams, kicking and hitting me while I hold her tightly in my arms.

"Nellie, you need to sober up." No matter how hard she hits or how much she squirms, I don't let her go.

"No, it's too much." This is what I was worried about. This is what I was fearing. That she wanted to feel less. That it was all too much for her. *I could control how much I felt.* Her words echo in my head. God, Nellie what did you do?

"No, you need this. Let me in, damn it. You need this."

"No. No. No. Let me out," she shouts, but she stops fighting me. "Let me out," she says in a broken sob. "I did this to him," she continues.

"You didn't do anything wrong. Just sh, sh, sh, I've got you," I soothe until she goes limp in my arms, and the only sound is the water falling over us. She feels so small, so fragile, and my heart breaks for her.. "You did everything right. I've got you. I've got you." Her soft cries fade in the background, but eventually, she puts her feet on the ground and wraps her arms around me. Her tears trickle down my chest as they mix with the water falling over us. I feel her heartbeat slowing and her breathing evening.

"You did nothing wrong," I say again, lifting her arms and removing her shirt, leaving her in nothing but underwear and despair. I turn the water to warm, bringing my hand to her back and holding her against me. Her cries break me too, little by little, and I just want to take her pain away. I wish I could take it all. I wish I could make her see it all from my eyes. I wish I could shield her from it all.

Time passes, and when she's quiet, I finally turn the water off and pick her back up. I walk us both to the tub, turn on the hot water, and let the tub fill without letting go. If there's one thing she takes from this, I hope it's that I'm not going anywhere. The water comes out with force, filling the tub quickly. She doesn't say anything, and for someone who likes to talk and share her thoughts, this is concerning, but she doesn't push me away. She doesn't kick, hit, or scream. She doesn't beg me to walk away. She doesn't ask me to leave her alone, so I'll take it. "I'm not going anywhere," I whisper against her hair, and the crying starts again.

This time, she pushes and kicks until I put her down, and then she runs to the toilet, falling to her knees and emptying her stomach in it. I move behind her and hold her beautiful damp hair away from her face, rubbing her back gently. "It's okay. Let it all out."

"Go away. I don't want you to look at me this way," she says before she throws up again.

"I'm not going anywhere, Nellie. I'm here. Let me be here."

She throws up until she's dry heaving, her hands hugging the toilet bowl. I help her up, and we both walk, hand in hand, until we make it to the tub. "I'm sorry," she whispers.

"Don't be. Let me take care of you," I reply.

"I'm a mess. Please, just go."

"Don't ask me to go, please. I'd do anything you ask me to, but please, don't ask me to go." She raises her eyes to look at me for the first time since I got here. The sorrow, the sadness, and the emptiness behind them are more than I can tolerate. It breaks me, but I can't let it consume me now. I need to be here for her.

The water in the tub is full and warm, so I turn off the tap and help her in. Once she's sliding in quietly, I take my clothes off and slide in behind her, resting both our bodies on the edge of the tub. The warm water is the best contrast to how cold it was before. It helps her melt her body into mine. We are both sinking under the warmth as her tears silently fall.

I reach out and grab the liquid soap, squirting some on my hand. "Can this go in your hair?" Let me not mess this up by putting something on her hair that she would never use. Specific products and shit.

She nods, so I lather it through her hair, softly spreading it until her head is covered in suds. Such a simple and mundane task, but it seems grand today. She's letting me. It feels like she might need it more than anything. I continue taking care of her, washing and touching, reminding her I'm here. I look at her, her eyes closed as she tilts her head back and lets me take care of her. Her tears are falling, but her breath is calming. Her body is melting. Her hand is grabbing my leg, holding me like I'm her lifeline.

I don't say much—I just touch, wash, and caress until I feel her shoulders relax, and she lays her head back on me. Her cries stop, but she doesn't losen her hold on me, not until moments later, when I massage her temple and rub small circles on her wrist scars. *I'm here. I'm not going anywhere.*

Her breaths sound heavy, and then they even out. She must be falling asleep again. I help her out of the tub and wrap her in a towel, carrying her to bed, letting her fall asleep in comfort.

"Don't go," she whispers when I try to get up from the bed, so I don't.

"Never again," I whisper back, kissing her forehead and pulling her flush to my body. I stay awake this time, not letting her out of my arms or my sight until I'm sure she'll be okay.

TWENTY-NINE

BE GOOD TO HER

FIRE ON FIRE, Sam Smith

GUS

"BENDICIÓN, MAMI. [1]"

"Dios te bendiga, mi hijo, ¿Cómo estás ?[2]" she replies. She's always available whenever we call, no matter what time it is. It doesn't surprise me that she answers on the second ring. It's late. I already told Manny Nellie's okay, and they're all breathing easier, but I needed to talk to her.

"Bien se podría decir. Necesito un favor[3]," I continue in Spanish. We moved a lot growing up, lived in different. countries, in different towns, but she always made sure Spanish was spoken at home at all times.

---

1. This is a respectful way to say hello to your elders in the Dominican. It translates to Blessings, Mom.
2. God bless you, my son. How are you?
3. You could say I'm good. I need a favor, though.

"Dimelo, mi hijo. ¿Como te puedo ayudar?[4]"

"You know when we were younger and sick, you would make us Sancocho, and it immediately helped?" I'm not about to tell her I need to nurse my—my what? Girlfriend? My secret I've been keeping from them? The love of my life? The woman I know I won't be able to ever live without? Or do I say her…her best friend's daughter? I guess I realize now how fucked up this whole situation has gotten. If only I would've told her. If only we would've come clean. I could tell her. But I didn't, and now is not the time.

"Yes…why?" she replies, her tone shifting from motherly to gossipy.

"Well, I would love to make it, but I don't know how." I never learned how to cook; none of us did, mostly because we always had our meals made for us growing up. In college, we had a meal planning service I just carried with me to adulthood. In the Dominican, we have Sonora, our house keeper, and she just made sure we were fed growing up and still when we go back. I highly doubt I'll be able to find Sancocho out here in this small Georgia town, though.

"You, Augusto? You want to cook?"

"On this occasion, I do. Don't act so surprised. I'm a grown man."

"Who's the girl?" she asks, because no matter how much I try to hide it from her, she knows. Moms always know.

"Mami," I reply. I don't want to lie to her, so I need her to stop probing.

"I know it's a girl. The only time your father would cook was to feed me, but if you don't want to tell your mother, I guess I'll die without knowing. Go ahead and keep things

---

4. Tell me, my son. How can I help?

away from your mother. Hijo eres y padre serás. Ya verás lo que se siente[5]."

"You're so dramatic," I reply, mocking in my tone, and she laughs. She knows what she's doing, but I won't give in. "I will tell you, just not today. Te lo juro.[6]"

"Mira muchacho dejate de estar jurando en vano.[7]"

"One of these days, you'll have to tell me who she is. Do you have a pen and paper?" I smile as I get ready to write the recipe of her famous stew everyone loves. I write down every ingredient and all the directions she has to give. She gives me examples on things I can substitute if I can't find all the ingredients here. I get worried I might not find them at all, so I put her on speaker while I order the groceries to be delivered. As she predicted, some of the root plants aren't available, but that didn't stop her from giving me tips on how to substitute or even use the pre-peeled frozen choices. According to the delivery app, I will have the ingredients here within the hour.

"Do you think I should call you when the groceries get here?" I ask her.

"Do not be afraid. You've got this. Call me if you get stuck. It truly isn't as hard as you think."

"Okay, Ma. Gracias." There's a silence after. I know she's there. I can hear her breathing, but she doesn't say anything. Even though I've been talking to her now for what seems like twenty minutes, my eyes have not left Nellie, who still sleeps on the bed just across the room from me. I don't let her out of my sight, too afraid of her slipping out of my hands and leaving again. The sun started going through the window a while ago, but it hasn't reached her face. I wish this cabin had curtains so I could shield her from the sunlight and let her

---

5. An idiom that translates to: a son you are, a parent you will be. It means that one day, you'll know what it's like
6. I swear.
7. Stop swearing in vane.

sleep, but it's not going to happen. At least I have ibuprofen ready for her whenever she wakes up. I'm sure she'll need it.

"Is this person someone I know?" she asks, and I freeze. How the fuck does she know? How does everyone know?

"Ma…"

"You don't have to answer if you don't want, but your brother was being cryptic when he called to ask if I knew where Nellie was. Then, he called back to tell me she was okay. I just hope that if you have her, you're keeping her safe." I don't say anything. I let the silence speak for itself. I can tell she knows. How? Who knows, but again, moms always know.

"I was with her mom all day yesterday until Manuel called. It's okay if it's her you're taking care of. I trust you. I trust I raised you to be a good man to whoever gives you their heart—to whoever you decide to give yours. Just promise me you two will let us know soon if it's serious, and if it's not… promise me you'll be careful. I would hate to lose the friend-ship of a lifetime over my son hurting her daughter, and you wouldn't do that, right? Grown or not." I swallow hard at her words.

"No, I wouldn't, and yes, I promise," I say.

"Te amo, Augusto. Be good to her."

"I love you too. I'll talk to you later." I hang up the phone and wait for one of two things to happen—Nellie to wake up, or the groceries to get here. Both will happen before I figure out what the fuck are we going to do from now on, especially if she doesn't feel the same way I do about her.

THIRTY
AFRAID, ANGRY, AND SAFE

US BY GRACIE ABRAMS and Taylor Swift & Good Luck, Charlie by Gracie Abrams

GUS

"UGH," Nellie grunts as the sun comes through the window onto her face, kissing her with its glow. She covers her head with a pillow, and all I can do is hope she'll go back to sleep but she doesn't. She sits up and holds her head between her legs, grunting again. If I didn't know the underlying reasons for her pain, I would laugh. She looks miserable. Miserably cute, but miserable all the same.

"Here," I say, holding out painkillers and a glass of water.

"Everything hurts," she says, still rubbing her eyes and not looking at me.

"I'm surprised you're even awake right now. Take it, it'll help." She follows directions and takes the four pills, swallowing them with a big gulp. Something tells me even the 800 milligrams of ibuprofen won't be enough for her to feel better, but it's a start. The groceries were delivered about two hours ago, and the Sancocho is cooking on the stove. The white rice to go with it is ready, thanks to two video chats with Mom to figure it out. After this, I'm going to be the Sancocho king.

"Close the curtains, Gus. I need to be in darkness. I shouldn't have to see the light." This. This is what I was worried about. Last night gave me insight into her feelings of despair, but it wasn't just the alcohol. It's what she's feeling right now.

"Sorry to break it to you, Trouble, but this cabin you love so much has no curtains." She grunts again, throwing herself onto the bed and wincing when her head bounces on the pillow.

"Wrong move," she whispers, making me laugh. At least part of her sass is here. I was worried I was going to have to call her sister if she was completely out of it. I don't want her to mask her pain and her thoughts with humor, but I also don't want her to feel like somebody else. My Nellie laughs. My Nellie cries. But my Nellie has to come back from this. She has to.

I sit on the edge of the bed but don't say anything, waiting for her to be the one to speak.

"I'm sorry I threw up last night."

"Why are you sorry? It's not like you could've avoided that. Are you sorry you threw up, or are you sorry you drank enough to make yourself practically pass out on the couch?"

"I'm sorry you had to witness it."

"Nellie, be thankful I did. Do you know how dangerous that was?" I told myself I wasn't going to bring it up. I told myself I was just going to be supportive of her today, but I would be lying to myself if I didn't say what I've been thinking: how reckless it was for her to drink that much alone. "You drank almost an entire bottle of vodka by yourself, in this cabin, away from everyone, without telling anyone where you were. That was reckless, even for you."

"How did you even find me?" she asks.

"I listen." *I know you. I love you.* All the words I want to say.

"Oh, so this was your first try? You listen so well, you knew you could find me here?" she sasses. I take a deep breath and clench my fists. I'm about to lose my shit. This is a game for her, and I'm about to lose it.

"No, Nellie. I wish I could say it was. I looked for you like a man starved. I looked for you until I had to stop and breathe because my heart rate was so high, I thought I was going to end up in the hospital. It took me entirely too long to figure it out, and then there was the drive here. Hours of not knowing. Hours of calling you and hoping you were here."

She stares at me with panic behind her eyes. Good— maybe she gets it now. "And I found you. Imagine your sister and your family. They were so worried. They *are* so worried. You need to call them. That was so reckless, even for you."

"I don't need to do anything," she snips. "All of you just need to leave me alone and stop scolding me."

"Someone has to. And no, we won't leave you alone."

"No?" she asks.

"No, we're not leaving you alone. *I* won't leave you alone. You have so many people in your corner, and we're all here for you." *Can't she see it? Can't she see we want what's best for her? That her family could've lost her because she was suffering in silence—alone? Can't she see I would give her my heart if I could, just so I could stop her pain? Can't she see I would take it all, all the pain, for her?*

"They're all mourning their friend." *Goddamn it, Nellie. She can't. She can't see it.*

"AND YOU WANT THEM TO MOURN YOU TOO?" I scream at her, and she flinches. *Fuck.* "I'm sorry, I just… We were all so scared."

"Don't yell at me." She crosses her arms over her chest and lets out a breath.

"I'm trying to keep my cool, but damn it, you're not listening. You're watching and assuming but not listening to all of us telling you we're here for you, telling you to trust us. I'm trying to be patient and be here for you, but damn it, Nellie, you scared me. What were you thinking?"

"I wasn't." She lets out a breath, and a tear falls down on her cheek. I'm surprised she even has tears to shed. "I wasn't thinking. It was too much."

"I have to ask you something, and I need you to listen carefully and answer truthfully," I tell her. Her eyes open wide, and she nods.

"Are you trying to hurt yourself?"

"No," she answers quickly—too quickly. I cock my head sideways as she lets out an exasperated breath. "Maybe."

I nod, softening my features so she knows I'm both serious and understanding. "Are you trying to kill yourself?" Be direct. Be honest. Be patient. These are all things I read online when I was researching self-harm. *Give them a reason but assess the situation to make sure you know if you can handle it.*

"No," she replies matter-of-factly.

"Is there someone you'd like to call?" My last question in the trifecta I saw I should ask. She shakes her head no and lies back down on the bed.

"Come here," I whisper. I scoot backward until my back hits the wall and help her climb into my lap. I cradle her against my chest. Her hair is ruffled, I'm assuming from going to sleep with it wet, but it's soft, just as it always is. It smells like vanilla, sweet and intoxicating. "I need you to be honest with me. I'm not going to judge. I'm not gonna go anywhere. Are you safe?"

"I am. I promise. I'm not going to hurt myself, but I'm not going to lie, I thought about it. It was just too much, Gus. It's too much."

"It is. You just went through something nobody should go through, but we need you here. I need you here."

She looks up, her eyes finding mine, searching mine. Her lips part like she wants to say something, but she hesitates. I feel her fingers grip the fabric of my shirt like she's holding on for dear life. My heart clenches.

"I don't know how to do this," she whispers, barely audible. "I don't know how to be okay after this."

"You don't have to be okay right now," I tell her, my voice steady but soft. "You just have to be here. You just have to let yourself breathe. But Nellie, you don't have to carry it all. You told me to let you help carry my health—do you remember that?"

"Yeah, and then you fucking dumped me like I meant nothing to you."

"You know what, Nellie…I wasn't going to do this now, but I'm done dancing around it. I didn't dump you. I did try to play it off as less than what we were…what we *are*, but guess what? I'm not going anywhere. It's not what you think, and *you* didn't allow me to say anything. You jumped to conclusions and came for my throat. I was afraid, okay? Is that what you want to hear?"

"Gus, if you're just going to lie to me, just leave. I'm so tired of the lies always told. I can't try to decipher—"

"Damn it, woman. I got sick," I interrupt. She sits up and brings her hands to hold my face, holding my gaze and reassuring me. So much for me being the rock she needed right now. "I'm okay, I promise, but I wasn't for a bit there, and I didn't want to drag you down with me. I was terrified."

"Gus—" I bring my hands up to stop her from talking. I guess we're doing this now. It's all or nothing.

"No, let me finish. They didn't know what was going on, and I just…I was scared. I was scared to tell you. I was scared it would be too much for you to handle, and you would end up too worried and too sad."

"You know what made me fucking sad? You pushing me away. You know what made me really angry? You disappearing on me and then showing up a couple of weeks later like nothing happened. Am I that disposable to you?"

"No. You're not disposable. I was trying to protect you, and if I recall correctly, you pushed me away too. I was giving you space. I was trying to protect your heart while mine was slowly falling apart. I didn't want to be a burden to you."

"Funny you say that—that's the same reason I'm here. Because I'm a burden to everyone around me." She brings her hands out to point at the cabin. "Why am I the one with these feelings, huh? I don't deserve to be this sad. I didn't lose my husband. I didn't lose my dad. I wasn't removed from my home and sent to live someplace else. My life will continue as usual…so why am I this fucking sad?" She exhales shakily, her forehead dropping against my chest. I run my hand up and down her back, slow and steady, grounding her, reminding her she's not alone.

"It was my fault," she admits, her voice raw.

"No. You don't get to say that. It wasn't. You didn't wake up and decide to bring a gun to work. You didn't pull the trigger. You didn't do anything wrong. Why do you think it was your fault? Why do you think you aren't allowed to feel sad? You're allowed to feel whatever it is you're feeling, Nellie, regardless of what you think, of what other people think." I stop because I haven't given her time to even answer one question. I wish I could get inside her brain and iron out all her thoughts, all her feelings. I wish I could pluck them out, one at a time, and shed some light on them, show them to her with a big ass magnifying glass so she knows the reality. Her brain is lying to her, just like it was lying to her about my feelings. "Why? You want honesty? Give it to me. Let me take it all. Tell me…why?"

She stays quiet for a long time, and I don't rush her. The weight of her against me, the way she lets herself lean into me, is enough to tell me she trusts me with this, with her pain, even if she doesn't have the words for it yet.

After a while, she whispers, "How much time do you have?"

"For you? A lifetime." She nods and pulls the blanket around her as she lays on the pillows so she can face me.

"How much do you know about what happened?"

"Not much. A kid brought a gun to school and shot Nick. That's all I know."

"Josh. His name was Josh," she exhales, rubbing a hand over her face as she musters the courage to say whatever happened. "I didn't know him personally, and honestly, I don't think most people in town did. Funny how that works, isn't it? How nobody really noticed him until now. He had football and school, and then school was hard because others didn't see him struggling. Just another jock in the background, not part of the popular crowd but not a loner either. He was with everyone, but nobody noticed him. Invisible—until he wasn't."

I lean back, looking at her, quietly waiting for her to continue. I'm not rushing her. I'm letting her share, in her own time. "His little brother, Cody, though…he was different. He was in my office all the time, every single day, sometimes twice. Funny kid. Sweet, too. Always had something to say but never anything too deep. It was mostly small talk—pointless stuff, I thought. I never thought twice about it, you know?. And now? Now, I see it. Now, I realize that's all he ever gave me. Surface-level things. He never let me in. I never pushed. Because why would I? He looked happy. He seemed fine. But you know what they say about people who smile the most."

I can see her swallowing hard as she shakes her head and wipes away tears. "Turns out, things at home weren't so good. Their parents…they had their own issues, though I don't know the full story. What I do know is that they controlled everything—food, toiletries, even clothes, locked them up like they were privileges instead of basic needs. If the boys wanted something, they had to earn it through physical labor. And if they spoke up? If they dared to tell anyone? They were threatened with starvation. And Josh…Josh got the worst of it."

She closes her eyes and lets out a breath before looking at me. I hold her hand and make the small circles she likes on her wrist, touching her scars gently, reminding her I'm here for it all. "He wasn't like Cody. He was quieter, more withdrawn, not as well-liked. But football…that gave him something. A place to be. A purpose." She lets out a humorless chuckle. "Didn't matter, though. Some kids saw him stashing food in his backpack one day and made a joke out of it. That joke lasted two years. Two damn years of taunts, whispers, laughter at his expense. And his parents found out, but instead of protecting him, they punished him. They took away even more. They starved him, Gus. Abused him. Not in the way people think—not through bruises or belts. No, they just…let him waste away. Quietly. Subtly. They never laid a hand on him, but they still hurt him, or at least that's what the principal shared with me."

I look up, meeting her eyes. "Do you know what that does to a kid? To be constantly hungry, to feel that kind of emptiness every single day? To be mocked at school and tormented at home? To have nowhere—no one—to turn to? He was starving, Gus, in every way a person can be. His dad brought the gun out the night before and threatened the family. The mom too. Suddenly, Josh had too much. He brought the gun to scare his classmates, to stop the bullying, but nobody knew that. In a time of school shootings and safety meetings, in a time of lockdown drills and everyone preparing for the worst, everyone thought that was his end goal. It happened during Home Economics class. Nick was his Home Ec teacher, but he was also his coach. He got in between Josh and the students, and when he thought he had the upper hand, he tried to snatch the gun away, and Josh accidentally pulled the trigger. It was an accident. Josh didn't even know it had a bullet in it, or so he told the police. Something that never should have happened, something I should've seen coming."

"How, Nellie?" I keep my voice low, steady. "How should you have seen it coming?"

She shakes her head, staring at the floor like the answer might be written in the cracks between the tiles. "I don't know," she whispers. "I just should have."

"Nobody could've predicted that." I lean in, trying to catch her eyes, but she won't look at me. "If anyone should have seen something, it's the high school counselors, right? Not you."

Her lips press together. Guilt sits heavy in her eyes, and I know she doesn't believe me.

"The kid you talked to—Cody?" I continue. "He seemed fine. You did the best you could with the information you had." I hesitate for a second then push forward. "It's not your fault."

Her shoulders stiffen, but she doesn't argue. Not yet.

"Who sent you that letter?" I ask.

Her head snaps up. "What letter?"

I don't miss the way her breath catches, the way her fingers tighten around the edge of her sleeve. She wasn't expecting that. I might not get another chance to bring it up.

"You know what letter," I say quietly.

She swallows hard. "Cody."

"He got pulled from his home," she continues. "Sent out of state to live with his grandparents. He must have slipped it through the door in my office. When I went to talk to the principal and he told me everything, I found it in there. His parents are under investigation, and his brother..." She exhales shakily. "He'll probably get sentenced after his trial. Cody is twelve. *Twelve.* And his whole world just collapsed. It's a lot," she murmurs.

"He's angry," I say. Suddenly, I get it. The letter. The blame. The sharp edges in her voice when she said she should have known. He's not just angry. He's heartbroken. He's terrified. And he's got nowhere to put it.

"You can't let this haunt you," I tell her. "He's a kid. You said it yourself. He's lashing out because he doesn't know what else to do. It's not your fault, and he doesn't mean it."

Her eyes flick to mine. "How do you know?"

I exhale, leaning back. "Because, for different reasons, I lashed out just like he did."

She doesn't move, but I feel her listening.

"I didn't understand what was happening to me. I blamed my parents for giving me genetic and hereditary conditions, like it was something they did on purpose. And my dad, well, he was controlling. He was always pushing for us to do the most, even when my body struggled. I felt like I was never enough. I mean, I always did, but in that moment, it was worse. If I'm being honest, my dad's still that way. I just don't care anymore." I let out a short, humorless laugh. "I didn't mean it, but I was hormonal, and sad, and afraid, and—yeah, angry. Angry at how unfair everything was. Angry I had to deal with it at all. I bet Cody feels the same way."

I shake my head. "You're just an easy target. You are who Manny was to me. Manny was there to be my punching bag when I needed it. You are that for Cody."

"Why?" Her voice is small.

"Because you care." I let that sit between us for a second. "Because the two people who were supposed to protect him didn't. Because he trusted you, and now, his brain is playing tricks on him. Because he's scared, and he doesn't know how to say it, but he knows you won't hurt him. No matter what he says, he knows you won't harm him." I hold her gaze. "You did your job. It had a terrible outcome, but, Nellie—it's not your fault. You did everything right, and the outcome still sucks, but that's life. You can't live with the what-ifs forever.

You did everything you could do with the information you had."

"And someone still died."

"Someone died. I'm sorry for that. I'm so terribly sorry, but it was an accident. A terrible accident. It's not your fault."

Her lips part, but no words come. I see it, though. The way her shoulders sag just a little, like maybe, just maybe, she's starting to believe me.

"He'll hate me forever. I told the police what he said, and that led them to look into it deeper. Cody's not in trouble, but his parents are. He won't ever forgive me."

"And while that might be true, you need to forgive yourself. You did everything you were supposed to do, as hard as it is. Maybe let him blame you. He'll hopefully get help, and he'll eventually see the bigger picture, but in the meantime, let him hate the one person who won't hate him back. Be that person for him, even if from afar. Sometimes, there are lies worth letting become truth, in order to protect our hearts. Protect *his*, baby girl."

"That's a fucked up way to put it."

"Maybe, but am I wrong?" She shakes her head and closes her eyes as he lets it all sink in. She doesn't answer. She doesn't say anything else. She just waits. I hold her hand and trace small circles on her wrist, on the spot where she once felt it was her only way out. I keep doing it so I can remind her she never has to go through things by herself again. I remind her with every touch how I will always be here for her, how I will always help her find a way.

"And when he's ready…be here for him, and you can talk. Even if that is in a year, or two, or ten. Maybe never, but at least he'll know he has you. When everyone else is a song, you can skip, be his eight-track, steady and consistent. Be his soundtrack."

I'm lost in thought, touching her skin, looking at her. I

almost miss her talking. "His shore. When everyone is a wave, I can be his shore." I nod, and she smiles.

She shakes her head. "I'm so lightheaded and my head feels heavy at the same time."

I chuckle and say, "Yeah, you have a hell of a hangover, and you need to eat. Come on. I have food for you."

THIRTY-ONE
LOVE IS

What A Time, Julia Michaels and Niall Horan; **Bleeding Love by Leona Lewis**

NELLIE

"I DIDN'T KNOW you could cook," I tell Gus as he serves me a soup-looking dish in a bowl. A stew, maybe? It smells fantastic, and it looks even better. The scent is warm, layered—hints of garlic, meat, and something earthy, like root vegetables, steeped in broth for hours. My stomach tightens with hunger.

"Neither did I." Gus chuckles, placing another bowl on the table before sitting across from me. His laughter is easy, light, a sound I haven't heard nearly enough.

I waste no time dipping my spoon in, the steam curling upward in delicate tendrils. My lips part as I bring the spoon to my mouth, only for my entire body to jolt the second the piping-hot liquid scalds my tongue.

"It's—" he starts just as I dramatically spit most of it back into the bowl, my tongue sticking out as I pant.

"—hot," he finishes with a smirk, shaking his head. "It's really hot." Laughter spills between us, a foreign sound after how rough the past week has been. Gus reaches for a roll of paper towels, dabbing at the table where a few droplets landed.

"Sorry. It smells great."

"Thanks. It's my mom's recipe." He nudges a small bowl of rice toward me. "Here, take some rice."

I frown slightly. "In the soup?"

"Sancocho, yes," he corrects, nodding as he demonstrates. He scoops two spoonfuls of rice into the broth, the grains sinking before puffing up slightly, soaking in the flavors. Then, without hesitation, he sprinkles some hot sauce over it and places a slice of avocado on top.

I hadn't even noticed the avocado on the table.

"This is the money bite," he adds, spooning a combination of all the ingredients into his mouth and smiling at me. I copy him, following the same steps and taking a bite. My eyes open wide as I moan at the explosion of flavors: salty, savory, liquid like soup, but with something to chew in between. It's perfect. I close my eyes as I swallow, and I hear him chuckle.

"Are you sure this is the first time you've made this? It's so good." He nods quietly with a soft smile.

"I can't take credit, though. She walked me through every step."

"Agh, I miss your mom. I need to spend some time with her soon."

"She'd love that." I mean it. I do miss her. I've seen her around with mine a few times since I moved back, but nothing like years ago, when we would spend days with the Zabanas, especially with her. It seems like a lifetime ago now.

We continue eating in complete silence, and I use the time to take it all in. How grateful I am he's here, bathing me, taking care of me, cooking for me. *Saving me.* He's the last person I expected to be here. He's been so icy and hot, pushing and pulling, driving me wild for months, but now he realizes he can be here? What changed? Was it the chase? Was it that I pushed him away again? What did I do? *Oh, God.*

"You're sick?" I ask, trying to remember what he said earlier.

"Eh, not really? Maybe? Not what you're probably thinking, though."

"Oh yeah, what am I thinking?" I ask.

"It's not some disease that will kill me, at least not now that it's under control. But eat. We can talk later."

"No. I want to know. Please. It'll help me. Let me be selfish." I know the moment the words come out of my mouth that he'll tell me.

"My medicine, for the HAE, was making me sick. It messed with my heart, and I was having some complications."

A chill moves through me. "What kind of complications?"

He's quiet as I take a sip from the glass of water he placed in front of me, his fingers absently drumming against the table.

"Nothing major," he says after a beat. "Just fainting, my heart skipping beats."

I nearly choke. "Nothing major?"

He shrugs, the nonchalance infuriating. "It could be worse."

"Oh, could it?" My voice rises in frustration. "Why do you play around with your health like this?"

"I don't, but Nellie, this is my life. It's my every day. I'm always thinking about what could be causing something. Am I tired just from life, or is it an indication of something else ? Am I excited, euphoric, lustful, in love, or is my heart failing? Am I catching my breath because I worked out hard, or is it a failed stress activity? Am I eating too much salt? Did I take my medicine this morning? My throat is tingling—is it a swell? Is it an attack? Is it allergies? I have to be serious about it, but I also have to be a little nonchalant, or it won't be able to live my life. So yeah, I had some complications. We figured it out."

My fingers curl into fists. "You were going through that, and instead of letting me help, you pushed me away? Why, Gus? Why?"

His jaw tightens. "Because I was a sinking vessel with a limited oxygen supply, and I wanted the chamber to be empty. I didn't want you near. I didn't want to hurt you."

"Well, guess what?" I push my chair back, standing abruptly. "You hurt me worse."

I walk away, out of the kitchen and onto the porch, my pulse thrumming beneath my skin. The air outside is cool against my heated face as I step onto the back deck, my eyes falling on the still water of the pool—the pool I didn't even get to use last time I was here because Gus hurt me so badly.

"I see that now," he whispers from somewhere behind me, but I don't move. Gus' presence is a quiet force behind me. I can feel him before I hear him, the warmth of him at my back. His scent—minty and clean, softened by the lingering vanilla from the soap in the tub—wraps around me.

"I didn't have any answers," he says softly. "We didn't know what was happening, Nellie. I know now how unfair that was to you, but at the time, all I wanted to do was protect you. I was scared, and, if I'm being honest, you jump to conclusions. You go from zero to one hundred, and there's no getting through that. You need control, and this was not only out of your control, but mine too. Hell, even out of my doctor's control. Last time we didn't have answers to symptoms affecting me this much, I ended up hospitalized."

I whisper, "I could have been there for you." Could I, though? If he would have told me this, would I have listened? He was scared, and I pushed him away.

His breath hitches, just barely. "I didn't want you hurting over something as frivolous as me, but now I see I hurt you either way. But, baby, I'm hurting too."

My heart clenches. I turn to face him, my voice shaking. "What I feel for you isn't frivolous."

His hands find my arms, his touch gentle, reverent. His chin drops to my shoulder, his warmth seeping into me.

"I was trying to protect you," he murmurs.

"Why? Why was it so important for you to protect me? Did you ever stop to think, to wonder that maybe in that situation, *you* were the one who needed protecting?" I don't drop his gaze, letting him see the anger behind my eyes. "Did you ever stop to ask whether, in that moment, maybe you needed to let someone help? To let *me?* I'm not brittle. I'm not fragile. The way I feel about you isn't either. Stop throwing rocks when you have a glass house, Gus."

"It's because of the way I feel about you that I want to protect you. It's a need to keep you safe. You said you hurt yourself so you could control the pain, so what was I going to do when everything I had was spiraling out of my control, huh? Was I going to let the woman I love suffer because she couldn't figure out what was wrong with me? When nobody else could?"

The woman I love. I open my eyes wide and take a step back with a gasp. "You should've trusted I wasn't going to hurt myself. You should've trusted I could handle it."

"Do *you* accept help, Nellie? Or do you keep everyone at bay? Do you share your thoughts, your feelings, your emotions, your struggles…with anyone?"

"I SHARED THEM WITH YOU! I kept *you* in the loop. I told *you* everything, Gus, and then you left me alone."

"You told me to leave!" he shouts.

"And you listened?" Oh my God. I sound insane. I stop and look at us, going in circles over the same thing over and over again. I stop in front of him, dumbfounded. The clarity I found that day before everything went down hits me again. He was scared… I was scared. We're both one fucking wave, pulling back and crashing at the same time. Not blending.

Not becoming one. Just parallels trying to coexist. Oh my God.

"Nellie..." He drags a hand down his face and shakes his head.

"Wait. I know you want me to listen. I get it now. I do. But oh my God. I was wrong, wasn't I? I was hurting, and I just didn't pay attention. You left me, but not because you wanted to. You left—"

"Because you told me to."

"Nobody ever listens to me," I reply, thinking out loud more than anything else. *I listen,* he said when he got here. "But you listen. You watch. You pay attention."

We wait, not saying anything, both of us suspended in time. So much hurt and loss has happened between us. So much pain. So much want. So much *love.* "I don't deserve you."

He holds my hand and pulls me to his chest, holding my head as he says, "You do. If I deserve you, you deserve me. We're two mirrors reflecting each other but incomplete without one another. Neither of us know how to let each other in. Neither of us know how to let each other heal, and love, and feel."

"You listened, even when what I asked wasn't what I wanted. You kept trying to be near me, and I just...I responded with sharp words and a cold shoulder. I pushed you away. I hurt us." My muffled cries hide my words when I don't move my face from his chest. I can see it all in my head. The way he looks at me. The way he cares for me. His dark eyes never leaving me, no matter where we are—always finding me in the room.

"I kept you out, Nellie. Out of one part of my life there's no controlling. One part of my life where there will always be questions and very few answers. I kept you out because I needed space to understand it before letting you in. I don't want to be a burden to anyone, let alone you. There was nothing you could've done. I'm sorry. I'm so sorry I did that, but I never stopped searching for you."

His rough hand caresses my back as his other hand holds my head. "I never stopped caring. I don't want you to push me away, and yes, maybe I should've fought harder, but Nellie, you didn't fight at all. I felt disposable too."

"I hurt you. I hurt him. I hurt everyone. I hurt—"

"None of this is your fault. Cody didn't share everything. His brother was unstable. None of it is true. Don't let your brain lie to you. You're hurting, yes, because you have a giant heart and you care. That's what I love most about you. I'm sorry I hurt you. I'm sorry I made you think I didn't love you. I'm so sorry, but none of this is your fault. Please believe me." I finally realize it. He wants to be the savior, but he doesn't want to be saved. Funny, because I hate feeling like I need saving, and now, we're here, in this conundrum. But he—wait? He loves me?

I look up at him, eyes glossy with tears, and ask the question that almost slipped my mind.

"Love? The woman you love?"

"I was really hoping you didn't catch that." He brings his hand up and cups my face, taking a deep breath and settling my own. "This is not how I wanted to tell you I love you." He wipes away a tear falling down my face. "I didn't want to tell you in the middle of an argument, but I can't omit my feelings. What I feel for you is so concrete, so real, that there's nothing holding it back. It comes so naturally to me, to love you, that my brain doesn't know I wasn't supposed to tell you yet. Loving you is so fundamental to my entire self, being away from you for those few days was torment. It was ripping me to shreds from the inside out. The day I came back for you, to talk to you, was because I felt like I was crawling out of my skin...and then I saw you, and everything was right. I could live an entire lifetime keeping you away from me, but it would be a life short-lived, because I realized very quickly, a life without you is not a life worth living. A life away from you is not something I can do. It's not something I want to do."

He kisses my forehead. I try to open my mouth to speak, but he brings a finger to my lips and whispers, "I'm not good enough for you, I know that. I know I'm damaged goods. You deserve better. I told myself I could let you go and let you fall in love with someone who didn't take up so much space, who didn't bring so much pain, but I'm going to be selfish and say that's not going to happen. I'm going to be selfish and keep you. I might not be the man you deserve, but damn it if I'm not going to die trying. Because you know what I realized?"

"What?"

"I realized you're mine, and I'm yours, and nothing else matters. I love you, Nellie. I'm sorry I didn't say it before. I'm so sorry I kept it from you instead of just letting you all the way in and letting you see it all—my fears and my love. But I do, baby girl. I love you, and I wouldn't have it any other way."

"I thought I wasn't enough for you. I thought you couldn't *love* me. I thought *I* was the burden. The weird one. The one hard to love."

He shakes his head and smiles. "Loving you is the easiest thing I've ever done." He lets the words float in the air, caressing all my doubts and easing any hesitation.

"I thought you knew, but maybe I just needed to say it, with words, once, twice, again. So, here I am, saying it. I love you. Wholeheartedly." Every word he says leaves goosebumps in its wake, comforting me and making me feel the way I always do around him—alive.

I rise to my tiptoes and kiss his lips. It catches him by surprise, but in no time, he does the same. He kisses me gently. He kisses me thoroughly. His kiss is communicating with me. His kiss makes me feel loved, cherished, and wanted. This one kiss means more to me than anything else. His lips are full and tasty, he always tastes so good. Salty, minty, and like him. Just perfect. His tongue dances with me. Slowly. Possessive. I'm his. He's mine. The rest, we can figure out.

"None of it was your fault, but Nellie, I'm going to love you through it. I know your heart, and I know you know mine. I see you, and I know you see me, but we both need to work on listening. We both need to believe, and this is where we need to be."

"I love you," I whisper, a weight lifting off my chest. I love him. I love him. I love him.

"I know. I can see it. It's good to hear it, though. And you know what? I'm going to love you so hard, there won't ever be a doubt in your mind about where your heart belongs and to whom. Where your body belongs. Where you belong. Who *you* belong with."

"Promise?"

"I promise."

"How are we going to face everyone? We basically lied to everyone. We've lied to ourselves, wave after wave of lies, to keep ourselves safe, refusing to accept help from each other. No wonder we were drowning," I whisper against his lips before he gives me another peck, before he kisses every tear off my cheeks.

He holds my face, and without any hesitation, he says, "You hold on to me. Let me be your anchor, my girl, and then, we face them together, one person at a time. But nothing else matters, as long as you're by my side. Everything else, we can figure out. I promise."

We kiss again. We kiss until my lips feel raw. We kiss until I don't want to shed more tears, until my own love for him is pouring out of every part of me.

"Hey Gus," I whisper against his lips.

"Yes, Trouble?" He smiles, and I can't help but do the same.

"I love you." He holds my gaze, his eyes darkening with intensity. This is not only lust. This is understanding and passion. This is friendship and patience. This is the way he holds me. The way his lips sync with mine is something I've never experienced. This is love, and suddenly, with his lips on mine and his hands roaming my body, I feel like I'm going to be okay. I can let him help me through this. I can let him love me, if he lets me do the same.

I walk us backward, not letting go of his lips and pulling him by his shirt closer to me. I keep walking, and when I finally reach where I want to go, I pull him even closer before I take us both down into the water.

He gasps after we resurface, and I laugh. What a foreign sound to my ears.

"What the hell?" Gus asks, shaking his head and taking his shirt off, tossing it out of the pool and onto the deck.

"I wanted the water, and the water wanted me, but I also wanted you, so here we are." I swim closer to him, sinking underwater, the place where I feel most at ease. He sinks under too, meeting me halfway and hugging my body tight. He kisses my lips before helping me and coming up for air.

"I can't swim a lot, not right now. My heart can't be working too hard."

"Oh shit, I'm sorry. I didn't think about it. Come on, let's get out."

"No, I didn't mean I can't be in the water. I just can't go for a swim, but you know what I can do?" he asks, lifting an eyebrow. I bite my lip knowingly, my body instantly coming to life under his gaze. I may be in the water, but the way he looks at me burns me from the inside out. He fits his hands under my ass and lifts me up, sitting me on the edge of the pool as he bites my nipple over the fabric of the shirt I'm wearing. *His* shirt.

"As much as I like to see you wearing my clothes, take it off." I obey his command, removing the wet shirt over my head and tossing it with his. The minute the shirt is off, his mouth is on my breast again, kissing, licking, biting, and pulling.

"Fuck," I groan, and he moans against my flesh, the most obscene, guttural, sexy, and delicious sound. I arch my back against him, pushing my breast deeper into his mouth as his hand lowers to pull my panties off.

"Lift your ass for me," he says with a mouth full of my breast. I set my feet on the edge of the pool, lifting so he can slide my underwear off. He lets go of my nipple with a pop and brings his eyes to me. He stares at me, starting with my eyes and lowering slowly as he adjusts himself underwater.

"Fucking hell, Nellie. You're perfect. I'm never going to be tired of this view. I'm never going to get tired of seeing you."

"Even when I'm old and wrinkly?" I ask, trying to close my legs, but he won't let me. His hands quickly go to my knees, pushing them open wider as he stares at my pussy.

"Especially if you're old and wrinkly, because that means we grew old together. I wouldn't have it any other way. I would still feast on my perfect pussy. I can promise you that."

"Your pussy, huh?"

His hands go up to my hips, as he pulls me closer to the edge. His hands roam up my belly, touching my breasts until he holds my face. "You are mine. All of you." He brings his hands down to my chest. "My heart." He continues lower until he touches the scars on my hips. "My pain." He continues lower, bringing his head closer to my aching core before he says, "And my pussy."

He closes his mouth over my mound, sucking hard and making me see stars. "All of you. I want it all." He takes one of my feet and places it on his shoulder, giving him more access to all of me. He licks, he kisses, he bites, he taunts. He flattens his tongue until he's touching dangerously close to my ass.

"And one of these days, this ass will be mine too." I suck in a breath the moment he says that. His tongue explores every-thing, every place he can reach.

"Mm, I'll never get tired of tasting you." He goes back to licking and teasing, and I moan and writhe under his touch. It feels so good, so *fucking* good. I feel the warm liquid pooling behind my belly, and with one scrape of his teeth on my clit, I come undone.

"Fuck," I groan once more, and he doesn't relent. He keeps going, stretching my orgasm out longer. Bringing me higher. Giving me pleasure.

"Take it all, Nellie. Take all the good. Give me the pain. Let it go," he says between my legs. If I didn't already know I love him, now would be the time. Not because of the earth-shattering orgasm or the way he's making me feel, but because he seems to know exactly what I need to hear. He seems to know exactly what I need.

I bring my hands to his face, lifting him from his favorite place, and the guy pouts. "Oh my God. Get over it. It's just a pussy."

"It's my pussy, and I missed it." I roll my eyes at him.

"You're so crass."

"You wanted honesty. How's that for honesty?" He removes his shorts and I take advantage of the moment to pull him closer to me. I hook my legs around him and hold his face. "You can give me yours too. Your pain. Your fears. I can hold them. They're not too much for me. You're not too much for me, I promise." He swallows hard.

"That was my biggest fear."

"I know it now, but you're not. You're perfect. You were made for me."

I caress his face, sliding my hands through his hair. "I love you. I want to love you through it too. Let me, please."

He nods, bringing his lips to mine. I whisper against them, "Promise, Gus."

"I promise."

We kiss again. This time, our kiss is both minty and tangy, salty and sweet, me and him. Us. The best way to be. He kisses me as he slides his dick inside me, meeting every lick of my tongue on his with a thrust. They're slow at first and then pick up tempo, just how I like it. I pull him closer to me, as close as I can. I thrust my tongue into his mouth, and he lets me. Tongues rush, nails scratching and dragging into his back. His lips kiss and bite my neck. My collarbone. My throat. I moan, I groan, I scream. He praises, he licks, he groans.

"Come for me, Trouble," he commands.

"Come with me, Gus," I demand. I want him so close to me that there's no air between us, so close, I can't move. I can't breathe. So close, all I feel is him. He wraps his strong arms around me as he thrusts again and again.

"I love you," I moan as I start to ride the wave of pleasure once more.

"I love you," he echoes, with everything he has.

PART 5

THE STILLNESS

And then, it was quiet.
A silence like never before.
Even the wind knows not to ripple the sea.
But in silence, we listen.
In silence, we grow.

THIRTY-TWO
THAT'S A FIRST

HOLD Back The River by James Bay

GUS

THIS HAS BEEN the second longest drive of my life. After Nellie called her parents and told them she was fine and messaging a very angry but understanding Cara, we decided it was time to go back. We both drove there, but I didn't want her to drive back alone, so Martin and one of the other drivers headed to the cabin. I have a very restless Nellie as we approach her home. She's looking out the window, her hands tucked under her legs, keeping herself from picking at her nails, I'm sure, but biting her lower lip.

"Are you nervous?" I ask, even though it's an obvious question.

She nods and turns her face my way as we pull up to her parents' house. Cara's van is in the driveway, and as soon as Nellie sees it, she lets out a breath and sinks into the seat.

"It's going to be okay. Just go with the wave," I say,

touching her necklace, reminding her of the meaning: life comes in waves, some high and some low, but they always reach the shore.

"We do it together, okay?" I grab her hand and bring it to my lips, smiling at her and setting the car to park.

The walk to the entryway of her house feels like a mile long. She's dragging her feet and looking down. I was the one worried about everything before, but now, I just want her to be happy. I know her parents will want her to be happy too. Our fingers are intertwined, dancing in a safe hold as we approach the door. She gets her keys and opens it as she squeezes my hand.

"I've got you, Trouble." We walk through the beautiful farm-style foyer and the swinging doors to the living room, where Cara, Manny, Nellie's parents, and my mom are all sitting talking. At least, they were talking, because when they see us, a hush falls over them.

"Hi," Nellie whispers, and Cara runs to her.

"You scared me shitless, Nells!" Cara shouts while hugging her tight, her arms wrapped around Nellie's neck, cradling her head with her hands. Such a protective hold, but I can see her almost trembling.

"Language!" their mom shouts.

"Sorry!" Cara shouts back.

"I'm okay, I promise," Nellie whispers.

"Still," Cara adds without letting her go.

I look up from them and find all the parents and Manny with their eyes on me. I smile softly and shrug. Nellie's mom shakes her head, and mine smile wider. I mouth "La amo[1]" to her, and she replies with a nod. Moms do know it all, it seems.

"Okay, let go now. I'm fine," Nellie says.

Cara lets go of the chokehold she had Nellie on and then

---

1. I love her.

smacks her on the arm. "Don't ever do that again." Then, she walks up to me and does the same with mine.

"What was mine for? I just brought her back in one piece."

"Sleeping with my little sister, Gus?! What the hell?" Cara stands in front of me with her arms crossed, her cheeks red. Oh, she's mad. She shares physical similarities with Nellie, like the same height and green eyes, but Cara's blonde hair makes her skin look lighter. The anger seeping under her skin shows like a bright pink blush on her cheeks.

"Language, Cara!" their mom says again.

"Let's have a seat," I say and walk to the couch with Nellie still holding my hand. I love that she's making a statement with something so small. We're in this together, and she won't let go. God, I love her.

We all take a seat, Nellie and I on the bigger couch and Cara sitting next to Manny.

"Anything you both would like to tell us?" Mom asks, for some reason hiding a laugh behind her smile.

"Mr. and Mrs. Thompson, Mom, Cara"— Nellie interrupts me.

"Oh my God, Gus, you make it sound like you're about to propose. Stop. We're together. He loves me, I love him, it started in April—" Cara gasps, and the parents giggle as Nellie continues "—nobody took advantage of anybody. We're both consenting adults. We're together now. Sorry we kept it from y'all. End of story."

Manny laughs, and that's the thing that tips the scale. Everyone but Cara starts laughing too.

"Did I get it all, babe?" Nellie asks me with sass behind her words.

"You forgot that I would never hurt you. I promise that to everyone," I add, looking around and nodding at her dad when he smiles at me.

"I know this is unexpected, and maybe not what you guys

wanted, but the truth is, I fell in love with Nellie the way you fall in love with music—with a note first, then with the whole melody. It was beautiful and loud, like how listening to your favorite song makes you want to dance or sing. I wish I could say it happened slowly, but it didn't. One look and a few conversations later, and I knew I was in trouble. We fought it, we did, because we knew it would be complicated, but that was a battle we were both going to lose eventually. I love her, and I'm honored she loves me back. I want to be here for her for everything, and these past few weeks just confirmed it. I'm sorry we kept it from all of you, but I'm not sorry I get to love her."

"We know, sweetie," Mom says, and with everyone else nodding and smiling, I know it to be true. They knew and they didn't care. I can feel a million pounds lifting off my shoulders, my hands loosening the tight grip they had on Nellie's. They know, and they don't care.

"Why is nobody surprised about this?" Cara looks at everyone and frowns. Manny softens his eyes at her knowingly.

"You all knew, didn't you?!" Cara shouts. Manny flinches and narrows his eyes at me. For a man who likes to talk as much as he does, he sure is quiet now. I open my mouth to say something, but Nellie's mom beats me to it.

"Not that they told us, Cara, but it was pretty obvious." Cara's mom turns to face us now. "I understand why you wanted to keep it from us, but truly, we're just happy you two are happy."

"You're not mad?" I ask, and she just smiles at us.

"Why would I be? Both my girls ended up with my best friend's sons. We will never need to fight over grandchildren. We can just have them all running wild and free between our houses."

"Mom, nobody's talking children," Nellie says, and we all laugh.

"One step at a time," I add. "I would like to date your daughter loudly now, so as long as you're all okay, I'm happy."

"Of course, we're okay. You're like a son to us, and now you get to be a son-in-law."

"Mom, nobody's marrying anyone," Nellie, clearly annoyed, replies.

"Yet," I say and look at Nellie, who's shooting daggers at me with her eyes. "Too soon?"

"Too soon."

"We're just happy for you. Hopefully, we can see more of the two of you instead of the sneaking around you've been doing." Cara spits her drink, Manny coughs, the parents smile, and Nellie's eyes are wide.

"You knew this whole time?" Nellie asks.

"Honey, this is a small town. Even the walls talk," Mom says.

"I didn't know anything, and I live here," Cara pipes in.

"You were preoccupied," her dad says, and although this is the first time he has said anything, it was the perfect come back, making us all laugh.

"Wait, I get that the elderly don't want to know how this happened, but I do, so spill. Now," Cara replies.

"How much time do you have?" Nellie asks.

"As long as you need," Cara says.

"THAT WASN'T THAT BAD, was it?" Nellie asks me, her head on my lap. After telling them how everything developed, leaving out all the filthy details, Cara understood, even thanking me for loving her sister. Eventually, their parents went to bed, everyone else left, and it's just us, sitting out back on the porch for a while now.

"I don't know why I was so afraid they would lose it when they found out."

"You were in your own head. I know the feeling too well. I think we were just so wrapped in our own fears, we didn't take the time to be vulnerable, honest, and logical with each other."

"When did you become so wise?" I ask her, caressing her cheek with the back of my hand. Her skin is so soft, and all I want is to keep my hands on her at all times.

"I was born a genius, don't you know?"

"A beautiful genius." She closes her eyes and lets out a sigh.

"I need you to promise me you'll be okay by yourself tonight." We've been dancing around this all night. Ever since I found her beyond drunk on the couch in the cabin, I haven't let her out of my sight. Tonight, it's time.

"I don't know if I will be," she replies honestly, eyes still closed and her hand holding mine. She looks so peaceful, as peaceful as she always does, as peaceful as I feel when I'm near her. It breaks my heart that she's hurting so much.

"I'm safe, though, I promise." That's what I wanted to hear. She's safe. She needed time. She needed to cry. She needed to feel. Now, she can heal. Slowly. A day at a time, and I'll be here for her every step of the way.

"Are you going to work tomorrow?"

"No, I emailed the principal on Monday. I'm taking the rest of the week off. I can't in good conscience go to school like this. I am seeing my therapist tomorrow, though. I should have gone weeks ago."

"Mm, then why don't you come with me? I could use some company."

I quirk a brow. "Could you now?"

"Mm-hmm. I get very scared when I'm by myself." She chuckles, and it's like music to my ears. I would give anything to always make her smile.

"Is that okay with you?" she asks, but this time, she opens her eyes and looks into mine. Her beautiful green eyes—I'm never going to get tired of seeing them, of looking into them.

"It's always okay with me, baby girl. I want to sleep by your side every night. I want you to be the last thing I see before I go to sleep, dream about you all night long, and wake up to you tangled with me in my bed."

"So clingy," she jokes.

"I'm in love with you. I can't get enough of you, love. Call me clingy if you want, but that's the truth."

"I love you too," she whispers as she sits up. "Are my clothes still in your drawer?"

"Yup, and your toothbrush on my bathroom sink."

"Then let's go. I would love nothing more than to fall asleep in your arms again. I love that feeling."

"Which one, my love?" I ask. I'm never going to get tired of calling her love, of telling her I love her. Of showing her I do, too.

"Safe. I feel safe with you."

"You are, Nellie, and you always be. Now, let's go home."

THIRTY-THREE
AFTER
SIX MONTHS LATER

Somewhere Over The Rainbow by Christina Perri

NELLIE

"I'M NEVER GETTING over you two together," Cara says, walking past me and Gus.

"You're never getting over it? I'm never getting over how you two—" Roe points at Cara and Manny, "—and you two —" she points at us "—did that. Two sisters with two brothers who also happen to be family friends? Too much to keep track of."

"At least the babies will stay in the family. No fighting over who will see them when, same set of grandparents," Gus replies, and I smack him on the chest.

"Babies?" I ask. Our moms won't stop bringing it up either, and I swear, I will start collecting a toll every time someone mentions kids.

"Yeah, I mean, not now, but, you know, eventually."

"A baby, yes. Babies plural, no." I don't want a bunch of

kids—or at least I didn't think I did, but the way his eyes are pure fire when he says *babies* might change my mind.

"Yes, plural. Ten of them."

"TEN BABIES?" I scream, and our friends laugh. Okay, that's too many. "We can practice making dozens of babies, but I think my vagina will be closed after two or three."

Manny spits out his drink, Jake shakes his head, and Santiago stays silent, as usual. "What? All of you know where babies come from, yeah? Don't act all surprised."

"Babies are great, but ten of them is a lot," Natalie says, walking by with baby Vero in her hands. Cara immediately takes her, offering a smile as she coos at Vero.

Natalie had Vero a month ago—Veronica Joy. *The one who brings the victory of joy*, a name fit for a princess, bringing happiness in the darkest of times. These past six months have been hard for this family they've made through love, joy, time, and heartbreak. Nick's death has not been easy to move on from, but we're all trying for Natalie and the girls.

Gus must see me with my eyes trained on them, because he squeezes my hand gently. I look at him, and he smiles softly, quietly, almost imperceptibly to everyone else but me. He has no issues showing me how much he loves me, but he knows I don't want him to make a big deal of how I feel.

When we left the cabin six months ago, the first thing he made me do was call my therapist, who I'm back to seeing weekly. The transition has been hard, but I have a great support system in place, including all these wonderful people.

"How can you say no to ten of these when they look this cute?" Gus coos, mimicking a baby until Vero lets out the loudest fart, and we all laugh as he scrunches his face.

"Because the cuteness is only so we don't eat them," Natalie says, trying to stand up to take Vero from Cara, but she doesn't let her.

"I got it. I'll be back." Cara goes inside, presumably to

change the baby, and the group falls back into easy conversation, setting the cadence of comfort and love.

"You good, Trouble?" Gus whispers in my ear, goosebumps breaking over my skin. Suddenly, I'm severely aware of how my body is molded to his. I sat on his lap a while back, and when I tried to get back up, he tightened his arms, keeping me in place.

I nod, turning my head to face him and drop a kiss on his nose. "I'm okay. I promise." We've been making each other promises since that night, not always with words, but with actions too. I keep my promises by making sure he takes his medicine every day without making a big deal of it, by going to doctor's appointments and asking questions when I don't understand. I keep my promises by going to therapy so I can work through some of the feelings and thoughts that won't leave my head, so I can keep learning strategies to cope.

He keeps his promises by showing up for me every day, reminding me he loves me no matter what. He gives me the space I need while simultaneously not leaving me alone when I need company, and he knows the difference between the two. We've talked about maybe moving in together in the summer so we don't have to make the hour commute between our places. Not because we don't already do it, but because it would just be easier.

Gus found some other passions that don't require strenuous activities so he can do them more often. One of them, I benefit from greatly everyday—cooking. I can't wait to live in the same place as that man so he can spoil me rotten.

I met Blair a couple of months ago, and although I didn't want to like her at first, she reminds me a lot of Bee, so we clicked right away. We've gotten close; even though Bee only lives an hour and a half away, her situationship with Abraham and Jean Luis consumes her free time when she's not at work. We talk every day, but Blair is physically there. Bee reminded me I'm allowed to love other friends, and I don't have to choose. She's living her own why choose life with her lovers, and maybe I do the same with my friendships. I welcome it all. The book club, brunch, dinners with Blair and her fancy friends. Daily chats with Bee and Victoria. A full life. A reminder I'm still here, and I need to want this to be better for me. Victoria is finishing school soon and moving to New York for work, living her dream, and I couldn't be happier for her. Bee and I will go visit her once she's settled.

Happy. I am truly happy. This is the first time in my life I don't feel out of place. I don't feel like I know too much or like I'm too young. I don't feel like I have to beg for attention or to be seen for more than my brain. Half the time, this group even forgets; they just care about me. Except Roe. That one mentions it every moment she can. I've learned to love her sassiness, so I don't care at this point. I am smart. It's part of who I am but not all that I am, and I love how all of them see that. I love how Gus sees that.

I love that he sees me. He sees my hurt, my happiness, my love, my struggles, and my passion. He sees my brain and my heart equally. He sees my body and my emotions. He sees it all, and he loves it all. I, in return, see and love all of him too. I never thought, at twenty-one, I would meet the love of my life, but I think I did. He's everything I've ever wanted, everything I needed, even when I didn't know it.

"Here," Cara says, stepping out of the house, the screen door creaking as it swings shut behind her. She balances the baby on one hip, a bottle of wine in the other hand. The air is thick with the scent of the garden—Nick's garden—where the flowers he planted still bloom, stubborn against the changing seasons.

She walks straight to Natalie, pressing a soft kiss to her forehead before carefully handing the baby back. Bella is with some friends, so it was the perfect time to do this. She doesn't want to talk much about her dad, and we all understand why.

"Get your glasses out, bitches," Cara says, her voice light

but steady as she uncorks the bottle. The wine flows into each glass, deep red and rich. Not Gus', of course. He gets water.

The small circle of friends stands close, their faces lit by the porch light and the flickering candles on the table. The night hums with the distant sounds of the neighborhood—laughing kids, a barking dog, the faint echoes of the pre-game show from inside.

"These past six months have been brutal," Cara begins, her voice carrying the weight of shared grief, "but especially for Nat. When I asked her how she wanted to spend today—Nick's six-month angelversary—she didn't want something somber. She wanted what he would've wanted. A night with friends watching the Superbowl. A night of laughter. A night of love. So, here we are." She glances around, eyes shining. "No tears—at least, not too many. Just good memories."

She lifts her glass. "To Nick. The best friend, dad, husband, brother, teacher, and coach this town has ever seen."

A murmur of agreement ripples through the group—the group of friends he left behind.

"Most of us grew up with him. We knew him as the boy who couldn't sit still, the teenager who drove us all insane, and the man who somehow found his way to Natalie like it was written in the stars. He's missed every single day, but he's never really gone. We see him everywhere." Her voice wavers just slightly before she swallows and continues. "We see him in our laughter because he wouldn't have had it any other way. We see him in Bella's kindness, in Vero's eyes. We see him in the flowers he planted with his own hands, in the home he built for Nat. We see him in the changes—better rules, better resources, the kind of things that might mean another family doesn't have to go through what we did."

She exhales a soft, shaky breath. Around her, people nod their heads. Some smile. Some don't even try to hide their tears. Livie, Alex's wife, presses her face into his shoulder, her body trembling. Alex—Nick's closest friend—stares down at the ground, jaw tight, eyes red.

"But more than anything," Cara continues, "we see him in Natalie. In her heart. In the way she loves us, in how she lets us in, even when grief makes it hard. In how she keeps his name alive, keeps his memory warm, and never lets him become a story of the past. For that, I'm grateful, and I know you are too."

A quiet beat. Then, she raises her glass higher.

"Long live our friend."

Everyone lifts their glasses as we shout after her.

"Long live Nick."

"Long live Nick!"

Clinks rings out into the night, and then, one by one, everyone tilts their glass, spilling a few drops on the ground—for him, for Nick. The wine is bitter and smooth, burning just a little, as bittersweet as this night.

Cara clears her throat, blinking fast. "Alright, before we all turn into a damn mess, let's go inside. The Tampa Knights and the California Cougars are putting on a show tonight, and I, for one, am not missing it."

Laughter, tired but real, breaks through the heavy air. One by one, everyone heads inside, drawn to the warmth of the house, the comfort of each other.

Everyone but Gus and me.

I never moved from his lap, and he never asked me to. The night wraps around us, the distant sounds of the game a low hum in the background. I take a deep breath.

"We can go," he says quietly.

"I don't want to."

"You sure?"

I nod. "I just need a minute."

His arms tighten around me, solid, warm, and mine. "Take all the time you need, baby girl. I'm here. I'm not going anywhere."

And he doesn't.

EPILOGUE
A YEAR AND A HALF LATER

It's Always Been You by Jessie Murph

NELLIE

"I THOUGHT you were supposed to be easy with my heart," Gus says, standing from the couch as I walk out of our bedroom, wedding ready. Allie is getting married today, and from what Cara said, it's the backyard wedding of her dreams. Cara and Manny got engaged last week, so this is their first major event as an engaged couple, and she's being insufferable about it. I'm particularly looking forward to having a good time with the man of my dreams, his family, and our friends.

"I'm always easy with your heart," I reply, walking up to him and landing straight in his arms.

"Not looking like this, you're not." I'm wearing a green bodice dress that shows off just a little cleavage. It wraps my body perfectly, and I look hot as shit. I knew what I was doing when I picked it. I know he loves me, I know he lusts after me, but even after moving in together, he still looks at me like he can't believe I'm his.

"You like?" I ask, taking a step back and twirling slowly so he can appreciate every inch of my body. "You don't look so bad yourself." And by that, I mean he looks hot as hell.

He's wearing a light grey tuxedo, a green handkerchief peeking out to match my dress. His skin is almost glowing, his eyes as beautiful as ever. I'm the luckiest girl in the world—I get to get lost in them every day and every night.

We've been asked so many times about when it will be our turn, but honestly? I'm not in a rush. The first six months of our relationship was such a whirlwind; I've just been savoring this man for the rest of it. We've been together for two years now, and I know I could spend a lifetime with him, so there's no rush. None at all.

"I'm about to look a lot better with the most beautiful girl by my side."

"Make sure you don't say that to the bride, you know, your sister?" He smiles before kissing me gently. He always kisses me this way, even when it develops into passion. He kisses me tentatively, as if he's asking for permission. He takes his time exploring my lips, as if they're not the ones he kisses every night. He does more than kissing—he memorizes. He treats every kiss as if it's the last one, and I love him so much more for that.

We walk to his car for the drive to the wedding venue. As soon as we arrive, I'm taken aback. It's a beautiful property by the lake in Magnolia Springs, about an hour from Baker. Bee lives here, and her company did the decorations. I'm in love with everything she did. It's subtle and cozy, with a mix of earthy colors and simple florals. Allie requested we all bring lawn chairs, so Gus carries ours. It's quiet; not many people are here yet, but I do see Natalie with Bella and Vero sitting nearby.

I've gotten closer to Bella in the past year and a half, and although I'm not really close to Natalie, we talk a lot. I help when I can, either watching the girls or taking Bella to the wine shop after work. We're all still mourning Nick, but nobody as much as them.

Natalie has the biggest heart. She talks about forgiveness, about how Nick would have loved for everyone to live life to the fullest. She's healing in such an inspiring way, and I can only hope to be like her one day. I heard from Cody about a year ago, after Josh was sentenced. Cody thanked me for everything I did, sending me a picture of him playing football at his new high school in South Carolina. It definitely gave me the closure I sought, and now, I can sleep in peace. I did what I could; nothing could've prevented the tragedy. Now, we live, we learn, and we heal, and we put procedures in place so nothing like that ever happens again.

The sun is shining, but the canopy of oak trees keep us from roasting. The soft breeze is perfect today, not too hot or too cold. We find our spot in the yard, and he places our chairs down. After I sit, he gives me a kiss on the forehead and does the same.

"You know...everyone else keeps asking us when it will be us."

I shrug. "Yeah, I know."

"Well...don't you want this too? The wedding, the celebration of love, promising we'll be together forever?" He looks so serious as he says these words. He's been joking about children and poking at the future since we got together, but this feels different. This feels like a serious conversation, one we probably shouldn't be having at his sister's wedding.

"I do, but we're so young," I say in the tone he hates so much. I love that he hates it.

"I'm being serious, Nellie."

"I know you are, babe, but now is not the time."

"I'm not proposing, love. I'm just bringing it up. Is this

something you want someday, maybe not too far into the future?"

I look at this man—a man who has taught me so much about myself, who has grown as much as I have in the past two years. A man who makes me laugh and smile like no other person. He has become my best friend in every sense of the word, and I'm so thankful for it. He makes me feel important and cherished. He understands me, and I don't ever want to be with anyone else.

"Of course I want to marry you one day, Gus. I'm the luckiest girl alive to be loved by you, and honestly, I want to make you happy too. If the wedding, the vows, the party, the grand celebration is what you want, then we can do that."

"What do *you* want?" he asks, and I know he means it. He loves me so much and so hard, my happiness front and center in his mind always.

"I want to be happy with you, and I want you to be happy, too. I want to love you for the rest of my life in whatever shape or form you'll have me. As long as I'm with you, nothing else matters. We don't need rings and a ceremony to know that, but if it's something you want, then I want it too."

"You're just gonna go with the wave, huh?" he asks, touching the necklace he got me that has become a daily reminder that life's too short. You have to take the opportunities when they come. Ride the wave until it reaches the shore, one at a time.

"As long as it's with you, I'm jumping in. Every time."

He smiles. "Te amo.[1]"

"Yo Tambien[2]. Now go, or your sister is gonna kill you." He looks up at how the venue is filling, the rows full of people waiting for the bride and groom. Manny stands in the back, signaling for Gus.

---

1. I love you.
2. I do too.

"Don't go anywhere. I'll be right back."
"Never," I reply.
"You promise?"
"I promise. Always."

THANK you so much for reading The Lies Always Told. Do you want to see Gus and Nellie's proposal?

Click here to read the bonus epilogue now or scan the qr code:

ARE you ready for Natalie's love after loss story? Keep reading for the prologue but you can preorder here.

THOL - COMING LATE 2025

Prologue

NATALIE

THIS WEDDING VENUE IS BEAUTIFUL, right by the water with a mix of earthy colors in the decorations. It reminds me of peace and good moments; both things we take for granted most of the time. As hard as it is to sit here—with my toddler on my lap, my daughter next to me, and an empty seat by my side—I still try to be present for my friends. My family that life gave me. An unfair life, but it still gave me them. It also gave me him, even if it ripped him away from me too soon.

Far too soon.

The gentle breeze caresses my cheeks as soon as I think those words. I look at the empty seat with a portrait of him smiling and one single leaf lands on my lap. *Is this you? Is this a sign?* Jake put a beer on the cupholder; always a good man looking out for his best friend even after his body is not physically here. I wish I could say it hurts less, but it doesn't. Nothing makes it hurt less.

The music plays, signaling the ceremony is starting, and we all stand up to see Jake walking down the aisle. He's smiling so big and tears threaten to trickle down my face. Looking at how happy he is reminds me how it felt to have my soul lit on fire once. It feels like you're walking on sunshine while there's a brightly burning flame deep within you, waiting to burst from your body at any point. But that doesn't exist inside of me anymore. The flame burned out and no match in the world will ever bring it back. There's no fire. There's no soul.

My heart was woven to his so deeply that every passing year, month, day, hour, minute, and second in which he's not on this earth with me, I can hardly breathe. I've been barely breathing for years now, and I don't know if I'll ever be able to take in a full breath again.

There are books, songs, movies, and poetry about true love. The one love of a lifetime. On how rare it is, and that when you find it, you must hold on to it and never let it go. Allie and Jake have that love and we're all here to witness it. It's beautiful, and although I wish I could believe that will again be me one day, I can't.

I had a love like that once. I knew so deeply in my bones he was the other half of me that, at just sixteen years old, I swore I would never see another person the same. I would never love another person the same. But fate would have it that when we vowed to be together until death do us part, it would be taken at face value and rip him away from me.

Away from us.

And the day that single bullet went through his heart was the day my heart started giving out, too. Except I have to pretend to be strong for the two little girls left behind, even if I'm dying inside. I never expected to live a life without him, yet here I am, trying and failing every day. But I smile, just like

I smile right now, holding our daughter he never got to meet. I smile, just like I am now as our best friends finally say their 'I dos'. *He should be here to see it, too.*

I wipe away a tear I can blame on the beautiful ceremony if someone asks, as opposed to the real reason I'm shedding them. Because his life got cut too short and it's not fair. It's not fair at all.

We live our lives creating memories. Every day in the mundane, we're creating what might be our last—whatever is happening. Our last cup of coffee. Our last drive down I-95. Our last first kiss. Our last goodbye. The sad part? We don't know it will be the last until it is. Until the moment is gone and all that remains are memories.

So, when the officiant tells Jake to kiss his bride, I try to commit it to memory, just like I've been trying to do with every single happy moment I've been a part of in the past two years. Even if it's a reminder that I'll never be kissed like that again. Even if I'll never be held like that again. Even if I'll never be loved like that again. I don't want to ever forget them. Any of them. I don't want to forget *him*. Even if it kills me in the process.

PREORDER THOL: A love after loss, plus size single mom, and retired hockey player small town romance

ACKNOWLEDGMENTS

You've made it! If you're here, it means you finished this book, and I can't thank you enough. Thank you so much for reading *The Lies Always Told*. I know I said it in the author's note, but this story has been rooted so deep within my soul that it feels like I put a little part of me in every single page, sentence, and word. Even each song has big meaning to me, and the fact that you finished it all makes me incredibly thankful.

As I'm writing these acknowledgments, tears in my eyes, Noah Kahan in my headphones, and a very sleepy Mr. Cordova next to me, I want to take a moment to say thank you. There are so many people who played a role not only in this story, but in my author career who I would love to take the time to say something to.

I want to start with YOU, because without your love for my stories and your support, I wouldn't be here. This story would probably not exist if not for you, so thank you. Thank you for reading, for recommending my books to others, for telling me how much my words mean to you, and for being there. I may not know who you are, but I want you to know how important you are to me and my dream.

To my husband, Joey—thank you for everything you do. I wouldn't be where I am now without your support. The late nights sitting by me so I could write. Taking the kids for hours on end when I was hitting writer's block and needed to focus. The countless dinners you cooked when I was in the groove. The smiles you pulled out of me when I was the grumpiest because I was so frustrated with Nellie and Gus. Just overall for everything. Thank you so much for always inspiring the male main characters in all my books. Thank you for letting me pick your brain with my million questions and for letting me steal your favorite car to give to my fictional character as his favorite car. Thank you for seeing me when I was so deep in grief, I couldn't see myself, and for showing me how loudly I deserve to be loved. I hope your music is always perfect and your car seat is always comfy. I love you with everything I have.

To my best friends and PAs, Adriana and Colleen—thank you for keeping me fed and caffeinated while I drafted this book with a million and a half signings in between. Thank you for being the ultimate hype girls and for wanting my stories so bad, you are willing to read them a chapter at a time in my notes app. Thank you for loving my stories so much, you would go to bat for me and them any day.

To my brand manager and PA queen, Cassie—I don't know how many times I reached out to you freaking out, and you gave me nothing but peace. I hope you know that every single time, I felt you were in my corner. I don't know how I would have written this book without you. Thank you for handling so much so I can breathe life into these stories. PS: you finally get to read this whole book as opposed to the hundreds of teasers I sent you one at a time.

To my alpha reader, developmental extraordinaire, and friend, Jayné Kirk—I hit the jackpot when I met you in that line at Apollycon almost three years ago. If I tallied how many minutes you and I spent talking about Nellie and Gus, their story, their hopes and dreams and fears, I'm sure we would have weeks, if not months. This story would have been a disaster without your input. Thank you for brainstorming with me and for believing in me. Thank you for everything you do and for teaching me more and more about showing and not telling. I'm so lucky to have you in my corner.

To my agent, Sadé—knowing you believe in me and my stories is definitely bucket list worthy. Thank you for your kind words and encouragement always.

To my alpha and beta team, Maeghen, Hannah Hayek, Jenn | La Bookish Latina, Anaika (Anya) Hidalgo Gomez Anderson, Erika, Julie Walker, Sky Kline, Ashley Boyle, Sophie, Jessica, Michelle, Ashley, Cait, Mandy, Erica @the-bookish.momma, Sam Parker, Brittany, Ycel, and Kendra, the biggest hype squad a girl could ask for—not only did you all give me hope when I didn't have any, but you also helped me turn this story into the best version it possibly could be. Thank you so much for your patience, understanding, and overall joy to read this story. I couldn't have done this without you. Special thank you to Jill Jones for giving me extra eyes for HAE. How small is this world that we both share this condition and are both book girlies?!

To my sensitivity readers, Ycel @icedcoffeeandabook, Jill and my other two who prefer not to be named—thank you so much for everything you did. This story is better because of all your input and care. Thank you!

To my author friends, so many of you who I adore, but especially to the ones who believed in me and practically held my hand as I drafted this book: Hollie, Rachel, Hailey, Sarah, Jenn, Erin, Alexis, Allie, Abby, Lo, Veronica, Mikayla, Nicole, Anastasija, and Emily—thank you for the endless sprints, hundreds of voice memos, the text messages, and the support. It takes a village, and I'm so lucky to have you in mine. Extra brownie points to Hollie Luckie, Sarah A. Bailey, and Anastasija White for all your help brainstorming, beta, or sensitivity reading some of this manuscript.

To my children, my biggest fans—you're so patient as Mami navigates balancing it all. I hope you're always as proud of me as I am of you, and I hope you never feel like you need to hide something from me, like these two did. I hope you know I'm always here for you, and when you read this book, at forty five years old at least, I hope you read this paragraph and smile.

To my cover designers, Kim with KBG designs and Acacia with Ever After Cover Designs—thank you for giving life to the most beautiful covers I've ever seen. We're not supposed to have favorites, but these covers are definitely mine.

To my editor, Alexa—I haven't even gotten the edited manuscript, and I already know it will be fantastic. Thank you for answering all my questions as I embarked in this adventure with you. Thank you for your kind heart and your listening ears. Thank you for easing my mind. I'm sure I should say thank you for turning all my words into the best version of themselves they could be…with proper grammar and all.

To the behind the scenes crew: Lemmy from Luna Literary Management—thank you for all you do, always. I'm so honored to be a part of Luna! Courtney from Marketing with Courtney—I could breathe more this time around with all your templates. Thank you. Sarah with Marketing with Sarah Anne—thank you for all your help narrowing down so many things for this launch.

To my content team—I love you all. Thank you for being the best hype girls and for going to bat for my books. Thank you for entertaining my shenanigans and for being as excited as I am about my stories.

To every arc or early reader—thank you. Thank you from the bottom of my heart. You play a huge role in authors' careers, and I thank you for that.

To every single reader who picked up this book—whether it was your first Ambar Cordova book or the fifth, I'm so happy you're here. I hope you stay a while.

And last but not least, thank you to Joey again—thank you for holding my crappy heart and loving it as if it was whole.

Now, off to cry in author tears and on to the next book.

143,

Ambar

JOIN THE BABE TRIBE!

Be the first to know when I have a new preorder or book ready to be released: Follow my Amazon Page Here!

Biweekly updates (and giveaways) on what's going on in my life and book recs? Join my newsletter Here!

Do you want weekly updates (and giveaways)? Join Ambar's Babes Here!

ABOUT THE AUTHOR

Ambar is the author of small-town and multicultural romance that brings emotional twists to her readers. Her debut novel The Truth Never Spoken, is book 1 in the Baker Oaks series: A small-town series based in Florida. Ambar is a wife and mom who has been living in Florida since 2015, and who loves the small town where she currently lives in. Born and raised in the Dominican Republic, she embraces cultural differences and brings that to her books,

When she is not writing, she is enjoying time with her family, traveling, and reading.

To learn more, scan or click here

Grab a book, fall in love, stay a while ♥